PROPHECY AND ALLEGIANCE

BOOK THREE OF THE FOUNDATION STONE SERIES

DEAN G E MATTHEWS

Contents

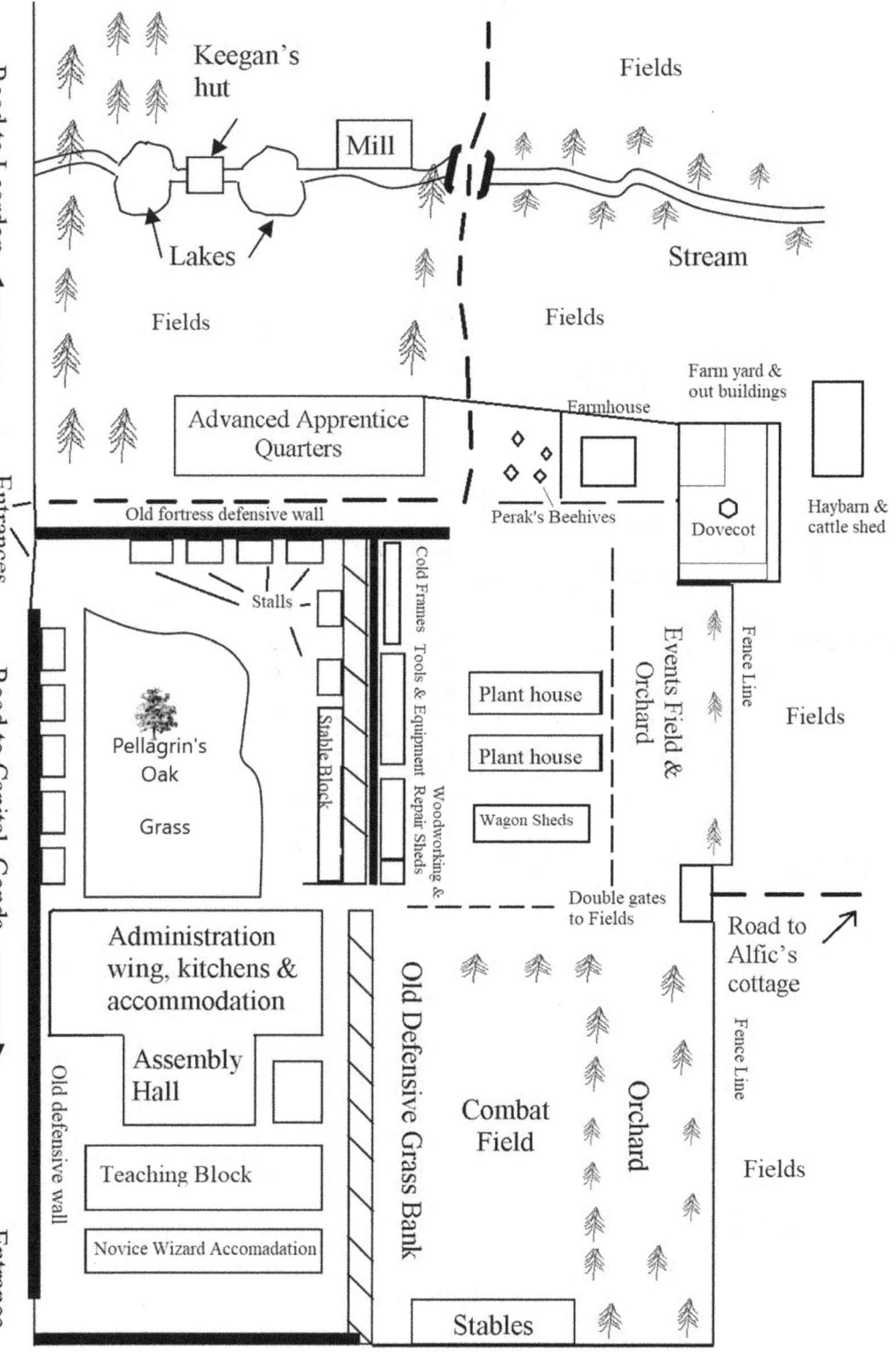

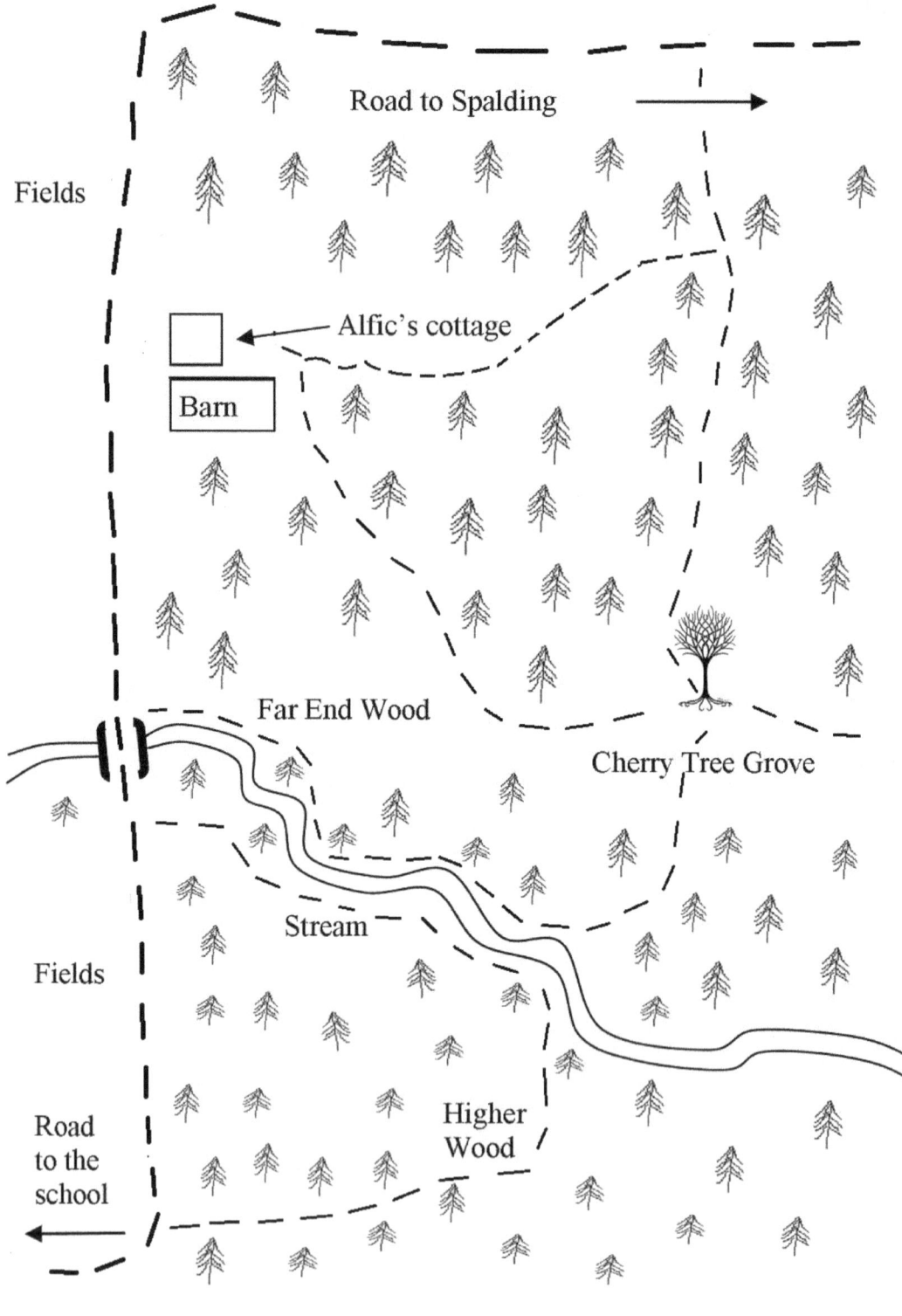

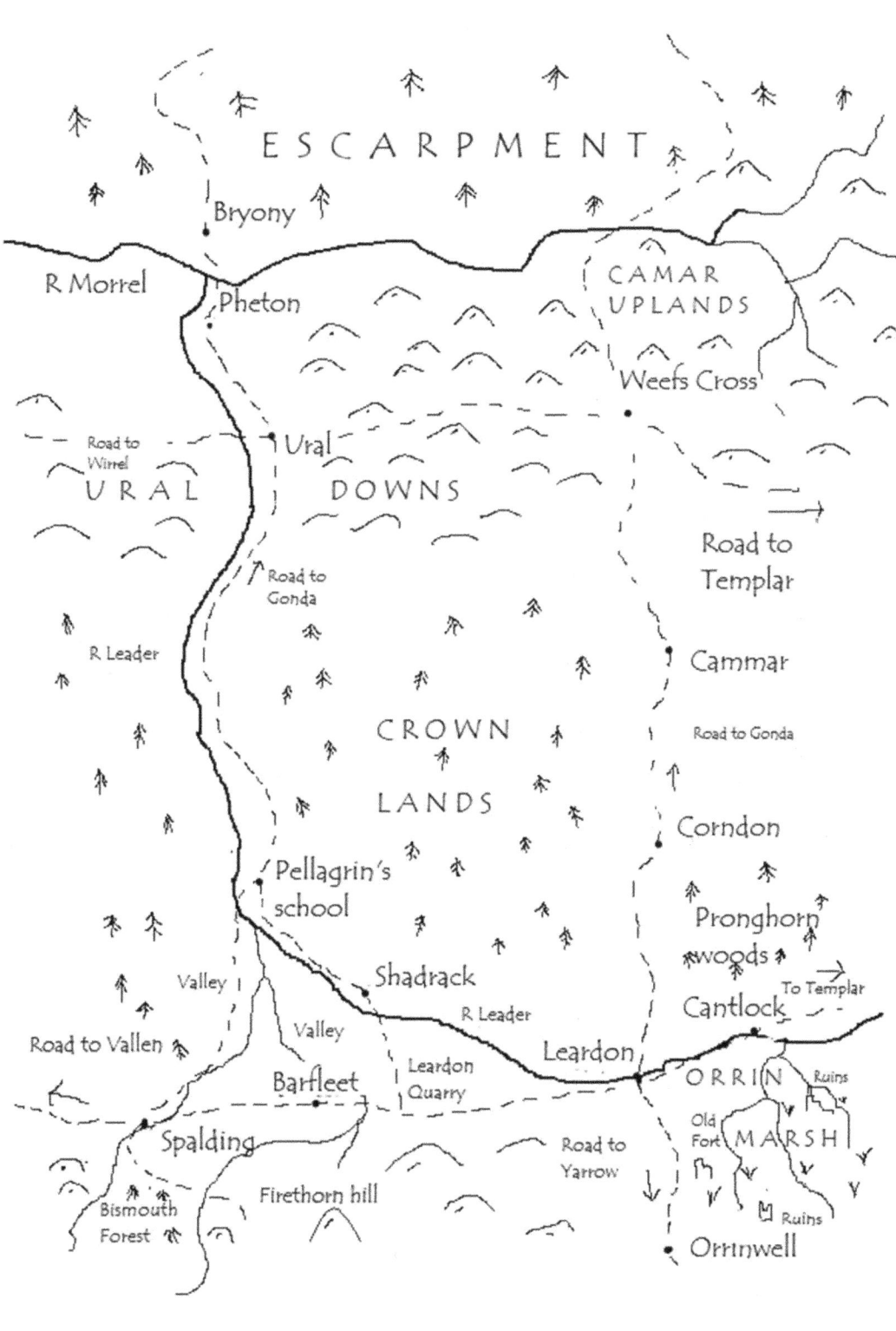

PREFACE

Before man discovered the stones, the first golden civilisation thrived in Vanhara, far to the south, across the Navas straight, in a place now called the Broken Lands, devastated by nucleonic war. The gods of light incensed, turned their backs on man, wiping any trace of their existence from the face of the land, and mankind's remnants were forced to live a simpler way of life. They lived in harmony with the land and the creatures of the world for a time, but the destiny of any species is to evolve and grow, otherwise it stagnates.

Fearful that man would follow the same destructive path as before, the goddess Seline, together with the gods Aquar and Praxis, created the Chimera stone. The stone was hewn from the forces found deep within the interior of the earth, in an attempt to better the human condition, to test man's fortitude, his will to survive and his goodness of heart. But, the god of the underworld, Fornax, objected, arguing that to better the human condition, there must be balance and adversity, so he created an opposite. Evil incarnate, this gem was called the Firebrand stone. Men and dragon-kind alike worshipped the stones peacefully for hundreds of years, until man's own powers began to blossom. They abandoned the stones, and once more began forging their own destiny. Legend then told that the gods, each passionately opposed to the other, created a defender to champion their cause, fearful they would lose their influence over man.

One was called Samuel, the other the first Dark Taal, both burdened to destroy the other and their talisman. These champions battled for an age, neither gaining dominion over the other, and locked in otherworldly combat, good and evil merged. Legend says they are fighting still, acting out their eternal struggle.

So consumed with each other were they, that they forgot what they were fighting for. Shortly afterwards, the Chimera stone was discarded as a fancy bauble and lost to history, whilst the Firebrand stone was concealed from the world by jealous greedy mages, consumed by lust and power.

But without the Chimera stone as a balance, the Firebrand stone, in the hands of men and dragon-kind began to influence history. In the desolate ruin of Vanhara, its resources now exhausted, a despot called Dacron, drunk with power, the Firebrand stone's evil whispering in his mind, turned his malicious eyes upon Aymara.

However, his plans of conquest were foiled by the wizard Pellagrin and his followers, who stole the Firebrand stone, in an attempt to destroy it. Failing, they instead split the stone into four and hid them from man's lustful gaze.

Peace reigned for a time, but as war threatens Durbah and the surrounding lands, the gods of light gaze once more upon the earth; their thoughts turning to the conundrum that was man and the talisman they had created. Championed by the goddess Seline, Aridain is born, his magic uncontrolled and unrestrained, tasked for one purpose only; to destroy the stones and bring order to the land once more. But her creation prompts Fornax to create a dark opposite, tasked with killing Aridain, salvage the stones, and usher forth a new reign of darkness; but they are not alone. Also seeking the stones is Aridain's evil uncle, a dark wizard called Kuelack, who also seeks dominion over the realm of Aymara.

With his dark opposite stalking him, Aridain, with the aid of friends and family, must quickly learn who he is, and control the magic that will aid him in his quest to defeat Fornax's dark champion, the Dark Taal, and then find and destroy the stones.

However, Kuelack has discovered clues to the whereabouts of the feared Firebrand shards, and sets out to find them, together with a disinherited dragon lord called Ramus, leaving his sadistic and power-hungry wife Gradine in charge of Pellagrin's school, who embarks on a campaign to kill and imprison Aridain's family and their friends.

But with each piece they unearth, Kuelack, and Ramus, begin to comprehend why the shards were so feared. Intent on spoiling Kuelack's plans, Ramus seeks the Balefires, a powerful sect of witches that the shards have no influence over, but his plans go awry.

It's at this time that the young Aridain Bruin stumbles across what he thinks are four pretty green stones hidden beneath the roots of a tree. However, like a moth to a flame, the Dark Taal, stalking the surrounding countryside, is drawn inexorably to Aridain. Battling against the creature for control of the shards, Aridain, together with the magic of the woods, defeats Fornax's champion, however the cost is great...

PROLOGUE

Looking around, Fornax, God of Chaos, perused Seline's earth, pleased that the creature called man, having bowed to his will and influence, had blasted the earth into fragments with atomic cancer.

Man, once held in such high regard by Seline, had not disappointed. Man's warlike nature had made him powerful, so powerful, in fact, that he, Fornax, was now the equal of his three siblings. Despite his brothers' and sister's efforts, his guidance and influence had brought them all to this, and, unopposed, Fornax roamed the scorched and shattered land alone. He breathed in the poisoned air and bathed in the polluted seas. He marvelled at the deformities made in his image that now roamed the twisted and tortured terrain at will.

Fornax did not turn at his brothers' and his sister's approach.

'Are you satisfied, Seline, now that you have sated your anger? You may have erased all signs of man's influence from the land, but you cannot erase man's proclivity for war.'

'They defy all logic; it's true,' said Seline. 'They are ruled by greed and do not understand that by raping the land, they inevitably harm themselves.'

'The precious jewel Vanhara, the land that you held in such regard, is now a shattered ruin, your so-called children, a shadow of their former greatness,' gloated Fornax.

'All because of your blighted guidance, Brother,' spat Praxis, God of the Sky.

'They are a warlike race and crave violence and war. This end was inevitable,' smiled Fornax. 'Although I am surprised at how little encouragement was needed.'

'There is good in them; they need guidance, a talisman, given a chance they can achieve great things,' stated Seline.

'A thousand years was not long enough? Their actions, their history, speak for itself; they don't deserve consideration.'

'I never could understand your inclination for hate and destruction, Brother. It borders on madness,' considered Aquar, God of the Sea.

'I never thought of my fascination for destruction as madness. If that's so, then perhaps we are all insane?'

'We only strive to preserve life. This beauteous world and the creatures living in it are our lifeblood, as its destruction is yours,' boomed Seline, her hands twisting in anger. 'Aquar is right. Your delight in destruction is madness. My realm was the one to suffer the most at your hands.'

'Who knows whose obsession is right, Sister? One God's insanity is another's paradise.'

'One day, when you are at your weakest Fornax, I will be there to look down upon your derelict body,' said Seline sadly, 'and before I send you back into the underworld, you will beg for my mercy, Brother.'

'Be careful, Sister, you may be the most powerful of us, but even you know when not to overstep the mark, and at present, you are in no position to dictate to me. Others of our kind have tried to contain my rage, to their cost.'

'And one day, their deaths will also be avenged,' promised Seline.

'You cannot destroy me, Sister, as much as you would like to. I am the dark personified. For every action, there is a reaction, and where there is light, there is also the dark; you know this.'

'Without hatred, men are not so easily swayed. Now you yourself are made weaker,' lectured Aquar.

'And the primitive mind cannot be easily swayed, at least for a few millennia. Man will rise again, more powerful than before, and with that power comes a renewed longing for war, for greed and dominance, and when their numbers become too many, they will, like a virus, turn against each other and destroy the very land that nurtured them, disregard the very gods that loved them.'

'Granted, life beginning anew can be a good thing,' pointed out Praxis. 'Life is reset, sometimes for the good and sometimes for the bad. This time, however, circumstances may turn in our favour.'

'Stop beating around the bush, Brother Praxis,' said Fornax.

'It was decided long ago that we would not influence man's minds or hearts. However, you, Fornax, broke that pact.'

'So, we have decided that we will no longer stand idly by whilst you secretly manipulate the minds of men,' continued Aquar.

'You have had your way for far too long, dark Brother. This time we will turn man's gaze away from greed and possessions; distract them from mechanical things, so as they can live in harmony with the world around them, introduce them to magic if you will, and make the world a better place,' lectured Seline…

'So, tread carefully Brother, you may be in ascendance, but without my waters, Praxis's oxygen and Seline's land, the very species that nurture you would not be able to survive.'

Bathing himself in fire, Fornax cursed. 'Do what you must, deal your cards and manoeuvre your pieces, but at the end of the day, greed and selfishness will always steer the human race towards destruction. I will see to that.'

Then, with a bright fiery eruption, Fornax disappeared beneath the molten rock, the ground quaking with his passing.

CHAPTER ONE

ABERRATIONS AND MISCONCEPTION'S

Examining Lascana's gemstone collection, displayed in an elegant glass-topped wooden cabinet, Vara with Aridain on her lap, sat quietly in the cottage in front of the fire. Sensing Lascana had walked into the room, she said. 'Impressive?'

'Lovely, aren't they?' nodded Lascana.

'Although I am surprised to see minerals and stones displayed here that I told you could be dangerous.'

'Vara,' Lascana said abruptly, 'I took all the necessary precautions. Now say goodnight to your grandmother Aridain; there's a good boy.'

Aridain looked up at her suddenly and said, 'Grandma, you need to wake up,' then abruptly he disappeared.

Thinking that strange, she looked up at Lascana.

'Your grandson's right, Vara, you do need to wake up.'

'But I am awake?'

'Then, Lascana's face, distorted and melted, merged and transformed into the face of... her husband, Perak.'

'Hello Vara.'

'Wait a minute, what's happening?'

Continuing as if she had not spoken, Perak said, 'Do you know that all I ever wanted was your love? Someone who would care for me as much as I cared for her. Was that too much to ask?'

She said sarcastically, 'It's called insecurity, lack of backbone...'

1

'So independent are you, that I'm beginning to think you're made of stone, and one day, your cold-heartedness, your independence and stubbornness will come back to haunt you,' continued Perak, as if he hadn't heard her at all.

'Perak, why are you saying these things...'

'You're also a stubborn, spoilt child from a wealthy dispossessed family who craves the finer things in life,' continued Perak.

'Insecure…, stubborn…, spoilt...heart of stone,' she said, offended now. 'That's not true; many of Spalding's residents turn to me for help; I've delivered their children, foretold their futures, tended their injuries. I am the hub around which village life revolves,' she shouted angrily.

Then Perak's face dissolved and transformed, and in his place stood Lascana once again.

'When we first met, you said I was the kind of girl who was too afraid to get my hands dirty. Do you remember?'

'Lascana, I've changed. You've changed. We're both different people now?'

'No, only I've changed. You haven't changed at all.'

Then suddenly, without warning, Lascana stepped closer and slapped her across the face.

Looking up at her angrily, Vara exclaimed, 'How dare you?'

'You always were very good at avoiding the issues at hand, Vara. Well, your daughter-in-law, the one who never measured up, is telling you to wake up and fight.'

Lascana then slapped her again, only this time harder.

Her mind suddenly cleared; *It was a dream, and a warped, spiteful dream at that!*

Vara slowly opened her eyes, but when she tried to wipe at a warm tear that had rolled down her cheek, she found her arms were stuck firmly to a small armchair, as were her legs when she tried to move them. Her eyes adjusting, Vara looked around in the diffuse light emanating from the strange glow globes arranged around the walls, and found herself in the pleasing familiarity of Almagest's old apartment.

Although dreams carry importance, some hold vital clues, whilst others are insignificant.... So why was I in my son's cottage with Lascana and Aridain? Surely if I craved security, I'd be in my house in Spalding with my mother, and why would my dream waker be Lascana? Am I arrogant? Am I obstinate? Has my stubbornness brought me to this?

Her eyes settled upon a figure sat opposite behind a large dark wood bureau. The figure, whose features were in shadow, sat studying a roll of parchment whilst slowly sipping at a dark hot liquid from a silver spoon.

'Ahhh, Mother, you're awake,' said the robed figure, lifting up his head to peer at her with eyes glinting in the strange, diffuse light.

'Kuelack, I should have known. I see you didn't waste any time moving in?'

'I now own these quarters. Its previous owner no longer needs them.'

Vara watched in silent anticipation as Kuelack, his face expressionless, dabbed at his mouth with a napkin. He then stared over his shoulder with dangerous intent. 'Report, Serac.'

It was then that a thin, diminutive figure detached itself from the shadows. Vara studied Kuelack's childhood friend, who looked more her age than a man in his thirties. Balding, with a spray of long ginger hair that sprouted from the back of his head, he turned and gazed at her with stark white pupils in blood-red eyes from a deathly white face.

'Karnack and his men searched the woods,' Serac continued, staring at Vara like a glob of sheep dropping wedged in the tread of his shoe, 'but they saw no evidence of Alfic's claim.'

'Do you believe him?'

'We know how resilient the creature was. If they did kill it, there's only one way.'

'Powerful magic,' agreed Kuelack.

Flicking her unruly hair from her face, Vara watched warily as Kuelack poured a measure of a dark liquid into two glasses. Handing one to Serac, they then drank them down in one. Vara knew that Kuelack's childhood friend, Serac, was a cruel and unfeeling individual committed wholeheartedly to Kuelack and his cause.

'The only one with any ability is the traitor, Kale, but his power is negligible.'

'I agree,' concluded Kuelack, it's the reason I chose him to track the creature in the first place.' He then looked intently at Vara, 'but I have a good idea who did.' Kuelack then took a sip of his drink. 'What of Tallus and Hogan?'

'For reasons unknown, they tried and failed to kill your brother's family and they paid the ultimate price.'

Fearing the conclusion Kuelack had reached, Vara returned his baleful stare, and with as much confidence as she could muster, said, 'OK, I confess, it was me. I created the creature. You said so yourself. Now I have destroyed it, destroyed the evidence.'

'Do you take me for a fool?' raged Kuelack.

'There is no one else in my family with the knowledge,' she replied, a bit too hurriedly.

'Family, knowledge,' replied Kuelack glibly. 'There's more going on here, more than you're telling us.'

Standing, Kuelack opened the top drawer of his desk, then picked out a small silken bag. Emptying the crushed fragments of a green stone onto the table, Kuelack then said calmly, 'Serac discovered you searching for something. What was that, I wonder?'

'The shards,' she said unabashed, 'but they weren't where they were supposed to be.'

'Don't lie to me, Mother; where are they?'

Watching as Kuelack's calm slipped away, like syrup from a spoon, Vara said cautiously, 'I don't know where they are, and no, I haven't got them.'

'As stubborn as always. Serac here has expressed a keen interest in discovering your pain threshold.'

Suddenly, Serac appeared at her side. Grasping her wayward mop of flame-red hair, he jerked her head backwards violently, subsequently forcing her to stare up into his skeletal face.

'It will be my pleasure to kill you, Vara, but before I feed you to my Piranha bats, I will wring the truth from you.'

Despite Serac increasing the pain, she hissed, 'Intimidate me all you like. Your threats will not gain you what I don't have.'

'Don't lie to me,' growled Serac in his deep, rasping voice. 'It would be an easy matter to have the shards removed by others, if you knew you were being followed, so who are your accomplices?' growled Serac, his stark sunken red eyes boring into hers. 'Was it Ramus?'

'I worked alone,' gasped Vara.

'Wrong answer,' hissed Serac, in his deep gravelly voice.

Then Vara gasped in shock as small sharp nailed fingers, like red-hot pokers, sank into her shoulders, and she felt dark power lance across her chest and back.

'I told you there would be consequences should you interfere, Mother,' spat Kuelack.

With Serac's dark power still cursing through her veins, Vara gasped, 'Regardless of what I say, you're going to kill me anyway, so get it over with.'

'So eager to die, Mother, don't you care for your grandson at all?'

Suddenly finding her strength, Vara thundered, 'LEAVE HIM ALONE, my grandson has nothing to do with this!'

'My, so much passion for your grandchild. Enough Serac; I think we're going about this the wrong way. Bring Byrak.'

Through pain-lacerated eyes, Vara watched Serac scuttle from the room and return a short time later with a short, stout callow youth dressed in long plain, beige breeches, shirt and a dark hooded cloak. But the most significant details of all was that his hands were tied, and he wore a bizarre-looking metal helmet on his head. She then noticed the golem in Serac's hand. Immediately, Vara recognised what was happening; this teenager was a thaumaturges puppet.

But what made this youth so dangerous that he needed an incantus to control him, and why was he wearing the strange helmet? She thought.

Nodding to Serac, Kuelack, removing the helmet, revealed a youth of no more than twenty-one years old with a thick mop of long, mousy hair. Despite the cuts and bruising, intense sea-green eyes stared out from dark sockets set into a severe, tanned, pockmarked face.

'Who is this? Why is he bound with dark enchantments?' she asked.

'Remove the helmet Serac.'

The youth, called Byrak, approached, his eyes boring into her very soul. Suddenly, Vara gasped as pain erupted in her head.

'Subtle,' cackled Serac. 'Now tell me psychic, tell me Vara's secrets?'

Tearing at her memories like a flail, the young psychic's exploration was painful, but brief. 'She doesn't know where the shards are,' said the youth morosely.

'You're sure?' threatened Serac, holding up the golem.

'Yes,' he said irritably.

'Did she have help?' demanded Kuelack. 'Speak truthfully now.'

'Yes,' declared Byrak wearily.

'Who was it?'

'It was Teacher Ramus?'

'I knew it. That traitorous scum,' hissed Serac.

Closing her mind, Vara whimpered in pain, and tried to resist Byrak, who, with a subtle sideways jerk of his head, discovered more of the truth.

'Ramus asked Beria if she could dispose of the shards.' He then continued, 'The Balefire witch said she couldn't, but knew of someone who could. She then met with Vara, telling her where to find them.'

Vara felt Serac's hot fetid breath upon her cheek as he squatted down beside her. Roughly grasping her face; Serac forced her head around so she was staring straight into his blood-red eyes. 'As well as a teacher here at the school, Beria's also a Balefire... but she refused to take them, and referred Ramus to you Vara, but why. Why did Beria refuse to take them?'

'What's the matter?' spat Vara, realising that Kuelack was close to discovering the truth. 'Is the almighty Kuelack scared of a single dragon lord?'

Suddenly, like a pouncing Maranta cat, Kuelack turned, and grasping Byrak by the throat, lifted him effortlessly from the ground. 'You impudent little... you're scanning me?' hissed Kuelack.

Holding up what was left of the golem, Serac threw it across the floor. Then dark, sinuous tendrils bore into Kuelack's back and chest, and Kuelack grunted out loud. Chopping downwards with his hands, the hastily erected barrier severed the strands of dark matter. Kuelack gestured then, extending the brightly glowing barrier outward towards the youth.

Vara watched as Byrak brought all the might of Serac's prestigious power to bear.

Serac was never in control. It was the other way around, thought Vara.

'Get out of Serac's head, release him, or feel the full force of my anger!' Kuelack bellowed.

Shedding angry tears, Byrak snarled, 'Never, you killed master Mass, Breuken, Maria and Nieta, you gave the order.'

Suddenly, Serac's attack intensified, and Vara threw herself and the chair to the floor. Closing her eyes, she gritted her teeth as sparks flew and conjured fluidic strands of dark force filled the room, searing her face and body. She watched as Kuelack sank to his knees, and blood began to trickle from his nose and ears, as he tried desperately to summon forth his own magic.

'You think me naïve, that I would allow a psychic to use Serac's prodigious power against me?' Kuelack thundered. 'I rule here, not your reviled kind.'

Time seemed to stand still, as a bubble of force formed around Kuelack and began to grow, pulsing, expanding and intensifying, as if possessed of a life of its own, until suddenly a horrendous explosion ripped through the apartment, its intensity destroying the chair and ripping at Vara's clothes and body.

Her panicked breathing, loud in the silence, Vara opened her eyes. The force bubble, together with the dark tendrils had vanished, along with the youth. Stood in the middle of the room, triumphant and imperious, Kuelack surveyed what remained of his possessions, now blasted against the wall in a wide arc, together with Serac now trying to extricate himself from the furniture's shattered remains.

Helping Serac to his feet, Kuelack said, 'You weak minded fool, you allowed that teenager to control you!'

'Keep in mind who you're talking to,' said Serac menacingly, 'in the past it would have taken more than one of your pathetic force bubbles to defeat me.'

'You were aware of the fight?'

Serac nodded and said morosely, 'I just couldn't stop myself.'

Kuelack stared at Serac in bewilderment. 'It's the reason why mind masters were so feared through the ages.'

'You still haven't learnt the lessons I taught you, have you, Kuelack?' lectured Vara. 'You're still an arrogant arse. When are you going to learn that you never take your enemies for granted?'

Kuelack then turned, as if seeing her for the first time. 'Ahh, Mother, you still live; more's the pity.' Looking her up and down, Kuelack picking her up from the floor and sitting her down in another chair warned, 'but for how long depends on how cooperative you're willing to be.'

Following Kuelack's look of distaste, Vara discovered her clothes were nothing more than rags, ripped and torn by his magic.

7

'So, what about Byrak?' queried Serac. 'He knows what we're about now.'

'He's a child, his classmates are dead, and he has nowhere to go. I seriously doubt he'll pose a threat.'

'What if he goes to your brother?' queried Serac.

'I hardly think that's going to happen. Alfic's as untrusting of psychics as we are.'

'We should issue a bounty for his arrest nonetheless,' suggested Serac.

'As you will.'

Looking around the apartment, Vara, smiling with a bravery she didn't feel, said nonchalantly. 'I'd say you have more pressing concerns, like redecorating this room.'

'Brave words for someone who's been abandoned by her friends and family with no means of escape. Now where were we?' Serac said threateningly.

It was then that she realised what the dream had been trying to tell her.

Cursing at his failure, his breathing coming in short ragged gasps, Byrak pressed against the corridor wall as teachers and retainers rushed past, totally focused upon the chaos that had emanated from Almagest's old quarters. Pulling his hood closer over his face, he hurried down the stairwell as calmly as he was able, and across the atrium.

He shouldn't berate himself; he knew. His former teacher, Mass Martin, a master psychic, had also tried and failed to kill Kuelack. As much as he mourned the loss of his teacher, he couldn't help but think Mass a fool. If only he had called upon the services of his students, his allies, the school would now be under their control.

Placating the two guards posted either side of the main doors with a word, Byrak, struggling to control his racing thoughts, exited the administration block. Striding out across the grass, he glanced sideways at the two Greyswords, Karnack and Jackamar, at the head of the school guard, rushed to cordon off the building. He then made his way towards the industrial sheds and glasshouses, and it wasn't until he was striding out across the playing field towards the farm and the fields beyond that he began to relax.

Thoughts of teacher Mass forced its way to the forefront of his mind then, of his lessons, and one in particular...

'Clear your mind, Byrak. Remember our goals, remember the plan, everything else will then fall into place.'

'You talk of serenity and composure, Master, but....'

'I was once a novice like you. I was also constantly bullied, regularly sporting black eyes and split lips, so I just lashed out. With no one to advise me at the time, I didn't realise what was happening, and had no idea how to control my power. As I assumed a modicum of control, I used my gift to save myself from more beatings, then rightly or wrongly, I began to retaliate, and intimidate. I also became cocky, so cocky in fact, that I sent two unwitting boys to retrieve a bejewelled knife I coveted from one of my tutor's desks, but my plan backfired.'

'So, what happened?' he had asked, intrigued.

'This tutor just happened to be a student of the great, recently departed Mind Master, Caberartus; she used my amateurish efforts as a pointer, leading her directly to me.'

'What did she do?'

'She steered me towards a more intellectual career, before I suffered too many 'mental problems.''

Turning to him then Mass had said, 'listen to me Byrak, I have realised a profound truth. We are the height of evolution. All roads lead to us. We are mankind's future; magic has chosen us to take this banner forward. If I should fail, it will fall to you to continue our legacy...'

At the time, he didn't realise what Mass was referring to. How could he, he was a psychic, not a prophet? Without Mass, without his teachings, he knew not how he would have turned out. He owed Mass Martin his life and future and would return that debt in spades.

His mind taking on a dreamlike quality. Byrak, having reached the cattle shed; sat cross-legged on the straw covered floor.

Whilst in control of Serac, he'd discovered that Kuelack was focused on Ramus's betrayal. His incursion into Vara's psyche had revealed an even bigger truth, that the dragon lord, having at first aided Kuelack, had turned against him. After Kuelack had failed to honour his promise to aid Ramus in his quest to avenge his family, and after realising the unquantifiable evil power contained in these four seemingly insignificant pieces of crystal, Ramus had switched the shards for fakes. He'd also discovered that Ramus hid these shards beneath the roots of a tree for Vara to find; only they weren't where he had promised.

Abruptly, the clinking of armour and the shouting of orders demanded his attention. Squatting down amongst the softly lowing cattle, he peered out into the grey, snow flecked day and concealed his presence as a contingent of the school guard marched past oblivious.

If anything was to come of his opposition, he must first gain knowledge of Mass's failure. Then, he must research the past and his kind's defeat, led by the Mind Master Caberartus. Only then would he be ready. But first he had to concentrate on his own self-preservation.

CHAPTER TWO

SAMUEL'S DIARY

After another busy day assessing students and checking paperwork, Beria closed the door to her modest apartment, and leaning back against it, exhaled slowly. Undoing the clasp from her shoulder, she hung her cloak, embroidered with vines and maple leaves, over her inlaid wooden privacy screen stood in the corner of her room. Restocking the range with fuel, she fanned the embers until the wood began to spit and pop. She then filled her copper kettle with water and placed it upon the range for a well-earned cup of honeysuckle tea.

Whilst she waited for the kettle to boil, Beria turned to look out through the window. The grey pine trees atop the old earthen bank, overlooking the stables, swayed crazily in the swirling wind, as did Pellagrin's oak in the courtyard beyond, performing a crazed drug induced ritual amidst the flurries of snow.

Momentous events were unfolding at the school, the enormity of which filled her with more than just momentary trepidation, events that she and many of the teachers would be unprepared for, events that would affect the world around them. She stared despairingly over at the austere brass bust of Acumen Gisela Brake, sat on her writing desk.

'What would you have done, I wonder, if faced with such a discovery?' she mused. 'Something inspirational, no doubt. It's why I will never be Acumen or even a Balefire Magnate.'

Rifling through the pages of the diary, she shook her head in consternation. A Male Balefire! She still could not believe it. As a

Balefire herself, she believed that only women could be a member of the surreptitious organisation.

She remembered watching the young boy many months ago, as he played and frolicked as did all young boys of his age, showing no outwards signs that he was at all special, allowed to take charge of a cart and a team of horses under his father's supervision, whilst Perak looked on.

Whatever the explanation for the Bruins' indifferent behaviour, it was plainly obvious, despite Vara's reassurances, that the boy had not been readied. Such a special boy should be away from the school and in a Balefires care, as the alternatives didn't bear thinking about.

The kettle shrilled its proclamation, and placing the diary on the table, Beria poured the steaming water into a teapot, then began readying her pastel colours whilst it brewed. She had been the same age as the Bruin boy when the letter had arrived, informing her she had been chosen to study at Pellagrin's. Her family had moved from Wirral, Durbar's main weapons and ore-producing town to Spalding, and in her naivety, she like many others had chosen to study what she thought were the more dynamic arts, like Natural and Elemental magic, scoffing when teacher Merle had first told her what a powerful and subtle art colour magic could be. It was at this juncture that her best friend Magen had introduced her to her mother Vara, who persuaded her to the subtleties of witchcraft. She, in turn, had persuaded her to try Colour magic once more, and since that day she had not looked back.

She held up the canvas portraying Keen's butchery table, located out the back of his shop. The sombre, taciturn butcher was probably still wondering how his de-boning knife had suddenly developed a severe layer of rust. Likewise, Amy Dickson, Pellagrin's head cook, who must have wondered how a beer barrel appeared suddenly upon the counter while her back was turned.

Colour magic's success depended on how good an artist you were. The more realistic the painting or drawing, the more successful the spell, although colour magic could never create life. As she became more adept, she would be able to make inanimate objects appear or add a flood of water, or paint in an open wound to kill with a few strokes of a brush. The only drawbacks were that it took time, and you had to stay with the paintings, but once you had the backdrops and backgrounds you needed, it was then easy to add or delete something, like the weapons she had created and left around Alfic's and Perak's homes for them to find during their recent troubles.

Having not practised colour magic since she was a student, her progress had been agonisingly slow at first. However, combining her witchcraft with her first love of painting, she had achieved varying degrees of success until her old ability had asserted itself. With greater and greater success, she had begun to influence people and events in very diminutive ways. Now it was time to take her art to the next level and try it on people who had the gift.

Pouring the hot water infused with honeysuckle flowers into a cup, she stirred, and blowing upon the hot liquid, took a tentative sip. She then picked up the diary, opened it, and began to scan the pages. The Shards were here at the school. How did she know this? The diary said so; the words appearing on the pages prophesied:

> *When the Dark Taal emerges from the peace, the Balefire man*
> *with compassion and steel will arise to challenge what the Child*
> *of Nightmare attempts to swathe in blackness; as the stone of*
> *darkness and fire reappears, in the ancient seat of learning.*
>
> *Then the dark creature, and the Male witch of the Balefires*
> *born of the storm, will battle for possession of it.'*

Then, turning a couple of pages, Beria continued:

> *To defeat the shadow without a shadow, the Balefire Taal must*
> *sacrifice his innocence and destroy the stone of light; only then*
> *will balance be restored...*

This, she surmised, related to the recent events in Farend Wood. But the more she studied the diary, the more engrossed, and the more frustrated she had become. The book interspersed with the odd coherent sentences, contained no dates and no time frames except a few historical references, and read like the ravings of a deranged mind. It indicated major events that had gone before, as well as others she had no knowledge of. Together with tantalising clues referring to the

13

future, the diary had even hinted at recent events, but as she continued to read, she came across pages that refused to be read. Perhaps they were passages only a male Balefire was meant to read. Turning to one of the legible pages, she opened it and again began to read:

> '*The stone of fire and darkness, now risen and the creature of the Dark undone, the Male witch of the Balefires born of compassion and steel will rise to challenge, what The Ancient One attempts to swathe in darkness.*'

Beria stared at the diary. The text had shifted again. It was almost as if once events from the past were settled; it predicted a future outcome, changing where necessary. It posed a serious question; does prophecy dictate how we behave or does behaviour dictate prophecy? One thing was clear, a reliable source of events, it wasn't. Turning the page, she read another short passage:

> *In the ancient seat of learning, the Male Balefire will attempt to reunite the stone, and banish the swathe of darkness cast across the land at the Child of Nightmares' hand.*'

Turning the page, she faltered, staring oddly at the text that yesterday she could have sworn wasn't there. Dismissing her confusion as tiredness, she continued reading:

> *The Balefire who covets the One, will gladly sacrifice all in the hall of dreams, as the evil blight swathed in yellow, attempts to reunite the darkness that has no influence upon them, extinguishing the light, and sealing his fate.*'

> '*United, the Taal once readied, will with fortitude and endeavour seek out the Chimera, but if The Ancient One unites the Siamang before the Balefire child is prepared, he will gain ascendancy and destroy all.*'

The Child of Nightmare, she was sure, was Kuelack, but The Ancient One? It couldn't be the creature, it was destroyed. Yet another name to look out for? Then it dawned on her, was the diary responding to her queries. After all, it was what she had been wondering.

'Who is The Ancient One?'

Words appeared on the blank page:

'A man of many names and guises.'

'I'm assuming the Siamang is another name for the Firebrand stone, so what is the Chimera?'

Materialising on the page, the words read:

'The balance.'

'Some clarification would be nice?'

She stared long and hard at the page, but no more writing appeared. Sitting back in her chair, she contemplated this new information.

If the current chain of events were left to unfold and the young boy was left without proper protection.... She shivered at the consequences for the school, its students and the world, should the boy be captured or, worst, killed. Magen had left the diary for her to find; her, a member of the coven who practised colour magic. Then clarity at what she must do gave her courage to combat her despair and make a decision. Beria finished her tea, packed a small bag with food and drink, then, donning her cloak, silently left her small apartment. Having managed to leave the school and the grounds undetected, she hiked through the fields in the rapidly diminishing evening light. Maybe she wasn't a wise choice, and she knew the coven wouldn't approve, but the gods had deemed her the one to discover the truth. It was a task she would carry out to the best of her ability.

CHAPTER THREE

A RUSH OF BLOOD

Wrapped against winter's chill wind, Perak stood in the late afternoon sun that filtered through the small stand of trees across from the house, but offered no warmth.

Glancing towards Kale, Perak thought. *Pay attention, this is not a game.*

Suddenly, out of the clear blue sky, a streak of white and grey skimmed overhead and Kale felt claws slicing his forehead.

'Owww, was that necessary....' exclaimed Kale.

Perhaps now you'll pay attention? smiled Perak innocently.

Perak steeled himself as the young Animistic felt at the wound and examined the trickle of blood.

Then Kale, smiling grimly, turned slowly towards him. His face a study in determination, he said, 'OK, now you've got my attention.'

A pulse of force sat Perak onto his backside, leaving him temporarily dazed. Shaking his head in exasperation, Perak climbed to his feet. 'You're supposed to be practicing your own art, not psychokinesis.'

'"Distraction is a weapon at your command", you said, so, whilst you've been talking, I took control of the goshawk.'

Out of the corner of his eye, Perak saw the hawk that, with a determined shriek, attacked, forcing Perak to the frozen forest floor for a second time.

'I'm just taking in your advice, "Use all the weapons at your disposal", I think you said.'

'Very droll, however, an opponent is not going to desist because of a distraction, or because you're feeling under the weather.'

Suddenly Kale coughed as a swarm of midges clouded his vision and flew into his eyes and mouth.

'Lesson three. Never let up until your enemy is either incapacitated or dead. Show no remorse, your enemies won't, you have to be ruthless!' Dispersing the insects, Perak puzzled at Kale's apathy.

'What is the matter with you today?'

'It's nothing; just tired, I guess.'

'It's more than that. You've been distracted all morning. That attack should not have succeeded, not against you,' concluded Perak. 'You must learn to overcome your physical shortcomings. Remember, commanding creatures is only the first step on the road to becoming a master of minds,' Perak lectured.

'I'll try to remember that,' Kale said ironically. Then, spitting out insects, he spluttered, '…. master of minds?' He then looked at Perak in surprise. 'What do you mean, master of minds?'

'Is it that hard to believe that creatures are so different from us? Some Animistics, not all, can become mind masters. I would have thought that Torsk taught you that.'

In an effort to draw him out further, Kale said, 'You knew Torsk?'

'Yes, why is that so hard to believe?' asked Perak, studying Kale's astonished look.

'Well, it's just that…, well, you know how it is…'

'No, why don't you tell me?' Waiting while Kale took his foot out of his mouth, Perak continued, 'I couldn't afford the schools fees, coming from a poor family in Cantlock village, so Torsk taught me on the QT. He sensed I had great potential, but despite his teachings, my mind could not make the leap needed for a mind master.'

'Does anyone else know about your, you know, abilities?'

'Oh no, no, no, no, better people think of me as good old reliable Perak. I just use my abilities to make my life a little easier, you know, like talking to my horse, Midge, or placating the oxen, or controlling Sorin's sheep dogs. Being myself has served me so well during my lifetime.'

Kale shook his head sadly. 'When it came to information, Torsk never was forthcoming. He always said that before you take the next step, you must look down to make sure both feet are planted firmly on the ground. You, however, have a unique style that gives me confidence; you approach our subject matter from a different angle. Your teachings have allowed me to process more information, allowed me to control my gift in ways I couldn't have imagined. Perhaps if Torsk had taught my class as you taught me, Tallus wouldn't have become a follower of Kuelack?'

'This is an art that suits a more mature mind. A settled mind is more stable, more logical, less volatile. It takes patience; however, this art also needs a young person's imagination and determination. Without both of these qualities, you're doomed to fail.'

Winter's blanketing chill now seeping into his bones. Perak blew into his hands. Plucking his works jacket from a nearby branch, he slipped his hands into the arms then arched his shoulders to make sure it was snug. Fastening the toggles down the front, he sat on a nearby log, immersing himself in the woodlands he knew and loved, and producing a small hip flask, popped the lid. Swallowing a mouthful of the dark liquid, he looked around the thicket, checking that they were indeed alone amongst the snow-covered trees. Then, in an effort to brighten up his gloom-ridden ruminations, he reached over-head to fondle the ripe red berries of a holly bush, then reached for the rattling seed heads of angelica and honesty to his right.

Offering the flask to Kale, Perak said, 'Velum brandy? I managed to procure a couple of bottles from Amy's kitchen.'

Sitting down next to him, Kale, raising the flask to his lips, wheezed, 'Blimey, good stuff.'

'Must be,' chuckled Perak, 'you look like a bulldog chewing a wasp.'

Kale, handing back the flask, persisted, 'All I'm saying is that had I the skills, perhaps I could have stopped this madness before it started, stopped Kuelack killing my mentor.'

Perak, looking at the youthful Animistic intently, said, 'Blaming Torsk is not going to solve anything. Have you thought that perhaps Torsk knew you would confront Kuelack ready or not, and that by denying you, he saved your life? Perhaps he was cannier than we both thought, knew we would meet and I would teach you.' Making up his mind, Perak said, 'Stand up; I want you to try something. Torsk always lectured that power is one thing, but to be a truly great wizard you need a good imagination, and I know you've got imagination.'

'You're talking about transformation, aren't you? Perak... I'm not ready!'

'With that attitude, you never will be.'

'Well, all right, I'll try.'

'Here, take another swig of brandy. It will help you relax. I know you can do it. You're greater than you think. Let it happen naturally,' encouraged Perak.

Taking back the flask, Perak watched as Kale closed his eyes and shook his shoulders loose in an attempt to relax.

'Now think about something that is your size and weight, an adolescent Ardent wolf, for instance. Now imagine yourself dashing through the woods, bounding through the undergrowth with effortless ease, over fallen trees, over brooks and hillsides, and over heathland, the smell of loam and earth in your nostrils. Yes, that's it,' he encouraged as to his astonishment, Kale's hands began to elongate, change, and fur began sprouting from his face and the back of his hands. 'That's it, let it come naturally, you're young and strong, let your imagination run riot, you can do it. No, no, no, now you're trying too hard,' warned Perak, recognising the symptoms. 'You have to relax, let it come gradually, imagination is the key, you're nearly there.'

But his instruction came too late as the thick padded paws, iridescent fur, and whiskers sprouting from his broad furry snout, began to distort and deform.

Grasping Kale on either side of his forehead, Perak stared into his citrine eyes. 'Kale, think about your form, think about you. Come back to me, now!'

'I can't do it,' growled Kale through sharp incisor teeth.

'Yes, you can! You are stronger than you think.'

Slowly but surely, Kale began to return to his true form. Falling prostrate on the floor, Kale, pounding his fists into the snow in utter frustration, cursed, 'It's too much!'

Smiling down at the young Animistic, Perak soothed. 'Hey, no one said it would be easy. That's why Torsk was a master Animistic. Your achievement, however, considering that's your first try, is a tremendous accomplishment. Most take months, even years. I never got anywhere near that, even with Torsk's help.'

Stiff now from all their exertions, Perak looked up towards the waning sun. 'Come on, let's get back to the house.'

Looking left and right, Beria approached the mansion and knocked. When Lascana opened the door she said, 'Hello, I'm here to see Vara.'

'Beria! I'm afraid no one has seen or heard from Vara in days. Anything we can do to help?'

Thinking for a moment, Beria looked at Lascana, nonplussed.

'You'd best come in.' said Lascana, taking her hand and guiding her through the solid oak door and into the small red and brown-tiled hallway.

'Does anyone know where she is?' she asked.

Lascana shook her head.

The smell of baking bread, and roasting meat assailing her nostrils, she followed Lascana through a twisting hallway, finally arriving into a kitchen/diner, where sat around a large oiled ash table eating, was Alfic, Perak, Aridain, and to her surprise, Kale.

'Help yourself to food?' said Lascana.

Nodding eagerly, and returning their greetings, Beria, smiling at the happy family gathering, ladled some of the stew onto a plate.

'Beria! Long-time, no-see,' smiled Alfic.

'Oh, by the way, thanks for the weapons,' said Perak.

Beria smiled sheepishly. 'As long as they served a purpose?'

'They were from you?' exclaimed Lascana.

'I did what I could, in service of the Balefire Taal.'

'The what?' said Alfic, bemused.

Beria turned reverently toward Aridain. 'The Balefire Taal?'

'Balefire Taal, what nonsense is this?' smiled Alfic jokingly.

'It isn't nonsense. Has Vara not told you?' said Beria seriously.

'Told us what?'

'Aridain is the chosen one,' interrupted Perak, 'destined to destroy the Firebrand and the Chimera stones.'

'This is some kind of joke, right?' said Alfic incredulously.

'No joke Alfic,' said Beria seriously, 'from what I can understand, Aridain has already procured the Firebrand shards. The creature somehow knew he had them and came for him.'

Nodding in understanding, Kale said, 'Don't you see Alfic? It makes perfect sense.'

'On the night of Aridain's birth, Pellagrin came to your mother, Alfic. He told her of Aridain's destiny,' confirmed Perak.

'So, let me get this straight,' growled Alfic, his voice raising several octaves in as many seconds. 'On the night of my son's birth, Pellagrin appeared to Vara, but not his mother or father. And you're telling me that you've both known of this for six years, but neglected to tell us; it seems Mother isn't the only keeper of secrets in this family.'

'That's unfair Son, it was all I could do to get this truth from her; and the price of that knowledge was to keep it secret.'

'Lascana said no one's heard from Vara,' said Beria, changing the subject.

'Yes, Mother has disappeared and, for her own safety, she should remain hidden. I am sick and fed up with her secret agendas,' growled Alfic.

'We've made inquiries,' continued Perak, throwing Alfic a harrowing look, 'but no one has seen her. Why, do you know something?'

'Personally, I think Kuelack has her.'

'You don't know that, Son.'

Beria reached into her cloak and produced a dark blue beaten and battered leather-bound journal. 'This is called, "The Prophecies of a Male Balefire", written and imbued by Aridain's predecessor Samuel, the first Balefire Taal. It's a special diary that only another Taal can understand. It recites prophecy and foretells the future. The words change when you ask it questions, they also alter as events unfold. It could tell us where Vara is!'

'So, what you're saying is that we ask the diary questions, it will respond?' mocked Alfic.

'Correct, but you have to be touching it.'

Picking up the diary and opening it, Alfic asked, 'Where is Vara Bruin?' To his astonishment, words appeared on the blank page...

'In a prison of her own making?'

'What's that supposed to mean?'

'The answer is for your benefit only.'

'Give that diary to me!' demanded Perak irritably. 'So what you're saying is, Vara is Kuelack's prisoner.'

The page remained blank.

'It is a frustrating read,' smiled Beria.

'So how did you come by it?' asked Kale.

'It was given to me by Magen,' said Beria.

'And how did she get it?'

'I'm assuming she stole it from Kuelack,' said Beria. 'Before Magen passed it onto me, it's the means by which Kuelack gleaned the location of the first shard.'

'Don't tell me, by reading it in the diary?' mocked Alfic.

'Precisely,' said Beria matter-of-factly. 'Recently, Ramus approached me, knowing I was a member of the Balefire cult. He wanted me to hide the Firebrand shards.'

'I don't understand?' queried Lascana.

'After procuring the shards, Kuelack fell into a wizard's sleep; so strenuous was the effort. With the realisation of how dangerous the shards were, Ramus switched them for fakes then sought me out.'

'Why?' insisted Alfic irritably.

'Because certain members of our cult are immune to its influence.'

'Like you, yes?' queried Kale. 'Because you're a Balefire?'

'Yes and no. I may be a Balefire, but I'm not immune! I do, however, know of someone who is.'

'Vara,' said Lascana. 'Vara is no ordinary witch, is she?'

'No.'

'Mother's a Balefire witch, isn't she?' exclaimed Alfic.

'And not just any Balefire, she's a Magnate, a member of the Balefire council,' continued Beria.

The silence was deafening as they all absorbed this new information.

'I've told Vara. Nothing good could ever come from keeping secrets,' said Perak, shaking his head in exasperation.

'So, thinking about this logically, if this diary could be mastered, it would give us a tremendous advantage,' said Kale.

'You said that this Samuel was my son's predecessor Beria; explain!' demanded Alfic.

'As Perak said, your son is the next Taal...'

It was then that Aridain climbed down from his stool and took hold of the diary. Closing his eyes and in a deep mature voice, he said, 'This diary passed down to me belonged to Samuel. This is his record:'

"During the first great age of advancement, the once progressive and proud cultures of man warred with each other, nearly wiping themselves from the face of the land. Watching as man destroyed themselves and their world, the Gods, in desperation, forged two stones, the Chimera stone imbued of light and the Firebrand stone imbued of darkness, but both equal. Enhanced with the elements created in the bowels of the earth, pressure, heat, flame, fire, sulphur and diamond, they were also infused with a primordial awareness. Replacing hatred and mistrust with peace, harmony and prosperity, the two stones restored balance through myth, legend and chronicle simply by being. Over the centuries, the devastated cultures of man, fairy and dragon kind alike, worshiped the stones as symbols of enlightenment and wisdom."

"But during the second age of advancement and reason, as civilisation developed apace once more, the stones were again consigned to legend; their purpose and influence forgotten, the Firebrand stone locked away in a forgotten vault whilst the Chimera stone vanished altogether. Many centuries later, the Firebrand stone was unearthed and, without someone to wield the Chimera stone, the powers of darkness gained ascendancy, and in the hands of despots influenced the greedy and the power hungry, returning the land to brutality and bloodshed. Angry with the God of the underworld Fornax, and his betrayal, the Earth Goddess, Seline, appalled at the chaos and anarchy rained upon her domain, fashioned me Samuel, into the first Elemental of light, a powerful human creature created to find and preserve the Chimera stone and destroy the Firebrand stone. But such is the balance of light and dark that Fornax created an opposite, a dark Elemental born to cement his hell on Earth, to battle and destroy me. But so finely balanced are our powers, that we are locked in continual battle, neither gaining dominion over the other. The Harmony stone however, seems more unattainable than ever before."

Then, as if nothing out of the ordinary had occurred, Aridain let go of the diary and stared at them mutely.

They all sat in stunned silence, each caught up in their own thoughts. Then Lascana, taking her son's young face in her hands, said, 'Aridain dear, what was that about? What just happened?'

'He was a very nice man. He wanted me to tell you his story; now two has become one,' said Aridain cryptically. Aridain then left the room, his trusty dragonlet following closely behind.

'The most powerful objects ever created. Imagine the power the shards give the possessor; you could do almost anything,' said Kale.

'The shards give you the feeling you are in control, but all the while, they corrupt your mind,' lectured Beria.

'So these stones, meant to bring balance and harmony, instead, fuelled man's lust for greed and power.'

'Only the paranoid lust after these things, Alfic. Only those who have no contentment within think everyone else is trying to take the things they lust after. That is what brought mankind to the brink of extinction,' said Perak grimly.

'Only Aridain can possess the shards without affect,' said Beria resolutely. 'The only solution, is to destroy both stones before man and fairy kind spiral downward, and drag the world down with them into ruin once more.'

'The day Aridain finds out could be a dark day indeed.'

'How so, Perak?'

'Imagine a mind, a gentle mind, discovering a destiny filled with horrors. Legend speaks of the Firebrand stone destroying entire cultures; look at Turkana and Chondite. It took all of Pellagrin's power and his most trusted people to split the stone into four, and that was with long-lost knowledge,' explained Perak. 'Imagine the knowledge of that responsibility on your shoulders. This is a little boy we're talking about, a boy who plays with wooden swords and performs hand stands with his friends, who wants to play Cabala, court girls and live a normal life. How do you explain to him that he holds the most destructive objects in the world, objects that could result in his death?'

'From that perspective, Pellagrin accompanying Aridain makes perfect sense,' assumed Kale.

'These Firebrand shards attract evil and are capable of nothing but creating chaos,' said Perak.

'And this Chimera stone could be hundreds of leagues away in, say, Navar, or Calabash, or in the Broken Lands thousands of leagues away?' said Alfic, 'and who's to say another creature won't appear someday? Aridain's already had to endure being turned into a mindless zombie.'

'I hate to be the bearer of bad news,' said Beria, 'but whilst trying to interpret the diary, it mentioned a being called The Ancient One.'

'Ancient One! As if we haven't got enough to worry about,' cursed Alfic. Picking up the diary, he opened it on a blank page. 'Tell me diary, I need to know, who is this, 'Ancient One'?'

Words appeared on the page: *A man of ages, and many faces.*

'What does he want?'

The thing we all seek, approval and worship.

'You useless piece of…, what sort of answer is that?'

When nothing else appeared, Beria, taking back the diary, said, 'If this Ancient One unites the shards before the Balefire child is prepared, he will gain ascendancy and destroy all. There was something else. On the inside of the back cover, I found a passage written by an entirely different hand,' said Beria. It reads:

Whoever reads this, beware, for in his attempt to destroy the stone, the mind of Samuel has been turned in on itself, but be reassured that even though the narrative may be complex, his insight is intuitive in the telling.

'I can tell you what that means. It means that this Samuel attempted to destroy the stone, but instead the stone destroyed his mind,' said Kale.

'So, what's stopping the same thing happening to Aridain?' exclaimed Lascana seriously.

'Nothing, but it's our purpose to make sure he carries out his task. We may not like it, but he's meant to have them,' confirmed Beria.

Alfic, throwing his head back, began laughing out loud. 'The fates certainly have a sick sense of humour.'

CHAPTER FOUR

TRANSHABIT

Having decided to get away from the complications of grownups, Aridain sat on a bench in his grandma's garden in silent contemplation, watching as the sun chased the retreating clouds and snow flurries towards the horizon; leaving the skies bright and clear.

Isn't the sky beautiful, Sabra? I never get bored looking up at the clouds. You're so lucky; it must be great to fly?

Sabra popped his head out from the compost heap next to Perak's shed. Shaking the soil from his head and licking his lips, having found several tasty grass snakes eggs, Sabra said, *I've never really thought about it youngling, it's just something I can do, but now that you mention it, yes, I am lucky.*

'Shoo, go away, I'm not in the mood,' he sulked, waving his hands irately towards a flutter of panther cap pixies that buzzed past his head; the pixies having flushed several water imps from the vegetation around the pond.

Alighting beside him, Sabra asked, *Why so cross youngling?*

'I miss my grandma, Sabra, and no one knows where she is.'

Youngling, your grandma can take care of herself, trust me.

Suddenly, the serene scene was interrupted by an explosion of feathers and claws, as a sparrowhawk swooped and took one of the pixies, scattering the rest of the pool's inhabitants. Aridain, reminded of how cruel the world could be, watched fascinated, as the hawk, its wings enveloping the struggling creature now grasped firmly in its claws, watched him silently before picking at the dead faerie creature.

Although Aridain felt sorry for it, he knew better than to interfere. His father lectured that it wasn't only the imps that were hungry this time of year.

Watching silently, his head on his folded arms across his knees, he stared into the sparrow hawk's eyes. *It must be so nice to soar on feathered wings,* he thought. Then, inexplicably, his pulse began to quicken and a wild, boundless energy possessed him. Standing, he found himself spreading his arms wide and leaning forward. Without knowing how, he became one with the hawk; looking back at himself, stood beside the pond. The hawk, then having had its fill, gained its bearings and suddenly took to the air in panicked flight.

Alarmed now, as the hawk's erratic flight took him low over the fields and tree tops, Aridain said, *Sabra, help me, what's happening?*

It's the shards, youngling, their magic is enhancing your own. Stay calm; it's something you would have been able to do anyway in time, but I can't keep up, the hawk is too fast, you'll have to slow it down.

How?

I don't know, experiment, I can't transhabit. The hawk won't mind as long as you're relaxed. It's sensing your fear and uncertainty. It's the reason for its erratic flight.

Focusing on the hawk's base feelings, the panicked creature began to relax. The pair, now working as one, started navigating the currents and eddies; the freedom giving him a feeling of invincibility; that the world was his to explore, that he could go anywhere and do anything.

Steering the hawk a little bit this way and that, he felt the bitter wind rushing through its feathers and over its back. Ignoring the taste of pixie in his mouth, he began to take an interest in the clouds and the world below, shrouded in white. He rushed over hedges and through trees, over Spalding common and the villagers' allotments, then over Spalding itself. Onwards, across the countryside, he flew to Firethorn hill, where his grandfather told him the dragon Haida, was slain. Flying onwards, he continued towards the forestlands beyond. His euphoria was interrupted as, all too soon, the hawk conveyed thoughts of hunger, hunting and food. His joyride curtailed, Aridain reluctantly returned to his body, leaving the hawk to go on its way.

Opening his eyes, he looked across at Sabra.

Welcome back, youngling, *well done.*

Isn't flying fantastic, Sabra? It's everything I imagined it would be.

Reaching into his pocket, Aridain produced the shards, and gazing into their depths, said, 'I just thought they were very pretty and they sang to me. What else can they do, Sabra?'

That is something you're going to have to find out for yourself, but be warned; too much experimentation can be dangerous.

Looking shrewdly at the dragonlet as it settled beside him, Aridain said, 'Sabra, how come you know so much about magic?'

I am born of magic and so is the Siamang, offered the dragonlet as if that were explanation enough. *As are you. Now, no more questions.*

'Now that you are officially my friend, I can tell you you're no fun.'

I do what I do for a reason. We dragonlets are hunters, not comedians, and don't keep calling me by that silly name, hissed Sabra defiantly, *and, once-and-for-all, I'm not your friend.*

Aridain smiled. Despite Sabra's protestations, he sensed the dragonlet was getting used to his name. 'You say you don't care, but I know you do, really.'

I don't care! The dragonlet stated regally.

'Then why did you save me in the woods?'

Because you keep saving me. How am I ever supposed to repay my debt to you?

'Because that's what friends do!'

Annoyed with the dragonlet, Aridain climbed to his feet. He would visit his friends in the grove, he decided; perhaps they could answer his questions.

'I'm going to the woods,' he announced decisively. 'You can come if you like?'

Then, without another word, he turned and walked to the end of the garden, purposefully not looking up when he heard the fluttering of leathery wings tracking him from above.

Having the dragonlet along for company suddenly made him think of his dog Chipper, and just how much he missed his friendly greetings, his wagging tail and how they would run and play together through the long grass, then curl up together by the fire after a thrilling day exploring and adventuring.

Skipping across Spalding Common, he slid down the inclined track, which was now covered in icy snow, bordered by the skeletal outlines of hawthorns and elderberries, then across the bridge and into the snow covered meadow. Suddenly, he skipped to a halt as a harvest mouse, flushed from cover by the ever hungry dragonlet, scuttled across the path in front of him. Watching the mouse as it scampered, terrified into the grass, Aridain realised that in the company of the dragonlet, his life would change dramatically. His dad said the teachers wouldn't tolerate Chipper running around whilst he practiced with his sword, so they would tolerate the dragonlet even less.

They would take one look at the fiery little creature, he thought gloomily, *and want Sabra killed out of hand.*

They can try, thought the dragonlet defiantly.

'If you keep following me around, they will catch you. Do you want to live in a cage again or worse, be killed?'

Better to die fighting than live like a lamb, youngling!

Picking up the pace, Aridain ran down the track beside the woody margin towards Farend Wood.

Aridain knew Sabra had to eat, but also he couldn't have Sabra eating his friends in the grove. There must be a way around this dilemma. Coming to a decision, Aridain stopped, and with hands firmly on hips turned towards the dragonlet as it skimmed low over the field.

'Pests!' nodded Aridain happily. 'You can eat vermin, like timber rats and scarrion lizards; and pests like magpies and crows. That way you'd be doing everyone a favour, even the school would like you then. But not the doves in the dovecote,' he said, wagging his finger sternly.

Hovering in front of Aridain's face, the dragonlet's long forked tongue exploring its mouth and glistening snout thought, *I'm not here to become popular.*

'Well, if you want to stay here with me, you'll have to behave.'

When the dragonlet remained quiet, Aridain smiled and said, 'I knew you liked me.'

Sunlight filtered through the trees, lighting up sections of the woodland floor as Aridain smiled proudly at his resourcefulness. He skipped along the path that wound between large sprays of feathery ferns, heavy with sporangia and stands of holly trees, now loaded with berries.

'Look Sabra, puffballs,' Aridain squealed, running and kicking at the large yellowy-brown papery spheres that exploded in a cloud of brown spores.

Very interesting, I'm sure, thought the dragonlet haughtily.

'Chipper would have been very excited and tried to catch them in his mouth.'

But there's nothing to catch!

'You're just no fun.'

Deflated once more by Sabra's lack of enthusiasm, Aridain shambled dejectedly into the stark woodland.

CHAPTER FIVE

DOES PROPHECY DICTATE HOW WE BEHAVE OR DOES BEHAVIOUR DICTATE PROPHECY

Alfic steered Midge around the cottages' boundary wall, applying the brakes as they descended the slope towards the stream, helping Midge cope with the heavier than normal passenger load. Curling his fists in anger, he parked the trap outside the blackened bones of his former home, illuminated by the winter sun and now covered in a layer of snow.

Inspecting the remains caused him to think back to the day he stood staring incomprehensibly at the still smouldering ruins...

'What possible benefit could the creature have gained from this?' He had asked, whilst consoling a solemn Aridain and Lascana...

'I don't know!' Lascana had replied tersely.

'It's OK, Dad, they're only things.'

'Do you know you have an annoying way with words, Young man?'

'Uh oh, Mum's angry. She called me young man,' Aridain had said seriously.

'In his off-the-cuff way, Aridain's right, Lascana,' he had smirked. 'We're all alive; that's what matters.'

'It's not as simple as that Alfic; we've nowhere to live. Our unborn child needs a home.'

Sifting through what remained of his cottage, hissing and sucking at burnt, singed fingers, he had held up Aridain's metal practice sword, together with the shield Keegan had brought Aridain for his birthday, all melted and twisted.

'It's OK Munch kin, don't look so sad. We'll buy you another shield and sword,' he had said sympathetically.

Pulling back a section of collapsed wooden beams and hot charred bricks from a collapsed interior wall, he had exclaimed triumphantly, 'Ah ha, Lascana, I know where the fire started, probably a stray ember from the range during the fight.'

'Does this mean we can move back in?'

'No need for sarcasm, dear. I'm just saying.'

It was then that he had discovered something extraordinary, and holding up a collection of wooden kitchen implements had exclaimed, 'Hey, look at this, they're untouched. Neither are the kitchen cupboards and sideboards.'

He had then begun pulling various items made of cherry wood from the ruins.

'Look, there's my rocking horse,' Aridain had squealed joyously, trying desperately to pull the wooden steed from the hot smouldering debris.

'Be careful, dear,' Lascana had worried. 'Alfic, do something with our son, would you?'

'Of course, here Son. Let me help you with that.'

Lascana had looked towards him then, annoyance etched on her face. She had then asked, dumbfounded, 'How is this possible? How can this be?'

'They are all made from the wood of the old ancient cherry tree....? Yes, that must be it...'

Drifting back to the present, Alfic wiped at a clandestine tear that had rolled down his cheek. Even now it was hard not to picture his cottage, tidy and picturesque in its own functional gardens, smoke rising lazily from its single chimney. Reining in Midge next to the burnt and blackened barn, Alfic insisted, 'Well, he's not here. I suggest we spread out and meet in the grove, and keep your eyes open for soldiers; we don't want anyone else going to jail,' he said tetchily.

Entering the woods, their footsteps crackling on the black frosted blight now dead beneath their feet, Alfic, Kale and Perak made their way between the majestic ash, silver birch, oak and sycamore trees. Reaching the grove, they stopped to peer into the interior, startling a herd of grazing deer and a family of wild boar feasting on fungi amongst the undergrowth. Despite the time of year, plants grew from the snow-covered floor with a renewed vigour, their leaves shimmering as if sprinkled with amber dust in the sun's rays. Spring flowers poked their heads through the snow and frost, and all around the grove, seemed alive with movement.

His voice echoing in the stillness, Alfic called, 'Anything?'

'No, nothing, but I think you should come and see this,' replied Perak.

Joining his father, Perak indicated the canopy above their heads. Wrapped around the branch of an old gnarly oak was a large, curled, spherical structure shaped like a snail's shell.

'It looks like it's made of mother-of-pearl. What is it?' exclaimed Kale.

'It's a harvestman's cocoon!' said Perak abruptly.

'I said nothing good would come of having those damn sapphire sprites here.'

'Honestly Alfic, you sound like an old superstitious fishwife,' accused Perak, his voice echoing through the stillness.

Then they heard the rasp of sharp claws and a loud, rapid clicking noise. Almost too late, they turned to see a glistening emerald and brown insect the size of a large goose, rushing towards them from the trees. Taking cover on the frozen ground, their arms covering their heads, they tried to locate the creature that once more dived for them from the trees.

Be gone parasites and I'll let you leave with your lives. It hissed in their thoughts.

'It's a queen! She's guarding her eggs,' bellowed Perak.

Then a blaze of emerald flashed through the trees accompanied by angry hissing, as with a flurry of leathery wings the dragonlet, spurting jets of white-hot fire, came to their aid. Ripping and shredding at each other's skin, eyes and underbellies, the pair spiralled to the woodland floor.

They stood back and watched, reluctant to intervene as the two creatures rolled around the frosted undergrowth biting, tearing and scratching. But the single harvestman was no match for the dragonlet that spewing flame spiralled into the air, leaving the harvestman lying burnt, broken and blackened amongst the vegetation.

Bursting into the grove, preceded by Keegan brandishing his Korda knife, Aridain screamed, 'Look out,' as with an ill-tempered hiss, another Harvestman flew towards them.

'To me, Keegan, Father,' shouted Alfic, who, with broad strokes of his sword, slashed back and forth.

'It's all right Alfic, belay your sword. With its queen dead, this one has no purpose.'

They watched warily as the remaining harvestman alighted next to its burnt and singed queen. Looking at them then back to its dead queen several times, the remaining harvestman with a hateful hiss, took to the air and flew from the clearing.

Approaching his son angrily, Alfic, grasping Aridain firmly by the shoulders, shouted, 'There you are! How many times, young man, do I have to tell you to do as you're told?' Indicating the burnt and blackened harvestman, Alfic continued angrily, 'This is why I told you not to bring the sapphire sprites here; this is what happens.'

'I'm sorry, Daddy.'

'This has nothing to do with Aridain, Alfic, this is Tallus's doing. He encouraged them here!'

The flutter of leathery wings overhead caused Alfic to look up irritably as the dragonlet, alighting upon a nearby branch, hissed menacingly, the spines along its back now standing upon end.

'Talking of dangerous animals?'

'Easy, Alfic,' said Perak.

'Dragonlets are only good for one thing, Father, and that's for harvesting fruit,' said Alfic testily.

'Don't keep picking on Sabra,' said Aridain brusquely. 'I told you he's not dangerous.'

I can defend myself, youngling, thought the dragonlet.

'Your dragonlet killed a man.'

'He deserved it!' shouted Aridain angrily.

'Whilst you're my son, you are subject to my rule,' Alfic shouted indignantly, 'and if your *pet* wants to stay with us, you'd best teach it some manners.'

'Hen's teeth! Alfic, when are you going to give in with this relentless tirade? Give the lad a break,' admonished Perak.

'And I don't need lessons in parenting from you, Father...' Alfic then turned towards Keegan as if noticing him for the first time. 'And what are you doing here?'

'Oh, and nice to see you too, by-the-way. Looking out for your son. We heard you calling,' said Keegan darkly. 'You don't think Mace and me would let him roam around the countryside on his own, do you?'

'Hello Keegan. Your wounds are healing, I see,' said Kale.

'Yes, all thanks to Lascana's cure all.'

'Tallus's two remaining harvestmen must have laid these eggs here,' said Kale.

'Drawn here, no doubt, by our new friends,' said Alfic derisively. 'Well, we can't leave that nest here. It must be destroyed.'

'No!' cried Aridain.

Bending down, Perak grasping his grandson by the shoulders, looked into his tearful hazel eyes. 'If they're allowed to hatch Aridain, there's no telling what damage they could do?' insisted Perak. 'We have no choice.'

'How do you know? They could be friendly harvestmen?'

'There's no such thing,' stated Alfic sullenly.

'Harvestmen are neither good nor bad, Aridain,' said Perak. 'They grow fast and with no natural predators, in six months we could be overrun.'

'It's OK,' offered Keegan, 'I'll do it.'

'No, you won't,' said Kale deliberately. Squatting and looking Aridain in the eyes, he said, 'come on, let's climb up there together.'

Aridain nodded silently.

They watched in silence as Kale, together with Aridain, began to climb, accompanied by the ever present dragonlet.

'Are you all right, Son?' asked Perak, turning to Alfic. 'You were pretty hard on the lad.'

'Just tired, I guess?' apologised Alfic irritably.

'No, that's not it!'

'Then what is it, Father? Tell me,' spat Alfic, shaking his head as if to clear his ears of wax.

'I don't know?' hissed Perak harshly. 'But the one thing I am sure of is you shouldn't take your frustrations out on your son or his dragonlet. Sabra is a godsend. He has come to your aid many times now.'

'You're right, I shouldn't,' agreed Alfic, his voice rising with every syllable. 'What I should be doing is confronting my brother. He is the cause of all our woes. Don't look at me like that, like I'm some kind of killer. I can see no other path; that's all I have. Everyone's looking to me for inspiration, for leadership, but on top of that, I have the responsibility of trying to keep my son safe.'

Suddenly, from above, there issued a sound like shattering crockery, and they were showered in glassy fragments.

'Everything all right?' enquired Keegan loudly, shading his eyes whilst trying to peer up into the bare branches.

'Yes, fine,' shouted Kale.

Waiting for them as they climbed down, Alfic noticed tears in his son's eyes.

'Grandpop was right, Daddy,' declared Aridain, 'so we destroyed the nest.'

'I'm glad, young man, that you came to realise life is not always so fanciful....' Sensing a fresh magical quality permeate the air, Alfic, troubled, began glancing about him. Engulfing him like an old friend, the woods called to him. Abruptly, he began forging his way through the undergrowth.

Perak watched nervously as his son strode across the clearing and stood at its centre beside the cherry sapling now grown to nearly four feet tall.

'Alfic, come back here. You don't know what you're doing,' whispered Perak harshly. 'You'll cause offence!'

'Don't fret, Father. I was summoned here.'

Pointing upwards into the spreading branches of an ancient oak tree, Aridain exclaimed, 'Look Grandpop, my friends are here!'

To Perak's astonishment, a myriad of sprites, imps, nymphs and pixies, tentatively at first, then with increasing confidence, filled the grove. 'This is unprecedented,' marvelled Perak, pointing to six glowing globes of light that had emerged from the trunk of the large oak tree overlooking the grove, their glow illuminating the surrounding trees. 'The wilds and the creatures in it are a constant surprise for sure, but they've never appeared when adults are present,' lectured Perak, now clearly perturbed. 'You can hear them, can't you Alfic?... calling out across the ether, calling to the woodlands all about them?'

Alfic nodded, dumbstruck.

'But how is this possible?' said Keegan.

'I don't know, perhaps it's my family's affinity with the wilds,' said Perak, aghast, 'that allows us to hear the sprites.' Watching enthralled as the softly glowing creatures flitted tentatively from branch to branch, Perak continued, 'Reading books and talking to knowledgeable scholars, I knew there were special creatures living in the wilds. Most of them are now very rare indeed. Creatures like these, driven from the land centuries ago, were capable of bringing about comprehensive changes,' declared Perak. 'If they are allowed to die, their magic, their link to the land dies with them and as a consequence, we all suffer. Now six of them are here in our woods. Thrilling times await,' he murmured excitedly.

Kale, smiling as though all his birthdays had come at once, exclaimed, 'They are absolutely beautiful.' He was surprised when their reply echoed in his head.

You are too kind, protector of the Elemental.

Alfic, watching sceptically as the sprites' strange whistling language rang like the peel of a bell through his mind, said, 'My name is Alfic Bruin. I'm Aridain's father,' said Alfic markedly, backing away as the glowing balls of light settled on the cherry saplings branches, no more than six feet away.

We know who you are. After all, we summoned you here. We also know you are angry.

'I only know that whilst Lascana and my son lay helpless upon the woodland floor, amongst the rot and evil filth with the Dark creature advancing upon them, you were nowhere to be seen!'

Your offspring is alive, is he not? Until you come to terms with yourself and your own magic, you cannot truly understand us, or your son's role in the events about to transpire. Destiny is not a choice. We help when we can. Destiny controls all of our lives. My brethren's role in the Taal's destiny is now seared into fairy memory, as is yours!

'Alfic,' hissed Perak, 'you are being disrespectful.'

'You call my son The Elemental. Why?' said Alfic, ignoring his father.

Because his child's mind, so accepting of the unprecedented events unfolding around us, represents the primal forces in all of us. We also understand that you do not comprehend the forces at work here.

'Alfic,' said Perak, trying another tact, 'I understand that to a practical man such as you, all of this must feel very strange.'

Shaking his head violently, Alfic replied, 'I can't help it, Father. I feel like a stranger in a world of my son's making.'

'His world is strange to me too, but it is what it is. The sooner you accept it, the better.'

Stood in sullen silence, Alfic thought back to the events leading to this point in time, recalling their fight for survival beneath these very trees, imagining the Dark creature hiding in every shadow, every hollow, preparing to pounce and kill them all. 'I just want magic to stay away from me and mine; it's caused us nothing but trouble.'

'That's impossible Alfic; everybody has magic in varying amounts and differing forms. Your mother's had magic as long as I can remember, as have Magen and Kuelack, and you, to a degree.'

So troubled is the Father of the Elemental, interrupted the sprites. *Are you not happy that the wild flourishes once more? We are grateful your son found us and returned us to our rightful place. Now the wild will return to the way it always was and everything is as it should be. Your progeny is fulfilling his destiny, his purpose.*

'His purpose? What is that?' demanded Alfic.

To restore the balance.

Frustrated now, Alfic asked, 'My father says that your kind enhances the world around us, for good and bad.'

Who is to say what is and what isn't beneficial? Take the harvestmen. They were doing what they must do to survive, nothing more, nothing less. The world is what it is. We all play our part, embrace it, revel in it, for the world is glorious if you only open your eyes and see.

'My son's confusion comes from logic; he is a practical man; these changes, what's happening in the grove is highly illogical; these things cannot be taken apart and studied.'

Magic is not the problem, Grandfather to the Elemental. Your son is. His fear of magic has placed a barrier in his mind. To break that barrier, he must conquer his demons.

The six sapphire sprites turned to each other and began conversing. Seemingly having made up their minds, they said, *We have decided; we will demonstrate to you what a wonderful thing magic is in the only way we know how.*

'What do you mean?' demanded Alfic.

Twittering in their strange language, the sprites began flying intricate patterns above Alfic's head.

'What's happening? Answer me, what are you doing?' demanded Alfic.

They all looked on dumbfounded as the sprites flew in intricate spirals, rooting Alfic to the spot. They then deposited sparkling blue dust over his head. The dance was over as quickly as it started, and Alfic fell back onto the woodland floor, stupefied.

'I can't see. Everything's fuzzy,' exclaimed Alfic, peering around the grove in an effort to locate the mischievous, glowing creatures that appeared abruptly in front of his face.

Your sight will return, Father of the Elemental. Trust your magic, trust your instincts and remember, plants are your favourite things.

Conveying their goodbyes, the myriad sprites and nymphs, whistling and chirping excitedly, followed the sapphire sprites up into the trees.

Hurrying over, the three friends helped Alfic to his feet.

'Wait, where are you going?' said Alfic dourly, rubbing furiously at his eyes. 'What have you done to me? What do you mean, plants are my favourite things? I need to understand... Is this why you summoned me here? I need answers?'

'Why should they, Alfic? Who are we to say what should or shouldn't be? These creatures have lived here for thousands of years. They see the world from a totally different perspective, their concerns are on a grander scale.'

'I'm not concerned with the bigger picture, Father. I'm only concerned about my family.'

'And how are we supposed to affect events unfolding at the school Alfic,' eulogised Perak, 'unless we start to consider the bigger picture?'

CHAPTER SIX

INAUGURATION

As the days grew shorter, flurries of snow from the east swept across the school, covering the grounds and the countryside beyond in an ever-thickening blanket of white.

Following the deaths of Hogan and Tallus, Kuelack had ordered a contingent of soldiers to be sent from the capital and a strict curfew had been imposed, the military now stopping and searching everyone travelling to and from the school.

'If it's not depressing enough,' moaned Alfic, having to attend my brother's bloody inauguration ceremony; now, the sun's disappeared. It's an omen, I tell you!'

'It's as if Praxis himself disagrees with this ceremony,' said Sorin.

'Will you two stop!' berated Lascana. 'Kuelack will officially be head of the school. Your whining is not going to change that.'

'You know, this is just an opportunity to humiliate our family in front of the whole school,' replied Alfic sullenly.

'We could always boycott his big moment?'

'And what would that achieve, Sorin? Nothing,' said Lascana.

'What else can we do, Lascana?'

'Better to stay and listen, Sorin, keep a finger on the pulse, so to speak,' said Perak despondently.

'I'm beginning to wonder if that's even possible,' Alfic countered. 'Despite our efforts, more and more people are buying into Kuelack's vision of the future and there's not a damn thing we can do to stop it.'

'They turn to him out of fear and ignorance, Son.'

Their greatest fear having come to pass, Alfic stood amongst the throng. His thick, bushy brows creasing deeply, Alfic thought darkly upon his younger brother, about to be installed as Head of the Sivan.

During his time at school, Kuelack had become intolerant of others and their opinions, failing to learn from the lessons that life taught him. With the trappings of greatness and wealth dangled in front of his nose like a carrot, Kuelack, Vara's greatest triumph and most spectacular failure, had chosen the easy, twisted, dark path.

As if reading his thoughts, Perak, studying his face, said, 'I tried to warn your mother, Alfic, but she would never listen. Now look what's transpired. I should have seen. I should have tried harder.'

'It wasn't your weakness, Father, it was Mother's,' said Alfic grimly. 'She was so eager to give my brother the things she had lost. By the time she realised what was happening, Kuelack had her twisted around his little finger. It was her stubborn refusal to acknowledge his manipulative ways that has brought our family to this. Do you know I suggested that me, Magen and my brother practise with our magic,' he continued, 'you know, defence and attack and all that, in an effort to hone our talents? But Kuelack refused. He said he wasn't going to be a stooge for me and Magen's ambitions. In his ignorance, he never saw it for what it was, an offer of help. He saw it as something else entirely, and when he challenged me, he could never understand why he lost, especially in a fistfight. After a time, I turned my back to spare him his blushes, but he accused me of being a coward. I remember congratulating Kuelack at his graduating ceremony,' said Alfic darkly. 'I think he actually expected me to go down on one knee and tell him he was the better man.'

'Since he first joined Pellagrin's, Kuelack frowned on anybody choosing to emulate you,' said Perak soberly.

His mood dire, Alfic gazed darkly around the assembly hall at the gathered teachers, students, retainers and administration staff. He then gazed up at the chandeliers hanging from the oak beams and their fiercely burning candles, then at the smouldering braziers of burning incense hanging from brackets protruding from the walls.

A concoction, no doubt, intended to pacify the uneasy crowd, he thought sullenly.

'Alfic?' asked Lascana, looking toward him, concerned. 'How are you feeling since your encounter with the sprites?'

'I feel more connected to everything around me, more alive, more aware of my surroundings, if that makes any sense, but beneath that, is an overriding sense of uneasiness and disquiet, I can't quite place my finger on what it is.'

'You don't fool me Alfic Bruin. Something's happened to Vara and you're concerned, admit it.'

'I'm sure Vara's fine Lascana.' said Perak.

'Yes, this is typical Mother, only thinking of herself,' argued Alfic. 'She's selfish, vain, and a self-centred bigot,' said Alfic grumpily.

'No, somethings wrong. It's not like Vara to stay away from her beloved home this long.' Disagreed Lascana.

Turning away angrily, Alfic studied Karnack, stood in front of the curtained dais with arms folded, and the youngest greysword, the severe-looking, flame haired Jackamar, stood by his side. Flanked either side by soldiers of the school guard, their anxious glances left and right reflected the crowd's guarded uneasiness. Soldiers were also evident beside the exits and along the sides of the hall, the increased reinforcements giving the hall the feeling of a military inquisition, rather than a celebrated inauguration.

At the sounding of a gong, Alfic stared towards the stage, the noise announcing to all to bow their heads and stand in silent reverence. Then, as was tradition, a choir consisting of students of various ages filed onto the stage, and in soft lyrical tones sang a lament to honour the recently lost heads of the school, Almagest and Exedra.

Amidst gentle weeping and shaking of heads, the assemblage joined with the choir in singing the melody, which, as well as sad and regretful, was full of high regard and respect. After a few choruses, a more upbeat melody replaced the gentle tunes; the change in tempo signifying veneration for the recently departed, whilst at the same time ushering in another chapter in the school's continuing narrative. The chorus then repeated and rose to a shattering crescendo, the abrupt ending corresponding with the curtains parting that revealed the council table, now divided into two, positioned either side of an imposing black and dark red gold inlaid chair.

From either side of the dais, four softly chanting teachers appeared, the necromancer, Arhass; the demonology teacher, Vargas; dark arts teacher, Serac and teacher of knife fighting and unarmed combat,

Dagan. Each swinging a smoking embrasure in one hand and a wooden staff of office in the other. Fashioned from hazel, the staffs were crowned with the elaborately carved wooden heads of a dragon, firedrake, wyvern and dragonlet respectively, in honour of the dragon lord, Pellagrin. Sporting ornate flame bejewelled headgear, made of Banth skin, embellished with multi-coloured scales, each teacher was dressed in black and red embossed ceremonial robes. Followed on one side by Magen and on the other Savarin, the teachers stood either side of the throne. Then Magen walked to the front of the stage and, holding up her hands for silence, she cast her gaze out over the assembled throng.

'Wizards, sorceresses, teachers and staff, please, be seated. We are here to witness the investiture of Kuelack Bruin, chosen by the Sivan to lead and guide the school and its students into the future, whatever that future may bring.'

Alfic shook his head despairingly. 'I think I'm going to be sick.'

'I think I might join you,' whispered Sorin sourly at his shoulder.

With a face like thunder, and arms folded deliberately across his chest, Alfic glowered at his younger brother, who emerged from the council chamber's door at the back of the rostrum and walked, saint-like, towards his lavishly decorated throne with his hands upturned.

'Oh please, spare me the hypocrisy,' cursed Lascana harshly.

'Shhh,' hushed somebody in the crowd behind her. 'Show some respect.'

About to reply, Alfic felt a hand on his shoulder.

'Easy, Alfic,' placated his father, 'let's not make a scene.'

Alfic, his anger bubbling just below the surface, watched as Kuelack knelt upon an embroidered, cushioned step in front of the chair as the four teachers approached. One of them carried an ankle length red and black bordered sash of office, decorated with a glittering red clasp, and held it over Kuelack's head. They then recited the words of appointment:

> 'Chosen One, you will defend the school, educate the ignorant, enlighten the deprived, and vanquish the wicked. This appointment, not taken lightly, is given to you to perform to the best of your ability, until your death.'

43

'Until your death,' responded the crowd.

'Here, here,' murmured Alfic.

Kuelack then took the oath:

> 'It is a burden I shall carry out with purpose, devotion and ardour. I solemnly promise that through discipline and strength, I will enlighten the deprived and endeavour to lead this school through adversity, and against all threats to its purpose. These responsibilities I will uphold and perform until my death.'

As the sash was placed over Kuelack's head and across his shoulders, Alfic, grinding his teeth, his breath coming in short angry gasps, felt Perak's grip firm on his shoulder, and his father's warning harsh in his ear.

'I know what you're thinking, Son, and believe me, I can think of nothing I'd rather see than Kuelack exposed for the tyrant he is, but remember, Mace and Keegan had evidence, and look what good it did them.'

The brief ceremony over, Kuelack stood to sporadic applause, accompanied by the sound of the choir's heavenly raptures. Then, the new head of the school raised his arms for quiet.

'Pellagrin's is the oldest and finest school in all of Aymara, and has a lavish history dating back nearly six hundred years. Consequently, it attracts the best students and luminaries. Teachers of the magical and combative arts, mathematics, philosophy, the written and spoken word, as well as art, history and the practical skills needed in the wider world, covet a position here. With its academic achievements, I've always counted myself privileged to live and work on its grounds. However, imagine what a force we would be now if, all those years ago, Pellagrin, in his ignorance, hadn't cast out the so-called dark arts,' he said vehemently. 'Imagine the breadth of the school's knowledge base; after all, the accumulation of knowledge is why we are here, is it not? You cannot embrace the light without understanding the dark,' sermonised Kuelack.

'Ahh, I think I have a headache coming on,' groaned Alfic.

'Shhh,' hissed someone close by.

Holding out his arms to placate the polite applause, Kuelack continued… 'Now that I'm head of the school, things will change for the better, and these changes will benefit everybody, especially the students, for they are, and I'm sure you'll all agree, why the school was created. This is my home and you are my family, and like my family, I will defend you and this school to the end. Together we can make this haven great, take it forward and defend it against all who dare to compromise its future, make it the centre of the civilised world once more.'

As the applause echoed around the hall, then died to nothing, Kuelack continued…, 'Now I would like to share with you a story, a story of a boy who despite his shortcomings was determined to make a name for himself and join the school's hallowed ranks…'

Alfic baulked, 'Shortcomings, you wanted for nothing you ungrateful cur.' Glaring at his Brother angrily, Alfic listened as Kuelack continued…

'I can recall my feelings of awe and terror, as I walked up the black marble steps towards the stout oak fortress doors that have stood firm for so many centuries. Don't be afraid, I said to myself, as I proceeded beneath the white marble columns and the mural of Pellagrin, leading his soldiers against the horde of outcast creatures, that threatened to destroy this bastion of culture. This is a place of learning and power and you will soon master both…, and with such an excellent array of teaching staff to guide me, how could I fail?'

Waiting for the applause to peter out, Kuelack, changing the subject, said, 'Now to business; we all know that the responsibility of taking the school forward should have fallen to the esteemed sorceress, Exedra, but Mass Martin and his underhanded schemes saw to that, and we will miss her dearly, as we will Almagest "the wise", vanquisher of Zakan the deceitful and avenger and subjugator of Tagor and his fighting Harajin. He was murdered by the traitor's Hogan and Tallus under the orders of Mass Martin, his body left to rot on the Blinks escarpment.'

'Initiated by you, Brother,' hissed Alfic.

Again, someone shushed him from behind and Alfic span around angrily, only to hesitate when he saw people in the crowd weeping openly.

45

'Alfic, no one told them. They have no idea how Almagest died,' hissed Lascana.

'Suffice to say, they paid for their betrayal with their lives,' continued Kuelack, 'as did the creatures under their control, which were all killed by my brother and his family. The Sivan offers them our heartfelt thanks; and I personally offer them a debt of gratitude.'

The crowd broke into spontaneous applause. Alfic studied the crowd uneasily as, with each well-rehearsed sentence, each carefully pronounced word, whispered agreement rippled through the crowd.

Holding up his hands, Kuelack continued, 'This gallantry, however, cost them their home, and for that aid, I shall give them accommodation at the school.'

More applause rang around the hall before Kuelack continued in a more subdued tone.

'As for our unfortunate confrontation at the fair, I'm sure Alfic will join with me in apologising to everyone who was unfortunate enough to witness a petty family squabble.'

Accompanied by cheers and whoops of joy, more applause broke out amongst the crowd, and through a deafening silence of anger, Alfic smiled reluctantly and nodded as hands pounded his back and people offered to shake his hand, accompanied by the congratulations from the staff, retainers and students closest to him.

'Petty family squabble?' Lascana hissed, smiling politely. 'He's had a bang on the head!'

Smiling and nodding compliantly as people slapped and pounded him on the back, Perak growled, 'He's telling the people exactly what they want to hear. Lascana, just smile and be grateful he hasn't had us arrested.'

When the applause and the handshakes finally diminished, Magen stood, and gazing out over the assembled teachers, said, 'With Rasbora having left for her homeland, and the traitor, Ramus, having fled the school, we have no choice but to offer the positions left by Exedra's and Mass Martin's passing to the next in line, Serac.'

Alfic, shaking his head in despair, stared into space as Kuelack's childhood friend walked up the steps to the centre of the stage, to receive his sash of office.

46

Turning from his position on the stage, Serac, in his crude rasping tones, replied, 'I accept this great honour with dignity and humility.'

'And who is to be your successor?'

'In my place, I commend my most gifted student, Sevan Banner.'

'Then come forward.'

Again, the crowd rallied to Kuelack's choice of candidate. Applause, led by the Sivan, reverberated around the hall once more.

When Serac had taken his position to Magen's left, Kuelack stepped forward and, fixing Alfic with his piercing grey eyes, announced, 'Now the formalities are out of the way, my first act as head of the Sivan is to denounce the traitors, Mace Denobar and Vanir Ulrich, who are not worthy of the weapons they possess, together with Keegan Fold and Kale Sim, who have brought shame on this school and disgraced its name.' Casting his gaze over the crowd, Kuelack said, 'Let me be clear, any sightings of these men are to be reported immediately and, if I discover anyone aiding them, they will suffer the full letter of the law...'

Feeling as though the walls of the assembly hall were pressing in upon him, Alfic looked around in disbelief as more agreement rose from amongst the crowd.

'The people are too willing, Father. Something else is at work here?'

'You know as well as I do, Son, that hardliners, cretins like Ryan and Gavin Torn have been placed evenly amongst the crowd.'

Alfic looked towards the ceiling, 'It's the incense burners.'

'Are you sure, Alfic?'

'What else can it be? If Kuelack was using magic now, I'd know.'

'That's all well and good, but what can we do about it?' hissed Sorin.

'Nothing!' agreed Alfic, staring intently at his brother.

Lascana said sadly, 'You know what offering us a room at the fortress entails, Alfic?'

'Yes, as a recompense for their generosity, we'll be required to service them and the fortress. It's just the excuse Gradine's been waiting for, to humiliate us further.'

'If you refuse the offer, Alfic, it's guaranteed they will come for you anyway,' said Sorin.

'Oh, please Sorin, stop sugar coating this, will you?' joked Alfic grimly.

'... I will restore this school to greatness,' Kuelack continued, the hint of a smile passing his lips as he glanced briefly in their direction. 'What I need to know is, will you help me, will you stick by me?' sermonised Kuelack.

'YES,' hailed the cry from around the hall.

'ARE YOU WITH ME?' Kuelack bellowed.

Once again, the crowd responded with gusto.

'I didn't realise the school was going to war,' stated Sorin ironically.

'I think you're closer to the truth than you know, my friend,' replied Perak.

CHAPTER SEVEN

FRIENDS AND ANTAGONISTS

In angry silence, Alfic, Lascana, Sorin and Perak were carried along by the crowd, amongst enthusiastic murmurings and mutterings, the ceremony now over.

'Alfic! Perak!'

'Gable,' Alfic acknowledged solemnly.

'It's a rum do and no mistake,' said the giant blacksmith dejectedly.

'No offense, Gable. Best not let the people see you associating with us?' said Alfic, grasping his arm and ushering him out of the crowd's way.

'Let them think what they will. Besides, you need all the help you can get.'

'What do you mean?'

His face severe, Gable replied, 'I've been commissioned to produce a quantity of swords together with a range of other weapons; we're expecting our first shipment of ore tomorrow.'

'Weapons! How can this be? Surely, Gradine knows you're no longer her willing servant,' queried Alfic.

'Only if I let on,' he said, pressing his finger to his nose.

Alfic smiled for what seemed the first time in days. 'You're a devious fellow, Gable Bagley. Do you know that?'

'Why thank you,' said Gable, his face and voice like stone.

'I'd like to see that manifest, if I may?' whispered Perak.

'So would I,' said Sorin.

'Sure, the order's at my forge. I'll meet you there.'

'Alfic, Lascana, we'll join you later,' affirmed Perak.

49

Watching as Perak and Gable, together with Sorin, left for the forge, Lascana and Alfic continued on.

'So, oh husband of mine,' said Lascana, 'how are your people taking the recent turmoil?'

'Coping well, despite the upheaval. They have mainly ignored Kuelack's slanderous propaganda and the tittle-tattle regarding our family.'

'And Micas?'

'He's like a chip off the old block. Last time I checked, he had the new recruits running around like flies, repairing roofs, fences and walls, that's on top of tending to the livestock. They probably hate him already. I'll bet he wished he'd never taken on the job of foreman,' smiled Alfic. 'What's so amusing?'

'You, giving responsibility to Micas, you normally don't like to relinquish control to anyone. I'm proud of you.'

'Actually, Father and I agreed it should be Micas. With a bit more experience, I'm sure he'll do a fine job. As you keep reminding me, it's time I trusted someone.' Then, changing the subject, he said, 'I watched Savarin sat upon the dais.'

'So did I. Is it possible they have coerced him?' offered Lascana.

'If he has been coerced, I'll eat my foot,' said Alfic abruptly. 'Somehow, we have to show him our support.'

'How? You know we're being watched constantly. Besides, just because he's a friend of yours doesn't mean he's above suspicion. Savarin's gruff adversarial manner would attract the very people you say he's fighting against.'

'I believe Savarin is better than...'

Abruptly, Alfic felt a sharp pain against his spine.

'Nice and easy, Alfic, just continue walking.'

'Keen, what are you doing?' Lascana exclaimed, starting towards her husband.

'Don't make a scene, Lascana. It will only get Alfic hurt,' said the greengrocer Bern, coming up behind and presenting the tip of his knife surreptitiously to her back.

'Janus, Milvus, what's going on?' cursed Alfic tersely.

'Before you end up in one of my boxes, we thought it was time you saw the error of your ways,' smiled Milvus, 'it's for your own good.'

'Is that a threat? Let me go,' insisted Alfic. 'Before someone does get hurt.'

'Sorry, no can do,' hissed Keen.

'You honestly think you're doing us a favour, don't you Milvus?' said Alfic incredulously.

'Bern,' demanded Lascana, 'this isn't like you? Can't you see what's happening? That thing in your pocket it's...' Lascana looked from Keen to Milvus. 'You know, don't you Keen? You know about Gradine's coins, as do you Milvus. At the stallholders' meeting, regardless of what we'd said, you were always going to oppose us.'

'No more talk,' insisted Keen, 'take her.'

Grasping Lascana roughly, Bern pinned her arms to her sides and Milvus wrapped a hand around Lascana's mouth, which she abruptly bit.

'Ahh, curse you, woman.'

'If you hurt her...?' threatened Alfic.

'Don't fret, Alfic; soon you'll both think like we do,' said Keen and he dug the knife point in, even further. 'Now walk towards the huts and don't cause a scene.'

'Bern, Janus,' pleaded Lascana, 'those silver coins in your pocket were given to you by Gradine. Throw them away, they're cursed. Keen and Milvus, they know all about it. They're playing you for fools.'

'You'll say anything,' sneered Milvus, 'won't you Lascana, anything in justifying your husband's envy towards his brother and his success?'

Against their will, Alfic and Lascana were marched across the grass courtyard and steered towards Bern's grocery store, one of the many shops that had originally been built to the same design against the old perimeter wall. With a long shop front backing onto two smaller rooms in the back, most of the owners had modified them, turning them into living quarters as well as selling their wares.

Forced through the door, they were grasped by more hands and, without ceremony; they were dragged kicking and screaming, then forced down into two chairs.

'Bind their hands and sit them down,' said Keen, angrily.

'One day you'll realise what a tyrant Kuelack is, and when that day comes, I hope you can live with yourselves,' cried Lascana.

Struggling to no avail, Alfic and Lascana looked up to see the school's stallholders, plus stable boys and retainers, stood watching silently from the shadows.

'Lawna, you agreed to this madness?' exclaimed Lascana.

'This isn't a game Lascana, this is about the future of the school,' insisted Lawna.

'So now what?' stated Alfic grimly. 'Do you intend to make us believe in a tyrant's lie by passing us enchanted coins?'

Keen turned to the small gathering, and holding up two silver coins said, these were given to me by Gradine. Once in a person's possession, they bring clarity and enlightenment... They are givers of truth.'

'So she says. So what, you're Gradine's willing helpers now.'

'For our loyalty, Gradine granted us immunity.'

'Granted you immunity, do you hear yourselves?' exclaimed Alfic disbelievingly.

'Don't fret Alfic, soon you will see that our way is best.'

'Keen, listen to me, please don't do this,' pleaded Lascana, 'you're being played; you're a pawn in Gradine's games. Question her motives, then you'll see!'

Then Milvus began to cough and spit as a cloud of midges filled the room.

The room's occupants then turned at a scuffling noise to see a scarrion lizard skitter into the centre of the room and look around. It then eyed the small throng curiously. It was followed by a black and white cat, that was followed by a second tabby cat, which bounded into the room, then leapt, knocking the coins from Keen's hand. Dropping to his hands and knees, Keen, searching desperately for the coins, also began swatting at a cloud of insects that buzzed around his face, eyes, and mouth. It was then that the scarrion lizard scuttled across the floor, and picking up the coins in its raptor like beak, swallowed them whole.

Then a bellow split the air as Perak, followed by Sorin, burst through the door wielding iron bars, swinging them this way and that. Surprise, combined with the lizard's and cats' bizarre cameo appearances, was all it took as the traders and retainers, unprepared or unwilling to fight, fled Bern's small hut.

Stood over Lascana, Alfic watched as Perak, darting this way and that, engaged Bern. Meanwhile, the scarrion lizard and the two cats leapt upon Milvus. With the undertaker's arms swirling around, windmill-like, in panic, the animals bit at his wrist, forcing the terrified undertaker to drop his knife. Perak then swung his iron bar and the undertaker, as if poleaxed, fell to the hard wooden floor.

His vision clouded by midges, Irvine strayed within striking distance of Sorin's metal bar. Yelping in pain, the fishmonger whimpered, 'You broke my arm.'

Janus, however, was a different kettle of fish and skipped expertly to the side. Then, shuffling forwards adeptly, Janus grasped Sorin's arm and, spinning him around, twisted. Forced to the floor, the bar wrenched from his grasp, Sorin, climbing to his feet, was forced to retreat against the wall of the shack.

'Perak! Alfic! I need help here!'

'Father, get these damn ropes off of me,' shouted Alfic.

His hands suddenly free, Alfic leapt to his feet. Looking around frantically, he picked a large pumpkin from one of Bern's displays and threw it. The wine merchant expertly deflected the missile with the crowbar taken from Sorin, as chunks of pumpkin sprayed all around. This was the distraction Alfic needed, and he launched himself at Janus. Rolling around, punching and kicking, the pair careered into another of Bern's neatly arranged displays, each attempting to secure the iron bar. Wrestling the bar away from Alfic, Janus, a look of utter fanaticism in his eyes, raised the crude weapon above his head.

'Take that,' shouted Sorin, smashing a piece of broken fruit stand across Janus's head. Janus's eyes glazed over and he slumped forwards on top of Alfic.

Grasping Keen by the scruff, as the butcher crept towards the exit, Perak growled, 'And where do you think you're going, you skulking worm?' Hauling the butcher to his feet, Perak, turning towards Alfic, asked, 'Are you all right, Son?'

Hauling the wine merchant's limp body from atop him, Alfic, feeling at the small bloody hole made by Keen's knife, replied, 'I'm fine, just a bit tender.'

'Lascana, are you all right?' asked Sorin, tying Milvus and then Keen to the same chairs occupied by Alfic and Lascana. 'You really should look after yourself, you know, after all you are'–

'What, pregnant! You know, I wondered what that bump at the front was,' said Lascana sardonically. 'Stop fussing, I'm fine.'

'Keen and Milvus, who'd have thought? I'll give them a sore, bloody head,' cursed Alfic savagely.

'Easy Son, they may think they're acting of their own volition, but they're not, not really,' said Perak.

'You're the one disrupting the school, not us,' shouted Keen. 'All we're doing is'–

'Oh, be quiet,' despaired Lascana, and she rammed an apple into his mouth.

Smiling at Lascana, Alfic, in pain, rubbed at his thigh. He then turned to Perak. 'So, Father, what are you doing here?'

'Yes, how did you know?' added Lascana.

'Well, that's gratitude for you,' smiled Sorin, hauling Janus to his feet and sitting him down next to the others. Then, binding the wine merchant's wrists, the farmer began rifling through the merchant's pockets.

Ushering Alfic and Lascana to the side, Perak explained, 'Still thinking Gable was under the influence of Gradine's coin, Keen informed him of this undertaking. So as not to blow Gable's cover, we thought it best that just the two of us come to your aid.'

'You knew of this?' exclaimed Lascana, staring at Keen and Milvus incredulously.

'Keen figured, with you and Alfic out of the way and Vara unable to act, it would then be a simple matter to coerce us,' declared Perak sadly, 'ridding Kuelack of our opposition once and for all.'

'I'll give them coerce,' growled Alfic, staring over at Keen and Milvus in disgust.

'Well, I'm just glad Janus was under the coin's influence,' said Sorin.

'Oh,' exclaimed Lascana, joining Sorin and helping him with the restraints. 'Why's that?'

'Not many people know this, but Janus was a captain in the army, he was an excellent swordsman. Under his own volition, who knows what damage he could do?'

'Have you got their coins?' asked Alfic.

'Yes,' announced Sorin darkly, holding up a leather pouch. 'It's as we suspected. Every one of them except Milvus and Keen had one.'

'I'll take them to the forge to be melted down,' decided Alfic.

'Alfic, do you think Casey and Elias had magic? After all, they were offered coins and refused,' surmised Lascana.

Disappointment clear in his voice, Alfic, looking upon Keen and Milvus, said, 'Lascana, there is no mystery here, it comes down to greed. Casey and Elias, however, come from a society raised to survive and live without wealth and possessions.'

'I don't know, Son. I've heard all sorts of stories regarding Korda agents' conditioning,' offered Perak.

'If that's the case, Father, how do you explain Elias Tan? He was just a baker.'

Having delivered the coins to Gable's forge, it wasn't long before Alfic returned. The sight of his friends of many years, now deprived of the coins, was a harrowing one. Tied securely to chairs, their faces had already taken on an unhealthy pallor, and sweat lay like a glossy sheen upon their skin, reminding him of the Sringarian priests his mother had told him about, and the frenzied fits they would suffer in order to contact their deities.

His anger needing some kind of outlet, Alfic turned and, grasping Keen roughly by the chin, snarled, 'Open your eyes, look, look at your friends. This is Gradine's doing. Does it make you proud to see them this way, lusting after those cursed artefacts?'

'Alfic I... we only wished for... what was best for the school...' stuttered Keen.

'And this is the result,' thundered Alfic.

Zombie-like Milvus droned, 'It is... for the good... of the school...'

Squatting in between Keen and Milvus, Alfic, now calmness personified, said, 'This is only the beginning. There is a lesson to be learnt here, I think, so together we will stay awake and watch and share, in part, their suffering as our friends recover from their addiction to Gradine's enchanted coins.'

They watched in silence over a number of hours as Bern, Irvine and Janus Loker, shaking uncontrollably, gritted their teeth in anguish, struggling and straining against their bonds, their clothing now soaked in sweat. Then, the three men, unable to stomach the anguish any more, cried out in agony.

CHAPTER EIGHT

FESTIVAL

Distracted, Perak looked up as, arm in arm, a happy couple emerged from the food hall, releasing the smells of roasting meat, warm bread and cooked pastries, into the chill afternoon air, accompanied by raucous conversation and laughter.

'A joyous foundation day to you, Perak Bruin,' they said in unison.

'And a joyous foundation day to you too,' smiled Perak, pushing his way through the thick wooden double doors into the smoke-filled atmosphere. But he was far from happy.

His friends may well be on the way to recovering from the effects of Gradine's coins, but there was still no news of Vara's whereabouts. In order to take his mind off of Vara's plight, he focused his attention on the festivities, now in its third day of four...

Foundation day, venerated each year in winter, celebrated the founding of the school; it marked a transition from the age of constant war, barbarianism and brutality to peace and culture. It was also a welcome distraction from winter's gloom.

Travellers from across Aymara also attended the auspicious occasion in order to celebrate the significance of this mark in history. They took the opportunity to sample the school's varied cuisine as well as enjoy the school's famed hospitality. But most of all, they came here to eat the meat of the Argol. Famed for its succulent life-sustaining properties, the rare wild goat, now found only in Navar, was eaten by Pellagrin and his followers on this very spot, whilst they constructed the fortress.

Approaching the serving counter, Perak ordered a beer. Then, through the smoky atmosphere, he sought out Alfic, who was sitting together with Micas and the rest of the grounds crew, enjoying a well-earned respite from the rigours of providing for and maintaining the school. Looking further afield, he saw Savarin together with Merle sat alone at a table in the corner.

Savarin was dressed in all his chintz finery across from Merle, who was dressed in a dark satin frock and light tan waist coat, staring into a glass of dark beer. She'd been crying.

'Savarin, Merle. Are you both drunk?'

'Yes, so, what of it?' said Savarin darkly.

'Oh, hello, Perak,' Merle sniffed, her eyes trying to focus as she looked up at him with red-raw eyes. She then tried to appear more sober, but didn't succeed.

'Are you all right, Merle?'

'Am I all right? Thas a very good quessshtion?'

Grasping Perak by his shirt, Merle pulled him close, her rum infused breath making him gag.

'Perak, I fear for the sschool, now your son is in charge. I have sheen thingsssh, heard thingsssh. I've known all along he'ssh been slowly disposing of the older teachers to make way for his own shupporters,' continued Merle. 'Kuelack is behind it all, and I said nothing.'

Reaching across the table, Perak, grasping her hands in his, said, 'It's all right Merle, you were scared to say anything. That is only human!'

'Hasssh Kuelack got shhome shhort of hold over Magen?' boomed Savarin. 'Becaush, if I find out Kuelack was behind Exedra's death...'

'Why? So you can go storming into Kuelack's quarters?'

'That snake, Kuelack, ordered Almagest killed, for Gronin's sake!' Savarin hissed savagely.

Perak, looking around the packed food hall, warned, 'Let's not cause a scene, not here on this particular day, all right?'

'Cruelack's nottthhhing like Almagest,' said Merle darkly.

'What did you just say?' smiled Perak.

'Crulack'sh nosshhhing like Almagest. Whahss so funny?' she asked, nonplussed.

Despite his dour mood, Savarin smiled. 'I think that name will stick.'

Merle, grinning, said, 'Oh, I see what you mean. I loved him, you know; just like you, Ssssavarin, loved Exedra.'

'Magen told me that she had to kill Exedra,' barked Savarin seriously, 'becaussh Mass, through Ex... Exedra... would have killed us all. I need to know, Perak, was this Kuelack's doing?'

'Keep your voice down, Savarin, there's more going on here than your need to avenge Exedra,' shushed Perak, looking around seriously. 'At first she was under Kuelack's thumb, but later on, well, we're not so sure.'

'Promise me, Perak, that should I fall, you will not let Kuelack turn this school into a haven of evil.'

'What sort of talk is that Savarin, "if I should fall?". Listen to me, Tallus was a smug, arrogant fool. He abused his power, turning the nuances of Animistic calling into something evil. That was my son's doing; that is the measure of the monster my son truly is. Consider that before you go wading in with your grief.'

'Almagest was also very brave?' continued Merle, as if they hadn't said anything. 'Do you know he was the one who discovered the traitor in our midst and foiled Zakan's attempt to infiltrate Pellagrin's? That was over a hundred years ago.'

'No, I didn't. He never mentioned it,' stated Perak, swallowing a mouthful of beer from his glass.

Now quite sober, Merle hissed, 'I was there that day, Perak... the traitor lay dead in the corridor and Almagest, having raised the alarm, stood steadfast as Zakan's men appeared through the rear door to the main hall. When I arrived, together with the fortress's soldiers, Almagest was standing within a glowing halo of power forging forwards and forcing Zakan's fighting Harajin back through the betrayer's door...'

'Betrayer's door?' questioned Perak.

'That was the name we gave the rear door to the fortress's old courtyard,' mused Merle. Anyway, with the help of the greyswords and the school guard, Almagest defeated the attackers. I later found out that Zakan attacked because he believed we were protecting something called the Harmony stone.'

'The Harmony stone, an interesting story, Merle,' said Perak, making light of it. Did you find anything?'

'After Principal Sakar and Almagest returned, having destroyed Zakan and his fortress at Orrin Marsh, we looked, but found nothing. The conclusion reached was that Zakan was mistaken.' Turning to Savarin and sidling up close, Perak placing his hand on his friend's shoulder, whispered, 'I swear, Savarin, we will avenge Exedra and Almagest, and all those victims of my son's avarice,' he hissed, 'but for now, please do nothing.'

Standing, Perak squeezed through crowds of people, making his way over to Alfic's table.

'Father,' greeted Alfic, 'glad you could join us. Are Savarin and Merle well?'

'As well as can be expected, recent issues withstanding, it's nothing a friendly face and a firm shoulder couldn't fix.'

'What about out there?' nodded Alfic, indicating the farm and the surrounding fields.

'Apart from a bit of broken fencing, everything's under control, Son. Don't worry, Drench and I took care of it.'

Indicating the benches and tables groaning under the plates of food, Perak, looking towards the rafters hung with foliage, said, 'I see Amy has outdone herself again.'

'Yes, she's a traditionalist, all right. Let's see now, as I remember it. Blackthorn berries represent winter; broom, plenty; and hazelnut, good health, whereas juniper wards against evil, as does holly, the rest of the foliage, as far as I can tell is just for embellishment?'

'Well, it's good to see my teachings were not in vain,' smiled Perak.

'I always *try* to listen, Father.'

'It's nice to see people happy again,' said Perak, indicating the throng sat around talking, laughing and revelling in the hospitable atmosphere.

'Yes, for the time being. Talking to a traveller from Calabash, he told me the people are worried, and full of unrest, and that the forces there are gearing for war, said it was rumoured they were headed for the Zapatian border; whilst a wagon trader, who transported the Argol meat from Navar, says that a number of clans are now ranging north, towards Srinigar.'

The tall, muscular Amus Holt, finishing his ale, said, 'It's as though the whole world's gone mad.'

'No, Amus, just my brother,' said Alfic sternly. 'If Kuelack has his way, the whole of Aymara will be at war.'

'You think Kuelack is responsible?' exclaimed Amus.

'Alfic, I'm going to the bar. Can I get you another drink?' Perak shouted over the general hubbub whilst chewing contentedly on a candied piece of fruit.

'No, I best be going, animals to oversee and all that, but thanks anyway,' replied Alfic. 'Hey, don't any of you go drinking too much? There's still work to do, and you know we'll only make you suffer,' smiled Alfic. 'Am I right, Micas?'

'I'm looking forward to it,' said Alfic's blond haired good looking protégé eagerly.

Micas's comment was met with a cacophony of derision from the workforce.

'So, Micas, are you looking forward to bossing the workforce around now you're promoted?' asked Perak.

'Oh yes, I'll have them hopping around like jack rabbits,' sneered Micas.

'I only hope in a couple of months' time, you won't be cursing Alfic's name,' smiled Perak.

'Father, there's nothing wrong with being up to your eyebrows in dung,' Alfic chuckled. 'Isn't that right, Micas?'

'It's no more than I'm used to,' replied Micas dryly.

His eyes narrowing, Perak stared at Micas. He had personally recruited the young, good-looking groundsman who had proved an invaluable member of the staff ever since he'd arrived, but recently a darker side had emerged. He had also put his faith in the muscular Simon Tubney. Hailing originally from Barfleet village a couple of leagues from the school, Tubney, who had repaid his trust tenfold, had recently worked for a wealthy baron in the capital. It had transpired that the daughter of the wealthy count residing at the estate in which Simon worked had, with time on her hands, demanded sexual favours from him, threatening that if she didn't get her way, she would plead rape. Fearing a jail sentence, Simon complied, and they had had several elicit rendezvous before they were discovered. But to avoid her father's wrath, the daughter accused him of rape anyway, and Simon had fled the capital. Seeking work at Pellagrin's, Perak had recruited the likeable lad.

Another, who had proved to be a hard worker and an asset to the school, was Amus Holt. Hailing originally from Navar, he was a wizard when it came to animals and livestock. And then there was the youngest of the new recruits, the conundrum that was Flullen Archer.

As if he'd been reading his thoughts, Alfic, smiling seriously, said, 'Good lad, that Amus. Have you noticed he's always munching on something?'

'Bloody good worker though, as is Simon Tubney,' nodded Perak.

'Flullen Archer, however, is about as useful as an Oscan bird with it's head buried in the sand,' complained Alfic. 'There's something about him that I just can't fathom.'

'I agree,' said Perak. 'I get the feeling he's never serviced a grand property in his life, and for that matter, never done a hard day's work.'

'Well, that's a conundrum for another day. Now I best go join Sorin and help him with any disgruntled livestock.'

In the chamber's unearthly blue light, Mace parried, then swung his sword. Advancing with a flurry of blows, he lunged, but the ordeal his body had endured in the dungeon once more came back to haunt him, causing him to overextend. Vanir sidestepped, then parried his sword as Mace ducked and rolled to the guard position, Vanir's sword whistling over his head.

'Curses,' spat Mace, wiping at the sweaty sheen on his forehead. 'Never thought I would fall for that one.'

'We can rest if you like,' said Vanir, twirling his sword skilfully.

'No! We keep practicing; I'm no good to anyone if I can't hold my own. I am a greysword, one of the four. I have sworn a sacred oath on this sword to uphold truth and honour,' growled Mace angrily. 'Now defend yourself.'

Again, Mace swung his sword, varying his attack, trying to catch Vanir off balance, but the blond-haired greysword defended with calm precision until, once more, he held his sword to Mace's throat.

Mace smiled then, and batting Vanir's sword aside, reached for a canteen full of water. Taking a long swallow, he said, 'I never realised how good a swordsman you were until now.'

'Well, it's down to you, you taught me everything I know.'

Frustrated, Mace said, 'Ah, training's one thing, but there's nothing like a real fight to hone your skills.'

Holstering his weapon, Mace strolled across the chamber towards the large sarcophagus sat upon a plinth above them in the middle of the chamber. Tracing the inscription on the side of the decorative tomb with his fingers, he looked around the vaulted chamber at the ornate marble pillars and thick roots, which spread across the chamber's roof.

'Do you think he did this?' asked Vanir.

'Who?'

'Pellagrin?'

'What? Give us this place to hide?'

'Well, this is his tomb and above us are the roots of Pellagrin's oak. Perhaps he's helping Kuelack's enemies in times of conflict,' chuckled Vanir.

'How can you be certain?' questioned Mace.

'You think Keegan just stumbled upon this place?'

'If I remember rightly, Keegan said he fell through the wall. That qualifies as a stumble.'

'And you believe him? So, how come no one else knows of this? Something must have compelled him to stumble upon this place?' considered Vanir. 'After all, others are now using the tunnels.'

'Look, all I know is we didn't choose this place; it chose us. Let's just be grateful for that,' said Mace.

'I didn't realise you were so superstitious?'

'It's called respect for the revered dead.'

'Well, meaning no disrespect, Mister Pellagrin,' said Vanir, bowing gracefully towards the tomb, 'but I'm beginning to feel like a rabbit in a warren.' Gazing skywards, Vanir said longingly, 'I'll bet the festivities are in full swing right now.'

'I know what you mean. It's been a real dick punch missing the festival.'

'Ahh, what I wouldn't do for a few ales right now, and the warm embrace of a serving girl wouldn't go amiss either? Instead, we venture out from this rabbit warren and observe, very rarely do we intervene. All work and no play makes Vanir a dull boy, Mace.'

Running his finger along his blade, Mace said, 'Well, perhaps it's time that changed. I've been thinking about my fight with Hogan, and who trained him; he was far more skilled with a sword than a half-giant assassin should be.'

'Well, it wasn't me, and it wasn't you,' said Vanir.

'Karnack or Jackamar then?'

'There is another possibility,' suggested Vanir. 'Arhass could be enchanting weapons and students.'

'So it seems we do have a purpose?'

Taking another swallow of water, Mace was about to hand the canteen to Vanir when they were interrupted by Keegan who appeared ghost-like through the wall. He had a satchel in one hand and a large flask in the other.

'Greetings, woeful warriors, I come bearing gifts. Take a draft of wine, Mace Denobar, and a chicken thigh, Vanir Ulrich.'

Kissing Keegan's forehead, Mace beamed, 'Keegan you beauty, where did you get this?'

'With a little help from Amy Dickson, I borrowed this meagre feast from the kitchens.'

'After all these years,' smiled Mace, 'your tracking skills have finally done us some good.'

'If ther'sh one certainty in life,' said the new recruit, Simon Tubney, addressing the friends in the food hall. 'It's that when you're part of a certain community, people form opinions, then you move to shhomewhere completely new, like here, people form different opinionsss. What's that all about?'

'I know what you mean, onceshh you're dubbed with a name, it sticksshh,' lectured Elimi, wagging his finger purposefully. 'Take me and my brother, for instance. Despite being the most experienced workers at the school, we'll always be known as the blunder boysss.'

'Oh, why's that?'

'Thathhsss not important, what is, is that once you have a nickname, people don't change their mindsss, oh no, shhhit shticks.'

'You have to learn the hard way,' agreed Simon, shaking his head vigorously.

'When things go titttsss up, all you can do is help pick up the piecsshes, am I right, Micas?' said Elimi, elbowing the taciturn foreman's arm and spilling Micas's drink all over the table.

'It's a term of endearment, Elimi, get over it?' said Amus, returning with his drink, and sitting his long lanky legs and frame down beside Simon Tubney.

Exasperated, Micas, taking a long swallow of what remained of his drink, glared at Elimi threateningly. 'People who have no backbone, no spine and take no responsibility for their mistakes deserve everything they get.'

'What isshh it with you, Micasshh? Why can't you drink beer and have fun? Why can't you act like a normal persshhon?' said Elimi, swaying to and fro and finding it difficult to focus.

'Because some of us have greater ambitions in life than to piss our lives up against a wall.'

Elimi now struggling to form his words, said, 'Hey, there'sh nothing wrong with a bit of gosshhip, Micas. Amy Dickson sayss the kitchensh have been hexshd, assh true as I sssit here,' insisted Elimi, despite a cacophony of heckling.

Standing, Micas announced, 'I'm going to talk to someone who speaks with some sense.' He then left the table.

'Oh well, itsss hissshhh loss,' smiled Elimi casually.

'So, why does Amy say the kitchens are hexed?' urged Flullen, intrigued.

'Ssheee sssays shhheveral thingss have moved when no one's around. Why, only a couple of hours ago sshhee says a flagon of ale and some food just disappeared.'

'I agree with Micas. Amy's almost as bad as Lawna when it comes to rumour and hearsay,' said Drench, placing his drink on the table and sitting down next to them.

'Hey Drench, glad you could finally join us,' said Perak.

'Just making sure that section of fencing along the furthest perimeter was secured.'

'Alfic blames the broken fencing on sapphire sprites. He thinks that they are influencing the farm animals and creatures of the woods,' said Flullen, sat next to the tall, wiry Amus, now intrigued. 'Does anyone know what he's talking about?'

'Perhaps the sprites are the reason Alfic was tossed over the fence by Sorin's new bull?' exclaimed Elgin.

'Don't exaggerate, Elgin,' warned Perak.

'Sorin's replacement bull, tossed Alfic over a fence?' exclaimed Amus.

'Yes, I've never seen anyone run so fast. Alfic was not too happy, I can tell you.'

'How did it happen?' asked Flullen, now riveted by Elgin's story...

'Well, Alfic was urging the bull towards the sheds with a wooden herding pole, but it just made it mad,' explained Elgin.

'I would have liked to have seen that,' Flullen chuckled. 'Was Alfic all right?'

'Hey, we're talking about Alfic Bruin here, the man who killed two Ardent wolves bare handed. Of course he was all right,' said Elgin proudly.

The friends all looked at each other strangely but said nothing, all except Elimi, who had slumped unconscious onto the tabletop.

'So come on Drench, we could do with an uplifting tune,' said Amus.

'OK, but first I need a drink...'

It was then that a figure suddenly blocked the way.

'Perak, may I join you?'

Surprised at the female voice, Perak looked up to see the tall, lithe stick fighting mistress, Crystal. 'Of course, take a seat.'

Her jet-black hair tied into a ponytail, Crystal was dressed in a white long-sleeved shirt with multicoloured braiding and dark, baggy trousers, whilst her eye-catching good looks were focused and alert. 'It's so nice to hear laughter,' she said, sitting down beside him. 'This place has been like a tomb recently.'

'So, what's a girl like you doing in a place like this?' Perak inquired accusingly.

'Say that to all the girls, do you?' she said candidly.

'Of course, I bring one here every night,' chuckled Perak. 'So, what's up?'

'It's Kale, as you may or may not know we're seeing each other.'

'Yes, I know.'

'Have you noticed anything out of the ordinary with him?'

'Like what?'

'I'm not sure really, I can't put my finger on it, his attitude is more serious, and when I ask him what was wrong, he just says he's taken your advice on board, to be more focused more resolute, but nothing specific. I have to say at the time I couldn't really argue with that. I know he's had a lot on his plate recently, even so...'

'He's young and still finding his feet, it could be that he feels responsible for our current predicament, his encounter with the creature, for instance. He also recommended Magen as Aridain's teacher,' explained Perak. Seeing the anguish on her face, Perak, making up his mind, said, 'I'll tell you what, Crystal, I'll see what I can find out.'

'Thank you, Perak,' Crystal smiled, her relief clearly evident, 'it would be much appreciated.'

His mind wandering, Perak watched Drench take his tayel from behind the counter and began tuning the instrument. Then, satisfied, and sitting down comfortably at the end of the table, he took a long swallow of his drink and began strumming a foot tapping tune.

As Linda, the smiling waitress, placed another drink before them, Crystal, watching several of the school's residents dancing, smiled as she sat forward.

'Do you know Keegan had a thing for me?' she smiled.

'He's not backward in coming forward, is Keegan,' agreed Perak.

Chuckling to herself, Crystal said, 'It was over a year ago, Drench was playing a foot tapping tune, just as he is now, and Keegan and I were dancing, he told me he admired a strong woman, one who can fight and who is fierce and true.'

'Keegan's got a thing for every female at the school,' Perak chuckled, 'he has a no ties, no compromise, no commitments philosophy.'

'Oh, don't get me wrong, Keegan's fun and good company, and I took it in the spirit it was intended.' Her foot tapping along to the feisty beat, Crystal then said loudly, so they could hear her above the clapping and foot stomping, 'Good, isn't he? Drench is one of my best students. As well as playing the tayel, he's good with a fighting stick, and according to Konya, he's good with horses. I'm beginning to wonder if there's anything he can't do, although I've always wondered how he came by the name of Drench,' she mused.

'Keegan, is how!'

'What do you mean?'

'Keegan found him when he was a boy wandering outside the school's grounds in the rain. Soaked to the skin apparently, and dressed in nothing but a pair of dirty pyjamas, hence the name Drench.'

'The poor lad.'

'Up until this day he can't remember how he got here or who he is,' said Perak. 'I wonder what sort of trauma blanks out a person's past like that?'

'Hello Crystal, Perak.'

Realising the music had stopped, Perak and Crystal turned as one to see the tall, handsome, well-built figure of Drench. Sporting high cheekbones and a full head of fine, dark, wavy hair, Keegan's understudy stood expectantly before them.

'Don't stand to attention, boy, take a seat.'

'Thanks.'

'You play the tayel well. Still no recollection as to how, ehh?'

'No! It's so frustrating.'

Leaning close, Perak whispered, 'I know you and Keegan were close, so I was wondering...?'

'I don't know where he is, if that's what you're asking,' said Drench warily.

'And I wouldn't ask,' assured Perak, 'knowing of your loyalty to Keegan.'

'All I can tell you is, Keegan is in good company, and that the supplies I leave are always gone.'

They turned around at a shout and a burst of laughter, and watched as one of the serving girls slapped at Ryan Delran's roving hands. Ryan, together with Kuelack's other two chief henchmen, Gavin Torn and Cordovan Harker, sat drinking along with some of their friends at the far end of the hall.

'I'd say by the looks of them they have consumed far too much alcohol,' said Perak. 'I see trouble brewing.'

'Since Kuelack's inauguration, those three have been nothing but trouble,' stated Drench angrily, 'strutting around as though they own the place.'

'I've seen this behaviour before. Autonomy makes certain people drunk with power,' said Perak knowingly.

'Hey orphan boy, what are you staring at?'

'Turn away and ignore them, Drench,' said Perak.

'Hey, I'm talking to you,' growled Ryan Delran, standing and approaching their table, followed by his muscleman, Gavin Torn.

'They're sitting in our favourite seats,' smiled Gavin.

Perak sensed rather than heard the room go quiet and realised the situation could quickly get out of hand if not handled delicately.

Standing, Perak intercepted Ryan Delran. 'Ryan, Gavin, let me buy you boys a drink.'

Returning his stare contemptuously, Ryan said, 'You think you're so wise and so clever with your words, old man, but you and your family are not clever enough.'

'It's said that youth is wasted on the young, so full of opinions and yet so naïve,' said Perak, his face a mask of stone.

'Things are changing around here, old man. Kuelack has made this school strong again, into a place worthy of note, so stand aside before I put you in the infirmary.'

Standing up, Drench growled, 'Now that's just rude.'

Suddenly everyone was on their feet except Elimi, his snoring loud in the deafening silence.

'I didn't ask for your opinion, orphan boy,' Gavin sneered contemptuously.

Crystal, her demeanour taking on the look of a female huntress, stood, and staring directly into Gavin Torn's narrowing eyes, said, 'Is there a problem?'

'Stay out of this Crystal; you have no say here, unless, of course, you're siding with these ingrates.'

'We are as loyal as you,' growled Perak.

'Oh sure, you and your friends are innocent, just like Vanir and Mace and... Keegan,' sneered Delran, looking directly at Drench.

'You tell him, Ryan. Almagest was also a tired old fool, his death a blessing,' spat Cordovan Harker, approaching together with several of their friends.

'Choose your next words carefully, Harker,' warned Drench, advancing angrily.

'Why does a gamekeeper's arse-wipe care who's running the school, anyway? You've always had your head shoved down a rabbit hole?' chuckled Ryan Delran.

Her face turning serious, her fists curling, Crystal sneered, 'Students, I don't know, their mothers have only just finished wiping their arses and they think they own the place.'

'Boys, boys, there's no need for this. Let's just have a friendly drink and celebrate foundation day,' smiled Perak.

'You know, you're right, Perak. We will share a drink with you.' Delran then threw his drink into Drench's face.

Wiping at his eyes, Drench, outraged, started towards Delran, who tried to push past Perak. Perak grabbed Delran's hand and twisted, pinning his arm up behind his back, then forcing him face down onto the tabletop.

'Curse you, old man,' hissed Delran, struggling violently. 'Get your hands off of me!'

'I could have snapped your wrist and your elbow, but I didn't. Now tell your hounds to back off,' Perak growled dangerously.

'Aaarh, well don't just stand there,' shouted a squirming Ryan Delran, 'get this piece of troll dung off of me.'

Suddenly, the room erupted as Perak's show of force, intended to stop their aggression, came to naught. He then choked, as a strong arm wrapped around his throat and another pinned his arms to his side, he was then wrenched violently backwards.

'I'm going to enjoy this,' grinned Ryan Delran, cocking his fist to strike.

Perak ducked as Ryan threw a stiff right hand and Gavin Torn caught the blow full on the nose, which burst into a bloody mess across his face. Perak, now free from Gavin Torn's grip, kicked out, and as Delran doubled over with a painful yelp, Perak followed that with a vicious uppercut that sent Delran crashing onto the adjacent table, scattering drinks and food all across the floor. Perak then turned, but not quick enough as with a snarl Gavin Torn launched himself from the opposite bench, and together they crashed onto the ground where the over-muscled youth rained blows upon him.

Grabbing his flailing fists, Perak said, 'You may have muscle, but you have a lot to learn about hand-to-hand fighting.'

Clamping his legs around Ryan's waist, Perak then levered him to the floor and rolled over on top of him. He then incapacitated him with a solid fist to his jaw.

Thank you for that, Keegan, he thought.

Looking around, Perak despaired as the fight, now totally out of hand, spilled across the hall, and food and drink flew in all directions. Simon Tubney flailed about with his shovel-sized hands assailed by two of Delran's thugs, whilst fighting back-to-back were Drench and the slighter built Flullen Archer. Meanwhile, Amus Holt had picked up the remains of a chair and, bellowing like a maddened fire lizard, ran to Simon Tubney's aid.

Crystal, restrained and reticent, was doing her utmost to calm everyone down when suddenly a chair hit her back and head, sending her to her knees. Helping her to her feet, Perak looked at her seriously. 'Now is not the time for procrastination, Crystal,' yelled Perak. 'It's time to act!'

'You're right,' she said, tasting the blood on her fingers that had dribbled down the back of her neck. 'I'll take care of this.'

Perak watched, mesmerised, as Crystal, with fluid, intricate movements of her body, weaved and danced, stripping a knife from one of the students and deftly disarming another. Pinning them to the floor and holding the points of their own knives to their throats.

Standing, she looked down at them.

'Go, get out,' she hissed, 'before I kill you.'

Perak walked over to Delran and, grasping him by the collar, pulled him close and looked into his blood-spattered face.

'I hope this act of insanity was worth two black eyes.'

'It's a small price to pay for ultimate power. Do the smart thing, Perak, and give in, for in the end, your pathetic efforts will count for nothing. As for Crystal, it seems she's made her choice.'

Standing back, Perak stared at Ryan Delran, dismayed. 'Is this what this is all about? You would incite a riot, just to ascertain who is for or against my son.'

Alfic was right, he thought. *Kuelack's followers were drunk with power. The war they had desperately tried to avoid here at the school now seemed more certain than ever.*

Suddenly, a wind powered pressure wave cascaded through the hall, flattening everyone and everything it came into contact with. It was at this juncture that armed guards led by Karnack burst in through the kitchen doors, in a clatter of armour and weaponry. Forming a cordon, they separated the combatants.

'Savarin, what is the meaning of this? What is going on here?' growled Karnack.

Holding his sore head and gesturing for Karnack to keep his voice down, Savarin replied, 'Just establishing some clarity.'

'To what purpose, a council member does not interfere in the school's security?'

'If you'd been here sooner, I wouldn't have had to,' said Savarin, staring at Karnack severely.

'Who started this?' Karnack demanded, looking around at the dishevelled combatants.

'Perak started it, he attacked me,' squeaked Ryan Delran. 'I want them arrested.'

'Yeh,' agreed Gavin Torn, feeling at his nose. He then pointed to Crystal, 'tooggeder wid her.'

'Why am I not surprised?' spat Karnack, his eyes narrowing.

'It seems to me they condemned these men for just being who they are,' offered Savarin.

'These men were protecting themselves from these morons, who'd had far too much to drink.'

'Silence Crystal, I'm asking the questions here.' Peering at Savarin critically, Karnack said, 'It seems they are not the only ones who have had too much to drink.' Karnack then turned his one good eye upon Ryan Delran. 'You may be a big noise with Kuelack, Delran, but not with me, understand? Now can anybody corroborate this statement?'

The rest of Delran's gang, led by Cordovan Harker, all replied as one.

'You lying, scheming pack of gutter trolls...'

'Easy Drench,' placated Perak.

'Hold him,' bellowed Karnack.

Drawing himself up to his impressive height, Savarin, rubbing at his chin, looked down at Karnack and hissed, 'Delran and his thugs deliberately goaded them into a fight. They instigated this whole thing. Perak and his friends were just defending themselves, that's all.'

Karnack then turned to Ryan Delran, and ushering him into the corner, they exchanged harsh words.

'Do the words authority and respect mean nothing to you at all?' hissed Savarin, sideling up to Perak.

'Only when the situation demands it,' Perak grinned conspiratorially.

'Perak, you will leave the food hall right away and your men return to their dormitory,' ordered Karnack, turning towards them and drawing his sword.

'Why us?' demanded Amus, feeling at the cut above his eye. 'They started it.'

'You will do as I tell you or I'll throw you all in the dungeons,' Karnack bellowed.

'Amus, guys, it'll be all right,' placated Perak. 'Just do as he says.'

It was then that Elimi decided to wake up. 'Hey, what happened? Did I miss something?'

'Get him to his feet,' urged Perak.

Feeling totally ostracised, Perak, together with his workforce, shuffled despondently from the kitchens. Suspended between Drench and Simon Tubney, Elimi said, 'Where are you taking me, guys? The night's still young.'

CHAPTER NINE

KORDA'S AND DISSIDENTS

Hitching lifts on wagons and carts, Casey Defray and Elias Tan travelled slowly northwards. They then headed east towards the small town of Templar, avoiding the capital and troops patrolling along the road to Gonda, and, more importantly, Kuelack's spies.

Thanking the farmer and his dog, transporting a wagon full of spices to the border town of Hemlock, for his assistance, Casey and Elias hiked northwards across the Galbanium expanse; an area of deep ravines, raging rivers, dry moor and scrubland.

'Not this again,' bemoaned Casey.

'I just think it was rotten to leave them in the lurch like that. They could have done with our help, especially after the kid saved my life.'

When Casey remained silent, Elias, stepping over a snow-covered tree that had fallen across the path, continued, 'After all the supplies they provided us with, after Perak arranged for Spalding's minister to shelter us in his house of worship, I can't believe you're still sceptical. That hamlet, for instance; the blacksmith, a man we didn't even know, took us in,' said Elias, 'and fed us, despite knowing we were from Calabash.'

'He didn't know!'

'Of course he knew!' exclaimed Elias.

'I'm intrigued,' enquired Casey, changing the subject abruptly. 'Why did you give up so easily? I pursued you because you were one of our government's foremost antagonists.'

'To see you eat your words. Perhaps I thought you had changed? Perhaps to see if you really cared?'

'You are a dissident, as are many others; that's the only reason I need.'

'Our government made us dissidents, Korda,' spat Elias, turning towards her and pointing his finger at her accusingly. 'People have the annoying tendency towards freedom of speech and freedom of actions, especially when the government rationalises their actions by labelling it with the words: governing the people. The only crimes us *dissidents* are guilty of is demanding equal rights for the citizens of Calabash.'

'Equality is what our government strives for!'

'Everyone's equal when it suits them, but behind closed doors, the best goods and services go to those in government, the government you support.'

'Why shouldn't the individuals working hardest for the people's welfare deserve more?' Casey stated candidly.

'That's a very Durbarian attitude,' said Elias.

'You are in no position to give me lectures on Durbarian society.'

'At least I didn't isolate myself from people.'

'I isolated myself because people always manage to throw a spanner in the works.'

'Unlike the Korda, of course.'

Sticking her chin into the air, Casey stated proudly, 'Bovid is a ruler who seeks perfection through production and conformity. People need to be reminded of these facts.'

'And the Korda are the ones to do it. I was out of Calabash, far away! I wasn't causing any trouble.' When Casey remained silent, Elias continued, 'Well, Bovid's certainly not ashamed of getting his hands dirty.'

'What you call inhuman atrocities, we call the purge, ridding ourselves of nonconformists in an effort to bring order to the land.'

'Every population, regardless of the regime or leadership, is at best three meals away from revolution. Can't you see that subjugating people who crave nothing but a life of peace and a full belly is wrong?' pleaded Elias. 'So desperate is Bovid, to control the way of life that he and his kin have created, that he formed the Korda secret service. Durbah has dissidents, but they don't persecute a whole society because of a few individuals, because they know that alienating their own people will only lead to chaos. Open your eyes, Casey,' insisted Elias. 'You are an individual. Ask questions, delve past the glossy sheen instead of following like an Agoti deer intoxicated on Rabidon fruit.'

In muted silence, they hiked across the rolling snow covered countryside. As the sun's rays lit up the tops of the trees like Roman candles, they entered an extensive patch of woodland as the temperature began to drop. Trudging through the snow and the undergrowth, they came upon a clearing that looked like a part of Fornax's realm come to Aymara. Dotted around were mounds of smoking bracken and earth and in the darkness two large pits spewed nauseous yellow gas into the air.

Hunkering down so as not to be seen by the gang of men sat around a fire eating and drinking, Elias said, 'Charcoal pits, used in slaking lime.'

'Yes, but unlike those kiln workers, we can't afford to sit around eating and drinking,' declared Casey, 'so we keep moving.'

Using the clouds of noxious gas as cover, they moved around the edge of the clearing, making sure not to make a noise in the late afternoon light. Keeping the setting sun on their left, they continued onwards through the stark woodland, until, in the distance through the trees, they saw lights moving slowly against the backdrop of a white wilderness.

'That must be the wagons transporting the slaked lime to the capital,' said Elias.

Waiting patiently until the wagon train had passed, they crossed the road, and with the sun now low in the sky, they hiked over low hills interspersed with brush and stunted oak trees, hawthorn and pine. It was completely dark when they came across the old empty ruin sat forlorn upon a raised hillock. Jumping a small icy brook that ran along the edge of the tumbled down building, they climbed the old defensive ramparts now overgrown with blackthorn and bramble thickets beneath a sky, blossoming with stars. Pushing through the thorny tangle, they crept up a stone stairway, and slowly, covertly, crept inside. Dark exits and entrances led left and right, and exploring one of these entrances, they found themselves in the base of a tower sheltered from the elements.

Her eyes adjusting to the murk, Casey said, 'This will do. I'll go and find us some dry wood.'

'Yes, ma'am!' saluted Elias sarcastically.

Whilst Casey was away, Elias searched the chamber and soon found an old, discarded torch. Wrapping a piece of pitch-soaked cloth around it together with some gathered moss and lichen, Elias, blowing on a smouldering section of beef fungus they carried and used as a firelighter, lit the torch. Searching the ruins, he entered a large anti-chamber and came across a rotted Banth carcass, the bones and fur burnt and blackened.

Peering wearily into the depths of the chamber, Elias hissed quietly, 'It seems you came to a fiery end, my hairy friend, probably whilst minding your own business and grazing too far from the herd, but it seems your attacker has long gone.'

Collecting the old bones and adding Banth wool to the torch for tinder, he returned to the chamber and soon had a fire going, slowly adding the old dry bones he had crushed up as well as some dead brush lying around the floor.

Casey reappeared and began adding dead wood found outside to the flames, and, when the fire was good and hot, Elias produced two cuts of preserved beef. Adding them to an old pan with some wild garlic and herbs, he proceeded to fry them off together with a pocketful of winter mushrooms that Casey had found whilst collecting wood. Half an hour later, with their bellies full and their bodies warm for the first time in hours, they sat quietly, sharing a canteen of pear cider.

'Poor Drummer, I wonder if he misses me?'

'No need to worry about that. From what I've seen, Alfic's family won't let anything bad happen to him, besides as long as they are being fed and watered, horses are simple beings.'

Producing a small pipe he'd fashioned from a piece of old bone, Elias began filling it with a small amount of tobacco. 'I still can't get my head around the fact that if it wasn't for Alfic's son, I would have died. I mean, Aquar's fishy bits! How did he do that?'

'Alfic's son is a true enigma.'

'Just think what you could do with power like that. Imagine the lives that could be saved. We could eradicate poverty forever; the people could start afresh.'

'Don't get any ideas Elias, he is but a child. Best not to wish for things that are unobtainable.'

'You're the one that was so insistent we leave. Anyway, it's all mute,' insisted Elias. 'The minute we step foot in Calabash, we'll probably be captured and tortured to death, anyway.'

They sat and stared at the flames in silence for a long while, and Casey's thoughts wandered to the people she'd left behind at Pellagrin's. As hard as it had been to admit, Elias was right. The people who she now called friends were not a horde of savages intent on ravaging and pillaging, as her government had portrayed, not as though she would ever admit it. In fact, they were no different from the people in her hometown of Poleen in Saran province. She smiled then and inexplicably; Keegan Fold's image popped into her thoughts. Shaking him from her head, she took another mouthful of cider, then offered it to Elias, who was calmly puffing on the bone pipe.

'I admit I was dismayed, having seen the change in our friends during the meeting at Sorin's house. But Alfic was right. Our presence there would only have complicated matters. Gradine, in her ignorance, told me of their plans. She had an uncanny knowledge of who we were and what we were doing at the school. Gonda and our government are communicating, but it's all a falsehood. In reality, Durbah is plotting our government's downfall, and on top of that, Kuelack has been seeking the Firebrand stone. For all we know, he could have found it.'

'Firebrand stone, you don't believe in that nonsense, do you?' scoffed Elias.

'To tell you the truth, I don't know what to believe anymore.' Sitting up, Casey fixed him with a serious expression. 'Listen to me, Elias. 'If we were granted an audience, together, as Korda and insurgent, we could convince Bovid to withdraw our troops, before they walk into Kuelack's trap.'

'Why this sudden change of heart?'

'I'm not sure. I only know my going back will help prevent a war. I can't explain it, but a compulsion is drawing me home, to our king, and you're going to help me.'

'Your very sure. What's stopping me from leaving you in the dead of night?'

'Nothing, but you won't, because the circumstances have changed.'

'Why, what circumstances? All I know is that there's a price on my head.'

'Because I know you, Elias. You have a good heart.'

'I thought I was safe living a new life away from Quelea,' grumbled Elias, 'that our government had forgotten about me. Now I'm being escorted by a Korda back to my country's black-hearted centre.'

They sat in silence for what seemed an eternity, each lost in their thoughts. Sometime later, Casey, throwing pieces of rotted wood into the fire, asked, 'When Gradine offered you a coin, you resisted; how?'

'Because, we underprivileged Calabashian's, put no faith in wealth.'

'Bullshit, I'm a Korda. They conditioned us to resist. That means you are either Korda or, more likely, you have magic?'

Elias remained silent, staring into the fire for a long while before replying, 'I was a Korda agent once, before I realised the hypocrisy of it all.'

'Who were you? What was your Korda name? Tell me.'

'My Korda name was Sujet.'

'Sujet, SUJET! The Korda agent who revolutionised our organisation's fighting techniques, the procedures that now shape our order; that man is a legend. If you are him, how come I found you so easily?'

'Perhaps I wanted to be found; perhaps I was looking for somebody in whom I could trust, instil some common sense, take on some new ideas, a Korda agent who doesn't just accept our government's doctrine blindly.'

With that, Casey stood. Then, walking belligerently to her bedroll laid upon a thick layer of straw, she lay down.

'Pellagrin's baker is the Korda Prime, Sujet, ha, the very thought.'

'You know you're right, I'm not him, I was just pulling your leg, I've had a bang on the head. Forget we ever had this conversation.'

Pulling the sheet over her head gruffly. Casey then turned her back to him and under her breath mumbled angrily, 'Sujet, Korda Prime, hah.'

CHAPTER TEN

ALTERED STATES

Yawning loudly, the effervescent Aridain trotting beside her, Lascana shambled through the empty halls of her temporary home, her footfalls echoing from the walls despite her best efforts to be quiet.

It had been another hard but rewarding day, tidying and sorting their possessions into some kind of order, whilst at the same time attempting to engage with the public in an effort to sell her goods.

Caressing her stomach for the umpteenth time that day, she looked down and thought guiltily; *With a new life on the way, I must be more measured and less reckless.* Calming her apprehension with an effort, she recalled her mother's words of wisdom as if she'd uttered them yesterday:

Why worry over things that you can never alter, or things that might never come to pass? What will be, will be?

'Muuuum hurry up, I'm hungry,' insisted Aridain, pulling heavily on her arm.

'Oh what a surprise,' she commented ironically and then smiled. 'I'm sure you've got hollow legs.'

Opening the thick oak door, she shambled along the stone-floored corridor and then stopped before a smaller wooden door. Inserting the large metal key into the lock, she turned it, and with a satisfying clunking of metal, the door swung inwards on silent hinges. Closing the door behind her, Lascana, astounded, stared into their new chambers and the many items of all shapes and sizes which laid around the apartment. Lying on the small round table in the middle of the room, amongst pots and pans, toiletries, and clothing, was a small piece of parchment.

Picking it up, Lascana immediately recognised the writing:

Just a few things, me and the workforce have managed to cobble together. Hope they come in handy. It was signed by Sorin.

With tears in her eyes, thinking about the generosity of loyal friends and colleagues, she began sorting through the donated items, and an hour later Lascana, with Aridain's help, had sorted the confusion and clutter into a semblance of order.

But the tears represented more than just the generosity of friends. She had taken as much time as she dare settling into the new apartment. Sooner or later, she would have to face up to her new duties, now that they were living in the fortress under Kuelack's protection. It meant servicing its many occupants, including Gradine's and Magen's chambers, leaving her little time to attend her stall.

'There we are, that's the last of it,' said Lascana, looking around the room sadly. 'How has it come to this?'

Twenty minutes later having diced some vegetables, and prepared a small leg of mutton, Lascana, rocking back and forth, sat quietly darning a pair of Alfic's winter socks, whilst Aridain, with tongue clamped firmly between his teeth, concentrated on stirring the vegetable and meat stew, cooking upon the small wood stove.

Admiring her handy work, Lascana stood and walked over to Aridain's rocking horse, unscathed apart from its mane and tail, burnt away in the fire. The rocking horse reminded her of their cottage now stood seared and derelict, and their good friends, Sorin and Celia, who had sheltered them, when they had appeared smoke-stained, tired and weary, on their doorstep, in their hour of need, with Aridain wrapped in a warming blanket. That same night, sat staring mutely into the fire, she had looked up with smoke-sore, bloodshot eyes at Celia's approach...

'I put Aridain in with Selva and Duran. Poor mite dropped straight off. He was exhausted,' said Celia.

'We're truly blessed to have friends like you,' Lascana had smiled, caressing Celia fondly.

'Think nothing of it, Lascana. Selva and Duran told us what happened.'

'The creature's dead now. That's all that matters.'

Then, putting a comforting arm around her shoulder, Celia had handed her a mug of chamomile tea. She had smiled and said, 'it will send you right off to sleep. Don't fret, deary, things will work out, they always do.'

Alfic tired and weary, and bearing the scars from the fight, his clothes bloodied and torn, had looked up and putting on a brave face, as he always did, smiled and said, 'I promise Celia we'll be out of your hair by tomorrow morning.'

'Nonsense Alfic, you can stay as long as is necessary. I can't imagine returning to find my home burnt to the ground. I think I'd be physically sick. Is this fight with your brother really worth the loss of your home, Alfic?' enquired Celia. 'The more you lose, the greater the impact. Kuelack knows this. Now all your belongings are gone.'

'Is that what you think this is, Celia, just a fight between brothers?' Sorin had said tersely.

Lascana had watched the Corvin's sympathetically as they listened in horror and confusion, Sorin more readily accepting of the situation, Celia not so much, the revelations challenging her practical outlook on life.

'Celia, there is so much more at stake here,' she had offered. 'If we're to prevail, if the school is to survive these events, then sacrifices will have to be made. We don't blame anyone for the loss of our home, it was our decision to fight. But the loss of their home had cut more deeply than Alfic had cared to let on. Independent, having to rely on Sorin and Celia for support, Alfic had felt the most uncomfortable...'

Back in the present, caressing Aridain's rocking horse fondly, the cherry wood vibrant and filling her with positivity despite its time in the fire, she began measuring for a replacement mane and tail.

It had been a strange sight, seeing the rocking horse, plus their cherry wood kitchen cupboards and utensils, standing unscathed among the ashes, she thought. *Their livestock had also survived the fire and now resided at the farm; it was as though nature, magic, call it what you will, had sought a balance. For everything lost, some things must be saved.*

'The pigs and the chickens hid beneath the trees in the woods Mummy,' said Aridain matter-of-factly. 'They wondered where you'd gone; they were so pleased to see you when you came to look for them.'

'What have I told you about eves dropping, young man,' warned Lascana tersely.

Aridain looked up at her and smiled. 'Sorry Mummy.'

Lascana knew you should never become attached to your livestock, but another tear trickled down her cheek at the memory, nonetheless. However, some precious objects hadn't survived, like her beautiful, reedmace moth silk rug, depicting an eagle clutching an oak branch stitched meticulously into a brown, red, and white background that Alfic had made for her birthday.

She smiled at the memory of him presenting it to her, an enormous grin on his face. 'It must have taken months to complete,' she said to herself quietly.

'What did, Mummy?' asked Aridain innocently.

Not realising she had spoken out loud, she said, 'The rug your father made, it was a work of… One day, when you're older, perhaps you'll understand that certain items are more than just objects. They bring with them precious memories and emotions.'

She then looked up and shook her head at the fate the cards had dealt them; now they would have to start again; from the ashes of destruction, life begins anew. But fate had also dealt them an unexpected card, a bizarre object buried beneath the cottage, and unearthed by the fire. It looked like a coat but without arms and was made from a dark black material like Banth skin but a lot finer, that shimmered in the light. To have survived the intense fire, this material must be something special indeed. Since its discovery, it remained hidden at Perak's house, and they hadn't spoken of it since.

Suddenly, the building trembled and shook, causing cutlery on the shelves and worktops to shake and rattle. This was accompanied by the sound of rending stone directly overhead. Rushing to the window, she poked her head out and looked up. With a yelp, she ducked back inside as chunks of masonry and stone rained onto the grass and flower borders, followed by Serac's body that impacted with the soft, snowy ground. She then watched aghast as a silver dragon swooped and grasped the dark mage in its claws.

'Stay here, Aridain, and don't let the stew burn.'

Rushing into the corridor, her footsteps echoing in the stillness, she sprinted across the foyer and outside into the late afternoon, just in time to see the silver dragon rise into the air, the dark mages body grasped in its claws. Released, she watched aghast as Serac plunged through the stable roof. About to assist, Lascana was grasped from behind and dragged back into the fortress.

'Alfic, what are you doing? We have to help. Let go of me!'

Like a broiling thunder cloud, Alfic said, 'This is none of our concern. We're in enough trouble as it is, without inviting more.'

Hustled towards their rabbit hutch sized quarters, Alfic manhandled her into the room and slammed the door shut.

'Uh oh, Daddy's in a mood,' warned Aridain.

'I can see that, Munch kin,' growled Lascana.

'You're damn right I'm in a mood,' confirmed Alfic.

Lascana could see Alfic's anger bubbling just below the surface, like the stew Aridain tended to. Wrenching her arm from his grip, Lascana said frantically, 'What's the matter with you, Alfic?'

Throwing his jacket onto the table violently and prowling around the apartment like an irate Ardent wolf, Alfic raged, 'A dragon has just destroyed Kuelack's apartment and the stables, and to top that off, I see you running towards the very danger you should be avoiding.' Calming himself with an effort, Alfic then said, 'I need to know you're safe Lascana, I can't keep you safe and cope with this increasing workload as well.'

Grasping him around the waist, Lascana looked sincerely up into his eyes. 'What matters is we're alive and together. Nothing else will matter in the months to come,' she said with certainty.

'Stew's ready,' announced Aridain hungrily.

Lifting the boiling stew from the small range, Lascana ladled it into wooden bowls just as Sabra, his nose twitching furiously, appeared silently through the window. The dragonlet, alighting next to Aridain, took its place at the table.

Putting on a brave face and walking up behind Alfic, Lascana placed his plate of stew in front of him, then kissed him on the cheek. 'There you go, dear.'

Suddenly, there was a knock on the door.

'Alfic Bruin, open up.'

Walking calmly towards the door, Lascana opened it and asked calmly, 'What do you want?'

Barging Lascana aside, Ryan Delran, followed by a contingent of guards at his back, ordered, 'Search the room.'

'What's this all about?' demanded Alfic.

Lascana watched as the gifts and equipment donated by their family and friends were casually thrown aside as Delran, together with the soldiers, waded through the apartment. After a thorough search, Delran turned to Alfic. 'Where is she?'

'I don't know what you're talking about?'

'Liar,' spat Delran, 'I have soldiers surrounding the fortress. The only place Vara could go was here.'

'Vara has escaped? From where?'

'Stop stalling for time.'

'We don't know, we weren't even sure she was still alive.'

Drawing his sword, Delran approached Alfic and pointed it at his throat. 'I will not ask again. Where is she?'

'Don't you believe your own eyes, Delran? She's not here, and even if we did know where she was, we wouldn't tell you,' said Alfic with venom.

'You are greatly mistaken if you think you can make a fool out of me Alfic,' spat Delran.

Under her breath Lascana hissed, 'Too late Delran, you've done that all by yourself.'

'You, guard the door, and you the window,' ordered Delran, spinning around on his heels and marching from the room, the remaining soldiers trailing in his wake.

Picking up the items strewn across the floor, Lascana said, 'Do nasty shits like Delran get some perverse pleasure from throwing things around? It's not as though Vara was hiding underneath these wooden bowls or these horsehair brushes.'

'People like Delran crave power and authority. It makes them feel important. It's due to a lack of contentment.'

They continued tidying the room in silence. It was then that Lascana said, 'It seems you were right about Vara, Alfic.'

'Oh.'

'It seems Kuelack *was* holding her prisoner.'

'Mother is like a tough old piece of gristle you can chew on, but never swallow,' grunted Alfic. Staring intently at the dragonlet sat beside Aridain on the table, Alfic said distractedly, 'There are three types of people Lascana, those that make the rules, those that like to live by those rules, and those that just want to be left alone to live their lives. Talking of rules, why do we tolerate that freeloader?'

'What are you on about?'

'The dragonlet. Why do we tolerate it?'

'Because, as you well know, Aridain's very fond of him,' said Lascana, 'and I'm sure Sabra loves him. He's quite charming when you get to know him, and he's a must if you want anything heated up. He's a cook's ultimate accessory,' she smiled in an effort to lighten the mood.

'Dragonlets are forced against their will to harvest catchfly tree fruit for the government,' said Aridain suddenly.

'Well, at least they're being put to good use, instead of lounging around people's houses doing nothing,' growled Alfic. Looking towards the dragonlet accusingly; he then started involuntarily as Sabra hissed at him menacingly.

'Sabra doesn't lounge; he catches all the pests around the school and eats them,' Aridain said indignantly.

'The dragonlet also saved our son on more occasions than I can remember. He even saved you,' persevered Lascana.

Staring glumly out the window at the combat field and the trees, now covered in thick frosted snow, Aridain said, 'Sometimes Daddy, I wonder if you really like animals at all.'

'So, both of you are conspiring against me now, is that it?'

'Alfic, how could you say such a thing? What is wrong with you?'

Holding his head in his hands, his fingers raking through his hair, Alfic said, 'I'm sorry Lascana, but all day long, soldiers have shadowed me, questioning and scrutinising my every decision, my every movement, and I'm getting sick of it.'

Aridain ran over to the window and opening the wooden shutters recoiled when confronted with a brusque, dark tanned soldier. 'Now there's another one outside the door, Daddy, and another one outside the window.'

'I know it's been difficult of late, having had our house burnt down around our ears, then being evicted from your childhood home Alfic, and I know you've tried your hardest not to risk making our lives even more difficult than it already is, but this is not the time for anger and recrimination. Without emulating the very people we swore to oppose, all we can do is what's right and hope people see the truth.'

'Lascana, Kuelack has targeted our family. We've done things the safe, easy way, and where has it got us, crammed into lodgings that's barely big enough to house a pixie clan, let alone two adults and a child,' bellowed Alfic frustratingly, throwing his hands in the air to indicate their cramped surroundings. 'And now, you're obligated to my brother and his wife, and we're supposed to be thankful!'

'Keep your voice down Alfic, the guards will hear you.'

'Let them hear, let them report to my brother that I will not submit...!'

'Daddy, why don't you like Uncle Kuelack and Serac?' asked Aridain offhandedly.

Turning abruptly, Alfic exclaimed angrily, 'What!'

'You just said that you would see them both dead.'

'No, I didn't.' Alfic rubbed at his face in an effort to massage some alertness into his worn and tired features. 'Aridain, how many times must I tell you not to keep looking in people's heads? It's rude.'

Aridain looked up, upset, and a little confused. 'I can't help it. I just forget that's all. What you need, Daddy, is false unicorn seed for your headache, and chamomile for your sore eyes.'

Standing, his face a mask of indecision, Alfic grabbed his coat. 'No, what I need is some fresh air.' Taking one final look around, he disappeared through the door, slamming it shut behind him.

CHAPTER ELEVEN

ESCAPE

Ramus's mind wandered to things that would never be again. Of him flying over the volcanic landscape, his children on his back, of waking up next to Sonya and her intoxicating smile, and all four of them walking through the gardens of his home. Abruptly, those images changed, his children's faces slowly melting, their bodies ripped and torn, as did the perfect image of his wife, burnt by dragon fire, and all three of them dying in his arms. Never again to feel Sonya's warm caresses and the texture of her soft silky skin, or the tender touch of her fingers as she drew them through his hair. Almost too much to bear, was the thought of never again seeing his children's welcoming smiles, hugs and kisses after returning from a long day's dragon training in the Sprawls.

Returning from a successful trading mission, he had found his castle home destroyed and his family murdered. Blinded by grief, and failing to see the trap set by the Protectorate, he had led several of his father's dragons and riders in retaliation, and they were burnt one by one from the sky until only he remained.

His dragon's heart skipped a beat, as quite unexpectedly, Sonya appeared through his delirium. Grasping his face, she hissed. *You were ousted from lands you were destined to inherit, dragon lord; what are you going to do about it? I am dead. Your family is dead, that is in the past, but there is still hope for you and Zapata if you choose to follow the correct path. The acceptance of what's happened is essential to the discovery of truth. You're a dragon lord; start acting like one.*

'Correct path. Start acting like a dragon lord?' The statement rang in his mind like the peel of a bell.

'*Sonya?*'

Your wife is wise, heed her words.

Focusing his thoughts, he whispered. '*You, you spoke to me before at the fair. Who are you?*'

You know who I am, and you know what's at stake. Make the choice, follow the One; he has already made himself known to you. Put an end to this ridiculous charade, fulfil your destiny.

Who? Who is this person? Who are you? called Ramus, but all he encountered was emptiness. His eyes snapped open.

His arms and feet were tied to a chair, and the metallic, tinny taste of blood was pungent in his mouth and nostrils. Through blurry, distorted vision he saw the surroundings were almost totally dark, and upon his lap, a smoking urn sizzled. He closed his eyes then and focused, opening them wide in surprise when he remained in human form. Suddenly, the door to his left opened and framed in the doorway was the dark arts master, Serac.

'I see our witch's infusion is wearing off.'

Ramus watched, detached but fascinated, as the dark mage walked toward him. Serac then clasped his jaw between thumb and forefinger.

'As you know, I am not a patient man,' purred Serac, staring threateningly into his eyes, 'so I will be plain. If you do not tell me what I want to know, I will kill you, here and now. Am I clear?'

'Disobeying Kuelack's orders, very bold Serac. What will your master think?'

'Don't waste your breath, Dragon lord, I need no one's approval,' spat Serac.

'Then get it over with. I'm tired of your inane posturing.'

'So feisty all of a sudden, what's changed, Ramus? What have you discovered?'

'My sense of dignity; I am a Dragon lord like my father before me and his father before him. We had lands stretching from Rabat in the south to the Protean Mountains in the north; from the River Priam in the east to the River Grabben in the west.' proclaimed Ramus. 'My family was held in the highest esteem.'

'A dragon lord's celebrated honour... hah, nothing but an encumbrance, if you ask me. So pompous, so dignified. Now Zapata's capital city is in the protectorate's hands, and your outmoded traditions have been cast aside. All that's left is a denounced dragon lord who has outlived his usefulness.'

'So, what was the price of this betrayal?' When Serac remained silent, Ramus continued, 'What's the harm in telling me? You're going to kill me, anyway.'

'It was quite simple, really, power and control. When the barons eliminated the most powerful family in Zapata, we would then range northwards and help wipe out what families remained and enslave their dragons.'

'But you didn't figure on Rasbora, did you, Serac?'

Walking up behind Ramus, and tearing his skullcap from his scalp, Serac jerked his head backwards. Serac's fetid breath then filled his nostrils as, despite his gaunt appearance, the emaciated mage, with uncanny strength, forced him to stare up into his skeletal bloodshot eyes.

'A minor annoyance. We suspected your treachery after Magen mentioned that you threatened her to join you or die, a suspicion confirmed when the fake shards you planted were crushed underfoot by Mass Martin. Mass also commented on Kuelack's weariness, and that the stones had been switched; now how would he know that? He knew that, because you were in league with the psychic. No more games; what are you planning now?'

'I am a disinherited dragon lord who has lost everything. I simply sought revenge. I thought it would be a simple matter to persuade Kuelack to crush the treacherous barons and their mages into dust in return for my services, but during our quest I saw the shards and Kuelack for what they are, evil incarnate, evil that deserves no place in this world.'

'The most powerful objects ever created and you would have them destroyed?'

'It was a calculated risk. I have tasted what it is like to be under the shards' control whilst in Kuelack's grasp. I would not wish that on any lord or dragon. But Mass discovered my plan to avenge my family and threatened me with a lobotomy if I didn't hand them over to him on my return. So, exploiting Kuelack's misguided assumption that he was immune to their power, I switched them with the fakes Mass gave me while Kuelack slept on the journey home. Swallowing the originals, I hid them to prevent another cataclysm, then arranged for them to be collected. That's it. There's no more to tell. The Hasp told Kuelack he is doomed, that for him it's too late. Now, the shards are in safe hands, and you will never see them again. It seems the hags prediction is coming true. You're on the wrong side, Serac.'

'I presume you're referring to the deal you made with Beria,' Serac sneered.

Suddenly the door opened, and dragged between two students he recognised as Gavin Torn and Cordovan Harker, was Vara Bruin, bruised and bloodied.

'I caught her searching beneath the same tree as you.'

Suddenly, clarity hit him like a slap to the face. Vara was the senior Balefire witch Beria had referred to. She was also the boy's grandmother. During his curious encounter at the fair, the impression Alfic's son had conveyed was almost dragon-like. Aridain was present then, when the voice had spoken to him the first time. The sorcerer Torkval also mentioned the Elemental, the one who will destroy the stone. He must have been referring to the boy as well. It all made perfect sense. Follow the One; he has already made himself known.

'So, despite my efforts, Serac, you are now in possession of the shards?' said Ramus, looking toward Vara.

'No.'

Ramus heaved a silent sigh of relief.

'All Vara kept spouting were the prophecies of The Hasp. More like the ravings of a sect of misfits, if you ask me,' spat Serac. He then fell into a fit of coughing. Studying the handkerchief and the specks of blood, Serac wheezed, 'Now look what you made me do.'

'My, that's a nasty cough you have there, the black arts taking their toll, are they?' scorned Ramus.

His voice rising with every word, Serac with finality, bellowed, 'You have been outmatched at every turn Ramus, your own betrayal has sealed your fate. Now that we have Vara, you're of no more use. Make your peace with your ancestors.'

Unthinking, Ramus opened his mouth wide, but instead of a bellow of defiance, a focused jet of white-hot flame issued forth, hurling the shadow mage out through the apartments shuttered bay window, out over the ornate balcony and onto the grass amidst a rain of shattered wood, glass and masonry. Stunned, and at a loss as to what just happened, Ramus melted the bonds holding his hands and feet, then strode to the shattered window frame. With a roar, and a starburst of flame, he jumped from the window whilst transforming into the silver dragon. Enraged, he grasped the emaciated warlock, lifting him into the air to the consternation of onlookers, students, and staff.

'You have fight in you still, dragon lord,' smiled Serac, 'but it's too late. You have cemented your guilt. Your culpability is now plain for all to see.'

Suddenly, black tendrils issued from Serac's hands, constricting and suffocating Ramus's eyes, snout and mouth. Burning at the tendrils and their creator, Ramus flew higher. Serac gripped the sharp razor claws holding him as Ramus shuddered and roared in pain.

'Your resistance is meaningless. You cannot defeat me. I am a master of the dark arts,' bellowed Serac.

Producing an intense ball of flame, Ramus flew through it, but Serac held on, delivering waves of pain that threatened to render Ramus unconscious. In desperation, Ramus performed a tight turn and, to his relief, the forces of gravity forced Serac to let go. Circling, Ramus roared as he dived towards Serac, now plummeting towards the ground, and once more spat fire that engulfed the helpless mage. Then, swiping at Serac with his tail as he passed, Ramus caused the dark mage to spin uncontrollably through the air.

'Give it up Serac; you're in my element now.'

For all his bravado, Ramus felt a cold, searing bolt of power pass by his tough, scaly skin. Banking sharply, he watched as with an almighty crash Serac tore through the thatched roof of the stables, causing horses to rear and buck, throwing their owners and dragging stable boys across the courtyard.

Alighting amidst startled tutors and terrified students, Ramus transformed, convinced he would find Serac's burned and broken body.

Pulling a large dagger-like splinter from his shoulder, Ramus bellowed, 'Where did he land? Where is he?'

'In there,' shouted a stable boy, trying to placate the terrified horses.

Searching through the debris, of Serac there was no sign. 'Are you sure?' Ramus asked, wiping at blood from a deep cut seeping into his eyes.

'Yes, scared me and my horses half to death.'

He looked around at the injured and bleeding teachers and students. It was no good; there was nothing more to be gained here. His actions would only damage the school and its students further. Then, knowing that this beloved school was now denied him, Ramus spread his arms. Transforming once more, he spread his thick membranous wings and took to the sky. Arriving at the gaping hole in the wall of Almagest's old apartment, Ramus lumbered over to Serac's torturer's chair and Vara slumped upon it. Severing the cords that secured her wrists and ankles with his claws, Ramus then carried her up into the dour overcast sky.

Allowing a carriage carrying supplies through the main gates, Tance, shivering noticeably in the chill wind, turned to Albain. Stamping his feet and blowing into his hands, Tance said, 'Chilly, isn't it?'

'You're from Turkana, anything is cold to you,' insinuated Albain, looking up at the chilly grey clouds rolling across the sky and wrapping his thick Navarian inlaid crimson and gold cloak about himself securely.

'Hey, just because it's now mainly desert, doesn't mean it's not cold.'

'Why are we talking about the weather?' said Albain, exasperated. 'It's no coincidence that we've been relegated to guard duty, and it's obvious why?'

'Is it? I don't see it myself?' hissed Tance seriously. Holding up his hand to halt yet another wagon full of supplies, then questioning the driver as to any weaponry he was carrying, he began searching through the wagon's contents.

Walking to the far side of the wagon, Albain hissed, 'The powers that be are trying to stop us from helping Vanir and Mace.'

'You're just being paranoid. Besides, they're wanted for crimes against the school. You know it's our necks if we help them.'

'It's the school that's overstepped the bounds of decency, not our friends, and when you do that, the boundaries of decency break down.'

'What? What are you talking about?'

'When do we conclude this isn't right, Tance? When do we say that enough is enough?'

Holding up his hand, Albain, fixing the driver with a no-nonsense-look, pulled aside the wagon master's thick cloak and exclaimed, 'You're armed, you're supposed to declare your weapons. Hand over your sword, now!'

'What seems to be the problem here?' said the Sergeant of the Guard, approaching from outside the gate.

'This man didn't declare his sword. I was just about to confiscate it.'

'It's all right Albain, I know this man, he's trustworthy.'

'Since when has this become school policy?'

'Drop it Albain. I can vouch for this man,' said the sergeant forcefully.

'So how many more have you allowed through without declaring?' continued Albain.

'I said drop it! Driver, you're free to proceed.'

The driver smiled, flashing tobacco-stained teeth. 'You're too kind.'

Watching together with Tance as the driver urged his two mounts onwards, Albain said darkly, 'Now do you believe me?'

'This was only one man,' Tance hissed guardedly, staring out intently from beneath his helmet with dark brown eyes. 'You can't base your distrust on finding one man trying to smuggle a sword into the grounds.'

Albain, not as tall as Tance but thicker set, in his deep voice replied earnestly, 'My father turned a blind eye to my family's situation, promising us that one day, when he hit the big score, we would all be living on the Kings Way in Gonda. In the end, he owed so much money through his addiction to gambling that the debtors took our house and all our possessions, condemning me and my family to a life of poverty and destitution. Even when the debtors came to take our father away to work off his debt, my mother still believed, convinced by my father's promises. She took her life shortly after that, leaving me and my two sisters without a father and a mother. So, you see, I hate people who spout lies. I can spot them a mile off, so whilst I have breath in my body, people like Sergeant Tanner will not prevail, not on my watch,' growled Albain.

Holding his hand up for Albain to be quiet, Tance hissed alarmed, 'Listen, that's dragon fire.'

Suddenly, a tremendous roar accompanied by a breaking and shattering of stone filled the night air. They looked towards the old fortress, now back lit by a ruby red fireworks display, as a silver dragon roaring as if in agony soared into the evening sky. It then plummeted back towards the flames, following a spinning, gyrating figure that crashed through the stable roof.

Sprinting across the snow-covered yard, Tance led them around the neatly trimmed hedges that enclosed the slabbed seating area, beneath Pellagrin's oak, as the silver dragon alighted next to the ruined stables. As they approached, the dragon's form shimmered and shifted, to reveal Ramus, as naked as the day he was born, stood amongst the flames. Slowing their pace, they watched, intrigued, as the dragon lord began searching through the debris. Turning to look around him, Ramus locked eyes with the pair, then transformed back into the lithe dragon, and took to the air. They then watched, mesmerised, as Ramus disappeared behind the fortress, to emerge a few seconds later carrying the figure of an elderly lady sporting a thick mop of flame red hair.

'Don't just stand there, you morons, help put out these fires,' bellowed Sergeant Tanner angrily.

'Now, do you believe me when I say something has to be done?' said Albain gravely.

As smoke billowed skywards in the still air, up through the grey barked pines, the two friends covering their faces, joined the staff now running around aimlessly, trying to put out numerous small blazes that had sprung up amongst the straw and hay, and the stables shattered rooftop. Half an hour later Albain, wiping at the grime-streaked sweat dribbling down his face, placing a firm hand upon Tance's shoulder, hissed, 'Congratulations my friend, thanks to our quick thinking it looks as if we may have the fires under control. Tance, are you OK?'

'I'm not sure. I thought I saw something, a disturbance in the air, amongst the flames, in the form of a figure, just before the dragon appeared. Ahh, it was probably a trick of the light.'

Suddenly surrounded by figures closing in to douse what remained of the flames, the pair turned towards the main gate.

Turning abruptly, Tance glanced down. Feeling at his hip, he felt at his pocket then reached inside. 'Will you look at that? How did that get there?'

'What is it, tell me?' asked Albain insistently.

'It's a silver coin!'

Suddenly, getting the urge to feel inside his tunic pocket, Albain exclaimed, 'Hey, I have one too!'

'Where did they come from, do you think?'

'I don't know. What I do know, however, is this is more than I make in six months? We have to return...'

Rolling the coin around in his palm whilst gazing at its all-pervading lustre, Tance said, 'Now hold on a minute, Albain, let's not be too hasty...'

Opening her eyes, Vara grasped, terrified, at the large clawed feet that held her, as she stared in shock at the countryside rushing along below.

'Where am I? What's happening?'

'Vara, you're awake, about time!'

With the cold winter wind buffeting her face, hair and clothing, Vara demanded, 'Who are you dragon, what do you want with me?'

'You have nothing to fear from me, Vara Bruin.'

'Ramus, is that you?'

'Yes, I'm taking you home,' rumbled the dragon. 'Spalding's only a short flight from the school.'

'No!' exclaimed Vara, struggling in the grip of Ramus's claws. 'I cannot go home. I know too much. They'll be waiting, watching...

'Then where do you suggest?'

'Leardon, I have friends there, but first things first. Put me down.'

'As you wish.'

Scattering sheep and cattle grazing upon winter straw, together with their terrified attendant herdsmen, Ramus, with a blast of snow-filled wind, alighted upon Spalding common.

'Climb aboard Vara Bruin, so that we can go.'

'Oh my, I don't think this is a good idea?' Vara quailed, climbing upon Ramus's back.

'You'll get the hang of it. Now hold on.'

Closing her eyes, Vara held on to the ridges along Ramus's back as, with a mighty thrust from his silvery wings, he headed straight up through the low hanging snow clouds, bursting through into a clear darkening sky. When it seemed they had levelled off, Vara slowly opened her eyes and looked around. 'For pity's sake, what is wrong with you?' she bellowed over the whistling of the wind. 'You nearly unseated me.'

'Swirls and eddies,' smiled Ramus, amusingly.

'It's not funny,' Vara bellowed, looking around in trepidation at the tops of the snow clouds that gave the illusion that they were skimming just feet from a grey field of thistledown.

'If people are watching, I don't want them tracking us from the ground,' said Ramus, settling into level flight.

'Just head for the Archer Estate, in Leardon. I'll guide you from there.'

Snow had begun to fall as Ramus, in order not to upset Vara's sensitive stomach, glided gently down through the clouds as the light faded. Vara, now more relaxed and much warmer, sat astride Ramus's back, as Ramus skimmed low over Leardon's rooftops in the winter twilight.

'Bit of a dump, and what is that smell? It reeks of old socks,' exclaimed Ramus, his dragon face turning sour.

'The dyeing works by the river,' answered Vara, pointing to gouts of smoke and steam rising from brick-built chimneys on the far side of the town.

Gliding silently across the rooftops, they came across a large estate. Sat in its own grounds, the large mansion, like an all-imposing behemoth, sat on a large hillock overlooking the town.

'Land here,' ordered Vara.

Dropping suddenly at the last possible moment, Ramus spread his wings, alighting on the manicured grass between mature oaks and ornate cedar trees.

'I suggest you look away.'

'Why..., on my, I never really thought about clothes,' exclaimed Vara, turning her back on Ramus, now stood naked in the snow.

'The cold isn't the problem. My dignity is,' said Ramus.

'I can see that. Well, come on, follow me.'

To hide her embarrassment, Vara striding ahead, said, 'That is Archer Manor, it was home to the Archer family, they were the wealthiest family in the area. They, more than anyone else, helped turn Leardon into a wealthy mining town until the rich seams of ore here about dried up. Now it's the Carnell's who own the dyeing factory. The garrison here is also larger than normal, guarding an important crossroads to the capital. Otherwise, apart from a small stone-built temple and a mediocre civic building, Leardon is an unpretentious, functional place, and not very colourful. Its only other claim to fame is its thriving marketplace.'

In the rapidly waning light, they followed a narrow path behind a row of horse chestnut trees, until they came across a small doorway set into the boundary wall that exited the property.

With Vara taking the lead, they turned right up a small track that wound beside one of several brooks that ran into the River Leader, until they came across a small cottage, nestled in its own small garden, beneath the stark snow-covered branches of a cherry tree.

'Wait here.'

Leaving Ramus hiding in the dark, Vara knocked on the old, weathered oak door. Several seconds later, a voice asked, 'Who is it?'

'Bridget. It's me, Vara.'

After a couple of seconds, she heard bolts being withdrawn. The door opened to reveal a small, rotund lady wearing a flowery pinny, tied around her waist and the back of her neck, over a thick, light blue cotton dress. From a central parting, grew straight, black greying hair that framed a rotund and weathered, friendly face.

Grasping Vara's hands, Bridget holding her at arm's length beamed. 'Vara, it's so good to see you. Come in.' Then, looking at the dried blood and soiled clothes, she exclaimed, 'What happened to you?'

'Nothing a nice cup of tea, a nice warming fire and a place to regain our strength won't mend, if that's all right?' smiled Vara, embracing the effervescent shop keeper.

'Who is it, Mother?' enquired a man's voice from inside.

Disengaging herself, Bridget smiled warmly, 'It's OK, Jacob, it's Vara. And who's this?' she asked casually, eyeing up the naked dragon lord as he poked his head around the door frame.

'This is Ramus. He works at the school; we need to borrow some of Jacob's clothes.'

'Of course,' said Bridget, throwing Vara a questioning look.

'It's a long story.'

'OK, follow me Ramus, let's get you out of the cold, and warmed in front of the fire.'

Vara averted her eyes as Bridget handed Ramus a set of clothes and he tried them on.

'These are far too small,' he said indignantly.

'Be thankful and don't complain!' smiled Vara, the dragon lord, looking like he'd just come out of a hot wash.

'This isn't funny, Vara!'

'Oh, believe me, it is.'

'So, what happened to your clothes, Ramus, your possessions?' asked Bridget.

Ramus, exposing sharp pointed teeth, said hesitantly. 'I was, umm… robbed.'

Eyeing him sceptically, Bridget said, 'Sit down by the fire. I'll go put the kettle on.' Returning with three steaming mugs of tea, Bridget, in her broad country twang, said, 'I know a dragon lord when I see one. So, is one of you going to tell me what really happened?'

CHAPTER TWELVE

THE CARPENTER

Seeking solace in the night, the falling snow deadening all sounds like a blanket, Kale walked the grounds silently and inconspicuously. Hiding himself and his magical signature when a patrol led by one of the gifted students ghosted past, he then walked silently and stealthily along the path beside the copper beech trees. Climbing over the twin gates, he then strode out across the fields into the wilds he'd always loved. Reaching a fallen tree that straddled the gurgling stream, he sat down upon the snow-covered bark. Ignoring the cold, he reached out to a small herd of Caracal, the small, timid, green-streaked, fur-covered deer walking over to him, eagerly eating the offered hazel nuts. He watched as fire sprites, unaffected by the cold, frolicked in the snow, whilst overhead a small murmur of starlings chittered whilst roosting in the branches of an old oak tree. After sitting and staring through misty eyes at the glistening stream for what seemed like an age, he lifted his face to the canopy and the heavens beyond, feeling the icy touch of falling snow upon his skin.

'Can you hear me, Master Torsk? What do I do now? How do I proceed? I tried to teach your class, to stop the creature, and failed at both. Perak says I'm making progress, but everything I say and do ends in failure. I feel like a humiliated, first year novice student sent home with his tail between his legs.'

The only answer he received was the trickling of water over the streambed interspersed with the warbling of water imps, and the soothing vibrato chirps of echo bugs.

He thought back to one particular lesson with Torsk; The master Animistic had brought in a cage covered in a thin material...

'I can see greatness in you Kale, you only have to apply yourself. Remember, the stronger the creature, the more powerful the wizard, and the stronger the spell or incantation has to be, tackle each problem separately and the rest will resolve itself.'

'There is so much to learn master, I sometimes wonder if I've chosen the right path.'

'Only you can decide that for yourself. The only reason you can't do something is because you haven't been told or you haven't been shown, and I have done both. Now, the only person placing barriers in the way is you. These are fire sprites, feisty little bleeders at the best of times. I'm going to let them out, then leave the room...'

'But...'

'No buts. They will seek vengeance, a focus for their anger at their incarceration, so I suggest you concentrate, then placate and restrain them, and order them back into that cage.'

Perhaps it was because he didn't have his mentor to back him up. Perhaps it was the imminent danger that broke the barriers, that triggered his response, saw him control and order the creatures back into their cage. Whatever the reason, ever since that day, his mind felt unleashed, the shackles broken.

According to Pellagrin, he had to stop Magen from discovering the young mite's secrets. On top of that, Kuelack thinks he's recruiting a powerful ally. 'So, what to do?' Ill-equipped to face them, his only hope now was that when Kuelack came for the little mite, he had the willpower to oppose him. Are you the one to aid him, Kale Simm. Will you be strong enough when the time comes to step up?

The brief flurries of snow had dissipated towards the horizon to reveal the stars and a crescent moon just showing above the horizon. Climbing down gingerly off of the fallen tree trunk, having received no answers or pearls of wisdom, he drank from the stream, then crept quietly along the road beneath the walnut trees. Suddenly feeling dizzy, he turned at the sound of hooves and the clattering of a wagon's iron clad wheels.

'Are you all right, son?'

Leaning against one of the tree trunks, he held on tightly as his world span. Looking up, he saw a small rotund man with thick, bushy eyebrows and greasy, grey hair. Jumping down from his wagon, the stranger grasping him by the waist and draping his arm over his shoulder, said, 'Here, let me help you.'

'Thank you for your kindness, but I'll be all right in a minute.'

Helping Kale into the rear of the wagon, the driver said, 'You look as if could do with Vara's help. She's a fine healer.'

'So I've heard.'

'Here, this is the last of it, but it seems you need this more than me.'

'What is it?'

'It's a cure-all. Vara made it for me.'

'Are you a friend?' replied Kale wretchedly.

'I am,' he said cheerily, holding out his hand. 'Been some strange goings on in that household recently,' he continued. 'Everyone in Spalding is wondering what's happened to Vara. You wouldn't know, I suppose?'

'Sorry,' Kale replied dimly, 'although after all this time we shouldn't be surprised. Well, thank you Mr…'

'My name's Gillion, carpenter by trade.'

'My name's Kale.'

'Kale. Ahh I know, you're a teacher at the school. Alfic told me about you. Are you sure you'll be all right?'

'I'm sure.'

He hadn't taken more than a dozen steps, however, when his world suddenly turned dark, and he felt himself falling onto the snow-frosted grass.

CHAPTER THIRTEEN

DANCES IN THE DARK

'Thank you, call again,' smiled Lascana, watching as the young couple, arm in arm, gazing into each other's eyes, strolled across the courtyard towards their ornate carriage parked outside the stables.

Not a care in the world, she mused. *What happened to those carefree days when nothing else mattered, to the days when mine and Alfic's worlds entwined and we were at the beginning of a journey to explore life's infinite possibilities and opportunities?*

'Excuse me, young lady?'

Roused from her musings by a small rotund man dressed in expensive finery, she replied, 'Yes, Sir, how can I help you?'

'How much is the nymph figurine on the brass water lily? Me and my wife have just bought our second home in Ural, you see. I think it will suit the decor.'

'That's four copper dektars,' said Lascana absently. 'A bargain. I think you'll agree?'

'Fine, I'll take it!'

'Yes, it's a lovely piece from the old Hasher province in Turkana, made during the reign of King Aries, I believe.'

'Ah, pre-devastation.'

Handing over the wrapped item, the man paid and left the shop, the bell above the door signalling his departure.

'Mind you, sometimes money does bring happiness,' she said to herself quietly, gazing at the coins in her hand. She then gazed out over the grassy courtyard to the guard, stood outside, his presence violating the one place she felt a sense of normality. She then stared out towards Pellagrin's oak, but even the setting sun shining through the pristine branches failed to lift her spirits.

Rubbing at her pregnancy, Lascana mused, 'What's the matter with me? I should be able to handle a simple relocation. After all, it's not as if I haven't moved before.'

But she knew in her heart of hearts that it was more than that. Her idyllic life was gone. She was terrified that she would never find that kind of happiness again, now that she was beholden to the head of the school. At the loss of their cottage, Alfic had tried to encourage her by telling her to focus her grief. Harness your frustration, he had said, let it empower you, use it to focus your energy against those who would besmirch our good name.

But that was his way. It was not her way.

Suddenly, she felt an enormous sense of guilt; here she was, thinking of her future, whilst Mace, Keegan and Kale skulked and hid for fear of capture. Also, since telling her of a bad man in his father's head, and Alfic's continual chastisement and unwarranted angry outbursts, Aridain spent more and more time outdoors.

To take her mind off of their plight, she re-entered the shop. Sitting down properly for the first time all day, she removed her shoes, and reaching down massaged her weary feet. Then rubbing the back of her neck, she looked around at her shop and the many rare and unusual goods on display. Unlike Bern's grocers, Keen's butchery, Elias's bakery, or Janus's winery, she had not turned her shack into living quarters, although that thought now had a certain appeal; her dwelling was a simple two-roomed affair, the rear used for storage whilst the room at the front was for display and trade as originally intended.

I'll be glad when you make an appearance, she moaned, looking down at her pregnancy tiredly. *Working whilst carrying around an extra passenger is no joke. Perhaps I could persuade Gable to make a giant shoehorn...* she looked up then as the bell above the door tinkled.

'Mrs Bruin! Mrs Bruin! I need to see you.'

'Elimi, can't it wait,' said Lascana. 'I'm very tired.'

'It's urgent,' said Elimi, a wild look in his eyes.

'Very well.'

Stood behind her well-worn wooden counter, she watched him curiously.

'I like your collection of rocks,' stated Elimi nervously.

Turning slowly and sensing things weren't as they seemed, Lascana focused. 'Rock's, Elimi what do you want, spit it out for Seline's sake, I won't bite,' she said urgently, watching him as he fidgeted uncomfortably.

Clearing his throat, Elimi said nervously, 'I'm here to collect five weight of iron nails; you've had some delivered, I believe,' he said, breathing loudly.

Lascana blinked. 'Nails?'

'Yes,' he said nervously. 'I've been instructed to pick some up.'

'All this fuss is over nails?'

'Well, yes.'

Taken aback by this sudden turn of events, Lascana said, 'For who?'

'A um… Mr Wintergreen.'

'Who's he?' she asked.

'I'm just being paid to pick them up and deliver them,' Elimi said angrily. 'He's not a patient man!'

'OK, keep your hair on. I was only asking. Stay here,' ordered Lascana suspiciously. 'I'll be back in a tick.'

Returning, Lascana, locking the storeroom behind her, said, 'Here you are, five weight of nails. Elimi?'

His behaviour completely out of character, and Elimi nowhere to be seen, she immediately knew something wasn't right. Surveying her shop Lascana realized that items were slightly out of place, a drawer wasn't shut properly, papers weren't stacked quite as neatly as before, and her adjustable stool had moved. Now either an unearthly spirit had taken up residence in her shop or…. she quickly exited the shop. Glancing about, she noticed through the snow a figure heading towards the school's main entrance.

Where is a husband or a greysword when you need them? She cursed.

With no help forthcoming, Lascana locked up her stall, wrapped her shawl around her shoulders, and followed.

Heaving an angry sigh of relief, Elimi hurried out the main entrance through the snow beneath the twin lamps that illuminated the entrance and the roadway beyond, his footfalls crunching the frosted snow beneath his feet.

You need a good kick up the backside, Elimi; he thought to himself. *You have a good deal here at the school. Why spoil it? Meeting people in dark alleyways, I must be mad. Just because someone does you a good deed, they shouldn't expect favours in return; especially one fraught with danger.*

Striding resolutely out of the main entrance, he pledged not to give anybody further justification to ask him to do anything like this again. Scuttling through the snow, he turned into the school's secondary entrance lit by two brightly burning lamps. He then crept quietly down the lane that led to the young apprentices' quarters and the farm beyond.

Compared to the simply furnished dormitories that he and his brother, Elgin, paid to sleep in, the students' two-storey building was a privilege, a privilege gained by the most successful students in their chosen subjects, their everyday needs paid for by teachers and sponsors who deemed them worthy successors or valuable assets. Nevertheless, he felt fortunate compared to those unable to afford to stay at the school or those who had to travel miles to attend lessons from the surrounding villages and hamlets. Although he drank most of his money away, he and Elgin had aspirations to better themselves, to be better than their father, who, having died in a knife fight, had achieved nothing his entire life.

When this distasteful episode is over, perhaps I'll ask Mace if I can train as a fighter and join the army, he thought. *Perhaps then all these years of working at the school might count for something?*

So deep in thought was he that he stepped noisily into a snow-filled hole and fell sprawling to the ground. The sound echoing in the quietness; he stopped and listened. Composing himself, he wiped the sweat from his brow and looked around. Satisfied that no one had heard his clumsiness, he strode down one of the narrow, paved paths that led to the dormitories' side entrances. Stood in the shadows, he hummed nervously to quiet his racing heartbeat, and peered out from beneath the sprawling branches of a large beech tree that grew close to the back of the building. Studying the farm's cattle as they cropped at the grass, he looked up toward the full moon as it emerged from the thinning clouds. *Not the best of nights to be skulking around,* he thought.

Suddenly, a shadowy figure wearing a dark, hooded mask stepped out from the trees behind him.

'You've been followed, you idiot,' the man whispered harshly.

Elimi looked around nervously. 'I can't help it. I'm not very good at this.'

'Was it there?'

'No, and frankly, I don't care; besides, I had little time, and I'm sure Lascana suspected? No more favours. I was crazy to do this and I'm not doing it again.'

'I will say if you do this again or not.'

Elimi stared malevolently into the eyes buried deep in the hood. 'You can't make me do your dirty work. It's not as if I've done anything wrong.'

'You're a nobody, a lowly farm labourer with no sponsorship, and until I say otherwise, you will do as I say, unless, of course, you want me to let slip to Alfic and Perak your many indiscretions, after all, they've been good to you, haven't they? Being the elder brother, are you prepared to incur their wrath?' sneered the figure. 'If they found out, think what would happen to your family, to your younger brother, Elgin.'

When Elimi remained quiet, the shadowy figure said, 'I thought that would shut you up. Now get out of here. I've got things to take care of.'

Shaking his head miserably, a look of despair etched on his face, Elimi hurried away down the lane.

Alfic stepped from the buggy as Perak brought Midge to a standstill. Tying Midge to a hitching rail, Perak looked up at Lascana's shop. 'It's closed. Lascana's probably finished for the day.'

'I'll go and check the rabbit hutch, see if she's there!' said Alfic tersely, looking meaningfully at his ever-present guardian in the form of one of Pellagrin's guards.'

Whilst Alfic disappeared inside the fortress followed by his ever-present sentinel, Perak, consoling Midge, glanced around the snowy, torch-lit courtyard. It was then that he noticed the slim female figure slip out of the entrance and out into the darkened lane beyond.

'Lascana?' He hissed.

Caught in two minds as to what he should do, curiosity got the better of him and he hurried across the courtyard. Reaching the entrance, he waited a few moments, then glanced around the corner. Watching as the slim figure disappeared inside the school's second entrance only a few feet beyond, he followed quietly.

Watching from the shadows, he realised with a start that the slender figure was indeed Lascana, but before he could attract her attention, she disappeared suddenly with a muffled scream. Perak, breaking cover, ran as fast as his ageing legs would carry him. Skidding to a halt, he came face-to-face with a masked man holding a wicked-looking knife to Lascana's throat. Perak, turning deliberately towards Lascana's attacker, raised his hands in compliance whilst covertly searching his surroundings with his mind. 'Steady there, fella,' he placated. 'Lascana, are you all right?'

'Perak! Where the hell have you been?' shouted Lascana angrily. 'Well, don't just stand there, help me.'

'Why don't you put the knife down, fella, before you hurt someone?'

'Give me one good reason why I should, old man,' grunted the figure, who began a detailed search of Lascana's clothing.

Struggling wildly, Lascana screamed, 'Get your hands off what you can't afford, you cretin!'

Frustrated, the masked figure in a deep, throaty voice growled, 'Where is it?' Pressing the knife to Lascana's throat he threatened, 'I won't ask again.'

Just then, raised voices and the sound of running feet issued from inside the student dorm. Suddenly, their attacker looked around in confusion and began swiping furiously at the air as night-flying moths and bugs flew into his mouth, nose, and eyes.

'Lascana, NO!' shouted Perak, as with a shriek of defiance, Lascana spun around and clawed at the attacker's mask. Slipping and sliding, Lascana's attacker thrust her toward him, and the pair landed in a heap on the frosted floor. To escape, the masked man leapt over them, but in desperation, Perak thrust out an arm, and the man fell to the icy ground with a grunt. Just then, the side door to the dormitory opened, flooding the path with light, and cursing profusely, their attacker rolled to his feet and sprinted into the darkness as a knot of students emerged from the doorway.

'What's going on here?... Perak?... Head Groundsman Perak?'

Jumping to his feet, Perak stated seriously, 'Please, stay here and look after Lascana, she's been hurt.'

Then, with a swiftness belying his age, Perak ran into the darkness after their attacker.

Following the rutted roadway, Perak, now totally focused, listened for movement in the moonlit night. He then probed the air, feeling for any insects or creature disturbed by their attackers passing, but strangely he felt nothing, the only disruption, a pair of tawny owls that conversed from the trees in the field beyond the lane. Confused, he failed to see the figure who leapt out of the darkness and forced him to the cold, stark ground. Rolling with the attack, he kicked his attacker away, his tunic and trousers soaking through from the saturated ground, but as he regained his feet, the man was upon him, slashing back and forth with a wicked-looking knife. Backing away, the knife narrowly missing his midriff, Perak tripped and fell, hitting his head hard against a tree stump, and with blurred vision watched as the figure shrouded in shadow, slowly approach with his knife held threateningly before him.

'You have interfered for the last time, Perak Bruin!'

Suddenly, with a shout, a figure appeared from out of the gloom and tackled the masked man to the icy floor.

'Are you all right, Father?'

'Alfic!' groaned Perak, his vision swimming.

'Are you hurt?' enquired Alfic, stamping on the masked man's wrist and kicking the knife away.

'I'll live, thanks to you.'

The night swimming in front of his vision, Perak watched as Alfic turned angrily to the figure laid upon the floor of the snow-covered lane, groaning in pain.

'What's going on here? Who are you? Why have you attacked my father?'

When the figure remained silent, Alfic bent down to pull back the hood. With shifting vision, Perak laid upon the floor in the pale moonlight, watched in morbid fascination as the figure began to expand and grow. He then gazed at an evil countenance, that looking like a crocodilian from hell, stared right back with dark, beady, tar pit eyes.

It then reached up and grasped Alfic by the throat, and standing upright on wolf-like appendages, it lifted Alfic, his legs kicking helplessly into the air. 'Father…, don't just lay… there… help me!' gasped Alfic.

Remembering the knife, Perak searched desperately in the dark until his hand came across the handle. Getting unsteadily to his feet, Perak charged. Avoiding the creatures' raking claws, he thrust the blade up to the hilt into the creature's body.

'Ahhh! Curse you human!' hissed the creature, dropping Alfic to the ground and reaching for the blade.

The creature raised its hand to strike and Perak, his vision still spinning, realised the inevitability of what was about to happen.

Then, a bellow split the air and Alfic, having found a thick log, swung it with all his might, sending the creature onto its backside. Then, to his relief, the creature turned and disappeared into the night.

'That was a close-run thing,' huffed Alfic, rubbing at his throat.

'Are you all right?' enquired Perak, climbing to his feet.

'I'll live,' croaked Alfic angrily. 'What the hell were you thinking, running blindly into the night?'

'I guess fighting lost causes, and seeking justice runs in the family.'

'Yes, well…, so, what was that, do you think?'

'How the hell should I know?'

'Well, there's only one way to find out.'

As if they had never been away, Alfic and Perak slotting seamlessly back into their army days, crept silently, stealthily, through the night, scanning the trees and the undergrowth for the tell-tale signs of their quarry. Abruptly, Alfic held up his hand and as one they froze, blending into the night. Then, without a sound or sign, Alfic disappeared into the surrounding trees. Minutes passed as Alfic returned to the same spot time and again.

Thoroughly frustrated, Perak crept up alongside and hissed, 'Alfic, what's the matter?'

'I don't understand. All the signs stop here,' he whispered fervently.

'Impossible, it couldn't have doubled back towards the school, we would have seen.'

'You and I know it, however…'

'What is it, Son?'

'I'm not sure. Something here doesn't feel right.'

109

'You're imagining things...'

Perak watched as Alfic, seemingly in a trance, stepped forward, a hand outstretched, as if attempting to grasp at something in front of his face. It was then that the sound of flittering wings filled the air, accompanied by a chorus of high-pitched shrieking.

'Run!' Shouted Alfic, as suddenly a horde of bat-like creatures having materialised out of the darkness, filled the air.

Picking a large log from the floor and swiping at their winged tormentors, Perak hollered, 'Piranha bats, but where did they come from?'

'Here, use this, it will be more effective,' shouted Alfic, handing Perak a spiky branch, whilst waving his own makeshift weapon above his head to discourage the furry assassins, that bit and tore at their faces, head and shoulders.

Alfic, leading the way, encouraged, 'Come on, Father, this way.'

Running through the woody margin, Alfic, followed closely by Perak, leapt over the fence that marked the school's boundary. Scrabbling down the bank, the pair, startling a herd of contentedly grazing cattle, ran across the field.

'Come on, Father, towards the walnut trees,' urged Alfic.

Hounded every foot of the way by furry winged creatures, each the size of a ferret, Alfic and Perak holding their makeshift shields above their heads, sprinted across the field towards the dark towering shapes of the walnut trees. With blood running from small, neat, bite-sized wounds on their arms and heads, they reached the trees and pressed themselves against one of the thick trunks.

'Now what? They can still reach us,' protested Perak, swiping at the grotesque razor-toothed creatures with his branch, as with unearthly determination, their teeth bared and their claws primed, the piranha bats attacked again and again. 'Your new magic Alfic, use the magic the sprites gave you.'

'No!'

Perak turned, and taking hold of Alfic by the scruff, shook him violently. 'What is wrong with you? We'll be torn to shreds. Is that what you want?'

'We've got out of worse situations than this without magic,' shouted Alfic angrily.

'If you don't use your magic, we're going to die here tonight, in this field,' gasped Perak, grasping one of the bats as it bit into his shoulder. Throwing it to the floor and stamping down hard he said, 'Embrace the magic as I've shown you, if you fight it, it will taste like a bitter pill, forever pulling you in different directions, like your body trying to reject its own innards, stop making excuses and silence your mind, listen and embrace your new gift,' he bellowed over the insistent screeching and twittering.

'No!' bellowed Alfic. 'I refuse to believe that magic is the answer to everything.'

Then, losing his patience, Perak slapped Alfic hard across the cheek and bellowed, 'JUST USE YOUR DAMN MAGIC!'

Alfic stumbled backwards, then fell to the floor. Rubbing at his face, he stared darkly at his father.

'Never do that again.' Then, picking himself up off of the floor, Alfic closed his eyes and said darkly, 'Just keep them off of me.'

Alfic concentrated and raised his arms. At first nothing happened, then slowly, gradually, a creaking noise above their heads could be heard, followed by a shower of snow as the two lowest branches began to move. Then, like a conductor directing an orchestra, Alfic, with eccentric movements of his arms manoeuvred the branches. With his huge twiggy hands, Alfic began swatting at the bats as they continued to attack. It wasn't long before the furry assassins began falling from the sky, until all too soon, the handful that remained were quickly and efficiently disposed of.

Breathing heavily from the exertion and wiping at the blood running from the many gashes about his face, Perak exclaimed, 'It seems our attacker had a backup plan.'

'No back-up plan? It was a membrane trap.'

'Then why didn't I trigger it? I must have walked through it several times,' queried Perak.

'Because it was affixed to me.'

'Alfic, are you all right?' Perak inquired, striding towards him, concern etched upon his face.

Holding up his hand Alfic said impatiently, 'I'm fine, just a little dizzy is all.'

'You'll get used to the magic eventually,' placated Perak. 'All you need is time…'

'I'm fine, just leave me be damn you,' blared Alfic angrily.

Leaping to his son's aid, Perak caught Alfic as he toppled forward. Hoisting Alfic over his shoulder, Perak stood up straight.

'Don't worry, Son, you'll be all right once I get you to the dorms. There are healers there.'

Sat in the dorm's communal area, sipping at a cup of hot tea, Lascana looked up as Perak, together with two students, carried the unconscious Alfic inside.

'What happened?' she cried, her face turning ashen as she hurried towards them.

'We were attacked by piranha bats.'

'What, here at the school?' exclaimed Lascana. 'Didn't you tell me these creatures are allied to the dark arts?'

'Yes,' confirmed Perak. 'As was your attacker, I suspect, it looked like a demented Ardent wolf that walked upon hind legs.'

'But Perak, I was attacked by a man?' said Lascana, dumbfounded.

'Believe you me, whatever it was, it was very good at covering its tracks, and we're still no closer as to what's going on here.'

Seeing the look of fear on Lascana's face, Erica Markeson, a young student of the healing arts, said, 'Lay him down over there.' Then, closing her eyes, Erica placing her hands upon Alfic's scalp, said reassuringly, 'He's fine, it's just exhaustion.' Suddenly, with a gasp, Erica snatched her hands away in alarm.

'Erica?'

'I thought I saw…'

'Saw, saw what?' asked Lascana, looking at Erica intently.

'Nothing, it's nothing,' apologised the young healer, who, taking hold of Alfic's arm, closed her eyes once more.

Several minutes passed before Alfic stirred.

'Selfish fool,' Perak said angrily.

'Really,' Alfic croaked.

'Yes, really.' Relenting, Perak smirked, 'After saving me, you had the indecency to pass out.'

Watching Lascana with a puzzled expression, Alfic croaked, 'Are you all right?'

'I'm fine, thanks to Erica here,' said Lascana, flexing her arm. 'The bump on my head has all but gone.'

'That's not what I meant.'

'I'm fine, really, now rest Alfic, you need it.'

As the young Erica attended to Alfic's head wound, Lascana turned to see Elimi, stood looking at them half-heartedly from the doorway in the diffuse light of the student's common room.

'Guilty conscience?' said Lascana severely.

'I came to see if you were all right!'

'We'll live. So, what were you really after, Elimi?' asked Lascana.

'I told you, nails,' he said fervently.

'Nails, really,' scoffed Lascana. 'We both know that's a lie, don't we, Elimi? You were searching for something.' When Elimi remained silent, Lascana said, 'Is your silence worth your freedom? Do you even know why you did this?'

Perak, in an effort to break the uncomfortable silence, said, 'So, what would you gain from this transaction, Elimi? Pride? Or is it the approval of the people you're helping?'

'Do you know how tempting it is for a man like me, a grunt, to be offered money for so simple a task?'

Wincing as Erica touched a sensitive spot on his forehead, Perak focusing upon Elimi, hissed, 'There's no need for that tone, we're only trying to help.'

Elimi reposted, 'It's not my fault Lascana followed me.'

'Quit it Elimi, while you're ahead,' hissed Alfic.

'With all that's going on at the school, all you can say is, "it's not my fault"? Alfic and Perak nearly died tonight over your so-called innocent actions,' Lascana howled.

'I didn't realise it would come to this.' Elimi lapsed into silence then and held his head in his hands.

'People never do, yet here we are,' said Lascana. 'Elimi, when are you going to realise nothing is for nothing? If it seems too good to be true, it usually is.'

'Well, one thing is for sure, Elimi; the questions won't stop until we find out what's going on. This isn't a game.' Starting to his feet and sitting down opposite Elimi, Perak said deliberately, 'Now I want you to tell us what happened tonight.'

'OK, so it wasn't nails, but I did receive an anonymous message, to pick up a small package from Lascana's shop for a Mr Wintergreen, then deliver it here for a price, that's all I know.'

'I don't believe you, Elimi,' said Lascana seriously.

'You searched my shop whilst I was distracted. This has nothing to do with money or packages. Who employed you, Elimi? Who is this person, this thing? Why did it choose you?'

'I can't tell you, Lascana,' despaired Elimi, now floundering, 'it's more than my life's worth. I swear, if I had known the trouble it would cause, I would never have taken the job on. I'm sorry OK, I'm sorry for everything. Can I go now?'

Perak nodded and stood up as Elimi, relief written all over his face, hurried from the room.

'Do you have it?' demanded the figure.

'No.'

'And the shards?'

'They weren't there either,' he then added quickly, 'but soon I will have both the diary and the shards, but to get them I will have to kill members of Alfic's family, it will cause an uproar at the school.'

'The school is of no consequence, only the items,' replied the figure in a grating, gravel-like voice.

'The Bruins are resourceful. They will try to stop us.'

'Then they will die,' the figure said confidently, 'for I will not be denied, not again.'

'If I may, lord, it would be better if I dealt with it.'

'You wouldn't have to deal with it if that bungling fool, Kuelack, had kept control of the shards and the diary; he is incompetent and stupid.'

'Kuelack is a fool, but I know the Bruins, and I know Alfic.'

'Very well, retrieve these items, and I will reward you handsomely. Fail, however, and you will leave me no choice but to destroy you.'

Bowing, the servant hurrying away through the darkness, said, 'I will not fail you.'

114

CHAPTER FOURTEEN

THE BALEFIRE CURSE

Vara opened her eyes and, yawning loudly, looked around in confusion. Remembering where she was, she climbed stiffly and painfully from the bed, the winter sun reflected from the snow, giving the flowery decor and white-washed walls a light airy feel.

Stumbling over to the wash basin, she plunged her hands into the water and drew a handful up and over her face, the cold water focusing her thoughts. Towelling her face dry, Vara looked into the bedroom mirror through the now familiar pink haze. The face staring back at her had changed. Her skin appeared rough and gravelly. Stark lines had appeared on her forehead and around her mouth, and bags had formed beneath her eyes. On the inside, conversely, she felt more alive, stronger, more mentally in tune with the world. It was as if her mind and body were at odds, her mind reconnecting with something long forgotten, whilst her body reverted to something primeval. It was a trade-off, power for life.

Vara had continued her steady increased dosage of dragon's blood in order to attain the dark magic needed to defend her grandson, but her increased stamina and new outlook on the world masked a deeper certainty. Sooner or later, even her mind would change, her thoughts darken, as her craving for blood became insatiable. She would start to devolve, become a yellow hag, a Hasp, for it was one thing to use dragon's blood in minute doses to retain your youth, but something else entirely to increase the dose to aid a Balefire's magic. She shook her head resolutely; it would be a small price to pay to keep her grandson from Kuelack's clutches. Her only hope was that when her mission was accomplished that her heart would give out, her liver shut down, or her kidneys fail as dragon's blood exacted its price.

Stepping down the narrow twisting stairs, Vara entered the warm and cosy living room.

'Ahhh Vara, you're awake?'

'Morning, Bridget.'

'Try early afternoon,' came the morose declaration from the large, comfy chair in front of the fire.

'Now Ramus, don't give Vara a tough time. She's been through a lot,' said Bridget.

'So, what are you doing here? I thought you decided to leave,' stated Vara.

'Some things have come to my attention, so I've decided to stay,' said Ramus.

'Like?'

'I'll let you know.'

'Jacob, warm up that stew, would you?' shouted Bridget. 'I'll get you a nice cup of tea, Vara,' she said kindly.

'Thank you, Bridget, you're too kind, as always.'

Yawning loudly, Vara sat down beside Ramus in front of the blazing fire. With the smell of warming stew suffusing the air, Vara, whilst sipping at a steaming cup of tea, studied the small, welcoming room that Bridget insisted, despite the room's apparent randomness, was the epitome of order.

Fixed to the walls were wooden shelves filled with numerous types of tin and wooden toys, shoved willy-nilly with books and everyday items into every nook and cranny. Some, it seemed, needed painting or repairing, whilst others were in pristine condition, ready to be sold from the shop out front.

'I never thanked you for rescuing me, Ramus.'

'Careful, Vara, you don't want people to think you actually have a heart.' Sporting the hint of a tired smile, Ramus asked, 'So what's the deal with you and these people?'

'When Jacob was born, he wasn't breathing. I resuscitated him, saved his life. Bridget and me have been good friends ever since. So, mind telling me why you were a prisoner in Almagest's old apartment?'

'Realising what it would mean if Kuelack possessed the shards, I stole them. Compelled by Mass Martin to retrieve them, Kuelack found out and caught me. And you?'

'I received your message.' Then, taking a deep breath, Vara said, 'As a Magnate I am the one best suited to dispose of the shards.'

'A Balefire Magnate! Well, I'll be?'

'Do you want to know what happened or not?'

Ramus nodded silently.

'When I realised the shards were missing from where they should be, I touched the tree trunk and discovered someone had taken them, but I'd been followed, I believe, by Serac.'

'That has a familiar ring to it.' Looking at her strangely, Ramus said morosely, 'Recently, I've been hearing a voice. This voice has been telling me it's my destiny to serve the One. It also said that I would know who it is because I've met him before. Whilst in Srinigar, the yellow hags at the Balefire temple welcomed me as the dragon lord who would serve the One. I now believe these clues were referring to your grandson, and that it was he who took the shards.'

'"The Ancient Balefire Temple in Srinigar"?' said Vara, now totally focused.

'Yes, the shards led us there to retrieve the third one.'

'Located in the Monad Mountains, right?'

With a questioning look on his face, Ramus nodded slowly.

'I knew it! I tried to find the temple during my Genesis questing, but I never did.' Seeing Ramus's questioning look, Vara said quickly, 'It's initiated by the coven to prove your worth as a Magnate, but that's not important right now. The voice you're hearing is Pellagrin, and before you say anything, yes, it's *the* Pellagrin. He's Aridain's constant companion these days,' said Vara, pointing to her head. 'It sounds like you've been tasked to aid my grandson.'

'It's not all good news, however, The Hasp addressed Kuelack as the Child of Nightmare,' mused Ramus. 'It was strange; they just allowed us to take it.'

'Because they would have no fear of whoever took it?' confirmed Vara. 'I assumed he ordered you to take the shard.'

'No, *he* took it; it was sat on a tall altar made of stone in the middle of a small henge. The Hasp said his coming was already written, but

Kuelack dismissed the prophesies as nonsense. He said once he'd secured the shards, he would wipe out their kind. It was funny..., during his speech they kept chanting....'

'One Balefire cannot harm another...' continued Vara.

'Yes, that's right. It was then that Kuelack tried to kill them, but couldn't. I won't kill any defenceless being; but dragons are servants of whoever possesses the stone. I tried to stop myself, but I couldn't resist Kuelack's command. I gave them my word, Vara,' said Ramus miserably. 'I gave them my word that I wouldn't harm them, and yet I did.'

In the silence that followed, Vara heaving a silent sigh of relief, put her hands together as if in prayer and closed her eyes. She then turned to look at Ramus, who was staring into the flames, his eyes far away, remembering.

'You're telling me that Kuelack took the Balefire shard from the altar?' said Vara.

'Yes?' replied Ramus glumly.

'Do you know what this means? It means that finally we have hope. It means that Kuelack cannot harm my grandson, or any other Balefire witch.'

'How so?'

'Because having collected the shard from the altar, Kuelack, like me, is now effectively a Balefire witch.'

Looking at Ramus's puzzled face, Vara said, 'my grandson is the Balefire Taal.'

'The what?'

'The Balefire Taal. He is supposed to have these shards. Never mind, it's a long story....'

'The clue's in the title, right?'

'Correct, but on the downside, Balefires can't harm each other, either; it's Pellagrin's curse. However, I'm a Magnate. Ramus, prepare yourself; we have things to do...'

CHAPTER FIFTEEN

HAIDA & SALOATH

Stood with Selva looking up into the branches of Pellagrin's Oak, Aridain watched as Duran climbed upwards through the sturdy branches.

'Isn't it brilliant, Aridain? Now you've moved to the school, we can play together all the time.'

'My mum's not really happy about it, having lost the cottage and all. Midge, however, is very happy about it. He didn't like all the extra work, trotting constantly back and forth from Spalding to the school.'

'What about your dad?'

'My dad isn't being very nice at the moment.'

'Why not?'

'He has a nasty man in his head, but when I say anything, he gets angry.'

'Have you told your mum?'

'She knows, but there's nothing anyone can do about it…'

'Don't stand and stare,' shouted Duran from the branches above. 'Follow me.'

'Come down, Duran. You know we're not allowed to climb this tree. It's sacred. It's Pellagrin's tree,' Selva shouted.

'That's what makes it fun, besides Pellagrin won't mind, he's dead,' replied Duran loudly.

'Take no notice Aridain, Duran's trying to get you into trouble again,' warned Selva.

As Duran continued to climb, Aridain looked resolutely up through the oak's healthy branches, his competitive spirit and the determination to humiliate Selva's obnoxious twin, threatening to spur him into action once again.

The afternoon had started innocently enough with fun and games in the snow and Aridain had, with Selva's help, reluctantly agreed to talk to her brother, and had managed to ignore Duran's annoying ways for the majority of the day. But as the day progressed, Duran, to Aridain's consternation, had returned to his old ways. Attempting to disregard Selva and leave her on her own, Selva and Duran, as was their way, began shouting and screaming at each other. When that didn't work, Duran refused to play with any of them until he sent the dragonlet away, although what he would do when he discovered he was climbing straight towards the diminutive lizard perched in the uppermost branches, Aridain couldn't wait to find out.

'Aridain no!' admonished Selva, looking around nervously and pulling at his leg.

'Let go Selva, do you want Duran to get hurt?' demanded Aridain.

'Well, of course not, but...'

'Selva, Sabra's up there,' insisted Aridain.

'You stupid boys, I hate you,' Selva squealed in her most spiteful voice.

Scowling, Aridain climbed rapidly up through the closely knit branches, knowing all too well that he shouldn't be climbing Pellagrin's oak, but disobeying the school's rules, anyway.

Catching Duran as they reached the top of the tree, the petulant youth suddenly started punching and kicking as Aridain reached for the highest branches.

Shall I teach him another lesson? intruded the thoughts of the dragonlet.

'No,' he shouted suddenly as all the months of putting up with Duran's nasty attitude exploded in one frustrated kick that threatened to send Duran spiralling to the ground below.

'Owww, that really hurt,' Duran shouted, grabbing despairingly for the branch above his head. 'I nearly fell out of the tree.'

'I don't care. Find another tree to climb. This one's mine,' declared Aridain triumphantly.

Staring at him spitefully, Duran poked out his tongue and in silence began the long climb down.

Aridain heard the dragonlet in his head once more.

If you loathe this youngling so much, why do you tolerate him?

Because Auntie Celia and my mum insist we play together, besides, someone has to look out for Selva. I've tried to be friends, Sabra, but Duran's just nasty all the time. My dad says the only way to fight bullies is to fight back. He says they are nothing but cowards.

The dragonlet, alighting on a branch close by, said, *I say it's no more than the petulant youth deserves. But be careful youngling. He's like a fury. They're no threat alone, but a pack of furies are aggressive and deadly.*

Abolishing all thoughts of Duran from his mind, Aridain stared out across the school grounds from his perch high up in the oak canopy. The gusts of wind rocked the branches gently to and fro, the motion caused his eyes to close and his mind to drift. It was then that an unfamiliar hooded figure, its features veiled, entered his thoughts and called his name. He watched in fascination as the figure pulled back its hood to reveal a face covered with an ornate clay mask. It wasn't a nasty dream, and he didn't feel threatened or frightened. On the contrary, the dream felt warm and inviting.

Caught in the strange dream, his mind's eye turned towards the horizon and a city adorned with domes, spires, grand palaces and ornate plazas. Floating above one of the blue, domed buildings, he suddenly found himself sat amidst soft cushions and fabrics dressed in unfamiliar clothes. Floating and drifting, the room took on a surreal quality as below him, strange looking creatures prostrated themselves at his feet, but when he tried to leave, their congeniality changed. Then, unknown to the gathering, two shadowy outlines invaded his dream, whispering his grandmother's name. Aridain, in a panic, then sought his grandparent's house. Soaring across the countryside in the still and clear atmosphere, it wasn't long before he was over Spalding. Phasing through the tiled roof and black and white-washed walls of the small mansion-house, he then found himself at the top of his grandmother's spiral staircase, and when he glanced outside, he saw a dark disfigured shape standing outside the front gate, looking up at him. Afraid to indulge this inexplicable dream any longer, his eyes snapped open and, breathing rapidly, he grabbed for the thin branches. Panicking, Aridain turned to find the dragonlet staring at him strangely.

Curious, it seems our connection is far stronger than expected. I too saw what you saw.

'What was it about?'

I wish I could tell you. I suggest, youngling, you consult your passenger.

I can't, said Aridain, closing his eyes for a moment. *He's not here.*

Feeling scared and out of his depth, Aridain wished Selva were here. She was always nice to him, but heights scared Selva.

'ARIDAIN, ARE YOU COMING DOWN NOW?'

'SELVA, YOU'RE STILL HERE!' he shouted, relieved. 'Well, at least Selva's not scared of you, Sabra,' smiled Aridain, 'if it wasn't for Duran's nastiness, we could all have so much fun together.'

Reaching the ground, Aridain's smile soon disappeared when he saw Duran kicking petulantly at the grass beyond the terrace and neatly trimmed hedges.

'Duran didn't want to go home,' said Selva.

'I wish he would. I don't want him to play with us,' shouted Aridain moodily. 'He's a big baby.'

Thrusting his hands into his pockets aggressively, it surprised Aridain to find the silk pouch containing the shards was warm.

'Can you keep a secret?'

'Oh yes,' nodded Selva, intrigued.

Drawing the bag from his pocket, he undid the drawstrings and opened the silk pouch. The two of them then gazed in wonder at the softly glowing shards.

'What are they?'

'Their called The Firebrand Shards, Sabra calls them the Siamang.'

'Where did you find them?'

'Under that tree, remember? The one we hid behind when we were chased by the nasty,' said Aridain.

'What's the big secret? What have you got there?' said Duran, suddenly peering over Aridain's shoulder.

Closing the bag abruptly, Aridain said, 'None of your business.'

His face taking on the look of a disgruntled warthog, Duran, staring with hate-filled eyes, growled, 'I hate you both. I'm going to find new friends, then we'll see.'

'Don't pay him no mind Aridain, he's always grumpy,' smiled Selva sweetly.

Despite Selva's words, Sabra's warning popped into his head. "Be careful, youngling. He's like a fury. They're no threat alone, but a pack of furies are aggressive and deadly."

'I know. We can go and visit your grandfather in Spalding,' said Selva enthusiastically.

'Why?'

'Well, we can play without Duran, and you can get away from your father. That's what you want, don't you? It will be fun,' said Selva in her most endearing voice whilst flashing her sweetest smile.

'OK,' said Aridain eagerly. 'But I have to go home first. I have chores to do now we're living at Pellagrin's, and I have to write a note, tell my mum where we're going. I'll meet you in the field beside the gates early in the morning.'

'OK,' she said. Kissing Aridain on the cheek, she then skipped happily towards the farm.

You do like getting into trouble for this one, don't you youngling? It's time you grew up, said the dragonlet, appearing suddenly overhead. *You have a destiny, as does Selva. Selva's birth parents will need her now more than ever; that is her destiny.*

Be quiet Sabra, you know nothing about climbing trees or having fun, said Aridain angrily.

Fun? queried Sabra.

Yes, fun, said Aridain, turning moodily and traipsing back towards the fortress.

Dragonlets have fun, said Sabra, his thoughts taking on a hurt demeanour, *but fun makes no sense when one's thoughts are on survival.*

What if I don't want to grow up, you grumpy old dragonlet? huffed Aridain.

You don't have a choice, hissed Sabra darkly, *you have a destiny.*

The early morning chill numbing their face and ears, Aridain and Selva ran across the field hand in hand, the frosted snow underfoot sparkling like a carpet of diamonds in the sunlight. It was only after they climbed over the neatly layered hedge that defined the field boundary, and entered Higher Wood, that they slowed down.

'You'll love it at my grandma's house, Selva. There's so much space to run around in, and the garden's really big,' Aridain said excitedly.

With an excited giggle, Selva turned and placed her small hand in his. Slipping and sliding down the path through the woods, they approached the sparkling stream underneath the frosted branches of hazel, and poplars blossoming with pussy willows, and hung with catkins.

'Look Selva, snowdrops.'

Picking one, he handed it to her, but instead of making her happy, Selva began to cry.

'Selva, what's the matter? I thought you wanted to stay at Grandma's with me. I thought it would make you happy?'

'Oh, I am. It's just that my mum and dad say we might have to leave the farmhouse,' said Selva, launching into a second wave of tears.

'But you can't. I've only just moved to the school! Why do things always have to change?' said Aridain, kicking at the ground grumpily. 'I just want to climb trees and play like we used to.'

'Me too,' said Selva sadly.

'Don't be sad, Selva, I know what will cheer you up. This is something Auntie Magen taught me.'

Walking over to a hazel tree, Aridain shook one of the branches. Dislodging several icicles, he thrust them into the ground, then stood back and watched. It took a few seconds, but slowly and surely, the icicles, despite the chill, melted, and in their place, small, green leaves pushed through the ground. Then, soon after, small yellow blooms burst into flower.

Picking one, Aridain gave it to Selva.

'Oh Aridain, it's beautiful.'

'They're called Aconites, they blossom...'

But he didn't finish his sentence as Selva hugged and kissed him firmly on the lips.

'You're welcome!' said Aridain, more than a little embarrassed.

They continued on in silence before Selva said, 'Dad does his best, and I help the best I can, but Mum's not sleeping properly. My dad doesn't know it, but me and Duran hear Mummy crying.'

'You are a healer, youngling,' said Sabra.' It is in you. You will find the strength to help your mother. Your brother, however, his heart grows darker every day.'

In surprise, Selva looked up. She smiled then as the dragonlet sat contentedly on a branch, hissed gently, and looked meaningfully down at her.

'Sabra, you talked to Selva!' exclaimed Aridain happily.

Smiling, Selva said, 'I always wondered what you sounded like, Sabra.'

'You are smiling youngling, my job is done,' and with that Sabra once more disappeared into the trees, leaving a bemused yet happy Selva staring after him.

'Sabra's right though. Mum and Dad don't know what to do about Duran.'

'Don't take it to heart, Selva. Sabra can be the voice of doom sometimes. Come on, let's go,' smiled Aridain.

Exiting the wood, they walked across the snow blanketed meadow, frosted snow crunching underfoot.

Looking towards the woods, Selva said, 'What was it like sharing your body with that creature? It must have been horrible.'

'I could see the woods and the sky, my friends and my parents, but I couldn't speak and I couldn't move,' said Aridain readily. 'It was like lying in a bowl of thick treacle. Things happened in me that I didn't like and everything felt dark and clammy, and after a while I felt really sad.'

'But you killed it anyway,' said Selva, kissing him soundly on the cheek. 'You were really brave.'

'Well, it wasn't all down to me,' said Aridain, his face now flushing red. 'My mum told me to be brave, and my friends in the woods helped me too.'

Suddenly, with a beat of its leathery wings, the dragonlet appeared.

'Younglings, I have something important to show you. Follow me,' and without another word the dragonlet turned towards the trees on the far side of the meadow.

'Where's Sabra going?'

'I don't know,' Aridain insisted, rubbing his hands together eagerly in an attempt to generate some warmth in his numbed fingers.

'But I don't want to.'

'If you knew Sabra, Selva, you'd realise that when he has something to show you, it's usually worth seeing,' said Aridain seriously.

Grasping Selva's hand, Aridain, following the dragonlet, led her from the meadow up a steep incline and over the brow of a hill. Eventually they entered a thicket, that was far from the beaten track and, with no paths to follow, they had to scramble over fallen tree trunks hung with moss, down overgrown gullies, and through the blackthorn's sharp twiggy branches as they struggled to keep Sabra in sight.

'This place feels old, like Pellagrin's,' concluded Aridain, gazing about in the half-light.

'What's all that?' exclaimed Selva fearfully, peering through the trees.

Rolling around in a large clearing, on a carpet of bright, red, spiky vegetation that grew on the woodland floor, Sabra hissed, *A dragon died here many years ago. His name was Saloath.*

'It won't come back to life, will it?' exclaimed Selva.

'Don't be silly,' admonished Aridain.

'Don't fret younglings, there's nothing to fear here,' assured Sabra. 'Out of ignorance, humans attach superstition to such places; like if you step on the firethorn grass, a dragon's spirit will appear,' explained Sabra reverently. 'But what humans don't realise is that dragon's mate for life. Once the carcass is found, my primitive brothers will not abandon the body for months, even years, afterwards. So, it's little surprise that people believed the dead dragon's spirit still resides over the carcass. If humans listened more to fact and less to meaningless tittle-tattle, this land would be a much saner place and humans and dragon kind could live side by side,' hissed Sabra angrily.

'Grandpop says the same grass grows on Firethorn Hill.'

'That's right, youngling, named after the red spiky plant you see on the ground here. It's nasty too. If you're not wearing thick clothing, one touch and it burns your skin. It only grows where a dragon has fallen and contains memory, information; like your death stones. It has to do with the makeup of a dragon's skin.'

'That dragon's name was Haida,' informed Aridain. 'She was the mate of Saloath, the last dragon in Durbah,' Aridain said solemnly.

'How do you know that, Aridain?' enquired Selva.

'Grandpop told me that when Saloath discovered Haida's body on Firethorn Hill, he induced the frenetic flame, and rampaged across Durbah.'

'Correct youngling,' said Sabra sadly. 'What is not recorded, however, is that Haida was killed by drug runners whilst she slept, then drained of her life's blood, and that she carried young.'

That's horrible!' cried Selva.

'Grandpop also told me that the wizard Adaxial was tasked with killing Saloath, and succeeded where many failed.'

'Anyway, I thought we should see this and pay our respects to Saloath, youngling, one of our own, who up until now has lain undiscovered and misunderstood,' said Sabra solemnly.

'So, even in death, dragon kind is revered and feared,' said Selva, looking around the thicket apprehensively.

'Yes, Selva, but treading on firethorn grass will not awaken a dragon's wrath,' chuckled Aridain.

'Or invoke the Dragon God Dragonhast's wrath,' hissed Sabra, who suddenly took flight and spurted a jet of liquid flame into the air.

'Sabra, you're scaring Selva,' said Aridain, watching the trepidation on Selva's face.

'I'm not scared, really I'm not,' smiled Selva, nervously.

They made their way back through the tangle of trees and undergrowth and all too soon they emerged back onto the meadow, causing a dozen roedeer cropping serenely on the grass buried beneath the snow to look about skittishly. Content the children posed no threat, the deer continued to root around in the undergrowth, as the pair ran across the meadow, performing cartwheels and rolling around in the snow. Failing dismally to copy Selva, bent over backwards and crab-walking across the snowy ground, Aridain, falling flat on his face, lay giggling upon the ground.

Sitting in the snow next to him, Selva said, 'Sabra's wonderful, isn't he? No wonder you're so happy. I wish it could be just the three of us all the time.'

'Keep your voice down, he'll hear you.'

'So, what's wrong with that?'

'Because Sabra's already far too clever for his own scales.'

'Well, I think he's cute.'

Cute and wonderful, I like your friend, youngling; she knows the truth when she sees it?

'Oh no, too late,' said Aridain seriously.

With tears in her eyes, Selva said suddenly, 'Aridain, if I have to move, will we ever see each other again?'

'Of course we will.'

'How can you be so sure?'

'Because I can fly.'

Now who's showing off, hissed Sabra.

'How?' asked Selva, perplexed.

'I just think of where I want to be and hitch a ride.'

'That youngling, is called passengering, and even though it appears like you are there, in truth you are not,' explained Sabra, appearing once more above their heads.

'Told you Selva,' whispered Aridain, 'a bit of a know it all.'

Whisper all you like youngling, I can still hear you.

'So, you're not there, not really?' said Selva sadly.

'But I can still talk to you,' smiled Aridain. 'I could even talk to you through Sabra, if you like.'

Don't even think about it, hissed Sabra dangerously.

'This isn't funny Aridain, I might never see you again,' sobbed Selva. 'I know; we could always run away together! We have the cute and wonderful Sabra,' she said suddenly, fluttering her eyelashes.

'Yes, we have the cute and wonderful Sabra,' mocked Aridain, eyeing the dragonlet hovering just out of reach.

'And I have everything I need in my satchel,' continued Selva.

'Selva, I just can't leave,' stammered Aridain. He then said more confidently, 'Besides, I have no supplies.'

'Then we'll get some from Spalding?'

'Spalding?'

'Yes, from your grandfather.'

Sabra, help me?

This is your problem, youngling.

If I say no, Sabra, she'll hate me.

If you had discouraged Selva right from the outset, this issue would never have arisen.

I was just trying to be nice, Sabra.

Sometimes, youngling, nice isn't the right thing to do.

CHAPTER SIXTEEN

GRAVE INTENTIONS

Drawing her hood back from her head worn against the freezing snow, Lascana approached her small merchandise shop. It was midday and having a couple of hours before her chores at the fortress began all over again; she stamped the snow from her boots and unlocked the door. Stepping inside, she twisted the cord as she had done countless times before, then tugged, heaving the reed shutters upwards, allowing the light to flood the interior of her shop.

Securing the cord around the retaining clip, she turned and let out a muffled cry. Clamping her hand over her mouth, Lascana, her heart now pounding in her ears, stood and listened, her mind at first refusing to acknowledge the carnage. Then, with her heart in her mouth, she entered the shop, peering nervously about.

Urns full of sand and slaked lime, as well as China cups and plates, were smashed on the floor amongst the scattered remains of her Calabashian glass jugs. Crates of nails and metal fastenings had been forced open as well as sacks and parcels containing ironmongery, their contents strewn across the floor. Also, the intricately carved wooden figure of a firedrake, made by one of the students to be sold on his behalf, lay broken in the corner along with a smashed rare ceramic powder box.

With her heart pounding in her ears, she crept tentatively into the storeroom and its gloomy interior, fearing the intruder would at any moment appear from the darkness. But after what seemed like an age, she heaved a sigh of relief as it became evident the intruder was long gone. With tears in her eyes, she looked up at the small side window and saw the intruder's point of entry. She walked stoically to the counter and, expecting it to be gone, searched for the pink rhinestone necklace, one of her more expensive items, only to find it discarded on the floor. Tears appeared anew as she picked up the empty Sringarian fairy tale lacquer box her father had given her. Kneeling and returning all the lucky charms together with her precious jewellery to the box for safekeeping, she set it aside on the counter.

Who could have done this? Was it the same figure who attacked Alfic and Perak? It was then that she saw the smashed display cabinet at the far end of the counter and her collection of minerals and stones scattered over the floor.

She pushed the open stock book aside and began to arrange her stones along the counter in alphabetical order, together with her collection of small green Peridot figures and wooden Pellagrin's souvenirs. She then swept up what was left of the smashed ceramic pots and, with a sigh, emptied the contents into a bin. Then, setting the dustpan and brush down, she began to cry.

Pull yourself together woman, you have to be strong for your friends' and family's sakes. Squaring her shoulders, she took hold of the manifest. Suddenly she realised why the book was open. She hadn't left it open; the intruder had.

She looked up at a knock on the door. Peering in through the window, his short blond curly hair giving him the appearance of a Gondian playboy, was Bern. Unlocking the door whilst waving and smiling reassuringly to the crowd, now gathered around outside, she let him in.

Smiling sympathetically, Bern said, 'Hello Lascana, I heard you had a burglary. I came over to see if there's anything I can do?'

Smiling tentatively, Lascana said, 'Thanks Bern, any help would be appreciated.'

Lascana then turned to the tall, sinewy greengrocer, minus his hessian overall, and threw herself into his arms.

'There, there Lascana, don't fret now.'

Shaking her head in annoyance, Lascana looked up at Bern, embarrassed. 'I'm sorry, Bern. After what you have endured, the last thing you want is a pathetic woman crying on your shoulder.'

'Nonsense girl, it's a natural reaction.'

'Who would do this? Elimi also came looking for something, but what, what are they after?'

'Come on, enough time for that later. Let's tidy this place up, then with a fresh perspective, we can try to solve this mystery.'

Taking up her broom, Bern began to tidy the shop in silence. For the next couple of hours they toiled, repairing and repackaging where they could whilst passing the time of day, and slowly but surely the shop returned to normal.

Sweeping the last broken remnants into a basket, Bern said suddenly, 'Have you talked to Janus recently?'

Blowing onto her cold hands, despite the thick woollen gloves she wore, Lascana replied, 'No, why?'

'I visited Sorin and Celia. They told me he's experiencing nightmares again.'

'But that's not right. He should be recovering. You don't think...'

'Gradine?'

'But if so, why? Why Janus Loker? Bern, what makes him so special?'

His face a picture of turmoil, Bern stared at the ground. 'Janus is a very private man. He's never told another soul about his past apart from Sorin, Celia and me. I'm not sure I should be telling you this, but you see, Janus was a soldier in the army, a good swordsman, too.'

'Yes, Sorin told us, making him ripe for recruitment,' finished Lascana. She then looked at Bern expectantly, as the greengrocer, taking a deep breath, continued...,

'When he was a boy, Janus's parents were killed by the blue painted barbarians. Consumed by revenge, Janus eventually joined the army, requesting a posting in the Mycean Highlands on the Zapatian border. He then went on a killing spree, slaughtering any painted tribesmen he could find. Then, many years later, whilst patrolling the countryside north of Hearkson, he met Sorin and Celia, who at the time owned a farmstead on the Zapatian border; whilst I had a provisions business in Hearkson. We all became friends, and together, with Sorin and Celia's help, we finally put Janus's demons to rest. When the painted men's raids became too much, we all travelled to Pellagrin's, where Janus became a wine merchant. Now, however, thanks to that bitch Gradine and her coins, I fear his demons have returned.'

'I never knew,' gasped Lascana, 'it must have been a terrible experience and taken a monumental effort to put those events behind him.'

'Yes, it did.' His brow creasing in thought, Bern asked, 'Gradine never offered your family a coin despite your opposition and all the trouble you've caused Kuelack. He has even given you a room here at the school. Why is that?'

'I have often thought about that. Maybe Gradine's coins wouldn't work because my family has magic. Perhaps it only works if you have something they need. The apartment could simply be down to the old adage, "Keep your friends close and your enemies even closer"? Come on, it sounds like we need to visit Janus, whether he wants company or not,' Lascana said cunningly.

With the heady aromas of cooking filling the kitchen, Perak placed the prepared ham into a pan full of vegetables simmering on the range. Then, reaching up, he plucked some herbs and spices from the rack hanging overhead. He then threw them into the pot together with the ham.

Grunting in satisfaction, he then walked down the hallway to the conservatory where the pigeon, coaxed from the wild, perched compliantly on one of the oak beams. Looking thoughtfully into its eyes, it landed on his arm and allowed Perak to tie a note written to Lascana, explaining that the children were all right, to its leg. The pigeon then looked at him one last time and flew out through the conservatory door into the cold winter sky.

Then, sitting down in his favourite armchair, he looked out at his garden, back-lit by the winter sun. He gazed beyond the pond holding his hibernating red-finned carp, and the patio, encased by wooden trellising to the deep borders, where his prized delphiniums and sweet-smelling roses grew. He then looked to the stable block beyond and the large, leafless rhododendrons to the rickety old shed stood at the far end of the garden that he had built before the house, now smothered by an overgrown clematis and honeysuckle, blanketed in a thick layer of snow.

His focus then returned to the glasshouse, and he perused the shelves packed with Vara's orchids and her Navarian grape vine, snaking its way through the wooden beams and supports; a vine that Vara claimed actually moved... when you weren't looking.

For years Vara had intimated her desire for a glasshouse so she could grow her very own exotic plants, instead of shopping in Spalding or travel to the school every time she needed ingredients. So, when he finally announced that he would build it, she was over the moon, but then Perak remembered Vara's impatience...

'If you want me to build this extension properly, you'll have to be patient, Vara. To finish quicker will only detract from the finished article.'

'It's not the quality, but your speed. By the time you've finished, I'll be old and blind.'

'Vara, it will be worth the wait, less haste, more speed.'

Conceding, Vara had left him to his slow and precise work and when at last it was finished, she was pleased, although she had never admitted it...

'Were back!' shouted Aridain as the pair bounded through the kitchen, followed by Beria.

'About time,' insisted Perak. 'Did you get it?'

Jumping up and down, her golden locks bouncing around like unruly springs, Selva handed him a small cloth bag tied with string. 'Yes, Mr Glassing was very nice.'

'Did you mention the breach birth?'

'Yes,' nodded Beria reassuringly, 'he said he would give you a healthy discount.'

'Good job. These ingredients aren't cheap.'

'Grandpop, can we go and play now?' pleaded Aridain.

'Yes, but before you go, I want to know if you are still planning on running away?'

'I told you it was a bad idea, Selva,' hissed Aridain.

'The thing is, if you run away, you won't be able to take any of this delicious liquorice ham I've cooked with you,' said Perak slyly.

'It does sound much more delicious than eating burdock roots, Selva, or eating dead squirrels,' said Aridain, holding his grumbling stomach.

'OK Grandpa Perak, we will not run away,' said Selva resolutely, 'at least not today. Tomorrow maybe?'

'Beria, can you give me a hand with these ingredients?' asked Perak. 'It's for a cure-all tonic I'm making.'

Watching whilst Aridain and Selva hurried out through the conservatory door, Beria suddenly stood stock-still, as if listening. 'Go and get the children, Perak, now!'

Then, sprinting into the hallway, Beria raced up the stairs to the second floor, and peered out into the garden.

She followed Perak's progress as he reached the children, now down by the old shed. However, as he herded them towards the house, something dark emerged from behind the stable.

'Perak,' she screamed, 'look out!'

Suddenly, Selva screamed and Midge whinnied a warning as the creature, looking like a dark, demented, moth-eaten Ardent wolf, grasped Perak by the back of the neck and threw him across the garden.

Sprinting down the stairs and into the kitchen, Beria began rifling through the kitchen drawers until she found what she was looking for. She then ran into the garden just in time to see Aridain place himself between the dark creature and Perak. With a shout of anguish, she watched as the creature lifted Aridain from the ground. Then, something strange occurred as the creature stood stock-still and stared at Aridain. Placing Aridain back onto the ground, the creature suddenly went rigid and turned grey. Then, its skin began to crack and split until it crumbled to dust on the floor.

'Aridain, are you all right? How did you do that?'

'Auntie Magen showed me how to move rocks,' said Aridain, as if nothing out of the ordinary had happened.

'Moving rocks is one thing, but turning things into rock, quite another.'

'I just remembered how the rocks felt and told the creature to be like a rock. I thought everybody could do it. Why are you looking at me like that?'

'You are the Balefire Taal,' intoned Beria, 'you are our'–

'That's enough of that, Beria Dearing.' Suddenly remembering what had happened, Perak said, 'Where's Selva?'

Selva, suddenly appearing from the conifer trees and staring at Aridain angrily, said, 'I'm fine, thanks for asking.'

'Thank you, Aridain, for saving us.'

'That's all right, Grandpop, you know I would never let a nasty hurt you.' Aridain, however, was looking at Selva's face. It was a look he hadn't seen before.

Lascana and Bern stepped out beneath the iron-grey sky as snow began to fall once more, covering the ground in a fresh layer of white.

Bent against the blustery wind, the pair made their way over to Janus's wine store, where a small crowd of people had gathered.

'What's happening here?' demanded Lascana, shielding her eyes against the light and peering in through the large, convex, multi-paned window in an effort to detect some movement.

'Janus isn't answering the door,' replied one of the anxious onlookers.

'Everything's burnt and blackened, Lascana,' said another, 'and there are smashed bottles and wine all over the floor.'

Concerned now, Lascana turned on the crowd, stood talking in hushed whispers. 'Did none of you think to help or call for assistance?'

Bern smashed one of the door's small panes using his elbow and, reaching inside, he unlocked the door. 'Stay behind me, Lascana,' he said quietly.

'There's no point in whispering, Bern. Smashing the glass has probably scared off any intruders.'

'You're probably right, but let's not take any chances.'

Walking cautiously through the shop front, they peered into the darkened nooks and crannies. When they reached the smashed wine rack, Lascana knelt down and inspected the darker splodges amongst the glass on the wine-soaked floor.

Pressing his finger into the blobs, Bern then tasted the substance. 'Blood!' he exclaimed.

Taking off her cloak, Lascana, treading quietly, walked past the bubbling stills into Janus's rooms beyond. She then screamed a warning, as suddenly a blood-stained figure leapt from behind the doorway, forcing Bern to the floor. Realising it was Janus, Lascana ran to seize his hand, now poised to strike with a knife.

'Two or twenty of you, it makes no difference to me devils, send your entire clan. I'll kill you all!'

'Janus, it's Lascana and Bern, your friends!' she screamed, but the ex-soldier wasn't listening and backhanded her with the knife handle. Lascana fell to her knees, clutching at her face, but it gave Bern the chance he needed, and turning the tables, wrestled Janus to the floor.

Backhanding the delirious wine merchant across the face, Bern yelled, 'Janus stop, it's me, snap out of it!'

Breaking free, Janus rolled to his feet, as did Bern.

'If you want revenge devils, attack me, not my friends. Leave them out of this,' Janus shouted, advancing once again.

Lascana climbed groggily to her feet, the anger she now felt clearing her head. Reaching for a half empty bottle of brandy, she smashed it over Janus's head, causing the man from the Mycean highlands to turn around angrily. He took two steps towards her, then abruptly collapsed.

'Thanks, Lascana. Are you all right?'

Waving him away, she said, 'I'm fine. Bern, look at his back! He's stitched the wounds he could reach himself, badly I might add, the others….' Wiping at her bloodied nose, Lascana searched his person. Finding nothing the wine merchant could use as an offensive weapon, she came to a decision. 'I'm going to search the shop. Watch Janus.'

Strewn with blood-soaked bandages and empty bottles of every kind, fouling what was usually a clean and tidy shop, it looked as though an enraged fury had run amok. The air smelled of stale sweat and alcohol, and more bandages were heaped in a basin full of bloody water together with kitchen utensils.

Finding a length of rope in an old wooden chest, she found more bandages and some thread in the kitchen. Handing the rope to Bern, the greengrocer sat him up, then tied Janus's hands and feet to a chair with the hemp rope.

'I've never known his aggression to be so intense,' said Bern, whilst tending to Janus's wounds. 'It's almost as if he's attaining some perverse pleasure from it,' he surmised. 'Perhaps something he saw or something he did triggered it. Perhaps he was scared he would be attacked again, and in his mind, he was back in the Mycean Highlands.'

'Or it could have something to do with this,' said Lascana, holding up a silver coin. 'I found it on the floor.'

'Not another one?'

'Gradine has a lot to answer for,' said Bern passionately. 'Get that cursed object out of here before it regains control.'

Nodding, Lascana disappeared outside. Returning five minutes later, she said, 'It's done!'

They both looked down at Janus, who twitched and jerked spasmodically.

'I fear his mind is broken,' stated Bern.

'Whatever the state of his mind, we can't leave him here like this. We have to get him away from the school.'

'I fear you're right, Lascana,' agreed Bern. 'But not whilst his mind is fuelled by alcohol and adrenalin.'

'Come on, let's clean this place up,' said Lascana.

Searching the property, they removed several bottles of Navarian brandy, all in various states of being consumed. They then began to tidy up the bedroom, pulling the bloodied, filthy sheets from the bed and sweeping half-eaten food on the floor into a pile.

'There, that's so much better,' smiled Lascana.

Then, from the back room, they heard inane muttering. Rushing into the bedroom, Lascana grasped Janus's face and stared into his bloodshot eyes. Seeing the demons cavorting there, she hollered, 'Janus, Janus, listen to me, it's Lascana!'

'No, I told you to leave them out of it. Just kill me and get it over with. I'm the one you want,' Janus stammered. Then his eyes sprang open, and he looked around furtively as if perceiving the world around him for the first time. He then reached into his trouser pocket. 'It's not there! Where is it?' He then began frantically looking around the room.

'Listen to me, Janus, you are having a delusional episode. Whatever you're seeing isn't real. It's all in your head,' Lascana soothed calmly.

'Where is it?' WHERE IS IT?

'I'm sorry Janus, I've destroyed it.'

The effect was as dramatic as it was instant. Despite being secured to the chair, Janus lunged towards Lascana, his eyes fixated on the object of his hatred.

Bern leapt and, manhandling the squirming wine merchant to the floor, said serenely, 'Hey buddy, how are you doing? You remember me, don't you, the good times we had together? Remember Gonda's sanatorium? We were refugees fleeing from the border skirmishes up north; Sorin, Celia and me helped release you from prison after three years. Also, recall that keg of nettle beer you brought around for Sorin's birthday, when you tried to insert the tap, the beer exploded over you and Celia's kitchen floor, and we all got soaked; or when you ran around Sorin's garden with Duran on your shoulders and he was sick all over your head.'

Lascana watched Janus's face crease up in puzzlement, the strong memories straining to break through the nightmares. 'It's working,' she whispered. 'Keep going.'

'And then… and then there was the brewers' seminar, held here at the school and you were the chief speaker, I remember the pride you felt when your blackcurrant mead won first prize, the judges were so keen on it they all got drunk, including the head judge, the obnoxious Mr Darsus, we all commented that it was probably the first time he'd relaxed in thirty years.'

Janus Loker blinked and looked around in confusion. He then dropped his head to his chest and sobbed uncontrollably.

Rushing to his side, Lascana said softly, 'It's all right, Janus, it's all right. We're here and we're not going to let anything happen to you.'

'Did I hurt anyone?' Janus sniffed.

Stroking his hair, Lascana placated 'No Janus, no one was hurt.'

Finally, Janus looked up at Lascana and said softly, 'What are you doing here? You must leave now, before they show up again.'

'Who, Janus?'

'The blue painted devils.'

'Hey buddy, there are no blue painted devils. You're at Pellagrin's,' confirmed Bern forlornly.

Gazing down at him in sympathy, Lascana, shaking her head sadly, said, 'I'm so sorry, Janus.' Lascana then turned to Bern and said dangerously, 'It seems me and Gradine have a lot to talk about.'

CHAPTER SEVENTEEN

MYSTERIES

Overnight, the grey snow clouds had cleared away to be replaced by chilling blue winter skies and windswept white clouds; the biting wind blowing the feathery snow across the grass.

Wrapping her out-of-control garments tightly about her person, her head bowed to ward against the stinging frost-bitten wind, Lascana, together with Bern, made their way beside the combat field towards the infirmary.

'By the way, thanks for what you did for Janus.'

'Don't mention it, Bern. We do what we can for our friends.'

Lascana glanced across the combat field and watched as students, coached by the archery teacher Martagan, and the stick fighting mistress Crystal, loosed arrows and attacked straw stuffed targets. Meanwhile, at the far end towards the stables, students coached by Horse Mistress Konya galloped back and forth, trying to retrieve a leather ball that scooted along the ground. Lascana watched as, in a spray of snow and mud, one rider leaned down from his saddle, scooped the ball from the grass, and then passed it to a teammate, urging his horse in the opposite direction. Wielding a short club, the rider threw the leather ball into the air and struck it, hitting the target area to the admiration of his teammates.

'Alfic tells me Aridain will make an excellent cabala player one day.'

'Believe me, Bern, I know. The garden is...., was far too small,' said Lascana sadly. 'Aridain's ball would regularly end up in the woods or in the cottage; I was always tripping over the damn thing,' she mused sadly.

Passing beneath the arched doorway of the sanatorium, Lascana focused on the interior.

Bottled pills, herbs, ointments, instruments, and utensils, filled shelves that were fixed against the wall. Dressings and bandages of every conceivable type hung above a row of large stoneware basins against the far wall; some of which were filled with bandages, soaking, she presumed, in a sterilising liquid. Beside wooden storage lockers stood a long marble workbench and a barrel of water, and beside them were several stitched leather stretchers, stacked in their separate divisions, together with beds pushed against the wall.

Marvelling at the vaulted windows, no doubt positioned to award patients and healers alike, a measure of contentment whilst they worked or recovered, Lascana, smiling warmly, approached Janus, laid contentedly on one of the five single beds.

At their approach, Janus opened his kindly dark brown eyes and smiled. Taking his hand, Lascana, sitting on the edge of his bed, asked, 'How are you feeling?'

'I'm good. Thank you for what you and Bern did?' he said, upbeat.

'It's our pleasure,' smiled Lascana. 'You were covered in blood and babbling about blue painted devils. Bern told me all about your situation. I think you deserve a medal.'

'Oh no, it's not Janus who deserves the medal.'

They turned as the large oak door to the infirmary creaked on its hinges. Stood in the doorway, dressed in a simple all in one thick silken dress, her hands clasped together as if in prayer, was the familiar gloating figure of Gradine. She was accompanied by Alsike, the school's serene healer. Often mistaken for Almagest's brother, he sported a kindly face covered by a thick grey beard and shoulder-length hair.

'So how is the patient today?' Alsike asked serenely.

'Much better thanks,' smiled Janus.

'I'll bet,' Lascana sneered, looking suspiciously from Alsike to Gradine. 'Explain to me why we found a silver coin on the floor in Janus's shop.'

'Well, I must confess, I don't know how that got there?' smiled Gradine, 'Perhaps Janus is richer than we gave him credit for.'

'Cut the crap Gradine, we know you're plying people with enchanted coins, especially those who refuse to toe-the-line.'

'I have no intention of explaining myself to the likes of you,' stated Gradine belligerently.

Her fists curling in anger, Lascana stood her ground and stared warily but defiantly at Gradine, who approached and stood before her.

'Besides Lascana, we don't want to upset Janus's fragile state of mind now, do we?' smiled Gradine serenely.

Gradine, her eyebrows knitting together, looked up at Lascana, then at Janus. 'According to Alsike here, Janus confessed that, on this day many years ago, his village was burnt to the ground. Is that not so Janus?' said Gradine solemnly.

'It is,' agreed Janus.

'What has that got to do with anything?' snapped Bern.

'This anniversary, combined with a student's sick joke, has had a profound effect on Janus's state of mind,' explained Gradine, 'as has your affection for him.'

About to reply, Lascana was cut off by Bern. 'I'm surprised he told you. Only a handful of people know about that?'

'I know what you're trying to do, Gradine,' Lascana hissed, sidling up close and looking down upon her angrily, 'You're just trying to cover up the fact that you have tasked students to play upon the mind of our friend here with a sick prank.'

'Or perhaps Janus should pick his friends more carefully,' Gradine sneered.

'Now wait just a minute!' protested Bern.

Moving closer, Gradine whispered, 'Face facts Lascana, you and your pitiful band are losing this struggle. Soon your son will be ours and you, your friends and family will be nothing but a sad memory.'

'And I swear, one day, Gradine,' hissed Lascana.

'You'll do what Lascana?' When Lascana remained silent, Gradine said, 'I didn't think so.'

'In the meantime, Janus will work his way through his problems,' said the aging healer suddenly. 'The best thing for Janus right now is for people not to confuse or cause him stress.'

Turning to the healer, Gradine smiled and said, 'I totally agree. He just needs time and some peace. Then, we'll soon have him working in the school's best interest again,' said Gradine smugly. 'Now I think it's time you got back to your chores, Lascana. After all, my privy won't empty itself.'

His voice, taking on a steely quality, Alsike, ushering them forcefully from the room, said, 'Now, I must ask you both to leave. Come on, off you go.'

'Don't trust Gradine, Janus,' insisted Lascana. 'Leave here now, whilst you still can.'

'Good day Lascana, Bern,' smirked Gradine. 'Have a pleasant day.'

The oak door closing with a solid thunk, Lascana, grasping Bern's arm to prevent him from running back into the healing centre, said, 'Think Bern, did Janus look as if he was in trouble, did he demand our help, did he heed our advice?'

'Well, no, but...'

'And have you ever seen that side of Alsike before?'

'Actually, no I haven't.'

Lascana watched Bern's face, as comprehension then understanding dawned on the greengrocer's face. He then looked up at Lascana. 'Are there no depths to which that bitch won't sink? 'Just how many of these coins are there?'

'Many moons ago, Bern, I listened in as Vara taught my son about enchantments. She lectured that sometimes in order to save time and effort, it's easier to enchant many small objects in one go, than bigger individual items on their own. So, I'm guessing there are many?'

'That's all well and good Lascana, but lessons on enchantment won't help us in the here and now. Janus needs our help,' said Bern resolutely.

She then took his hand in hers, and focusing on his steely blue eyes, said, 'Of course Janus needs our help, Bern.' *I just wish I knew how*, she said under her breath.

She looked to the sky then, but the winter sun failed to lift her spirits, or provide any inspiration. Then, bowing her head, she followed Bern as he strode determinedly out into the icy winter wind.

Woken suddenly by a noise, Perak, dressed in his woollen under garments, climbed out of bed. Taking up the quiver stuffed full of bolts, together with the crossbow saved from the battle at the cottage, he tiptoed out onto the landing, and was surprised to see Sabra, his skin now a medley of red and green, sat alert, watching him from one of the railing finials.

'You heard it too. Beria's asleep. What about the children?'

'Asleep,' replied Treerinks, his tongue flicking agitatedly.

Walking downstairs, Perak, with Treerinks in close attendance, moved through the house, checking each room in turn. Stopping suddenly, Perak sniffed at a pungent smell of freshly chopped herbs, accompanied by a faint bubbling noise emanating from the kitchen. Approaching quietly, Perak peered into the gloom, the crossbow pulled to his shoulder in readiness. He then span around at a muted scream followed by the sound of gushing flames and muffled voices coming from the hallway.

Perak, alert now, burst into the living room. In the shadowy candlelight, a very tall figure, accompanied by a short stout female, were running around, flapping their arms above their heads as Sabra swooped and dived above them.

'Stand still, and turn around, slowly, with your hands in the air or I'll fire a bolt into you?' said Perak with purpose.

Standing, the figures slowly raised their arms.

'So, are you going to lower your crossbow, husband, or are you going to shoot me?'

'Vara, and who... Ramus?' snapped Perak, lowering his weapon.

'What are you doing here, Perak?'

'I could ask you the same question?'

'I live here? We've been at Kuelack's mercy, but we escaped, thanks to Ramus here,' said Vara sullenly.

'And your faces? What happened? Did Kuelack do this to you?' You look like you've been in a fight with Fornax.'

'Yes, and Serac too. But I don't want to discuss it?' said Vara morosely.

'Oh no you don't!' raged Perak. 'You're gone for weeks and now I find you here in the middle of the night, covered in scars, and you don't want to discuss it! I want answers. Ramus, help me out. What are you doing here?'

'I'm not exactly sure,' said Ramus, nonplussed. 'Vara didn't tell me anything.'

'Stop being so melodramatic Perak, it's nothing you need concern yourself with!' said Vara abruptly.

'Vara…?' bellowed Perak.

Heaving a deep, silent sigh, Vara concluded, 'Be content knowing that what I do is in our grandson's best interest, and that sometimes along the way we have to bear some scars.'

'You know there are people watching the house, spies working for Kuelack?'

'Of course there are, it's why we arrived in the night. Circumstances have changed Perak and I need certain items.'

'I don't need your bag of tricks to determine that!' spat Perak angrily.

Vara, shaking her head, said almost inaudibly, 'People always jump to the wrong conclusions.'

'Jumping to the wrong conclusion is nothing to what I'll do if you don't tell me what the hell you're doing here?' Perak growled.

'You wouldn't dare,' threatened Vara, looking shrewdly into Perak's eyes.

'Try me,' Perak growled.

'Haven't you realised yet that the less you all knew, the less you could divulge if caught? Despite what you might think of me, my actions are those of a caring grandmother safeguarding her grandson.'

Looking intently into Vara's eyes, Perak watched as her normally calm, unwavering confidence floundered like a drowning person grasping at straws.

'I may have told a few mistruths over the years, but I have never lied.'

'Like you being a Balefire Magnate, for instance?' exclaimed Perak, 'and that you're drinking dragon's blood.'

Glancing covertly towards Ramus, Vara nodded. 'How did you…?'

'You can't stay that young without…, put it this way, I've known for a while!'

'I never lied about that. I just didn't tell anyone.'

'You're drinking the life blood of dragons!' exclaimed Ramus.

'Yes, it's the only way I can protect my grandson. Not doing this could cost me his life, and many others besides.'

'YOU'RE DRINKING DRAGON'S BLOOD!' raged Ramus!

Perak placed himself in front of Vara as Ramus advanced dangerously.

'There are risks, I grant you, but nothing any of you say will stop me, I've decided.'

'Then you're no better than the Hasp,' said Ramus, outraged. 'Do you know how many dragons die each year, so people like you can indulge yourselves…?'

'This is my decision.'

'But that's just the point. It isn't up to you, don't you see?' raged Ramus. 'Nothing can justify your lust for the exotic liquid.'

'Or you're turning yourself into a depraved witch!' declared Perak. 'This substance turns a Balefire into a yellow hag.'

'Actually, it's the other way around. Balefires evolved from the Hasp,' corrected Vara.

'Fornax's fires! Vara, this is just another game to you, isn't it? Your priority has always been yourself and your agendas. Well, I, for one, am sick and tired of your games and your secrets.'

'I thought that keeping my identity secret would keep Aridain safe.' Seeing the misgivings in his eyes, Vara said, 'When I found out about Kuelack's obsession with finding the Firebrand shards I went to see him, hoping to dissuade him, and if not, kill my youngest son, but he was too strong, my Balefire magic failed me and subsequently all of us. He then threatened me to silence with Aridain's life if I mentioned a word of our conversation to anyone, and that I steer Aridain away from wizardry, despite my pride in what he could become. You may not agree with my views or my methods, but it's a pledge I've taken. I would lay down my life to protect my family, so please trust me to do what's right,' she exclaimed, looking up at Perak with intent.

'I know that look. What is it?' exclaimed Perak.

'Actually, I'm glad that my secret's out, because I was wondering how long it would take for you to own up to your own secret,' said Vara with venom.

'I don't know what you mean?' said Perak innocently.

Standing, Ramus said meekly, 'I'll just leave the room so you love birds can argue in peace.'

'Stay right where you are, Ramus. You need to hear this,' ordered Vara. She then turned to Perak once more. 'You see Ramus, I always wondered how my husband calmed Midge so easily, especially during a certain stampede in the woods. And I always wondered, in the height of summer, why there were never any flies around us or Midge, when we rode the buggy, even on the hottest of days. How is it that a simple farmer's son could be an Animistic?'

'So, ingesting dragon's blood is OK, but me being an Animistic…?'

'That's different.'

'No, it's not. I never asked for this gift. All I wanted was to go about my business covertly, attracting no attention.' Perak remained silent for a few moments before he said savagely, 'You may be proud to proclaim you're the last word in Balefire law, but did you honestly think that status determines a predisposition to magic? That our children only inherited their talents from you?'

As if about to spit fire, Vara, standing to her full height, hissed, 'No, of course not, it's just that…, that I feel useless in my present guise, helpless against our evil counterparts.'

'Ramus, be the voice of reason, will you? Talk to her.'

'I've got a headache,' complained Ramus, walking out into the central hallway. 'Have you got anything to eat?'

'Thanks, thanks a lot,' said Perak dryly.

CHAPTER EIGHTEEN

THE COME OF AGE BALEFIRE

Famished, Beria pushed her plate aside, having finished her breakfast. Opposite, sat Vara, Ramus and Perak, and to either side were Aridain and Selva.

'Don't look at me like that, Vara,' she explained, 'I am here to aid the One, The Balefire Taal, nothing more.' Then, sidling over to Aridain, Beria watched as, with his tongue clamped firmly between his teeth, he finished drawing a surprisingly lifelike picture of an orchid on a piece of parchment. 'Aridain's very much like his father. They both have a certain quality.'

'Yes, headstrong and opinionated,' commented Vara.

'How can you say that? Your union resulted in this remarkable young man,' said Beria happily.

'Urrhg, you make the act sound so clinical, Beria. Nevertheless, lately, Aridain's father has become far too big for his boots,' murmured Vara, 'and secretive.'

Standing, Beria looked out of the window upon the snow-covered garden. 'Regardless of your feelings, Vara, Alfic and his son are the ones to whom we should invest our efforts.'

'I agree. Aridain and, despite his recent erratic behaviour, Alfic, are of great value. Of all of our children, he is the one child who has retained a modicum of common sense. He is also the only one who has grown up appreciating the beauty and true riches of this world. He is the one we cannot lose to Kuelack's schemes and enticements.'

'My dad is very clever, and he's wise,' said Aridain, nodding appreciably, 'but now he has a bad man in his head.' Then, more upbeat, Aridain reached into the book and, plucking the hand drawn flower from the page, handed Beria a perfectly formed orchid and said, 'I like you Beria. This is for you.'

Dumbstruck, Beria thanked him, then stared at the blank page.

'Vara, did you see…'

'He brought another picture to life, did he?' said Vara casually.' He does that.'

'It's destiny, Vara, he is the' –

'I'm sorry, Aridain! What did you say?'

'I said, I like Beria, Grandpop.'

'No, no, before that.'

'What, that Daddy has a bad man in his head?' said Aridain hesitantly.

'Care to elaborate?'

Aridain stared back at Perak blankly.

'Do you know who it is?'

'No, he stares at me with nasty green eyes. He's not very nice,' said Aridain sadly.

Perak looked towards Vara, who shook her head, nonplussed.

'It could be a psychic?' queried Ramus, picking at his teeth with his long fingernails.

'But Kuelack had them all killed, didn't he?' asked Vara.

'So everyone thought,' said Perak grimly.

They all stared into their now empty plates, the quiet deafening in its silence.

When Vara stood and began collecting their plates and cutlery, Beria, taking the silence as a cue, asked, 'What are you reading, Aridain?'

'It's a book Grandma makes me read.'

'Yes, I know that feeling,' Beria said, sitting down next to him. Then, glancing with purpose towards Vara, she smiled, 'but I'm glad she made me.'

'She made you read this? But you're a grownup!'

'I wasn't always a grown up. I was only a teenager when I started, and before that, I studied colour magic.'

'My cousin Linden is studying colour magic!'

'Yes, I know; he'll be one to watch in the future.'

'Selva says colour magic is really boring magic.'

'It is to begin with, but it's easier if you have an aptitude for art, like you. It takes years to become a good artist and it can be really frustrating. Some of us have the magic, but not the patience. But when the art catches up to the magic, it's a powerful talent indeed,' said Beria with flamboyant sweeps of her arms. 'Those bumps and grazes, Aridain; how did you get them?' asked Beria, changing the subject, and studying Aridain's hands curiously.

'I fell through the roof of Grandpop's old shed.'

'What were you doing in there?'

'Me and Selva were playing?'

'We were playing house,' said Selva proudly.

The frantic noises of dishes being washed suddenly ceased and from the kitchen Vara exclaimed, 'Playing house?'

Shaking his head deliberately, Aridain, looking at Selva disappointedly, said, 'You said you wouldn't tell, Selva, now you've got me in trouble.'

'But it's true,' said Selva.

'Well, I don't want a queen who can't keep a secret,' said Aridain angrily.

'And I don't want a husband who's nasty all the time. I hate you, Aridain Bruin,' shouted Selva, and she fled the kitchen.

'It's all right, Aridain,' grinned Ramus. 'She'll get over it.'

'It certainly is not all right,' exclaimed Vara seriously. 'I've seen the way Selva looks at my grandson. He's far too young to be playing those sorts of games.'

'But... but she's my friend...'

They all looked up suddenly at a knock on the door. 'Open up Perak, you know we have to do this!'

'Soldiers! Ever since you escaped, they call at least twice a day. You have to hide both of you,' hissed Perak, getting to his feet. 'I'll delay them the best I can.'

'What are you waiting for? Vara, we have to hide,' whispered Ramus harshly.

Seemingly making up her mind, Vara, gesturing to Ramus from the kitchen, hissed, 'In here.'

Walking towards a blank wall in the kitchen beneath the spiral stairway, Vara placed her hand on the wooden panelling. Closing her eyes, she uttered one word, 'Raceme'.

To Ramus's astonishment, a panelled section opened and slid sideways, revealing shelves stacked with vials full of exotic liquids, ingredients, strange items and materials.

'Stop gawking, Ramus, and get in. Beria, you'll have to close the door.'

'We'll never fit in there?'

'Yes, we will,' gasped Vara, forcing herself and the dragon lord into the limited space.

From inside, Beria heard a muffled yelp as she slid the panel across, which shut with a reassuring thunk.

Later that day, having released Ramus and Vara from their claustrophobic cage, Beria, warming her hands by the fire in the living room, glanced upwards and studied the dragonlet, perched silently on the ceiling beams. 'At least the Taal is in good hands,' she murmured.

Her mouth now set in a permanent grimace, she approached Vara and Perak, who, as usual, were arguing.

'A secret panel containing Seline knows what, right here in this house! What else don't I know about?'

'Don't be so melodramatic Perak, it was the only place I could put these dangerous ingredients in order to safeguard our children and grandchildren.'

'For Gronin's sake! Can't the pair of you put your egos to the side for one moment? There are more important issues at hand, like your grandson's safety.'

Vara and Perak looked away awkwardly.

'Of course we know,' said Perak sheepishly. 'We also know he is still a child and the one thing we will not do is cancel his childhood because he is this so-called saviour.'

'Oh, and Beria, please don't keep calling him the Balefire Taal,' whispered Vara severely. 'There are certain cultures that if they knew of his identity, would take him without hesitation.'

Reaching down into her leather rucksack, Beria produced the small blue leather-bound diary and placed it on the kitchen table.

'What's that?' asked Selva, now all smiles and sweetness again, Aridain having once more talked the cold and shivering temperamental girl back into the Mansion's warm interior.

'This diary is called "The Prophecies of a Male Balefire",' explained Beria. 'Aridain's predecessor, a Male Balefire called Samuel, wrote this diary.'

Ramus sat up suddenly and exclaimed, 'Predecessor! So Aridain isn't the first?'

'The diary was supposed to be our secret, Beria, remember?'

'This story needs to be told, Vara. We cannot do this alone. Having heard nothing from the coven in months now, we need help.'

'I make the decisions here, and I say we can do this without help.'

'You are a Magnate, and I have to obey, but I believe that none of us will survive the months to come if we don't seek help.'

There was a short uncomfortable silence, then Perak, looking accusingly at Vara, said, 'So, you've seen this diary before?'

'I confess I have,' said Vara tersely. 'Beria presented it to me after the summer fair. According to Beria, Magen left it for her, to aid us in our struggle.'

'But now they are intent on retrieving it,' said Ramus, pulling contentedly on a thin clay pipe.

Shaking her head and sighing, Vara said despairingly, 'So Beria, have you deciphered any of the passages?'

'Yes. I'–

'What does it do?' asked Selva excitedly.

'It predicts the future; it also tells of the past,' explained Beria.

'You called me the Balefire Taal. What's a Balefire Taal?' asked Aridain.

'Now see what you've done,' said Vara, shaking her head irritably.

'We are Balefire witches Aridain, you and me, and your grandma too,' continued Beria, undaunted by Vara's slant. 'We are also historians, healers, and a force for good. It's only occasionally we have to use our powers more...' and she searched for the right word, 'assertively. In time, you'll understand that despite our convictions, we have to do things we don't want to, regardless of our wishes.'

Nodding in understanding, Aridain concluded, 'Like Grandma's devil's claw recipe, it can be used to either strengthen bones or weaken them.'

Perak chuckled. 'You asked for it, Beria.'

'Correct.' Taking a deep breath she continued, 'Once a Balefire has control of an object or substance, she can do with them as she pleases. For instance, to take control of a person or an element, all we need to do is to touch it, or gain a small sample of that person. Then a Balefire's natural magic takes over, allowing her to control or affect that person or that element. Cures can become infections or ailments, and beneficial creatures can become harmful organisms. Take that bissy nut there for instance,' said Beria pointing to a glass jar with one solitary kernel in it, 'normally it's used to alleviate gout and rheumatism, in a Balefire's hands it becomes a painful weapon, or alternatively whilst holding the object, we can just touch the area to be healed; but once we're done with the spell, it goes away and we have to start all over again.'

'You, young man, are far too clever for your own good,' interceded Vara. 'Continue studying your books, and remember....'

'I know, Grandma, knowledge is power.'

'So, Beria, how does this diary work?' insisted Ramus.

'I'm not sure; I'm still discovering its secrets... but so that you can get a feel for the diary, I will... Actually, Ramus, you read it.'

'OK,' replied Ramus sceptically.

'Aridain, Selva, I want you to go outside.'

'But Grandma?'

'Now, do as you're told. This is not for young people.'

'Aww.'

'Come on, Aridain. Let's go and play,' smiled Selva.

Waiting until the children and the dragonlet had left the room, Beria, opening the diary and licking her finger, began flicking through the pages. Finding the page she was looking for, she handed the diary to the reticent Ramus. 'Take it, it won't bite.'

Ramus began reading:

'When the stone of fire and darkness appears in the ancient seat of learning, the dark creature born of the storm, and the Male witch of the Balefires, will battle for possession of the destroyer that the Child of Nightmare attempts to conceal.'

'Pellagrin's is often referred to as the seat of learning,' offered Ramus.

'And the creature was born of the storm,' said Perak, amazed. 'This is referring to Alfic's fight in the woods.'

'Read on;' encouraged Beria, 'The diary hints at what your grandson has to do in the future.'

Ramus continued:

'The stone of fire and darkness now risen, the Male witch of the Balefires, born of compassion and steel, having defeated the shadow without a shadow, must sacrifice his innocence and rise to challenge what The Ancient One attempts to swathe in darkness.'

'I've reasoned that the shadow without a shadow is the creature, and I'm pretty sure that the Child of Nightmare is Kuelack,' announced Beria.

'That would be right, the yellow hags at the old Balefire temple referred to Kuelack as the Child of Nightmare,' confirmed Ramus.

'Who the hell is The Ancient One?' asked Perak annoyed.

'I don't know,' said Beria. 'But according to this diary, Aridain's destiny is fixed. Not only must he face Kuelack and his allies, but this Ancient One as well.'

Having stayed silent, Vara, snatching the diary from Perak, said frustratedly, 'Well then, let's ask it. After all, it seems to react to its environment and the people around it.'

They stood and watched amazed as suddenly words formed on the blank page of the diary, but it wasn't what they were expecting at all.

The long-lost sister, slave to the Turkanian sands, resplendent and renewed, will lead the blooded Magnate to the star circle, where she will confront her disfigured past and bring about the downfall of the ancient order.

Ramus began chuckling.

'Something amusing, dragon lord?' sneered Vara.

'The diary can read minds, it seems.' His chuckles swelling into fully fledged guffaws, Ramus looking at Vara said, 'There's a lesson to be learnt here, I think it's, "be careful what you wish for".'

'Some call it poetic justice,' agreed Perak, and the two of them broke into howls of laughter.

'What am I missing?' asked Beria, nonplussed.

'So, are you going to tell her, Vara, or shall I?' stated Perak, having finally recovered from his fits of laughter.

Vara looked at them blankly. 'I'm the blooded Magnate, Beria, it's because of my use of dragon's blood.'

'You're the blooded Magnate!' said Beria, flabbergasted. 'The diary also mentioned the long-lost sister, slave to the Turkanian sands.'

'You wouldn't happen to have a long-lost sister we should know about, Vara?' asked Ramus.

'My sister is dead to me.'

'Doesn't mean Mira isn't involved?' said Beria ominously.

'This diary and you, Vara, you are a perfect match. You both speak in riddles,' mocked Perak.

Vara turned to Perak intently, but before she could speak, Ramus said, 'So, assuming Vara's the blooded mistress, and you obviously have a long-lost sister, who or what is the disfigured past, and what ancient order is the diary referring to?'

'Whatever it means, we, Vara, will have a conversation!' barked Beria angrily.

Vara looked up at Beria's approach, then continued to fill a pot with water. 'I know what you're going to say, Beria.'

'No doubt, but I'm going to say it anyway,' said Beria angrily. 'What's the matter with you, taking dragon's blood! You're a Magnate, for Seline's sake, you're on the Balefire council!'

Selecting glass vials containing ginseng, horsetail, golden seal and skullcap, Vara threw them irritably into the pot. 'No one knows of the burden I carry; I decide what is in the best interests of the sisterhood.'

'So, knowing the consequences of your actions, you took the substance anyway?' alleged Beria.

'I would journey to the ends of the earth to protect my grandson. The night of Aridain's birth, the Dragon Lord Pellagrin, as an apparition, appeared to me.... In this very house, his spirit warned me of the significance of the events about to unfold,' continued Vara. 'He said to prepare Aridain for the struggles to come, that together we could protect my grandson. I believed keeping his secret was protecting Aridain, but I failed him, you see.'

'No, you didn't, you just made the wrong choices, but together we can make the right choices.' Leaning close to the fire to warm her hands, Beria said seriously, 'Vara, I understand your sacrifice, but he should have been readied for his role in the future! Sending him from the room every time you think he might be upset or offended doesn't help him. It is the Taal's destiny to find and destroy the stones.'

'The creature's task was to kill my grandson and preserve the stones,' said Vara passionately.

'The creature is now dead, killed by your grandson despite your protective blanket,' said Beria, 'proof that he doesn't need protecting, proof he has been born for his role,' informed Beria coldly.

'His role...,' gasped Vara, 'Powerful and instinctive Aridain may be, but he's still a six-year-old boy.'

'This isn't right,' exclaimed Beria. 'The sequencing is wrong, but prophecy never is.'

'You almost sound disappointed,' said Vara.

'No, not at all, but something here isn't right. The only reason the creature would appear is if it were drawn to the stones, which means...'

'As you said, Beria, prophecy will have its way.'

Beria looked up at Vara sceptically. 'As far as I was concerned, you had the shards in your possession. I recommended you because I thought you would hide them away. But the creature didn't come after you. It came after Aridain. Don't you see, your grandson must have the shards?' she exclaimed. 'Vara, what happened?'

'I was approached by Ramus. He told me he had left the shards beneath a certain tree for me to collect, but when I arrived, they weren't there.'

Nodding in understanding, Beria said softly, 'Your grandson found them first.'

'Very perceptive, novice.'

'As you said, prophecy is a strange bedfellow. Vara, you know what you have to do?'

It was then that they heard the sounds of laughing and squealing children, followed by the ever-present flapping of leathery wings.

'Aridain.'

'Yes, Beria?'

'Can you come here, please?'

She was actually proud of the novice Balefire, now exhibiting the courage and ingenuity she had seen within her psyche as a child, now ignited in a time of need and danger.

'What's going on?' asked Perak.

Bending down whilst staring into her grandson's eyes, Vara took his shoulders firmly in her lithe but sturdy hands. Pulling Aridain close, she lessened her grip but didn't let go. 'Aridain, we need to speak to you about the shards. You know the pretty green stones you found?'

Immediately, Aridain's demeanour changed from a compliant, affable adolescent to a protective, distrustful guardian. He then looked from the dragonlet to his grandmother and said flatly, 'You can't have them!' he warned.

Scowling at Vara, Perak said, 'Is this really necessary?'

Ignoring Perak, Vara continued hopefully, 'Aridain, we know you have the Firebrand shards; we don't want them, we only want to see them.'

Aridain looked around at the expectant faces uncertainly, then unbuttoning his tunic pocket, Aridain felt around inside. Opening his hand cautiously, he revealed four dull-green stone segments.

'Enchantment, Ascendancy, Enslavement and Domination,' said Aridain, pointing to each.

'And the true Elemental will know their names,' proclaimed Ramus.

'Yes, yes, enough of that prophecy twaddle,' said Vara uncomfortably.

'What are they doing?' Selva enquired, as the dragonlet and Ramus closed their eyes and slowly bowed their heads in silent reverence.

In a voice that was not his own, Aridain said, *The Balefire Taal holds the four segments allied to the stone of darkness, known to dragon kind as the Siamang,. This stone has ignited dragon kind's primeval desires for centuries. They crave it as much as they fear it; its possessor can control them. But ultimately, he who holds the stone will be consumed by it.*

'Dragon Lord Pellagrin,' said Ramus reverently, bowing.

'Yes, Pellagrin made the connection when he touched Aridain's forehead, when he was born,' confirmed Perak.

Glaring at her grandson, Vara said, 'Nice of you to make an appearance, dragon lord. A word, a hint of what you were planning to do, would have been nice.'

Turning to Aridain, Beria asked, 'If you are who you say you are, then show yourself?'

I cannot, to do so would jeopardise everything. It's the reason I reside within the Taal. His life force is what masks my existence and the shards from the world. I arranged his meeting with the dragonlet, and with my help, he, together with his mother, defeated the creature.

'So, why tell us this now?' demanded Perak.

To help you all guide and protect the Balefire Taal.

'Then enlighten us as to these accursed stones?' insisted Perak.

Very well. Know that before man discovered the stones, the first golden civilisation thrived in Vanhara, far to the south, across the Navas straight, the place we now know as the Broken Lands. Depraved and immoral, the first race of men destroyed themselves. The gods turned their backs on man and what remnants remained were forced to live a simpler way of life. They lived in harmony with the land and the creatures of this world for a time, but the destiny of any species is to evolve and grow, otherwise it stagnates.

'But what has this to do with the stones?' demanded Perak.

In truth, there was only one stone, created by the gods of light, Seline, Aquar and Praxis, to better the human condition. The Chimera stone was created to test man's fortitude, his will to survive and his goodness of heart. But Fornax, the god of the underworld, objected, arguing that to better the human condition there must be balance and adversity, so he created an opposite. Evil incarnate, you know this gem as the Firebrand stone. Men and dragon kind alike worshipped the stones for hundreds of years until man's own powers began to blossom and the stones' true natures were revealed. It was then that the gods, each passionately opposed to the other, created a defender to champion their cause. It was shortly afterwards that the Chimera stone was discarded as a fancy bauble and lost to history.

'Samuel and the first Dark Taal,' hissed Perak.

Yes? But without the Chimera stone as a balance, the Firebrand stone in the hands of men and dragon kind began to influence history. During the second age of chaos, the first men, drunk with power, having destroyed what was left of their lands, turned their malicious eyes upon these shores.

They all looked on at the dull green stone segments in Aridain's hand.

'All those lives sacrificed for four tiny pieces of stone!' exclaimed Beria. 'To look at them, you wouldn't think they could contain so much power?'

They normally glow an intense green, but the Taal's power suppresses them. This power, however, comes with a price, proclaimed Pellagrin. *It takes energy and life force to dampen the Firebrand stones' power.*

'Life force, what do you mean?' exclaimed Vara.

'I think what he means is that these shards are slowly killing our grandson?' confirmed Perak sadly.

Sometimes we have to do things for the greater good. He is the Elemental. He has been born for this.

'Then give the shards to me,' exclaimed Vara fearfully. 'They have no effect on me.'

Your hypothesis is sound Vara Bruin, but the outcome would be the same. It is his destiny to destroy them.

'I don't care about that. I only care about him.'

You could not mask the shards' evil. In your care, the shards would attract the sinful, malicious, and the greedy, putting your friends; your family, and the very land at risk. This is why Aridain must have them, to keep them secret.

'At least he would have a life, meet girls, have children.' Turning abruptly towards her grandson, Vara ordered, 'Aridain, give them to me!'

Overriding the voice in his head, Aridain bellowed, 'No, you can't have them!'

Stuffing the shards and the silken bag back into his pocket, Aridain buttoned it up.

'Young man, I order you to give them to me,' cried Vara, clawing desperately at Aridain's pocket. Without warning, there was a flash and Vara was catapulted across the kitchen, colliding with the whitewashed wall.

'No, they're mine. No one else can have them!' shouted Aridain savagely.

'Come on Vara, up you get,' said Perak tenderly, offering his hand.

'Leave me alone!' cried Vara.

'It's no good snapping at me, Vara Bruin. Now what are you doing?' hissed Perak. 'Come back here.'

'Do you want to save our grandson or not?'

'Of course, but he won't let us,' hissed Perak desperately.

'So, the great Perak Bruin is just giving up. I thought you craved danger.'

'Danger yes, stupidity no.'

'Well, I'm not giving up,' announced Vara, who, getting to her feet, strode across the kitchen floor towards Aridain once more.

With no choice now, Perak tackled Vara to the floor. He was joined by Ramus, the two together pinning Vara to the floor.

'Perak is right,' agreed Beria. 'If you persist, Aridain will kill you in defence of the shards.'

'He wouldn't dare!'

'I'm as unhappy about this as you, but this is how it must be,' argued Perak.

'The die has been cast, Vara,' hissed Ramus. 'Give it up.'

'Vara, please,' pleaded Perak.

Ceasing her struggles, Vara composing herself said, 'Leave me alone, don't touch me.'

One more thing I can tell you before I go is that the one called Magen has placed a magical tracker on your grandson.

'Magical tracker? That crafty two-timing...I was wondering why he alone has been allowed such free rein?' said Perak. Well, can't we get rid of it? Pellagrin, can't you do anything?'

I'm sorry, I cannot.

'You're going to have to come out of the shadows sometime Pellagrin; fight for your corner.'

Choosing when to do so, Perak Bruin, that is the trick. Now I must leave; farewell for now. And with that, the voice fell silent. Aridain then stood and smiled up at them as if nothing out of the ordinary had occurred.

'Removing the tracker would be a grave mistake,' said Ramus cogently. 'No need to make matters worse by revealing we know of its existence.'

Grabbing his leather cabala ball, Aridain, smiling, said, 'Come on, Selva, let's go and play?'

159

Following the three of them into the garden, Vara stood and watched as Perak threw Aridain's small battered and beaten, leather cabala ball to him and Selva. Aridain then launched it at a target that overhung the garden from one of the branches with unerring accuracy.

Strange times indeed, thought Vara darkly.

Ominous clouds built in the gathering darkness like a harbinger of doom, and Beria, her keen senses searching the night, perceived nothing. No creatures rooted through the undergrowth and no winged things skimmed overhead in their relentless search for food; all was still. Coming up short, Beria sensed rather than saw Magen's silhouette in the darkness.

'Hello Beria.'

'Magen! what can I do for you?' she said guardedly.

'You were seen returning from my former home.'

'I am allowed to visit, or is that something else your brother frowns upon?'

'No games Beria, the diary, do you still have it?'

'No, I've hidden it.'

'I thought I was doing good by leaving you the diary; instead, my so-called selfless act has caused me nothing but trouble. If you return the diary to me now, you just might live, because I guarantee that if Kuelack realises you have it, he will kill you.'

'If I'm in that much danger, then the diary is my only bargaining tool.'

'You fool. Do you think he cares about bargaining tools?' hissed Magen angrily. 'Give me the diary and live, keep it and die.'

'People are dying all the time it seems, Serac, for instance, was incinerated and your brother shed not one tear for his childhood friend. This is the mark of the man you would serve.'

'I have made my bed and am prepared to lie in it. Are you prepared to lie in yours?'

'What happened to you, Magen? Allying yourself with someone who would torture his own mother?' Suddenly, Beria said, 'Do you remember your first attempts at magic?'

'A strange question, considering the circumstances.'

'Regardless whether I have the diary or not, I'm bound for the dungeon anyway, courtesy of the soldiers you have waiting to pounce from the shadows. So, what is there to lose by answering my question?'

Relenting, Magen said in a clipped tone, 'It was a steep learning curve.'

Beria considered. 'I will never forget Acumen Delia's frustration at teaching me how to infuse a potion with my gift or to take control of another's. And now I'm teaching it here at the school I love so much. The new girl, Maria Harkness, tried to endow Gavin Torn from Ural with love lust. Luckily, I turned around just in time to break the spell, otherwise he would have gone around the school trying to mate with every female he could find,' laughed Beria.

'I can imagine the look on Mistress Merle's face, seeing a ten-year-old reciting his undying love for her. She'd have had a seizure,' considered Magen.

'Did we do any better when we were their age?' smiled Beria. Thoughts suddenly flooded her mind of young Aridain Bruin and his family, of her loyalty to the Balefires, and of Vara's belief in her as a young girl. Now why had those memories suddenly popped into her head?

Because I put them there, Beria Dearing, to remind you that together with a select few, you will do what's right when the time comes.

'Pellagrin?' she whispered softly, knowingly.

'What did you say?'

'Nothing that would interest you, Magen Breed,' she said stubbornly. Realising that now was the time to return Vara's trust, she said resolutely, 'Do those memories, this place, our history and the students here at this school mean nothing to you?'

Looking at Beria seriously, Magen said distantly, 'Our interests are different now, as are our futures.'

In the silence that followed, Beria studied her childhood friend. Magen had changed, as if a darkness had germinated within her; she had become a stranger. She chuckled then; however, it lacked mirth.

'Something funny?'

'Just thinking about our differing paths, how I would fight and die for something that is right, whereas you defer to anyone with power.' Squaring her shoulders and looking at Magen sternly, Beria announced,

'I will not give up the diary. It is a powerful tool that, in the hands of your brother, would cause devastation.'

'Perhaps Perak has it?'

A bit too hastily she said, 'Do you think I would be foolish enough to take it to Perak? As I said, it is hidden.'

'Then I will ask again, where is it?'

She remained silent.

'Nothing to say Beria Dearing? Very well.' Then, in a voice that demanded attention, she said, 'Then you leave me no choice.'

At a sign from Magen, the soldiers slowly emerged from the shadows.

CHAPTER NINETEEN

ECHOES FROM THE PAST

Edging through the night like a coiled tiger in the fading light, Crystal crept silently through the orchard beside the outer wall of the farm. Passing the circular stone trough, used to crush the fruit for cider-making, she dropped silently behind a figure crouched there.

'Not bad, Crystal, but I heard you moving several trees back.'

'How did you know it was me? I wasn't making any noise,' she insisted.

'Don't beat yourself up. I'm very good at what I do, but you did well to find me.'

'What are you doing here in the dark, Keegan?'

'I've been keeping tabs on Elgin and his brother. They're being very secretive these days.'

'I agree,' said Crystal, shifting her weight. 'It's so obvious something's wrong. Avoiding Alfic, I can understand; but the rest of us? Also, they tense visibly whenever Micas is around, they avoid the man like the plague.'

'So, why are you creeping around in the dark, Crystal?'

'Oh, this and that.'

'Oh, like that, is it?'

'Drench has resumed his lessons with me,' continued Crystal.

His gold tooth glistening in the dark, Keegan said, 'Well, that's good.'

'Perak mentioned Drench's chequered past during the festival, that you found him when he turned up in his pyjamas in the middle of the night.'

'Did he now?'

'Now don't get bent all out of shape Keegan, Drench deserves to know. During one of my lessons, he suddenly held his head and collapsed. When he recovered, he said he'd had a flashback to his past. When I asked, he says a memory popped into his head, but the moment he focused on it, he blacked out. I think he wants to remember, but something's preventing him. These blackouts, Keegan, they're only getting worse. I feel that with you out of the picture and the Bruins under constant surveillance, the burden of looking out for his welfare has fallen on me. So, I was wondering if you could, you know, tell me anything about him?'

Reaching a decision, Keegan said, 'Perhaps it's time I gave this mystery to someone else. I owe him that, at least. After all, the situation I find myself in doesn't lend itself to solving his past.' Sitting down on the frosty ground opposite Keegan, Crystal sat and listened silently.

'He was ten years old when he turned up here with nothing but the clothes on his back,' said Keegan. 'Since that awful night, I cared for him, taught him everything I know. Then two years ago, the black hole that was Drench's past resurfaced, be it in confusing flashes, their meaning tantalisingly out of reach. However, the one thing I do know is who his family is,' explained Keegan. 'You see, on that night, all he had on him was a ring sewed into his pyjama pocket.' Fumbling around in his trouser pocket, Keegan produced a thick gold ring. On it were two cherubs holding a wreath over a falcon with its wings outspread. 'It has the Archer family crest. I know it sounds incredulous, but on the underside is a capital A,' smiled Keegan, 'for Archer.'

Her eyes opening wide, Crystal exclaimed, 'He's a member of the ARCHER FAMILY FROM LEARDON?'

'Are you sure you couldn't say that any louder?' hissed Keegan, peering about nervously.

'But why didn't you tell him? He deserves to know.'

'He was happy here, and he'd suffered enough. I'm many things Crystal, but I will not give false hope to a man who doesn't need it.'

Early the following morning, Crystal, bringing her sweating, puffing students to attention during the morning's practice, announced, 'After a quick assessment, it seems some of you are practicing sloppy techniques.' Looking around the distraught faces, Crystal said, 'I will not tolerate this lack of discipline. We have to remember at all times that practice does not make perfect, only perfect practice makes perfect. How can you progress, be the best you can be, if you do not adhere to the fundamentals of staff fighting? On a lighter note, I am pleased to welcome Drench back to our practice sessions.'

'With all respect, Crystal, the outcome is what matters. We're here to learn the fundamentals because we want to defend ourself, not to become fighting masters. It's all about self-preservation now.'

'Simon, step out here, will you?'

'I can see your point of view, Mistress, but taking out your frustration on me will solve nothing,' cautioned Tubney.

She watched as the thick-set man from Barfleet stood and faced her. Tall with thick, dark eyebrows and short, thick, black greasy hair tied back from an acne-scarred face, he had been another stray who had fled to Pellagrin's seeking sanctuary, in order to escape the wrath of a wealthy family's irate father, after his daughter had pleaded rape.

'Simon, hold your staff at the ready.'

Attacking with speed and precision, Crystal forced Simon back who, to the class's astonishment, staved off the attack.

'As precise as I was, the main reason Simon could counter my attack is because I telegraphed my movements. Subtlety, deception and cunning are the key, especially against a sword. Observe... Staff at the ready, Simon.'

As before, Crystal attacked, only this time she feinted a swing, hitting Simon's midriff with the end of her staff instead of the length. Simon doubled over in pain, caressing his stomach silently. 'Swinging your staff willy-nilly will only get you killed. It is more than just a blunt, club-like instrument. Nine times out of ten, your staff is longer than a sword. Jabbing with the end is more efficient and tougher to counter.' Making sure he was all right and helping Tubney to his feet, Crystal said, 'Natural ability will only get you so far. Be precise, and accurate, like so,' she said, demonstrating with ethereal fluidity, 'that is the reality you need to ingest. Back in line, Simon,' she encouraged softly.

'We saw you during the fight at the festivities. I will not take orders from someone dating a traitor,' said another of her students.

'Is this what this lacklustre performance is all about? Me dating Kale has nothing to do with my loyalties,' said Crystal dangerously. 'My loyalty is to the school and you, as students.'

'It speaks volumes,' said another. 'It points to only one conclusion.'

'Speak freely, then,' she said.

'If you are loyal to the school, you would turn over the traitor, Kale.'

'So, you're asking Crystal to become a snitch?' said Amus Holt, turning to the student angrily. 'I, for one, will not question Crystal's loyalty. She fought to maintain order in the food hall.'

Crystal turned to Amus, who, after the fight in the food hall, now sported the nickname, Tall, lean and mighty mean. Amus was a tall, wiry individual, displaying an impressive set of teeth and gums when he smiled. Sporting short light wispy hair, he had suntanned craggy skin from working outdoors in the fresh air.

Crystal looked around at her students. 'You think you know me? Know where my loyalties lie, but like my fighting technique, you only see what I allow you to see. You don't know my subtleties, what is in my heart. The issues at the school are not about choosing sides. We have to come together, fight against the common enemies, fear, hatred and paranoia. Once we recognise these, only then can we move forward. Class dismissed,' ordered Crystal angrily. 'All, except you three.'

Waiting until the younger members of her class were out of earshot, Crystal turned to Amus, Simon Tubney and Drench. 'Thank you for what you said. Trying to secure students' loyalties is hard, especially with the enticements on offer.'

'Why do you let the students talk to you like that?' contended Drench.

'It is of no concern, and besides, the less I have to hide, the more people will trust me, well that's the plan, anyway.'

'Begging your pardon, Mistress, but, you're normally so self-assured, so positive, this doubt is not an emotion we'd normally associate with you,' said Tubney.

'Bless you, Simon.' Taking a deep breath, Crystal said, 'I have also come to look upon you three as friends.'

'Is it Kale, Mistress?'

Silent for a moment, Crystal, making up her mind, said, 'Kale's avoiding me. He's failed to turn up at any of our rendezvous'.'

'Perhaps he's just changed his mind,' offered Drench.

'Or perhaps you're too domineering. Some men can feel threatened by a strong woman, you know. Then again, some men love to be dominated,' hinted Amus, nudging Simon knowingly with a wicked smile.

'Sometimes, I seriously wonder about you, Amus,' said Simon solemnly. 'We don't all walk around with our mind in our pants. Some men just want to fall in love and live their lives with a good woman.'

'Here, here,' agreed Drench.

'That's enough for today,' said Crystal forcefully. 'It's time to get back to your work before you're missed. Drench, can you stay for a moment? I have something I want to show you,' explained Crystal.

'Very well.'

'See you later back on the funny farm, Drench,' chuckled Simon.

Fishing inside her leather trousers, Crystal, presenting Drench with the ring Keegan had given her the night before, said, 'This ring has a family crest embossed on the surface.'

'Nice gold band. Must be expensive.'

'There's also a capital A inscribed inside. Do you know what it stands for?'

Drench shook his head.

'Keegan found it the night you arrived here. The A stands for Archer.' She then pointed to the engraving. 'This is the Archer family crest.'

'OK, but what has it got to do with me?'

'Everything, it's yours.'

'What do you mean, mine?'

Watching as Drenches face screwed up in puzzlement, Crystal enquired, 'Drench, are you all right?'

Staring at the insignificant item, Drench, holding his head, slumped to his knees.

'Drench!' hissed Crystal.

'What's wrong with him?' inquired Simon Tubney, appearing suddenly together with Amus.

Trying to revive Drench now knelt on the floor, rocking back and forth with his arms over his head. She replied, 'I don't know. I presented him with this ring. He stared at it for a moment, then collapsed.'

Taking the ring from Drench's hand, Amus gave it back to Crystal.

Coughing, Drench opened his eyes and looked around. 'What happened?'

'I think you had another flashback,' said Crystal, concern written all over her features, 'triggered by this ring.'

His eyes focusing on something they could not see, Drench said, 'It hit me without warning, a powerful memory; people running in the darkness with torches, together with urgent, frightened voices. It felt surreal; it's like my eyes have suddenly been opened.'

CHAPTER TWENTY

VESTIGES OF A NORMAL LIFE

V ara peered through the kitchen window at Perak, whilst stirring a large boiling pot full of washing in soapwort and carbolic. Perak's breath was clearly visible in the cold frosty air as he busily chopped wood, and like so many times before, despite her attempts at indifference, her morbid fascination towards him had emerged like a never ebbing tide, perverting her attentions as it always did.

I'm even doing his washing again, for Fornax's sake.

He was still a charmer, although she would never tell him that, and at the time of her impoverishment, his vivacity and rugged good looks had enticed her like a Hasps craving for blood. Even now he kept that compelling innocent that she had found so appealing. However, over the years, her art had become more important than their marriage, and their relationship had become fractious at best. To salvage what they could, Perak had built her, her mother and sister, this house to live in, and provided her with three children.

Having nurtured her children's extraordinary talent for magic, she had enrolled them at the school, where they advanced quickly in their chosen fields. That was when Kuelack began nurturing his rivalry with Alfic. She had hoped this was just a passing phase, but with Kuelack's desire to prove he was superior, the rivalry continued on into Kuelack's teenage years, becoming all-consuming. Then Alfic had announced he was forsaking magic to join the army, a setback admittedly, but nevertheless she pinned her hopes on Magen and Kuelack. Only Kuelack took Alfic's desertion personally, and ever since, his hate for his brother had festered like a malignant cancer, together with her plans that had evaporated before her eyes as surely as a mist in the morning sun.

Vara thought upon her eldest and youngest children, drawn to power and ambition like moths to a flame, inheriting her weakness for all things shiny and lavish. But unlike his brother and sister, Alfic had rejected these things. The irony now was that after all that had transpired, Alfic, according to Perak, now possessed potent magic. So why couldn't she deal with it? Why wasn't she proud? To see Alfic as Magen and Kuelack's equal was what she had always wanted and hoped for, but she felt betrayed and rejected instead. Perhaps it was due to him receiving this gift without her involvement or consent...... It was ironic; before she had discovered Alfic possessed magic, she, Alfic and Perak had had nothing in common. Now that they had, it had become a bone of contention. It was because in her eyes, each had known their place. Now the order and constancy she had strived to maintain was yet again crumbling around her, and none of them really knew where each other stood or what the future held. She knew Perak deserved a better spouse; she knew she should be better than this, but her desire to keep a hold of what she perceived of as hers, and her version of normality, always got the better of her. It was a trait she was not proud of. Shaking her head irritably, Vara continued to stir his washing.

'Does it hurt?'

'What do you mean?' asked Aridain curiously.

'Having another person in your head?'

'Of course not, silly?'

'I don't think I'd like another person in there,' she said, poking Aridain's forehead. 'Do you like me, Aridain?'

'Of course, silly, you're my best friend?'

'So, when are we going to run away together?' she demanded.

'We have, were in Grandpops old shed, this can be our home, and Sabra can be our trusty pet.'

Dream on, youngling!

'No, I don't mean pretend play, Aridain, I mean for real.'

Be careful, youngling.

It's OK, Sabra. I play along most of the time, but I can put my foot down when I have to.

Very grown up. You sound just like your birth father.

'Selva, we have already run away once to my grandfather's house to get away from your brother. Running away once in a week is enough. Now I'm going in there.'

'Well, I'm not. Tell him, Sabra, that it's all dusty and dirty,' squealed Selva.

'This is a much better idea, and we won't get into trouble. No one has been in this old shed for ages,' assured Aridain.

I agree with Selva, youngling; I don't think you should go in there.

Why not?

The structure looks unsafe.

The structure looks unsafe, mimicked Aridain melodramatically. *Sometimes, Sabra, you sound just like my dad.*

I don't want you to get injured youngling. Your birth mother and father would never forgive me.

Sabra, you are worried about me. I always knew you cared.

If it makes you happy youngling..., thought Sabra indifferently.

Don't worry, Sabra, I'll be fine. Aridain then turned and disappeared inside.

Having overheard the ephemeral conversation, Selva screamed, 'Aridain, come out here at once! If you don't, I'll tell your grandma!' Then, her demeanour changing like the passing of a sudden squall, she smiled sweetly. 'If you do, I'll give you another kiss.'

Aridain, peering out from the shadowy doorway, stared at her blankly. 'This is so much more fun. Come in here, there's all sorts of weird stuff.'

Stamping her feet, Selva squealed angrily, 'Then I won't give you anymore kisses.' She then turned and stomped up the garden path towards the house.

'I don't understand what's wrong with just being friends, Sabra, like I am with you.'

I'm not your friend, remember? I'm here to tell you when you're walking into danger, like now, said Sabra decisively.

'Don't be such a grumpy old dragonlet. It's perfectly safe.' Watching Selva as she disappeared behind the ornate conifers, Aridain said, 'I don't know, Sabra, you'd think kissing was the most important thing in the world, the way Selva behaves.' Then, making a ghastly face and shivering, Aridain said innocently, 'Kissing is all slimy and stickiness.'

Human females seem to demand a lot of attention. Now, if my kind become too demanding, a good scolding with flame now and again always does the trick.

'Sabra!' laughed Aridain. 'She's a human, not a dragonlet. Besides, I'm far too young to have a mate.'

I totally agree, however the young female is right, you should vacate the shed.

Ignoring Sabra, Aridain disappeared inside. 'I love exploring old places like this. You don't know what you'll find.'

Honeysuckle and clematis fronds hung all around through gaps in the old slate roof and dust covered cobwebs hung from the roof, and over old cupboards and shelves.

'Wow, this place is fantastic, Sabra,' said Aridain, opening up a drawer and finding a load of old woodworm-ridden tools.

Only if you like dust and decay, youngling, replied Sabra, settling on top of an old dusty cupboard.

'Phew, what's that smell?'

What smell, I don't smell any smells, replied Sabra too readily.

Running his hand along the surface of an old set of shelves, Aridain's hand met with something wet. Lifting his hand to his nose, he said, 'URGH, that's disgusting.'

Then, a noise caught Aridain's attention.

'What was that?' said Aridain fearfully.

It's just the creaking of an old shed, said Sabra stoically.

'Sabra, don't tell lies.'

When Sabra remained silent, Aridain said, 'Very well, I'll find out for myself.' He then began slowly making his way into the darkness at the far end of the old shed. It was then that he heard chittering, clicking, and subtle hissing. Realising that Sabra hadn't followed, Aridain said, 'OK, I know you're here. Sabra's a miserable old dragonlet and won't tell me who you are. But I promise I won't harm you. I've....'

They know who you are, youngling, said Sabra.

Then, to Aridain's astonishment, several large black fly-like creatures, the size of a cabala ball, appeared together with woodland imps and water sprites. Also, another creature, half bird and half lizard with the wings of a bat, appeared together with a slightly smaller winged creature that looked like the melding of a bird and large rodent.

You saved them from the evil Animistic at the fair, youngling. Like me, they were also locked in cages.

'But what are they doing here, Sabra?'

I am not their mother, youngling. They do what they feel they have to. Ever since you saved them from the evil Animistic, they have been here close to you. I believe they wish to repay their debt to you.

Staring intently at the creatures hovering before him, Aridain said seriously, 'I want you all to leave. If I found you, then someone else could, then you won't be so lucky.'

The creatures, hovering at head height and standing on the surfaces, stared at him defiantly.

'You could be captured or, worse, killed. You should be far away.' Aridain then turned to see Sabra glaring at him.

'Don't look at me like that. You know I'm right. The wild is where they belong, Sabra, not hiding here in the dark in my grandparents' old garden shed. My dad says that if animals become too attached to humans, then you will never know the good ones from the bad. Better you don't become attached at all. Not everyone is as friendly as me and my family.'

'Alighting on Aridain's shoulder, Sabra said, *I have a compromise, youngling, if they're willing. They could stay in Farend Wood, after all, you're always passing through, and that way they will know you're safe.'*

Nodding eagerly, Aridain said, 'That's settled, then. You will all stay in your natural habitat along with your own kind, and I promise I'll come and visit. Do you know Sabra? Sometimes you have really good ideas.'

Suddenly, perking up his ears and sniffing the air, Sabra warned, *youngling, we are about to be visited by Dragon Lord Ramus.*

'Quickly,' warned Aridain, shooing the strange menagerie back into the shadows, 'Go. Oh, hello Mr Ramus, you scared me,' said Aridain, as the dragon lord, parting the profuse tendrils of honeysuckle and clematis, appeared in the doorway and peered into the gloom.

'I doubt that Balefire Taal,' said Ramus sceptically.

Bending almost double and peering around the interior disdainfully, Ramus said, 'You attend the school soon, don't you? Are you looking forward to it?' said Ramus reverently.

Nodding his head, Aridain said, 'Oh yes, I can't wait to play cabala and learn to fight with weapons.'

'And learn magic?'

'Magic is all right and all, but it's not as exciting as sports or combat.'

It requires discipline and patience, something the youngling here lacks.

'What Treerinks is trying to tell you, Aridain Bruin, is that some people struggle with certain disciplines, whilst others don't. Whilst others, with help, can achieve great things.'

'That's not what I meant at all, Mr Ramus.'

May I ask what you are doing here, dragon lord? asked Sabra, inclining his head but keeping his eyes on Ramus.

'Sabra, don't be rude!'

Staring at the dragonlet, Ramus said, 'It's all right, Aridain; dragonlets are proud creatures, more so even than dragons. Treerinks here has obviously bonded himself to you, and is, as you say, concerned for your welfare, and rightly so.'

'Treerinks, is that your real name? You don't look like a Treerinks, you look more like a Sabra.'

Youngling, I wouldn't care if you called me the God Praxis.

'Hm, actually that's not a bad name,' Aridain concurred, looking at the dragonlet that shook its head in despair. Then changing tack, Aridain said, 'You see, Mr Ramus, Sabra says he doesn't care, but I know he does.'

I don't, insisted Sabra, automaton-like.

'What if I told you that my dragonlets, the ones you watched performing at the fair, need your help?'

'My help?'

'Yes. They are prisoners locked in my quarters. They need releasing.'

'But you're a teacher, and I'm only six. Why can't you help them?'

'Because I'm not welcome at the school anymore. Tell me, Aridain, would you like a ride on a dragon's back? It's not a privilege offered lightly. I could take you on a journey even.'

'Would I ever, Mr Ramus! That would be neat,' Aridain exclaimed excitedly.

The dragonlet's eyes narrowed, and he stared up at the dragon lord. *Youngling, you need to exhibit caution. If you're caught, I may not be able to help you.*

'Sabra, stop being rude. Mr Ramus likes dragons, and he likes you. Why don't you like him?'

'It's OK Aridain, it is of no concern.'

'No, it is not all right. Sometimes, I don't understand you at all, Sabra. Dragonlets, just like you, need saving.'

'Then you'll do it?' asked Ramus.

'Yes,' said Aridain, looking at Sabra resolutely, 'every creature deserves freedom, not just grumpy old dragonlets.'

'Excellent.' Taking Aridain's small hand in his and shaking it firmly, Ramus said with a smile, 'I'll be in touch.' And with that, Ramus span around, and crouching beneath the old wooden door frame, exited the shed.

You hold the Siamang, youngling. You could compel the dragon lord to take you wherever you wanted to go. You don't need his permission.'

'I'm surprised at you, Sabra. Making people do what you want without their permission is wrong,' lectured Aridain.

'And that, youngling, is why I will never leave or abandon you,' whispered Treerinks.

Stood in the kitchen, bathed in the winter sun's waning light, Vara, smiling contentedly, sorted through the winter veg, listening as Selva read a passage from a book called, *The Balefires, A History,* together with Ramus and Perak, basking in the kitchen's warmth, the pair puffing contentedly on clay pipes. Meanwhile, her grandson, attended by the ever-vigilant dragonlet, sat quietly reading a book on Balefire remedies and how to reverse them.

Vara realised that as nice a girl as Selva was, she was also very demanding. She also knew how to manipulate her grandson. A game to Selva; she knew her grandson took things much more seriously. It was not what he needed right now.

'It says here in this book that many centuries ago, the Balefires were driven from the land of Srinigar,' explained Selva. 'Where's Srinigar?'

'Srinigar is the land to the west. It's a land of religious zealots, and its capital city is Alerium. My sisterhood originated there. The first Balefire temple is located somewhere in the Monad Mountains, far to the west.'

'Say it as it is, Vara, blood sacrifice, it still goes on. I experienced the Hasp's unique ceremonies, saw the carnage. I would not wish yellow hags on any civilisation,' said Ramus gravely.

'Blood sacrifice, urgh, sounds disgusting,' said Selva.

'Back then, our practices were uncommon. Back then we were the Hasp. But despite our cult being one of Srinigar's founding religions, our art was outlawed, because of our unusual practices, the ceremonies regarded as an affront to the righteous teachings of the new Sringarian priesthood. So, the Hasp was given a choice, choose a more moral path or be banished.'

'Sounds like a horrible place?' said Selva, screwing up her face.

'On that day, the yellow hags split from the Balefires, both reflecting humans' base urges. One was caring and sympathetic, the other required them to prostrate themselves in front of statues with blood offerings. The worse the predicament, the younger the blood offerings,' criticised Vara angrily. 'Hah, the Sringarian priesthood are bigots. The so-called religious rights they perform behind closed doors were as bad if not worse than the Hasp ever performed. Balefires are more in touch with reality than they ever were. At least some good comes from what we do.'

'When you sit upon the Durbarian throne and conquer Sringaria, I'll be your queen, Aridain, if you like?' smiled Selva sweetly.

'Huh, what?' said Aridain, looking up from his book.

'You know, when you defeat evil and take Aymara for your own,' said Selva proudly.

'Aridain won't be conquering anybody or anything,' announced Vara tersely, 'or sitting on any throne. At least not today, that Selva, I can assure you.'

'Vara, there is no big conspiracy here. When are you going to learn that children are just being children?'

'You're doing what you always did, Perak, confusing and clouding matters. Do you remember us walking upon Spalding common and picking bluebells with the children?' smiled Vara.

'Of course,' said Perak. 'I think of it often! I miss those simple days filled with fun and laughter.'

'And how the children delighted in the ice cream I used to make on a hot-summer's day.'

'Uh huh, your ice cream was legendary,' said Perak, looking at her suspiciously.

'That is how six-year-old children should behave, not trying to steal kisses with boys in the woods or old derelict sheds.'

'So, what's brought on this attack of nostalgia, a guilty conscience? The stark truth is Vara, that these so-called rose-tinted days were interspersed with Kuelack snapping his fingers and you running around after him; with you and Magen disagreeing and arguing all the time; and with your head nearly exploding when Lascana began dating Alfic, as well as Gradine stealing away your baby boy…'

Just then, there was an insistent knocking on the door. 'Perak Bruin, open up in Kuelack's name.'

'Here we go again,' bemoaned Perak.

Waiting until Vara and Ramus had hidden themselves away, Perak said, 'I'm coming. Keep your hair on.'

Vara crept through the halls of her home. Making her way to the kitchen, she approached the large panelled wall beneath the iron spiral staircase, only this time it wasn't to hide from soldiers. Running her fingers lightly down the shuttering of overlapping panels for the last time, she whispered, 'Raceme.'

There was a subtle click, and the shuttered panel swung open, revealing the rows of bottled ingredients and liquids. Along the top shelf were many powerful poisons like foxglove seeds, ground mandrake root, snapdragon thorn, ground Navarian black orchid, hellebore powder, liquid skullcap, henbane and lily-of-the-valley, a plant not only used for scenting sweet smelling soaps. But she wanted none of these. Tracing her finger along the rows of bottled secrets and potions, she paused briefly by each jar until she found a shelf filled with stoppered vials of red liquid. Selecting several, she closed the panel with a snap and turned to the kitchen and her rows of neatly ordered ingredients. She then entered the living room and approached the mirror hung above the large marble fireplace, and studied the aging image framed by a wealth of blue rinsed hair staring back at her.

'I'm not weak,' she said, 'I do this, not for the Balefire Taal, but for my grandson.'

She then turned and headed out into the hallway and up the stairs. Reaching the children's bedroom, she squatted down in front of Aridain. With the ever-vigilant dragonlet watching from the end of the bed, she leaned close and kissed his forehead.

A tear trickling down her cheek, she whispered, 'I don't know if you can understand me, Aridain, but this may well be the last time we see each other. I just want you to know that although we may be apart, I will always love you, never forget that.'

'I know, Grandma,' said Aridain sleepily.

Tearfully, she looked up at the dragonlet and said, 'Take care of my grandson and his family, you hear?'

'Yes, Aridain's Grandmother, with my final breath,' replied Treerinks sincerely.

She then made her way quietly down the stairs and strode out into the garden, through the thickening snow, past the pond and the trellising and ornate trees, to the small hardstanding by the stables, to where Ramus waited in the dark, his deep powerful breathing, the only sign that a dragon squatted silently in the shadows.

'Goodbye, Midge,' said Vara, wandering sadly over to the stable and scuffing his mane, 'take care of my grandson, OK.'

'Are you sure you know what you're doing, Magnate Balefire?' rumbled Ramus in his deep dragon voice.

'It is the only way to protect my grandson.' Taking one last look towards her home, Vara said, 'I am convinced of no greater necessity.' Then, without another word, Vara climbed upon the dragon's razor back. Ramus then launched his sizable bulk upwards into the snowy maelstrom.

CHAPTER TWENTY-ONE

DAGGER STORM

Angrily, Alfic wiped the back of his hand across his forehead. Looking to the trees of Farend Wood that disappeared down to the stream from the field, furthest from the school, he thrust his spade into the soil. He then straightened up to look at the ominous clouds building overhead.

'The winds getting up, those clouds will drop more snow soon,' he said grumpily.

'What do you reckon, Flullen, good for sledging but no good when trying to feed animals, right?' observed Amus.

Blowing into his hand, all Flullen said was, 'My fingers are like blocks of ice.'

Alfic observed Amus, who, together with Flullen Archer, dug the turnips from the ground, and threw them into the wagon. Transported back to the school, the turnips would be diced in a mangle, then fed to the livestock during the winter.

He had concluded that Flullen Archer hadn't done a hard day's work in his life, despite his claims to the contrary. He could tell just by looking at Flullen's blistered and torn hands and dirt-ingrained manicured nails. He was a good foot shorter than Amus and had a pale complexion, and where Amus was wiry and strong, Flullen looked as if he would break if he dug the spade into the ground too eagerly. He seemed to carry an almost regal bearing that looked totally out of place amongst the muddy vegetable beds, but he tried hard enough, which was all anyone could ask.

As if he'd been reading Alfic's mind, Amus asked, 'So, Flullen, what are you doing here? It's evident you're not used to this digging lark. Did your family dispossess you as well?'

'Oh, why do you say that?' replied Flullen guardedly, who, as hard as he tried, could not disguise his high-born accent.

'It's just that Pellagrin's seems to be a haven for runaways,' said Amus indifferently. 'Take Drench for instance...'

Suddenly, as if on cue, the intense wind predicted by Alfic suddenly appeared, but not from the east or the west, but directly from above, and accompanying it was a deluge of snow.

'Well, that's that, there's no point in continuing,' hollered Alfic over the rising wind.

With the snow now stinging their faces and hands, they threw their tools into the wagon, now almost full with winter feed.

'Alfic, get in, we're leaving,' said Amus, jumping up after Flullen, and taking the reins. As Amus spurred the shire horse forward, Alfic leapt into the wagon. Suddenly, there was an ominous cracking of wood as one of the wagon's wheels collapsed in a spectacular shredding of wood, spewing all three together with their load across the field.

'Are you both all right?' asked Alfic, extricating himself from the mound of turnips littering the snowy ground.

Pushing Flullen from atop him, Amus, shaking snow from his clothes and hair, announced, 'We're fine.'

'Look at this,' cursed Alfic, raising his hands to the sky. 'How are we supposed to work with wagons this old? We should condemn them for firewood.' Then, tearing a rotten strip of wood away from the disintegrating tailgate, he said, 'Parts of it are so rotten that if the woodworm weren't holding hands, it would crumble to dust.'

'We need to commandeer one of the other carts,' said Flullen.

'They're needed elsewhere,' mumbled Alfic indignantly. 'We'll have to wait until the storm has passed and come back in the morning to recover this load.'

It was nearly dark when they'd finished unhitching Roscoe from the ruined wagon, and completely dark after they fashioned a makeshift carryall for the tools.

Raising the hood of his cloak over his head, Alfic, shielding his face from the blinding snow, took the reins and led Roscoe across the fields until they came across the Spalding Road. Sheltered now to a degree by the trees of Farend Wood, they made better time following the track past the ruins of his old home. Any signs of traffic that had passed this way had now disappeared, as if erased from memory, so the only means to find their way was by familiar landmarks and objects.

Gritting their teeth against the cold, Alfic, Amus and Flullen, placing one foot in front of the other, followed the boundary of Higher Wood, knowing that eventually they would come across the fence line that would force them to turn right towards the orchard and the school. Frequently, when they hid their faces from a particularly strong gust, they lost their bearings and had to loop around in expanding circles until they came across the fence line in the dark; the effort sapping their waning strength further.

His breathing came in brief gasps now. In a blizzard that tingled strangely when it hit bare flesh, Alfic could feel his extremities going numb with cold despite his thick clothing. 'Are you two all right?'

Pulling his thick robes tighter around his person, Flullen smiled and nodded that he was.

'Don't worry about us, we need to get Roscoe out of this weather, Alfic,' shouted Amus over the howling of the wind.

Amus was right. Alfic could now feel that the shire horse was becoming fatigued by the cold.

Then through the snow, Alfic glimpsed the twin gates to the school grounds, and beyond, the ghostly trees of the orchard and majestic chestnut trees swaying crazily in the blizzard. The freezing wind searing the back of his throat, Alfic placated, 'Nearly home now, fella. You and Flullen take the tools and ride Roscoe to the stables. I'll follow."

'But….'

'That's an order, Amus, now up you get.'

Closing the last gate behind them, Alfic took one last look at the snow driven fields. As if alive, vortices swirled and gyrated, and in the relative calm beneath the apple trees it seemed like figures were cavorting in the snow.

Seeing figures in the storm, he mused, *I need to find shelter and fast.*

Alfic pressed on, his hands and feet now numb with cold. He hadn't taken more than a dozen steps, however, before he collapsed. Enveloped by a white shroud, he felt surprisingly warm and at peace. His world was now reduced to a snowy sphere ten feet in every direction, his mind wandering as he peered calmly into the maelstrom towards the school.

I'm perfectly OK, I hope they have the good sense to stay indoors on a night like this, and not to come looking for me.

In his delirium, Alfic smiled at shadowy outlines hurrying about in the storm, coalescing and then dissipating, floating on the wind like ghostly apparitions; some even seemed engaged in a snowy dance. Then, one of these apparitions approached him, and began exploring his body with ephemeral fingers, the search causing the hair all over his body to stand on end. Then the figments of his imagination disappeared, as if they had never been there.

The sun had set, as Vara, beside the tall figure of Ramus, strode determinedly through the swirling, stinging snow, along the road beneath the walnut trees. She usually tried to avoid visiting the school and its ornate surroundings; it always ignited her yearning for her former home in Gonda and her sumptuous lifestyle. She couldn't explain it; but the halls of power had a beguiling effect, empowering her with a lavish intoxicating desirability, compelling her to pursue the wealth and standing she once possessed as a child. However, tonight she would accomplish a task only a desperate mother could perform, that was to kill her youngest child. If they needed proof of the Firebrand stone's mesmeric influence, Kuelack's mania and single-minded compulsion to threaten violence against his own family, was it.

I'm sorry, my son, but you are now beyond madness. I cannot allow you to possess the shards or manipulate my grandson. If your death means his and the realm's survival, then so be it.

A mother's love was unconditional, but when a child's very nature had been corrupted and that child's moral code gone astray, she believed it was the parents' responsibility to act, no matter how disagreeable.

Hunched against the sudden squall that swirled through the naked trees, their bare branches swaying dramatically in the sudden intense breeze, the pair made their way past Perak's dormant beehives, onto the grounds proper. Hurrying across the road, they crept along between the cold frames and allotments, past the glasshouses, to the large stone-built barns housing the farm's working implements. Once inside, they made sure they weren't in danger of being disturbed, and Vara made her way to the very back of the shed behind the hay-wain and wagons.

'Go, keep a lookout, Ramus. Once I begin, I won't have much time.'

Producing a large candle, Vara lighting it, set it under a small copper pot suspended by a simple A-frame. Reaching for the bottle filled with the diluted dragon's blood, she blended it in the copper pot, one drop at a time, with the ingredients mixed earlier. As the air began filling with a metallic tang, she heated the mixture until it was bubbling. As the mixture thickened, she chanted, 'Mantrodee, instrum, wormswood, abtinum, willowing, firesting, brusuim, oust Kuelack.' Then, drinking down the exotic mixture, she chanted the words over and over, louder and louder.

Unlocking and drawing the shutter of her cabinet upwards, Magen took the bottle of brandy and a glass from her drinks' cabinet, and pouring the dark liquid into a glass, looked into its amber depths.

'Just one,' she reassured herself, 'just one drink to help steady my nerves.' Magen then drank it down in one. She then poured a second and, drinking that down, hastily placed the bottle and the glass back in the drinks' cabinet. She then turned to the mirror over the fireplace, and, making herself presentable, headed out of her apartment to her meeting with Kuelack.

However, when she approached her brother's apartment, she heard the sound of raised voices.

... 'My father reports that Rasbora has reached Zapata's borders. He says that if she reaches the rebel forces, she will tip the balance of power in their favour, and all because of your failure to stop her.'

'Our "search and destroy" strategy was based on your father's intel Gradine, we lost scores of men trying to stop her,' bellowed Kuelack, his voice rising with every word, 'besides, when Calabash's forces arrive her power will count for nought, they have the numbers and they have dragons... until then we will consolidate our positions.' There was a brief silence before she heard her brother's voice, once more, 'I seem to remember it was your plan to expose a much larger rat's nest by allowing Mace and Keegan to escape from the dungeons, that was your failure.'

'I'll have you know, I learnt strategy from my father and the plan will work.'

Suddenly everything went quiet, so she knocked on the door. Receiving no response, she entered gingerly, mystified as to what had happened. Making her way into Kuelack's inner chambers, she found Kuelack and Gradine in a tempestuous embrace.

Coughing and smiling conspiratorially, Magen said, 'I see you are both fully recovered from your encounter with Mass Martin.'

She then walked serenely across the room and stared out the window in order for the pair to untangle themselves and straighten out their clothes.

'A stake through the heart was no less than that weasel deserved,' stated Kuelack casually.

'It's a shame that the psychics your father placed at the school failed in their mission to control Mass, Gradine. If they had, we could have avoided all that unpleasantness.'

'There is no mystery here,' stated Kuelack casually. 'It is well understood that psychics stick together.'

'What happened to them, by the way?'

'We terminated their positions, permanently,' smiled Gradine severely, 'as will you be, Magen, if you don't hold your tongue!'

'Don't make empty threats, Gradine,' said Magen, spinning around on her toes. 'My brother knows I'm on board, so I suggest *you* hold your tongue.' Turning to her brother, Magen enquired, 'So what are we doing to counter the resistance and their dragons?'

'*We* have a weather wizard accompanying the army. It's standard practice,' said Gradine.

'But not that effective from what I'm hearing,' said Magen severely. 'We have the best here at the school.'

'Savarin has set out his stall very clearly.'

'If that's the case, then send more; she can't battle them all,' insisted Magen.

'Your sister has a point, husband.'

'It will take too long.' Slamming his fist onto the table, Kuelack cursed, 'If only I had the shards, with the dragons under my control, my plans would come to fruition in a matter of days.'

'But they haven't, have they?' sneered Gradine. 'Another failure on your part.'

Kuelack turned savagely, and, grasping Gradine around the throat, pinned her against the wall.

'Distracting though you are, I am becoming increasingly tired of your impertinence. You think all of this, these plans, are all so simple.' Releasing her and taking a deep, calming breath, Kuelack glided across the room. Grasping a decanter full of dark liquid, he poured it into a cut glass goblet. Lifting the glass to his mouth, he drank the liquid in one, then said, 'How rude of me, brandy, Sister?'

'No, not for me,' she smiled calmly, looking around at the wooden shuttering and half-finished repairs. 'Now that Serac is dead, who do you have in mind to liaise with Agrestal, in the capital? After all, Serac was privy to the army's efforts and mediated closely with the spy master, I believe.'

'Serac's death will set us back not one iota; he knew the risks as did we all.'

'Callous aren't we?' admonished Magen. 'Serac was your only childhood friend, after all,' offered Magen sitting in one of the sumptuous tweed chairs.

'Do you think you can have war and not be tainted by it? Stay sterile whilst its stain infects all around? There are plenty more willing candidates to choose from, his next-in-line, for instance, Saven Banner.'

'The fact that we've not heard from Mother worries me,' said Magen, 'we'd do well not to dismiss her.'

'Vara knows she is no match for me. She and that snivelling dragon lord have fled; we will have no more trouble from them.'

'How can you be sure, Brother? Our family and especially Alfic may be many things, but quitters they are not.'

'We've had people watching Alfic and Perak for weeks now. If Vara contacted either of them, we'd know. Believe me when I tell you she is not a threat.'

Walking over to his desk, he poured himself another drink, emptied it, and span around to face them. 'The Hasp mentioned a being called the Elemental who will destroy the stones and, before I destroyed him, the Wizard Torkval talked about prophecy and my meeting with a Male Balefire. I assumed they were all mad.'

'And now?' enquired Magen.

'It is the reason I keep his family close. It is the reason I gave Alfic an apartment at the school, so that, Magen, you can continue to teach Alfic's son. But mainly it's because I've come to realise that this Balefire Taal seeking the shards, that this Elemental the yellow hags warned me about, is here at the school. As impossible as it sounds, I think they were talking about Aridain.'

'You jest!' exclaimed Gradine.

'My brother could well be right. During our lessons, he has exhibited extraordinary talent,' claimed Magen.

'That doesn't mean he is this Elemental,' declared Gradine. 'Many of the students exhibit extraordinary talent.'

'Surely you are not jealous, Gradine,' smirked Magen.

'Of a family of pigs living in a pigsty, I think not!'

'Regardless of your feelings regarding my brother's family, Gradine, his son was present during both of the powerful magical outbursts,' concluded Kuelack, looking at Magen. 'Me and my sister both felt the magic ripple through our beings.'

'Then, there's only one way to settle this?'

'Yes, bring him too....'

Clutching suddenly at his stomach, Kuelack's face creased up in pain. Rushing to his side, Gradine said, 'Husband, what's the matter?'

'Aaarrrhhh, blood magic.... incantatttion.'

Abruptly, Vara's voice echoed in Kuelack's mind... *You would torture me, put people's lives and the lives of your own family in danger? For these crimes, my son, you must die.*

Kuelack's eyes suddenly opened wide in surprise, and he glared up at Magen. Then, through pursed lips, he spat, 'Vara... it's Vara! He gasped, 'She must be.... close.'

Rushing to him, Magen took his face in her hands. His skin looked pallid and his eyes bloodshot, whilst the veins in his face and hands stood out as if they were about to burst from his skin.

We both know I can do it, Kuelack, continued Vara in his head. *I've given life to an abomination, and abominations have to be put down.*

'Aaarrrhhh, blood magic.... incantatttion.' Kuelack's eyes suddenly opened wide in surprise, and he glared up at Magen. Then, through pursed lips, he spat, 'Vara... it's Vara! He gasped, 'She must be.... close.'

Collapsing to his knees, Kuelack bellowed in pain, 'Arrghh, it feels as if my very blood is on fire....' he then began writhing around on the floor. He managed an amused grimace then spat, 'My... we mussst be getting desssperate... Mottther.'

It's time to pay for your crimes, Kuelack. Witty retorts will not save you; your time is over.

His eyes then rolled backwards up into his head and through pain-locked teeth, Kuelack roared in anger, 'It's never over... Mother, first you have to... kill me.'

'Blood magic, how is this possible? Only the cult use blood magic,' said Gradine incredulously.

'Motherrrr... sssheee must be a ... Baleffffire....'

'But you said one Balefire cannot ...'

'I know what I sssaid,' he hissed curtly.

'The only way to stop this is to kill the conjurer. Keep him alive,' ordered Magen desperately. She then sprinted out of the apartment, gathering members of the school guard around her.

Gradine took Kuelack's despondent face in her hands and stared into his dark grey eyes. 'Fight! You must fight this. Fight for all you're worth.'

On the periphery of his pain-wracked world, Kuelack tried desperately to respond to Gradine's muted mumbling. However, he realized that, if he didn't act, his mother's conjuring would result in him losing his life. Focusing his mind, he called on the dark realm for help, mumbling in a tongue long since forgotten. Pain erupted in his veins once more, as the venom conjured from the dark ethereal world battled against his own, now contaminated blood. Leaving an appropriate period for the poison to work, he turned to Gradine and mumbled weakly, 'Quickly.... in my desk drawer, get the vials labelled.... burdock, liquorice and gentian root, ahhhrrr..., grind them together in a pestle.... and then steep the mixture in hot water, quickly.'

'But I've never....'

'Now is not the time…., hurry, Gradine, my own dark magic is now trying to kill me. Let me know when you're done.'

Closing his eyes, Kuelack trying desperately to stave off unconsciousness and death, tried to still his sense of rising panic.

'Kuelack, KUELACK!'

He opened his eyes to see Gradine, panic etched on her face, holding a stoneware cup.

'How long have I been out?' he asked. 'Never mind, is it done?'

'Yes, but don't blame me if it's not right. I've never done this before.'

'Well, we'll soon see, won't we? Give it to me,' he ordered desperately.

Lifting the cup to his lips, Kuelack swallowed deeply of the liquid. Nothing happened at first, but then suddenly Kuelack bellowed in pain, his body heaving and bucking until his thrashing subsided. Smiling up at Gradine, he opened his eyes wide in surprise and then went still.

'Kuelack, are you all right? Kuelack, answer me,' spat Gradine. 'KUELACK!'

CHAPTER TWENTY-TWO

TRAGEDY IN THE SNOW

Peering into the storm, his dragon ears searching for any sign that they may have been discovered, Ramus, alerted by the sounds of muffled voices calling to each other through the darkness, hissed urgently. 'Whatever you're going to do, Vara, do it now; we have company.'

'I need to be closer,' gasped Vara. 'Kuelack's resisting me.'

Ramus, peering into the darkness as the sounds of urgent voices moved ever closer, bellowed, 'You said you could do this?' Abruptly, he sensed the swirling of magic and, walking to the entrance, he peered into the night. Before he could react, however, he felt his arms clamped to his side as he was lifted into the air.

'Hello, Ramus, you did say that we would meet again, that there was unfinished business between us. Only this time, you're facing a very different opponent.'

Unable to move, Ramus stared at Magen, trying to gauge her mood. Indeed, she had changed and the events of the last year had left their mark. Savage eyes peered out from gaunt, hardened features, the soft friendliness they once possessed strangely absent.

Magen then made a fist, and Ramus, his insides feeling as if they were about to burst, groaned in agony.

'Where is she? Where's Vara?'

'I don't know what you're talking about; I'm just out for an evening stroll,' grunted Ramus.

'Corporal, you and your men search these buildings. I'll deal with the dragon lord.'

'Yes, Mistress Magen.'

'I won't ask again, where is she?' demanded Magen, lifting Ramus into the air so his head was nearly touching the thatch of the roof.

Abruptly muffled bangs and thuds could be heard from within, then, just as quickly, everything went quiet.

'Corporal, talk to me. Do you have her?' demanded Magen.

'No need to shout, Magen, I'm here.' And before Magen could act, Vara belched flame.

Ignoring Ramus's incredulous stare, Vara, helping him to his feet, said, 'Come on. We have to go before more soldiers appear.'

'Oh, it's not over yet,' hissed Magen, who, like a phoenix from the flames, stood facing them, surrounded by a halo of raw power. 'Did you really think you could harm me, Mother? I'm not the little girl you couldn't wait to marry off, not anymore.'

'What are you talking about?'

'I'm talking about the daughter you wished had been another son. Another son you could feel proud of, who you could dote on. Instead, you couldn't wait to ship me off to the first man who showed an interest. Was it no wonder I couldn't wait to leave?'

'That had nothing to do with gender, and everything to do with pride. When you were younger, you reminded me of me at that age.'

'So, envy, then?'

'Yes, I couldn't look at you every day, growing more and more like the way I used to be, whilst I grew more unlike the woman I remembered, as you became the strong, resilient woman of the family.'

Looking around in bewilderment, Megan said, astonished, 'So, instead of talking to me, like a mother and daughter should, you pushed me away?'

'As tender a moment as this is Vara, we need to go,' said Ramus. Gesturing, he drove a flame straight at Magen who, taken momentarily by surprise, was forced backwards out into the yard, but she quickly recovered, the scorching flames affecting her not at all.

'Do you honestly think you're a match for me?' said Magen, gesturing dramatically. Immediately, farm implements gathered from inside the building, flew towards them, forcing the pair back against the barn wall.

'Magen, daughter, don't do this?' pleaded Vara.

'Really, Mother? Whereas it is quite acceptable for you to resort to blood magic to kill the apple of your eye, your favourite child?'

'We both know he's a monster. I do what is necessary.'

'You turned him into a monster. Now I'm looking out for my brother; which is more than you ever did for me!'

'I tried to instil in him confidence, resilience and fortitude, something that my father never had; the confidence to take on the world and not bow to those who would take everything from you,' insisted Vara, 'but Kuelack's taken those principles and twisted them into something obscene.'

'Your father, Vara, was a coward; this is your son. Yes, you showered him with gifts; yes, you spoilt him, compensating him for your perceived broken upbringing. But now I see that all of your pampering damaged him beyond repair.'

'I saw in him a potential for greatness, but he lacked Alfic's strength and your kindness. You always were the mother he never had.'

'Don't try to appeal to some invisible bond between mother and daughter. It's too late Vara, it always was.' Pressing the sharpened farm implements closer, Magen growled, 'Now surrender, or I will kill you both.'

'Alfic?'

Roused from his warm, cosy blanket of snow, Alfic looked up and saw a shape approach through the maelstrom. 'Oh, back already, shadow, there's still nothing for you here.'

'There you are. Thank Seline, I found you. Come on, up you get.'

'Sorin, is that you?' murmured Alfic, trying and failing to stand. 'It's OK..., I'm fine..., I can manage.'

'It's OK Alfic, I've got you,' placated Sorin. 'You're fine now.'

Despite his detachment, Alfic felt himself being helped to his feet. 'Amus and Flullen, are they OK?'

'They're safe at the farm, as is Lascana.'

Guided through the storm, Alfic felt the reassurance of a thick blanket wrapped around him as he was helped into the back of a wagon.

As Sorin urged Aussie, another of the shire horses, through the snow, he lay back. Snowflakes caressed his face, and Alfic, remembering the apparitions in the storm, said tiredly, 'Sorin, something's wrong, this storm, it doesn't feel right. It has an almost supernatural feel about it,' he gasped. 'I can't explain it, but we need to do something, find our friends..., our families..., they're in danger...'

'You're delirious Alfic, you're imagining things. Besides, you're in no condition to help anybody,' insisted Sorin.

'No Sorin..., you don't understand..., there were ghosts in the storm, even I didn't believe it at first...., you have to believe me...'

It was then that the jangle of armour and the sounds of laboured breathing could be heard in the dark. Urged on by persistent bellowing, a contingent of the school guard ghosted past across the playing field.

Sitting up, Alfic suddenly reached forward and, tugging on Sorin's thick coat, said, 'Follow those soldiers, Sorin.'

'Alfic, are you mad? We need to get you into the warm.'

'Sorin, something's going on.'

Just then, across the field, the yard, the equipment sheds and the glasshouses lit up in a blaze of light, followed immediately by the hiss of flames.

Closing his eyes. Alfic exclaimed, 'It's Magen... and Mother!'

Sorin drove Aussie through the darkness, the wagon's wheels hurling clots of snow into the air. Then, reining the excitable shire horse to a stop, Sorin stepped down from the cart and said aghast, 'You're right, that's Vara, and Magen together with...., Teacher Ramus!'

Peering into the storm over the wagon's freeboard, Alfic wheezed, 'Sorin, where are you going?'

'You said we have to do something, so I'm going to do something and stop this madness before anyone gets hurt.'

'Sorin, don't be a fool! Come back here!' gasped Alfic. 'Sorin, come back here, please, you don't realise what's going on..., you never did,' he pleaded desperately, falling from the back of the cart, as he attempted to follow Sorin.

'Don't worry Alfic, I'll be fine,' said Sorin calmly.

Clinging to the wagon's side, parked beside the glasshouse, Alfic stumbled forward through the blizzard.

'Step back Alfic,' ordered a soldier, turning towards him with sword raised, 'this is not your concern.'

'Sorin! What are you doing?' gasped Vara. 'Get away from here!'

'Mother!' bellowed Alfic desperately, trying and failing to barge the guard aside. 'What's happening?'

'Alfic, get Sorin out of here; he's in grave danger.'

'Don't try it Alfic!' warned the soldier, pushing Alfic backwards.

Alfic watched helplessly as Sorin, holding up his hands in supplication, walked slowly towards Magen.

'This is madness, regardless of what's going on here. This is your mother, Magen, and you are her daughter. Don't you think this has gone on for long enough? This conflict is tearing friends and family apart.'

'Vara tried to kill Kuelack, who is on the council, and Ramus helped her. They must pay for their sedition,' said Magen dangerously, 'as is the law.'

'Your mother is fighting for what is right. Is it really worth losing friends and family over one man's lust for power?'

'Sorin, I have no choice,' voiced Magen sadly.

Shivering, Alfic listened in trepidation. Lessons learnt from the past had taught Alfic that the situation was on a knife edge, and that at any moment, the slightest word could tip the balance. It was then that the balance tipped, as a contingent of guards led by Ryan Delran suddenly appeared out of the storm.

'Vara, Ramus, you're under arrest. Sorin, stay where you are.'

'The situation is under control, Delran,' warned Magen. 'Now stand down, that's an order,' commanded Magen, taking several steps toward him.

'If you cannot deliver Kuelack's justice, Magen, just step aside so I can,' said Delran confidently.

The tension was palpable, as was the silence. It was then that, intermingled with the howling wind, a low chanting could be heard.

'The witch is weaving an enchantment!' cried Delran, drawing his sword. 'Stop her!'

Everything happened at once, Magen gestured; but Vara, with a word of power, was quicker. The farm implements fell to the ground with a loud clatter as Magen, holding her head, doubled over and then collapsed to the floor with a groan of pain. It was the distraction Ramus needed. With a rending of wood and thatch, Ramus roared, and in his place stood a magnificent silver dragon.

'Kill that dragon lord,' bellowed Delran, running with his sword raised towards Vara, who was reaching into her multi-coloured cloth bag.

Alfic sought the cover of the cart, as Ramus's flame blanketed the yard, the glasshouse exploding in the heat, together with soldiers that were cooked instantaneously in their armour. As glass shards fell all around, Aussie, bucking and rearing in fright, span around and fled into the night together with the cart. Looking up from beneath protective arms, Alfic watched as Ramus, with a roar, grasped a burning roof beam from the glasshouse, then swung it to and fro, scattering Ryan Delran and the soldiers.

Crawling painfully to the end of the decimated and burning glasshouse, Alfic watched through the flames as Vara, glancing his way momentarily, climbed onto Ramus's back, then held on to the raised spines as Ramus disappeared into the cold darkness.

The storm, an unusually savage one, raged over the school, completely blanketing its grounds and the surrounding countryside in a veil of white. Whilst the populous huddled in their homes fearing that all the black magic in the world had united to destroy them, Ramus, with Vara clinging to his fiery skin, battled against the savage wind.

'We should be through this by now. It's almost as if the storm's following us.'

'Don't be ridiculous,' scoffed Vara. 'It's just a bad storm blowing in from the west; it'll pass.'

Ramus shuddered, 'Mock me all you want, but I'm flying higher; this storm is making my skin itch.'

Bathed in moonlight as they rose above the snow storm, Vara began retching.

'What are you doing?'

'The sooner I expunge Kuelack's blood, the better.'

'But do you have to do that over me?' complained Ramus, making a face.

Vara retched again. 'I could wait twenty-four hours for the blood to leave my system. However, to guarantee Kuelack's blood isn't used against me, I must do this now.'

'And Magen?'

'You don't want to know.'

Licking at one of the small wounds inflicted by Magen's magic, Ramus said, 'Somehow, Kuelack countered your magic, care to elaborate?'

'Balefire magic differs from hasp magic, as it is conjured through blood. With it, as a Magnate, I thought to bypass Kuelack's acquired Balefire magic, but I underestimated his resistance,' admitted Vara grimly.

'Has your life always been so complicated? I mean, a senior Balefire not of the coven, living a life of secrecy, now embracing hasp practices, that would drive me to despair?'

'I can be selfish, I know, and secretive, and I can be over sensitive when people question my motives, but my upbringing, my past, have forced me to erect stalwart defences, but I've never regretted my choices.'

'Some choices are our own, others are forced upon us,' countered Ramus. 'The true test is how we survive those choices thrust upon us and how we come out the other side.'

Vara turned her thoughts to her former life; she too had made a choice. Deliberately turning her back on the coven's offer of Acumen, and the responsibilities it entailed, she had instead dedicated herself and her skills to tending the people of Spalding and the surrounding villages and hamlets.

She remembered her first case like it was yesterday. His name was Bodeas Stone, and he had been badly wounded defending his homestead from a gang of thieves who had raped and killed his wife and daughters. His wounds had been not only physical, but mental as well, and had defied all attempts by the local physician to heal. Hearing of her formidable skills, she had been sent for. His physical wounds she had repaired fairly quickly, his mental ones, however, they had taken a bit longer, but with a pinch of wisdom and a smattering of knowledge, she had had him up and about.

Her life, it had been so simple before Aridain's birth; now it had been turned on its head. Taking a deep breath, she centred herself and said calmly, 'Head back to Bridget's, Ramus, we have plans to make.'

Struggling to his feet from his position, sheltering behind what was left of the glasshouse, and using a crumbling wall now smashed beyond repair for support, Alfic looked around at the carnage. Burnt and singed soldiers walked around in confusion, turning over lifeless bodies, searching for their comrades amongst the debris and burning plants, thrown from the blazing glasshouse by the explosion.

Alfic then looked up towards the motionless silver pines, growing steadfast on the bank atop the old fortress wall, to Pellagrin's oak beyond, that only moments before gyrated crazily in the wind as if in the grip of a drug induced trance. He then turned to see Magen, standing stock-still amongst the wreckage, her head bowed, her shoulders shaking. It was then that he realised Sorin was nowhere to be seen. Shambling across the yard, he called out, and when he received no reply, he became increasingly concerned.

'He's here Alfic,' called Magen, sadly.

Staggering towards his sister, Alfic knelt. Removing the wreckage, he saw his friend's burnt and wrecked body lying face down amidst a pool of slowly expanding blood, a large wooden splinter protruding from his back. He turned him over. *Tambours' fingers,* he thought, *it must have been instant. What am I going to tell Celia?*

Wiping away tears of rage, Alfic staggered to his feet. Seeking an outlet for his anger, he turned towards Magen.

'Is this what you envisioned when you surrendered your soul to Kuelack?'

'I am under no illusions about what's happened here, Brother. However, it was not I that brought Sorin to this; it was you. If you hadn't involved him in your little crusade, he'd still be alive.'

'Little crusade! He was your friend, and in your desire to please our brother, you killed Sorin. His death is on your hands, this is your doing!' he cried, sinking to his knees beside Sorin once more. But even as he uttered the words, Alfic knew Magen was telling the truth. *He* had convinced Sorin that their cause was just, and of Kuelack's tyranny.

'Go home Alfic, go home to Lascana and your son. Explain to them why Sorin is dead. Perhaps then you will see the folly of supporting our mother.'

'Mother! You think this is about Mother?'

In silence, Magen turned and left the yard, as more soldiers and medical staff appeared together with Amus and Flullen.

Alfic looked down from his kneeling position and, reaching out with hands shaking from rage, closed his friend's dark and bloodied eyes. He had seen death before, had dealt with it daily, but this was different; this was Sorin, a family friend. He looked up then and all he could picture was Kuelack's face and felt a desperate compulsion to kill him. He realised somehow that the compulsion wasn't his, but looking at his friend laid dead on the ground, he didn't care. Grasping the splinter in anger, he pulled it gingerly from Sorin's lifeless body.

Those that survived the blizzard dubbed it the Dagger Storm, due to the fact that anybody caught out in it, said that the snowflakes stung like a thousand tiny daggers when they touched your skin. Others called it the Ghost Storm, so called because of the claims of ephemeral figures seen dancing in the snow. Many, however, did not survive, buried in some places by drifts up to six feet high, or killed by the cold. The one thing no one could agree on, however, was what had triggered such a savage storm.

CHAPTER TWENTY-THREE

THE BONDS OF FRIENDSHIP

After a busy night clearing and organizing, Alfic, Amus and Flullen, having transported Sorin's body together with the soldiers, to Milvus Bloch's mortuary, walked listlessly towards the farmhouse, the pair arguing that it was only right they accompany him, as it was, they who had gone to Sorin for help.

Pushing hard on the farmhouse's garden gate, now choked with snow, Alfic strode through the deep drifts, and clearing the snow piled against the front door, knocked hesitantly.

'Alfic, what happened to you? Where have you been?' exclaimed Celia, opening the door and peering about. 'Where's Sorin?'

'Well, you see Celia that's....'

'You look frozen. Go around to the outhouse, you can tell me what happened when you come inside. I'll put the kettle on, we'll soon have you warm.' Celia then shut the door with a solid thud.

'Celia wait, I...'

With a sense of guilt weighing heavily, Alfic, followed by Amus and Flullen, walked around the side of the farmhouse. Entering the outhouse, he hung his coat on one of the black metal hooks screwed into the wall next to Amus's and Flullen's, then stepped out of his thick leather boots. Making his way through to the lounge, Alfic shambled towards the window. He stood and watched the sun reflecting from the snow that had drifted up against the garden fence and the farmyard's outer walls.

'Alfic!' Throwing her arms around him, Lascana cried, 'Alfic, thank Seline, you're safe.'

Hugging her soundly, he said, 'Lascana, I'm so glad you stayed here last night.'

'I came to keep Celia company and when the storm blew in I was…, wait a second, how did you know? Alfic, what's the matter?' insisted Lascana, concern now evident in her voice. 'Alfic, what's happened?'

Celia, placing the cups and saucers on the table, said simply, 'It's Sorin, isn't it? Something's happened.'

Feeling Amus and Flullen move closer to him, Alfic, struggling to get the words out, said simply, 'Sorin's dead.'

Lascana, holding her hand to her mouth, gasped, 'What do you mean, dead?'

'He was killed during the fight at the tool sheds last night.'

'You were there?' cried Lascana. 'Wait a minute, what a stupid question? Of course you were there.' Calming herself, Lascana said tearfully, 'Just tell us what happened.'

'Sorin found me in the snow,' despaired Alfic, 'he saved my life. Celia, I'm so sorry…. I told him not to, but he insisted… he was caught in the crossfire and…

Alfic watched Celia as she shambled forwards shaking her head; she then looked around as if confused. 'I don't know, you men. You're always doom and gloom. We will remember last night as just another quirky snowstorm, and everything will be as right as rain. Do you boys want some tea?'

Amus and Flullen looked to Alfic, a look of perplexity on their faces.

'We are as much to blame, Celia. We could have stopped him going out into the snow looking for Alfic,' said Amus despairingly.

'Don't be ridiculous, Amus,' said Lascana savagely. 'Alfic would have done the same… thing…' relenting as she realised the absurdity of her words.

Disappearing into the kitchen, Celia appeared shortly with five large cups of tea. 'There we are; drink this. A nice cup of tea always makes things better.'

'Celia, stop fussing with cutlery, did you hear what I said?' cried Alfic loudly.

'Sorin said that this weather is going to put a stop on everything,' continued Celia, 'that he'd be back shortly after he'd seen to his beloved oxen. Everything's going to be...'

Grasping her shoulders and shaking her vigorously, Alfic, tears in his eyes, shouted, 'Sorin's dead Celia, and it's my fault.'

'But what about his beer and his mole traps?'

Celia suddenly stopped, and to their astonishment she placed her tea on the kitchen table, turned and slapped Alfic hard across the face. 'Of course, this is your fault, you filled his head with false hopes, you told him that if we stuck together, we could make the school a better place, and he believed you, trusted in you.' She then collapsed to her knees and began weeping uncontrollably.

Alfic stared ahead stoically, as Lascana, consoling Celia, looked up at him sympathetically. He felt at his face; it was no less than he deserved.

It was then that Alfic felt a wind, not hot, but not uncomfortably cold either, rush through the kitchen.

A few moments passed, then deliberately, Celia looked up and smiled through tears of happiness. Climbing unsteadily to her feet, Celia disappeared into the utility room that led from the kitchen. She reappeared moments later holding a stoneware demi-john.

'This is Sorin's homemade potato brandy,' she announced grandly. 'It's only fitting we toast the life of my husband with his home brews.'

'Mistress Celia, you're a godsend,' smiled Amus.

'You'd do well to remember that,' said Celia, who, lifting the jar to her mouth, took a long swallow.

'I think these will suit us better,' suggested Lascana, appearing with several small stoneware cups. She then filled them with the potent brew.

'To Sorin, never to be forgotten,' toasted Amus.

'Here, here,' announced Flullen.

Celia, with tears in her eyes, smiled. 'Bless you both.' She then disappeared into the kitchen, leaving the jug on the table.

'What just happened?' hissed Flullen, a puzzled look on his face.

'Don't look at me!' answered Amus. 'One minute she's slapping Alfic around the face, and now she's offering us some of Sorin's home brew?'

'Celia's very confused right now. She needs time to process the information,' said Lascana knowingly.

Having made a toast to the likable farmer, their mood turned more reflective as Celia, plying them with slices of cake, recounted stories past and present together with Alfic and Lascana, the two young men listening enthralled. Finally, Celia fell asleep on the couch, and Amus and Flullen, buoyant on Sorin's potato brandy, said their goodbyes and returned to their duties.

Warming his hands by the fire, Alfic stared into the glowing embers, his sight wavering due to too much alcohol. He then got up, went into the kitchen and looked out the window, a faraway look in his dark brown eyes. Smelling a familiar fragrance, he smiled as Lascana appeared and wrapped her arms around him. Turning to face her, he kissed her tenderly.

'Are you all right?' she asked.

'I'm fine.'

'Don't give me that. Sorin was your friend.'

'My grief is nothing compared to Celia's.'

Reaching for a cup on the table, Lascana said. 'Here, drink this.'

'What is it?'

'A herbal infusion, it will help you sleep,' said Lascana, giving him a look that brokered no arguments.

Alfic, his face, akin to a young child's biting into a lemon, swallowed the sleeping draught. He then said, annoyed, 'Why does medication always have to taste bad? What's wrong with adding a spoonful of honey?'

'My mother always says, "If it tastes bad, it's doing you good,"' said Lascana resolutely.

'We both know that's poppycock.'

'So, have you any idea as to what happened?'

Placing his empty glass on the kitchen table, Alfic said, 'Savarin's the master of storms bar none, but I've seen nothing like this. I thought it was delirium, but the more I think about it, the more I'm convinced the storm wasn't natural, and that what I saw wasn't a dream. Just before

Sorin found me, I thought I saw figures in the snow. Lascana, I need to know why Sorin had to die. I want to know who conjured that storm, and what Mother and Ramus were doing at Pellagrin's in the sheds in a snowstorm, in the dark?' shouted Alfic angrily.

'That's a mystery that will have to wait. Right now, you need to sleep. Take Celia's room. I'll stay down here. Celia needs me right now.'

The effects of the herbal mixture, combined with the alcohol, caused Alfic to yawn loudly; sleepily, he climbed the stairs. Stretching out on the bed, he immediately fell into a deep sleep. He dreamt of his friend Sorin and ephemeral figures dancing in the snow. What they had failed to see, however, was the door to Duran's and Selva's room slowly closing...

CHAPTER TWENTY-FOUR

PORTENT'S AND
SNOW GOBLIN'S

Cursing, Perak reached out to the insects of the stream and surrounding fields and began directing them to congregate around Hogan.

Blinking and peering around frantically, as if trying to locate something in the dark, the half-giant in an ominous, deep, resounding voice boomed, 'You think a few insects will stop me?'

'No, but it means that you can't see what I'm about to do next.'

He struck at Hogan with his sword, but despite the insect swarm, Hogan still managed to parry his blow. Cutting this way and that, he continued attacking, driving the flailing giant backwards.

'Pathetic. Once Alfic and your friends are dead, who's going to stand in our way, that sword-wielding buffoon, Mace? He couldn't figure his way out of a four-sided room if there was a door on each wall, or that pretty boy, Vanir, who's only claim to fame is bedding women and playing drinking games. Or could it be Vanir's comrades in arms, Tance and Albain? Now where have they been hiding, I wonder?'

Wrenching the weapon from his grip, the half-giant reached out a hand and engulfed his head, and his world turned grey...

'Grandpop, Grandpop, wake up!'

Perak opened his eyes suddenly to see Aridain looking at him with a puzzled look on his face.

'Yes, Aridain, what is it?'

'You were shouting in your sleep!'

'Bad dreams, that's all.'

'Grandpop, come and look at the snow,' said Aridain excitedly.

'Yes, yes, I will. Just give me a moment, will you?'

His eyes refusing to focus, his head felt fuzzy like the morning after the night before, and if he had closed his eyes, he knew he would have fallen straight back to sleep. He looked around groggily. *I must have been tired,* he thought, *falling asleep in the chair?*

'Morning sleepy head,' said Selva seriously, carrying a cup of piping hot tea.

'Why thank you Selva, I need this?'

Rubbing at his face vigorously in an attempt to wake himself up, he drank his tea. Then, standing and bathing in the bright sunlight streaming in through the living room window, Perak began wriggling some life into his extremities. Walking out into the kitchen, he grasped a large water jug, then cursed when he saw the snow piled up against the door.

'The storm!' he exclaimed.

Then, to the children's consternation, he opened the door and plunged his hand into the wall of frozen snow.

'Grandpop, what's the matter?' asked Aridain.

Looking up strangely, a confused frown on his face, he mused, 'I'm not sure. I would have bet my life that it was not a normal storm, but there's nothing, very strange!' Returning to the kitchen, he sat down at the table in silence and poured himself another cup of hot tea from the pot. Then, having consumed some of the leftover stew, he joined the two children digging away with their hands at the wall of snow blocking the conservatory door.

'Where's Sabra, Aridain? He'd melt this snow in no time,' queried Perak.

'He's out catching breakfast.'

'Well, we can't wait for him to come back.'

Disappearing, Perak donning his thick coat, reappeared moments later holding the coal scuttle and a small ash pan. Giving the ash pan to Aridain, they began burrowing through the snow.

Encouraged by the morning sunlight shining through the diamond like snow, Perak, an intense look on his face, pushed the remainder of the drift out into the garden together with the giggling children. Brushing the snow from his clothing, he chuckled, 'You both look like miniature snowmen.'

Suddenly, with mischievous looks, the two children, gathering armloads of snow, proceeded to cover him from head to foot. Now in fits of laughter, Perak, chased the two children around the garden. This culminated in a snow fight and soon all three of them were laid on the ground, covered from head to foot.

'That was fun, Grandpop Perak,' laughed Selva.

'It was Selva, really it was.'

'Perak Bruin, what's happening here?' asked a soldier peering over the hedge from the lane.

Holding up his hands, Perak, still chuckling to himself, whilst trying to shake snow from the parts that snow shouldn't really be, replied, 'It's OK corporal, we're just having fun in the snow.'

Looking him and the children up and down disdainfully, the soldier said, 'Very well, carry on.'

'Stay here kids, I won't be long,' said Perak.

His mood turned darker, the soldier, suddenly peering over the hedge, reminding him of life's stark reality. He ploughed his way through the fresh snow that covered the patio area and the pond. Making his way through a particularly large drift underneath the trellising, now groaning under the weight of snow, he proceeded on down the path towards the small stable block between the flower borders.

Returning with a shovel and a couple of large trowels, Perak together with Aridain and Selva, began clearing the paths of snow, promising that when it was done, they'd be free to play.

Collecting up the tools, Perak, about to return them to the stable block, turned at a female voice.

'You always were one for fun!'

Stood in the lane facing him was a figure wearing a voluminous hood and a thick Balefire cloak.

In a puzzled voice, he replied, 'Vara, is that you?'

Removing the hood, a heavily tanned and weathered female face was revealed, topped by a head of greying hair tied back in a ponytail at the base of her neck. It wasn't Vara; however, her face had a familiar look that Perak couldn't quite put his finger on.

'A penny for them?'

Looking the strangely familiar figure up and down, the mature voice implied years of hardship. 'Do I know you?'

'You should do, Perak Bruin.'

His eyes narrowing, Perak stared agog at the tall, slender figure stood before him. 'Mira? Mira Corvus, is that you?'

'In the flesh, Perak Bruin.'

'I don't believe it? How are you? Where have you been?' he cried, taking her in his arms and squeezing her tight.

'Better, now I've seen the face of my favourite brother-in-law, as to where I have been; that's a long story.' After a suitable amount of time, Mira said, 'Well, are you going to release me? I've been on the road for three days, Perak. I could murder a strong cup of tea.'

'Of course, go inside and sit down and I'll make us a drink,' said Perak self-consciously. 'You still know the way I presume?'

'How could I forget?' said Mira, striding through the entrance. 'This was my home too, remember? There are soldiers everywhere. Two of them stopped and questioned me.'

'Yes, that is also a long story.'

Sipping at his tea, Perak studied Vara's long-lost sister from behind the kitchen counter. 'So, what are you doing here, Mira, and why are you dressed as a Balefire?'

'I thought that was obvious.'

'You've joined the cult?'

'Yes, I'm here on cult business. I need to see Vara.'

'You know she never forgave you for running away?' implied Perak.

'Nevertheless, I need to see her.'

'She's not here!'

'When will she be back?'

'She won't be. She doesn't live here anymore.'

'So, you two finally came to the right decision?'

'Oh, it's nothing like that. She's had to leave. The last time I saw her, she was going to kill Kuelack.'

'Kuelack!' queried Mira, a searching, puzzled look on her face. 'Ahh, now I remember, he's the new head of the school, right, he's also your youngest?'

'Correct.'

'Talking of family, is mother....?'

Peering over the thick oak counter at Vara's tall, rangy sister, that he hadn't seen in nearly thirty years, Perak said stoically, 'You must understand, the burden your mother carried weighed heavily on her mind and body. Pion passed away from an infection even beyond Vara's skills. Vara even tried to administer dragon's blood, but your mother wouldn't accept it. She said that it was her time.'

Sitting down heavily on a stool in front of the range, Mira nodded slowly then said sadly, 'I shouldn't be upset I suppose, being away for so long it was always on the cards.' Staring around the walls of her old home, Mira said matter-of-factly, 'This place hasn't changed at all, still feels exactly the same, old and settled, like a well-worn sofa. You always said that the only way they'd get you to move out of here was in a box.' Then, taking a drink from her cup, she purred, 'Hmmm, there's nothing like a nice cup of tea; I can't remember the last time I had a decent one. This is the first time I've been warm in three days. You wouldn't have anything to eat, would you?'

'I'm sure I can find something,' said Perak. 'So have you anywhere to stay for the night.'

'Well, I....'

'That's settled then. You're staying here.'

'OK, I guess one night won't harm.'

Taking Mira's empty plate and placing it in the stoneware sink, Perak washed it and stood it up to dry. He then sat opposite, and looking thoughtfully at Mira, chuckled.

'What's so amusing?' asked Mira.

'Do you remember when your father first appeared in the village, roaring drunk?'

'How could I forget?'

'When your mother refused to see him, his childish slaps were hardly a challenge.'

'Are you basking in your own ego?'

He smiled sheepishly. 'No, of course not. I was only saying!' He then lapsed into silence.

'Prison was the best place for him, and I, for one, was very grateful. Helping you build this place after you took us in helped me to appreciate the simple things in life, appreciate simply being alive again.'

'It was a pity Vara didn't have your attitude, she can be, "demanding". I loved your sister and my intentions were honourable. I thought she loved me, but for Vara, however, love is just another inconvenience, and what was contentment for me was merely another stepping-stone for your sister. She was never satisfied, as her favourite statement of, *'it will do for now'*, echoed in my ears time and time again.'

'I've had no time to think on the ups and downs of relationships, but I do know things change, feelings change, Perak. I know our upbringings should make no difference, but as a child I realised long ago what Vara's like. Vara often talked about marrying into wealth and power, to someone with goals.'

'I have goals, Mira, but being married to your sister entailed social climbing, power and status, and there was no room in her heart for anything else. In fact, I can't understand why she married me at all?' said Perak pensively. 'I envy my son, Alfic, married to Lascana. She's house-proud but satisfied with what they have, and they love each other despite their circumstances.'

'You are a passionate man, Perak, a loyal man, and you shouldn't torment yourself. Obligation was always my sister's master. Vara's one of the most senior Balefire Witches in Gonda. The sooner you come to terms and understand that, the more content you'll be. Her art has taken an entire lifetime to study. Together with our beliefs and traditions, Vara has a duty to uphold. It's simply the pride of a Balefire, of dedication, and of service.'

'You're right, of course. I always had more in common with you, whilst Vara has more in common with Gondian high society, and our marriage has always been a sham.'

'I know what you're thinking, Perak, but do not think for one moment that because of your upbringing, you are any less than Vara. Growing up as an orphaned serf with nothing, you've attained so much more than I could have ever imagined. Head Groundsman at Pellagrin's is a grand achievement, I'd say.'

He looked up sheepishly. 'I'm sorry Mira you return to your home, and all I can do is whinge to you about your sister.'

'Nonsense, you were my best friend growing up, Perak, you still are, I could always count on you in times of trouble, so believe me it's no burden, just because I'm a Balefire, doesn't mean I'm unsympathetic.'

Standing, Perak looked out into the garden. Overseen by the dragonlet, the children were busily building a snowman.

'Come on. I'll introduce you to the children.'

'Children?'

'Yes, Mira, children.'

'But…, I wasn't expecting to…, I didn't know the Taal would be here.'

'Grasping Mira's shoulders, he looked at her kindly. 'He's just a boy. Please, treat him as such.'

Donning his thick cloak, Perak led Mira out into the snow.

Aridain, Selva, this is Mira, your grandmother's sister.'

'Hello Mira, we've built a snow goblin,' yelled Aridain.

'Ahh, I wondered what it was; it's very ugly,' smiled Mira, bending down and shaking Aridain's hand.

'That's what they look like,' admonished Selva.

'It's not as ugly as the bad man in the storm,' said Aridain matter-of-factly.

'Bad man in the storm?' queried Perak. 'Do you know who it was?'

'No. I tried to push him away, but he kept coming back. But it was all right in the end; Uncle Sorin helped me.'

'Sorin… helped you?'

'Yes, Grandpop. He said, don't be sad, I'm at peace now and with friends. He also said he doesn't blame Daddy, and to try to help Duran.'

All three of them stared at Aridain.

Her bottom lip beginning to quiver, Selva asked, 'What does Aridain mean?'

Tears stinging his eyes, Perak, drawing Selva to him and hugging her tenderly, whispered wretchedly, 'I think what Aridain is saying Selva, is that your father's dead.'

Engaged to be married, Lascana remembered vividly her shock when Alfic had announced he was quitting the army.

'Not because of me, I hope?' she had declared defensibly.

'Of course not. I figured it was time I settled down, although Mother wasn't too pleased. She said that I lacked ambition and vision, that you had turned my head; she also went on extensively to remind me of my siblings who'll be in charge of the school one day. I told her it's a decision I stick by...'

She smiled at those recollections, but the innocent, every day memories seemed a lifetime away. Two nights previously, however, whilst laid next to her in bed, the dependable ex-army captain that everyone looked up to, who everyone depended on for leadership, had confided in her that he'd been having strange, violent dreams...

'I feel frustrated and angry all the time,' Alfic had confessed, looking about him hesitantly with fear-filled eyes. 'Certain times of the day are blank. But when I try to remember, I can't recall where I've been or what I've done. I feel like there's a shadow hanging over me, a shadow just out of sight and just out of reach, ready to pounce at any time. It's like I'm walking around with one hand tied behind my back. I dream over and over of my hands around my brother's throat. What's that all about?'

Grasping Alfic's head in both hands, she had stared desperately at her husband's grey and drawn features and into his bloodshot eyes, despairingly. The change was alarming, and with no help forthcoming, she'd felt alone and helpless.

'I don't know what's happening to you Alfic, but you have to fight this. You have too.'

Just then, Celia intruded on her thoughts...

'Duran's not in his bedroom. He's gone. We need to find him!'

'Of course, I'll be right with you,' smiled Lascana buoyantly, although she felt anything but happy.

Lascana watched as Celia, distraught and dressed for the weather, milled about with no purpose or plan.

'Why are you stood around? My son is missing,' snapped Celia, opening the front door angrily, but she was soon stopped in her tracks as she came face to face with a wall of snow. Panicking visibly now, Celia cried, 'Now what do we do?'

Setting her shoulders and putting her own concerns to the back of her mind, Lascana, shuffling towards the kitchen, emerged with two of Celia's brass tea trays. 'Calm down, Celia, take a deep breath and start shovelling.'

Having created a hole in the snow, Lascana, with Celia's help, began clearing the snow, until finally, daylight streamed in through the front door. They were surprised, however, when through the void, peered a tall, clean shaven, youthful looking man dressed in a thigh-length leather coat, hat and trousers.

'Drench,' exclaimed Lascana, taking a step backwards.

'Morning, Mistress Celia, Mistress Lascana,' smiled Drench.

'For what do we owe this pleasure?' enquired Lascana.

Pushing Duran to the fore, Drench said. 'I believe you are missing this one.'

Hugging him fiercely, Celia cried tearily, 'Duran?' She then clipped the moody youth around the ear, exclaiming, 'Where have you been? You had me worried sick!'

'I am truly sorry for your loss, Mistress Celia,' said Drench sincerely.

'You're too kind. However, you, young man, have a lot of explaining to do.' Thrusting a lavender biscuit into his hand, Celia marched Duran upstairs, grumbling about how he will have plenty of time to contemplate the consequences of his actions whilst locked in his bedroom.

'Come in,' said Lascana, 'you look half frozen. Where did you find him?'

'I found him down by the mill,' answered Drench, stamping the snow from his leather boots and stepping into the warm, cosy kitchen. 'When I asked what he was doing there, he told me he'd been for a walk.'

Noticing Drench's rueful smile towards the stairs, Lascana asked, 'Why the sad face?'

'Strange dreams and flashbacks!'

'Oh!'

'I can't remember my childhood, Lascana, or my family, and I can do things without knowing why or how. I have glimpses, but when I do, they're replaced by pain. I often wonder if it was something I did, something so horrendous, that I have deliberately shut it out?

211

'I wouldn't fret so; your memories will return soon enough.'

'But what if they don't? Then what?'

'The mind is a complicated place. It works in mysterious ways. You just need to give it time. If I were a mind master, I would help you, but I'm not.'

'Do you know, you may have a point there?'

'About what?'

'Mind masters.'

'Take my advice. Don't go there, I know. Besides, we don't know any; they're all gone. Now, I'm about to make breakfast. Would you like some?'

'I wouldn't say no.' said Drench, more upbeat.

'I'll get on it right away,' smiled Lascana.

Just then, Celia hurried down the stairs. 'Alfic's gone!'

'Gone?' exclaimed Lascana with a start. 'What do you mean, gone?'

'The bedroom window's open,' offered Celia.

'That's not the sort of thing Alfic would do,' said Lascana, knowingly.

'Lascana, what's going on? What's happened to Alfic?'

'If I knew, Drench, I would tell you?'

CHAPTER TWENTY-FIVE

DOWN THE RABBIT HOLE

Byrak looked on stoically as a figure appeared through the trees.

'Ahh, there you are. Come here, Alfic?'

Gesturing and closing his fist, Byrak concentrated, and brought his mind to bear.

Alfic let out a muffled agonised scream, then dropped to his knees.

'Your family and friends have been busy, it seems!'

'Why.. are you.. doing this…., what do you… want?' Alfic hissed.

'I thought that was obvious. I want you to kill Kuelack, then I want you to kill Serac.'

'No,' Alfic hissed.

'As impressive as your resistance is, your struggles will only cause you pain.' Silent for a moment, Byrak looked down upon Alfic and said, 'Frankly, I don't understand your resistance. It's not as if I'm asking you to do anything you haven't already considered yourself.' When Alfic remained silent, Byrak continued, 'Nothing to say, no words of wisdom or defiance? Very well then, to business. Thanks to you, I have recently discovered that Kuelack has lost four precious items, that Vara is a Balefire witch, and that Ramus sought her help regarding these items; items she failed to procure. Also, through you, I have discovered that Pellagrin's spirit resides in your son, leading me to believe that he has the Firebrand shards.'

'Firebrand shards,… you're mad!'

'Do not test me, groundsman.' Grasping Alfic roughly by the chin, Byrak, peering deeply into Alfic's eyes, said, 'Your son has the ability to mask his mind from me, but you do not. Lascana and especially Perak are beginning to realise that there's more to your irritability than simple tiredness, and if your family's past record is anything to go by, it won't be long before they discover why.'

'I don't understand....'

'Enough! Forget subtlety and timing; kill the arrogant mage and his sidekick now. Then I want you to bring me the Firebrand shards before your family discovers my plans.' Byrak then closed his eyes for an instant. 'If you fail, picture your son lying dead and mutilated at my feet.'

'Byrak...., don't do this, join me,' Alfic gasped, 'and we can defeat... Kuelack... together.'

'Join you! Why would I join you?' Byrak sneered, 'I am a member of the master race, tasked by Master Mass to take up his mantel. Once I've unearthed the manner of my kind's defeat, I can complete Mass's and Grand Master Caberatus's grand plan, and lead the mind walkers to greatness.'

'That's... the past... talking,' gasped Alfic painfully.

'They are wise words from men of vision; compared to them, you are an insect. I mean really, what have you to offer me?' spat Byrak.

'Strength in numbers.., strength in... unity, and because... no man is an island....'

'Enough,' snarled Byrak, clamping Alfic's mouth shut with his words. 'Kill Kuelack, retrieve the stones. You are a resourceful individual. You will find a way.'

Watching from the shadows, Keegan, scrutinised Alfic as he left the trees. He looked bewildered and confused, then with renewed purpose, strode across the fields. Resisting the urge to charge into the clearing after Byrak, Keegan, squatting amidst the sparse vegetation, waited to follow the young psychic, who moments later emerged from the trees and strolled confidently through the snow across the fields towards the school.

Confident in his abilities, Keegan, as imperceptible as a ghost, shadowed the young psychic covertly as he disappeared behind the apprentice dorm. Darting across the road, following the psychic, he peered around the corner, then flattened himself against the old perimeter wall, as Byrak turned in his direction. Creeping silently down the path between the small glasshouses built against the old perimeter wall and the allotments, Byrak's voice abruptly filled his mind.

Did you really think you could follow me, Keegan Fold?

Darting quickly into the last of two cold framed greenhouses, Keegan replied. *I will not stand idly by whilst you use my friends as tools for your twisted ambitions.*

Commendable Keegan Fold, but a futile gesture. I know your thoughts the instant you do.

And I should have killed you whilst I had the chance, Keegan thought aggressively.

Keegan then studied his surroundings. Against the far wall were benches and shelves containing pots and wooden trays ready for cuttings and seedlings. Planted along either side of the central aisle were two rows of large leafy chandelier plants laden with yellow teardrop shaped fruit. Also, in the corner was a folded light canvas sheet next to the wooden containment boards, together with a large wooden prod with a hook on the end used to open the skylight windows. It was then that he became conscious of a low humming noise issuing from above; the noise saturating the crisp morning air.

Oh, great, hibernating hornet flies, he thought, *dammit Drench, why haven't you moved them on?*

His eyes narrowing, Keegan focused on the task at hand and gripped the hilt of his knife tightly. Checking on the undulating mass one more time, he slowly eased himself behind the chandelier plants and tried to still his racing pulse. He should abandon his fruitless plan, but how do you make any kind of plan when Byrak could pluck it from your mind? No, all he could do now was try to prevent Byrak from reading his thoughts.

His senses finely tuned, he scanned the world outside, from the frozen water barrels to the tops of the cold frames and the glasshouses, to their snow-laden roofs evaporating in the winter sun, but of Byrak there was no sign.

It was then that he heard a strange indiscernible scuffling sound, accompanied by the unmistakable smell of rotting grass. Spinning around, he saw a large male scarrion lizard the size of a small dog that had appeared from a hole in the old fortress wall. Glaring at him with unnerving intelligence from piercing yellow eyes, the lizard, without warning, shuffled forward. Then, raising the deep blue frill around its neck and back, it leapt towards him. Before Keegan could react, the scarrion lizard, hissing loudly, dug its claws into his thigh and bit down hard. Crying out in pain, Keegan grabbed the frenzied lizard by its neck and thrust his knife into its rib cage, then with an angry curse, cast it to the floor. Horrified, he kicked out, as the lizard twisting upright scuttled back towards him, regardless of the gaping wound in its side. Pinning the lizard against the wall with his foot, Keegan severed its warty head from its scaly body. Grimacing, he produced a cloth handkerchief. Then, to stem the blood seeping through the fabric, he pressed it to the large V-shaped wound in his leg.

'Is that your best? You'll need to coerce something much larger if you want to stop me, because if you don't, Byrak, rest assured, if I get the chance, I will kill you,' he bellowed.

I don't need to do anything more. The creature has done its work. You're already dead.

Sweating profusely now and trying to ignore the toxic rot coursing through his veins, Keegan leant wearily against the old perimeter wall.

Skulking in dark places? Too cowardly to confront anyone face-to-face, stabbing people in the back; is this the way of the master race? Encountering only silence, he continued confidently, determined not to show any weakness. *Does it rankle that Kuelack killed Mass and laughs at you, as he concocts his schemes?*

Keegan turned as Byrak appeared from the doorway opposite. The vehemence of his words cutting through the air, Byrak spat, 'If it's the last thing I do, I will see that..'

Keegan, not waiting for him to finish, gripped his knife tightly and charged, his blade angled towards Byrak's throat. The young psychic, caught totally off guard, threw up his hands in defence, but Keegan's lightning like charge faltered as his infected leg gave way. From the frosted floor, he then looked up at Byrak determinedly.

'You humans are pathetic. Ooh, a brick wall, how cute, that's first-year student stuff,' laughed Byrak. 'I'm far beyond brick walls.'

Squirming beneath the young psychic's psyche, Keegan felt his body torn from his control as his mind became smothered as if in a thick blanket. Then, suddenly, Keegan opened his eyes, his fogged mind clear once more. He was back in the cold frame again, with no idea how he got there.

Physical strength is one thing, mental strength is quite another. Let's make this encounter more exciting, shall we?

Keegan stilled his breathing as two men approached and entered the small greenhouse with him; it was Amus Holt and Simon Tubney.

Picking up the window prod, Amus poked at the swarm that rose like a dark apparition to defend their queen, but there was no outcry or pain wracked shouts, as the two men standing quite calmly were stung repeatedly by the enraged swarm.

'Amus, Flullen,' he bellowed, 'don't just stand there, get out!'

Did you really think you could stand against me? I am now the foremost mind in the land; I can cut through wizards defences like a hot knife through butter. So what chance do you stand?

'If it's me you want, then kill me,' snarled Keegan loudly, 'but leave these two out of it. They have done nothing to you.'

Don't feel too bad, Keegan, just take comfort in the fact that you were beaten by a superior being.

Angry now, Keegan charged, rugby tackling the two men to the ground, the impact hurling all three of them into the corner, where he quickly covered the dazed pair and himself with the hessian sheet.

Now that's not very noble of you, I'll have to order your two friends to kill you instead.

'Byrak, you sick bastard, I swear...'

Abruptly, the angry buzzing receded, and after a short period, Keegan cautiously uncovered himself and the two dazed workers. All around, hornet flies lay dead and dying.

'Gronin's beard! I'm covered in stings,' exclaimed Amus in a pain wracked voice.

'Me too. What the hell happened? What are we doing here?' cursed Tubney.

Keegan looked up to see a figure standing in the doorway.

'Kale, thank Seline!' Looking at the swarm, lying dead and dying on the floor, Keegan said cautiously, 'But was it really necessary to kill them?'

'It was a very aggressive swarm. What happened here?'

'Byrak tried to kill me, through Amus and Simon.'

'Interesting!'

'What do you mean, interesting? He's the reason for Alfic's state of mind. He's tasked Alfic to kill Kuelack. We have to stop him.'

'Yes, yes, of course, but first we need to get you and your friends some medical attention.'

'Where is Byrak, by the way?' gasped Keegan, looking at Kale strangely, then about the yard.

'Oh, no need to worry about Byrak. I'll deal with him,' said Kale with certainty.

'What do you mean, deal with him?'

'That's not important right now. You and your two friends need medical attention.'

Leaning heavily upon Kale, Keegan said, 'Are you mad? You do remember the bit about us being fugitives?'

'Then what do you suggest?'

'I know, I'll take you to the cavern.'

'The cavern?'

Keegan, looking at him, knowingly said, 'Of course, you wouldn't know about the cavern, would you?'

Ordering Amus and Simon, looking like a pair of warty toads, to the infirmary, Keegan, the toxin from the lizard's claws, together with the painful stings making his head swim, said irritably, 'Help me up here, it's this way.'

Aided by Kale, Keegan, hobbling significantly now, said agonisingly, 'Strange how we've seen no guards? You'd have thought someone would have heard the commotion.'

'Your right, it seems luck is on our side.'

'Well, we could certainly do with some.' Glancing at Kale, a puzzled look on his face, Keegan asked, 'So how are Molly and Mo? Is Drench looking after them properly?'

'Molly and Mo?'

'Yes, Molly and Mo, my ferrets. Honestly, I knew the love of a good woman can tire you out, but I didn't know that all of that blood draining from your head could give you memory loss.'

'Of course, Molly and Mo! What am I thinking? They're fine.'

Glancing quizzically towards Kale one more time, Keegan said jokingly, 'Honestly, what is Crystal doing with you of a night-time?' But there was no humour in his expression.

Relying heavily upon Kale now, Keegan directed them to the woodworking shed.

'What are we doing here?' Kale asked irritably.

'Open the door and get inside before we're seen,' Keegan slurred.

Entering, Keegan instructed Kale to search behind an old broken pole lathe.

'What am I looking for?'

'You see those two old water barrels in the corner filled with an assortment of wooden off-cuts. Move them from atop that old leather tarpaulin sheet, but mind your step.'

'I've found a hole!' exclaimed Kale.

'Not just any hole, it is a hole to an underground world. I discovered it six months back, trying to catch a particularly nasty scarrion lizard, put my foot right through the floor. It's dry rot.' Indicating a knotted rope tied to an old iron ring secured to the wall, Keegan said, 'Right, down you go.'

'You first,' said Kale warily.

'As you wish.'

Sweating profusely, the lizard's toxin coursing through his veins, Keegan somehow managed to lower himself down into the dark void, falling the last foot or so onto the dusty floor. Immediately, the tunnel flooded with light.

Following Keegan, Kale lowered himself down into the tunnel. Marvelling at the bizarre lights, he said, 'Strange magic indeed!'

'Magic? I'm not so sure?'

Wrapping his arm around Kale's shoulder for support, Keegan directed them down another dusty section of tunnel until they came to a crossroads. Turning left, they continued down another old section of tunnel until Keegan raised his hand. Pushing lightly against the tunnel wall, his hand disappeared, followed by the rest of him. Then a few moments later, Keegan's disembodied head reappeared, followed by his arm.

'Well, don't just stand there gawping, come in,' insisted Keegan, and grasping Kale roughly by the wrist, pulled him through.

Kale closed his eyes and, with a feeling akin to passing through a thick skin of treacle, he instantly retched.

'I'm not clearing that up, Keegan, that's down to you,' said a voice that Kale, through his nausea, recognised as Greysword Vanir.

'Don't be so squeamish and help me here,' demanded Keegan.

'Bloody hell, Kale. You look like death,' said Mace, taking his arm and helping him towards a small spring of water that flowed through a rocky pool.

Feeling as though his insides had been extracted from his body, mixed up in a bowl and then put back again, Kale, wiping at his mouth, coughed irritably. 'I'm fine, just need to get my bearings.'

Sipping at the cold clear water, Kale scooping some in his hands, doused his face and hair. Then, lying back upon a strange shimmering outcrop of rock, that looked remarkably like a bench, he took in his surroundings.

He was in a voluminous cavern hung with stalactites. Met by upward thrusting stalagmites sprinkled with quartz, the limestone pillars sparkled in a soft blue hue that permeated the cavern. In between the stalactites, roots grew, worming their way across the ceiling from the cavern's highest point, some disappearing through the thick cavern wall. Thick strands of ivy hung from the cracks and crevices, and all around the strange fruiting bodies of a fungus that coated the walls gave off a strange blue light. But the most notable feature was the large, lavish stone sarcophagus laid upon a rock platform at the rear of the chamber. Steps led up to the front of the tomb, supported by thick granite pillars decorated in marble, and edged by decorative pilasters, and adorning the ornate cornices around the tomb's lid were embossed images of dragons of various sizes. It dawned then that the roots belonged to the oak tree in the courtyard and that this was Pellagrin's long-lost tomb.

'How are you feeling?' asked Mace.

'I'll survive,' said Kale forebodingly.

'Well, this is a turn up for the books. One minute we're being tasked to investigate the rumours of a strange creature roaming the grounds, the next…'

'Things change, Mace. We just have to roll with it.'

'Never a truer word spoken,' agreed Vanir.

Trying his hardest not to retch, Kale studied their appearance. The friends looking as though they had been dragged through a hedge backwards and then trampled on, their clothes frayed and worn; they looked healthy nonetheless and had plenty of food and water.

'Whoa, take it easy, you pathetic excuse for a greysword,' hissed Keegan, through clenched teeth.

'Stop squirming! If you want more than basic healing, you should have gone to Alsike?' admonished Vanir.

Taking another swig of brandy, Keegan said, 'Just stitch my wound, will you? Basic healing is preferable to having my head chopped off.'

They sat in silence as, with a needle and thread, Vanir began closing Keegan's wounds.

'There, done, that should hold,' said Vanir, snatching the leather skin flask from Keegan and taking a mouthful of brandy. Seeing Keegan's longing stare towards the flask, Vanir said, 'Oh no, this isn't for you, you're drinking this. It's some of Lascana's cure-all, and apply this salve to the wound.'

'I don't think much of your bedside manner. Heartless, that's what you are.'

'So, care to explain?' said Mace, pointing to Keegan's wounds.

'Pissed off scarrion lizard, controlled by Byrak.' Keegan said wearily.

'Byrak! I thought Kuelack murdered all of Mass's students?'

'Not this one, Mace. Byrak survived. He discovered me watching from the trees and tried to stop me.'

'What were you watching?' exclaimed Vanir.

'Alfic, he met with Byrak.'

'Cronin's beard! This is all we need,' pondered Vanir.

'What was Alfic doing meeting Byrak?' demanded Mace.

'Your guess is as good as mine,' said Keegan.

'Have you considered that Alfic may be working with him?' said Kale.

'Have you learnt nothing? Alfic would willingly lay down his life for us and we for him. He would never work with that cockroach.'

'I was only going to say that this could be the reason for Alfic's recent irritability,' said Kale.

'Unless we kill Byrak, Alfic will have him in his head, constantly reminding him of his assignment,' said Vanir.

'That's not the way it works,' explained Kale. 'Byrak's death will not alleviate Alfic's burden.'

'Well Kale, you found Byrak,' said Keegan. 'Can't you persuade him to withdraw his command?'

'You have Byrak? Then what are you waiting for, Kale? Do something!' insisted Vanir.

'And perhaps it's time that two of the greatest greyswords in Pellagrin's history stopped skulking in the shadows beneath the school,' accused Kale angrily.

'Keep your whiskers on,' stated Vanir.

'Yeh, steady on Kale,' finished Mace.

'I give you my word that Byrak will be dealt with. Leave it with me.'

The chamber fell silent as each became lost in his own thoughts, and Kale couldn't help but be impressed by the bonds the three friends had forged, or the love they retained for Alfic.

'Talking of unforeseen complications, there has been a lot of activity along the main tunnel leading to Higher Wood recently,' said Mace grimly. 'Whoever they are, they're wearing armour and carrying heavy loads.'

'That's speculation, surely,' postulated Kale. 'How can you tell?'

'Well, during our night-time forays, I haven't noticed strangers running around the school fully armoured, carrying armloads of weapons, have you?' insisted Vanir.

'Whoever they are, they're using the tunnels as a means to travel back and forth to the woods,' announced Mace.

'Which means they've repaired the steps,' stated Vanir frustratedly.

'Whoever they are, do they suspect you're here?' asked Kale wretchedly.

'No,' mused Mace, 'Which is surprising.'

'Why would they?' smiled Keegan. 'We'd be stupid to stay here, right? Hiding right under Kuelack's nose is the most satisfying part.'

'So, it's obvious what we have to do.' Then, picking up and studying his body armour, Mace said, 'Talking of weapons and armoury, I need to contact Gable. My armour is in dire need of repairs.'

'So is mine. It's a pity Gable can't forge our armour the way our swords were forged, eh,' supposed Vanir bleakly.

'I need some fresh air,' announced Kale wretchedly.

'Still not feeling better?' suggested Keegan.

Standing, Kale shook his head, then, putting on a brave face, he enquired, 'Have you told the Bruins about any of this?'

'No,' confirmed Mace, 'and we don't intend to.'

'Good.' With that, he strode up the incline towards the cavern wall. 'I'll be in touch.' Then, closing his eyes, he stepped through the cavern wall.

Furniture burst apart, and personal items, books, and paperwork exploded in showers of flaming debris.

Grasping Delran around the throat and hauling him into the air, Kuelack raged, 'Incompetent fool, my mother tried to kill me and you let her get away. She should be here, now, whimpering at my feet, she should be....'

'He is not to blame, Brother!'

Releasing the choking Delran, Kuelack, spinning around, inquired slyly. 'Oh..., then who is, Sister?'

'It was a series of unfortunate events that led to the farmer being killed and Vara escaping.'

'I am not interested in unfortunate events.' Calming himself with an effort, Kuelack said, 'The lie crosses your lips so easily. But attaining results is not so easy or painless. If I can't get results through kind-heartedness, then I must use alternative methods. Someone will have to pay for last night's incompetence, Sister.' He turned to Gradine. 'Let them in.'

Magen watched as Gradine, rubbing her hands together and grinning like the cat that got the cream, opened the door. Escorted by Karnack, four guards, looking about warily, entered the apartment.

'Gentlemen,' smiled Kuelack. 'Magen has called her failure, a series of unfortunate event's, what say you?'

'If I may, My Lord,' interceded Delran. 'When the witch attacked, it was I who ordered these men forward. In the confusion'–

'Quiet, Delran, you did what you thought was right,' said Magen.

'Yes, credit where credit's due, and thanks to you, Sister, Vara failed. She will not try again, I wager.'

'You said that after the last attack, Brother.'

Taking a deep breath, Kuelack turned to Karnack and, the teacher of enchantments, Arhass. 'Vara escaping, no shards and no diary, it's a shame it's come to this, but an example must be set.'

Realising Kuelack's intent, Magen said hastily, 'I agree, an example should be made, but it was my incompetence that led to mother's escape. I'm to blame, Brother, punish me if you must.'

'Sister. Sister..., I understand your feelings in the matter. You are a compassionate person. It is one of your many failings. The rewards of success and power, entail more than the cutting out society's grimy, dirty cancer. Acquiring power, however, is not a sterile process. Failure infects everything we do and say.' Turning to the soldiers, Kuelack, strolling down the line, looked into their eyes one by one. 'You understand, don't you? That if order is to be maintained, I must make an example of someone. This time, however, I will be lenient.'

The soldiers visibly relaxing, Magen watched as Kuelack turned towards her. She watched in fascination as his eyes turned the colour of onyx. Then, with a twitch of his claw-like hand, Kuelack snapped the neck of one of the soldiers, who flopped jellyfish-like to the floor.

Looking at her with intent, Kuelack said ominously, 'Let this be a lesson well learnt.'

Kuelack had been determined to take his anger out on someone, it seemed, regardless of how hard she had protested.

'Gradine, have that removed, will you, and display it for all to see? I'll leave the details to you. Meanwhile,' he announced, 'I will change.'

An almost lustful look upon her face, Gradine replied, 'Of course, husband. You three take up the corpse and follow me.'

Magen sat down heavily upon one of the opulent chez-longues, trying and failing to avoid looking at the soldier's body, as it was carried from the apartment. To distract her thoughts, Magen sat and studied Karnack's and Arhass's faces.

The contrast couldn't have been more stark. Karnack, morose and serious, his chin in his hand, stared ahead forebodingly, whilst Arhass Vydra, the school's teacher of enchantments and curses, gazed around the apartment as if perusing a local shop for trinketries, his basset hound features affected not at all by the spectacle they had just witnessed. Highly individual, Arhass, although secretive, had destructive tendencies, so was the perfect fit for her brother. A troubled individual prone to fits of rage if things didn't go his way, his enchanting magic, although imaginative, was for his intended victims, lethal.

Appearing from a door to their right, Kuelack, fondling the weaved red and black bordered ankle length sash of office, embroidered with glittering red clasps, said casually, 'This is the new, Head of the Sivan's sash of office, I had it made especially. This sash will be the new symbol of my authority. It shows my determination, my willingness, my desire to rule, and lead the school into the future without the shackles of the past,' boasted Kuelack.

'Why?' exclaimed Magen. 'The old official sash has been the symbol of power here for generations.'

'Yes, it has served as a symbol of distinction and excellence,' announced Karnack. 'But not anymore. This is a new era, a new era deserves a new sash.'

'Is this really the way you want to go, Brother, discipline by death and reinventing the Sivan?'

Magen watched as her brother, who, with barely contained anger, said frustratedly, 'The people will except it, and my rule, and so will you!'

'Well, I like it,' announced Arhass gleefully.

That speech has Gradine's slimy fingers all over it, thought Magen. *Speak of the devil?*

'Ahh, Gradine,' smiled Kuelack.

'It is done!' she announced joyfully.

'Excellent. Now that unfortunate business is out of the way, we can proceed. The storm was not natural, we all felt it. It wasn't Mother. She hasn't the power or the knowledge, neither has Ramus.'

'What about Savarin? His ties to the Bruins are common knowledge, as is his opposition.'

'As is yours, Karnack?' suggested Arhass.

'Lascana's son!' announced Gradine. 'If as we suspect he has the shards, he could easily conjure the storm.'

'He has power, yes, but I suspect, not the knowledge,' countered Magen.

'How can you say that? According to my husband, he was present during both disturbances in Farend Woods,' insisted Gradine.

'Be careful Gradine, that your hatred for Lascana doesn't cloud your judgement,' countered Magen.

'Do not lecture me on'–

'Ladies, ladies, we will investigate both lines of inquiry.'

'So, what is your fascination with this diary, Kuelack?' queried Arhass.

'It predicts the future; it also teaches us lessons from the past.'

'An enchanted object; right up my alley. Perhaps I can assist,' smiled Arhass.

'I still don't understand,' queried Magen, throwing Arhass a stern look. 'You may have needed it to find the shards, Brother, but now...'

'We need it if we are to triumph. The rest is none of your concern, Sister. Your priority is to find the diary. You, Gradine, seeing as your schemes regarding the coins with Arhass's help was not a total failure, will assist Karnack in recapturing those traitorous greyswords, and that duplicitous gamekeeper.'

'As you wish, husband.'

'In the meantime, I want you, Arhass, to persuade the people still leaning towards Alfic and his friends, to our way of thinking. Failing that, I want them disappeared. Do I make myself clear?'

'Perfectly,' smiled Arhass.

Magen turned to her brother. 'What of Rasbora?'

'What of her?'

'She's free and heading for her homeland!'

'Don't fret, Sister, it is all part of my new plan.'

'New plan?'

'Yes, you see, it has come to our attention that Rasbora has acquired some dragons loyal to Ramus's family, but it is of no mind.'

'This is a consequence of inciting the Barons Protectorate to revolt, and kill Ramus's family?' worried Magen.

Throwing Magen a harrowing look, Kuelack continued, 'Instead of confronting her, we will simply drive her and her dragons northwards towards the protectorates' clutches, killing two birds with one stone.'

'I hope you know what you're doing, Brother? Rasbora is no ordinary sorceress. Alfic's son is also a powerful individual. Fall foul of either and you may well regret it.'

'Thank you for those words of wisdom, Sister,' said Kuelack sardonically. 'Now go, get to it; you have your tasks. Oh, one more thing, Sister, regarding the diary. I don't suppose you saw anyone suspicious snooping around my old apartment. After all, you were the most frequent visitor?'

Magen turned and, looking directly into her brother's eyes, said with confidence, 'If I had, you would have been the first to know.'

Kuelack sat back in his opulent black chair, and leaning heavily upon the polished tabletop with his chin in his hands, thought on his sister's warning. As much as he hated to admit it, the Hasp was right. Their inane chanting, that he dismissed so easily as the ravings of the demented, had proven true;

You are the fated herald. One Balefire cannot harm another.

With no protection, Vara's attempt on his life should have killed him. How did he know this? His mother's teachings as a child? Also, if he was the fated herald, it must follow that the Male Balefire and the Elemental he'd learnt about during his quest, was true also, and they were the same thing. It all pointed to Alfic's son. Why him? Why was he so special? Why not his son Gabion? After all, he was the son of the most powerful sibling, the youngest wizard to sit on the Sivan?

He thought back to his encounter with Mass Martin. Even if the shards Mass had destroyed had been real, the realisation that he couldn't have used them sat like one of Alfic's unattested challenges. Thanks to the Balefire shard, the fated herald, whoever it may have been, could never have united the stone, let alone use it. It was Pellagrin's ultimate sardonicism.

Cursing, Kuelack slammed his fist down hard upon the tabletop. This put a whole new slant on things, he would have to change his plans, find another way to gain Aridain's trust and turn him into an ally, or, now that he was a Balefire and could wield the shards without any effect, find some way of taking them from him. Again, his sister's warning reverberated through his head.

"Do not underestimate Alfic's son, or fall foul of him. He is a powerful individual."

CHAPTER TWENTY-SIX

IRIDIUM

Beria Dearing looked up from her position sat upon the straw and dirt covered floor with soft brown eyes, as light appeared outside the bars of the door penetrating the darkness of the cell block. Her auburn hair was unkempt, as were her dirty clothes, and her normally well-rounded kind face looked gaunt, and had an unhealthy sheen. Residing with her was the butcher, Keen, and Bern the greengrocer, who looked up with barely disguised anger. Followed by the jailor and two of the school guards, the traitor that they all recognised as Kale, entered. He strolled between the rows of cells lit by the flickering torchlight and peered at the decrepit souls within. When they stopped outside her cell, Beria got to her feet.

'Have you gleaned any useful information?' asked Kale.

'Nothing of use,' replied the jailor. 'They just keep spouting the same mundane rhetoric about how the righteous will prevail, and how Kuelack will not succeed, blah, blah, blah…'

Beckoning to the dirty, sweating student installed as a jailor, Kale said, 'I want our guests kept healthy, idiot. Mistreatment will only make them more defiant.'

'With all due respect, Master Kale, I'm not their nursemaid,' said the student, looking at Beria disdainfully. 'I was put here to gain information, by any means.'

'You'll be a dead student if you don't do as I tell you!'

Withering under Kale's gaze, the jailor quailed, 'Of course.'

Indicating their surroundings, Beria said, 'So this is Kuelack's new utopia, his vision for a better, more prosperous school. Attained by torturing loyal workers and using them as bait.'

'Very clever, quite the spoof, aren't we?'

Grasping the iron bars forcefully and pressing her face against them, Beria said with vehemence, 'This is wrong, our imprisonment here is unlawful.'

'Unlawful, well let's see, shall we? As I recall, Bern talked with Alfic on numerous occasions. The butcher is now a sympathiser of Alfic's family, despite our efforts to convert him, and Magen caught you, Beria, before you could rendezvous with an accomplice. Hardly above-board behaviour.'

Shaking her head, Beria said sadly, 'What happened to you, Kale? I never took you for a turncoat, never thought you could betray your friends like this. You were a staunch supporter of Alfic's. What made you turn to Kuelack? What has he got over you?'

'It's simple, really. I saw the light! I came to realise that..., our resistance could only end in failure, and that it was only a matter of time.'

'I wouldn't be so sure of that,' said Beria knowingly.

As if Beria had not spoken, Kale continued, 'With Sorin now dead and Keegan, Mace and Vanir soon to follow, it's only a matter of time until we try Alfic and his family for treason. Then, when they are executed, Alfic's son will be ours. But there is still hope, for all of you, if you make the right choices. Swear fealty to Kuelack and all will be forgiven.'

'As long as we give you Vara and Ramus!' spat Bern.

'Just treat it like pulling weeds from a garden. Once the "weeds" are gone, they can't spread anymore seeds of insurrection, then we can all get on with our lives.'

'We will never join you, traitor,' roared Bern.

'Or compromise our self-worth,' said Beria with finality.

'I thought not. So here we are, you locked in a cell, and me, out here, fishing for information.'

'Where I come from, it's called torture,' hissed Beria.

'I'm sorry you feel that way; however, I need information.' Turning to the guards, Kale ordered gruffly, 'Bring me the greengrocer!'

'Leave him alone!' shouted Beria, jumping to Bern's defence, and received the flat of a blade to her forehead for her troubles.

Dragged from the overcrowded cell, Bern, kicking and punching desperately, bellowed, 'Bastards, get your hands off of me!' Restrained by the burley guards Bern rasped, 'Torture me all you like, I know nothing of these Firebrand shards or Vara's whereabouts.'

With the cell's occupants looking on, Kale produced a wickedly curved knife.

'What are you doing?' demanded Beria, feeling at the bruise forming on her forehead.

'What I have to do,' said Kale sincerely. 'You see, finger nails grow back and skin heals, but take away a person's senses, well that's something entirely different. Now hold him down.' Pointing the blade at the greengrocer's right eye, he demanded, 'Now tell me, where are the shards, where are the insurgents hiding?'

'Don't do this, Kale,' pleaded Beria. 'Damnation awaits you if you do.'

'It's too late for that,' said Kale indifferently. 'Fornax awaits me with open arms.'

Bern screamed in pain as Kale pressed the knife's point into his eye. 'Tell me what I want to hear.'

'I don't know, damn you,' cried Beria.

'How many of your friends will lose their eyes before you're forced to tell me?'

'OK, OK, stop and I'll tell you.'

'WHERE ARE THE SHARDS,' repeated Kale forcefully, thrusting the dagger's tip further into Bern's left eye.

'I DON'T KNOW,' she retorted, but what I do know is that Vara has Kuelack's diary. You want that too, right?'

'How did she get this diary?' demanded Kale.

'I gave it to Vara in Spalding.'

'And where is she?'

'Vara's a Magnate. In situations like this, she's under no obligation to tell me; that's the truth.'

'So, how did you get a hold of this diary?' asked Kale threateningly.

'Magen gave it to me!'

'Really!'

'Yes, she stole it from Kuelack, but that was before she chose her brother's side, before she captured me and threw me in here.'

Returning the knife to a belt around his waist, Kale ordered, 'Return the greengrocer to the cell and feed them. You have earned you and your friends a reprieve, but should this information prove false...'

Catching Bern, as he was tossed casually back into the cell, Beria and the rest of the prisoners were plunged into darkness once more.

'We mustn't underestimate Kuelack. If he gains knowledge of our plans or someone overhears...'

'But he won't find out Byrak,' threatened Mass, his eyes narrowing as he stared into the sea-green eyes of his student shadowed beneath his mop of mousy hair.

'If we're to stand any chance, Master, your man must kill Kuelack before he can master the shards,' said Byrak darkly.

'Very true, but a smart man keeps his options open. I have safeguards in place and when the time is right, I will unleash those options.'

'Like Hogan and Tallus?'

'Very good Byrak. It seems I have chosen my successor wisely. It will be a simple matter to make a few adjustments so that Hogan and Tallus implicate Kuelack, leaving myself in control. When he returns from his quest, he will be weak, vulnerable, and I'll have the satisfaction of killing Kuelack myself. Then, before his allies realise what's happening, I will take the shards. After all, there's no point in ruling over a blasted desolate ruin. Should I fall, I'm counting on you to see the plan through.'

'If you should fall, the school will suffer my wrath,' growled Byrak...'

Abruptly Mass's quarters began to collapse, retracting and folding in on itself until only his master's face filled his narrowing vision. He prayed for darkness, but his wish wasn't granted, as Mass's face wavered, his features melting and twisting before disappearing abruptly, leaving him with the feeling of being locked in a metal shell. It had been a dream, hadn't it? His mind was playing tricks.

Mind walkers don't have dreams, we invent them; we control them.

Byrak looked out through a narrow slit and it was a few moments before he remembered. He was sitting in the dungeon, strapped to the torturer's wheel, wearing a helmet made of metal.

A face suddenly appeared in the helmet's narrow slit, and he looked into the youthful eyes of Kale, leering at him a few centimetres from his face.

'How did I get here?'

Images of cold frames and hornet flies flashed across his vision, before coalescing and becoming clear, and of Keegan trying desperately to save his friends. He had turned at a noise, but even the speed of thought didn't save him. Before the pain and blackness took him, he had felt his core, his very bones, go cold. He looked up at Kale strangely.

'So, you do remember?'

'Yes, I remember. What I don't understand is how?'

'What is not on this plane of existence, the living can't control. Controlling a living person's mind is one thing, but the dead?'

Again, Byrak looked at Kale strangely. 'What do you want with me?' he enquired. 'Why am I here?'

'You're here to die, but first I need something from you. I want you to rescind the compulsion you placed in Alfic's mind.'

'I will never relinquish my control over Alfic, not until Serac and Kuelack are dead!' Despite his weakness and delirium, Byrak focused in an effort to gain a foothold in Kale's mind, but nothing happened.

Stepping away, his head bowed in contemplation, Kale said, 'Then we both know where we stand. I would have granted you a quick and painless death, but now you will continue to suffer. Now, for you, death is not an option.'

'Gloat whilst you can,' croaked Byrak. 'You're Neanderthalic minds are no match for mine. When I break free'–

'Minds? Who needs minds?' Kale chuckled. 'When are you going to realise that you are no match for Kuelack? The reason your powers will do you no good in here is because we possess one of these,' gloated Kale, banging on the silvery helmet strapped to Byrak's head.

Byrak looked up tiredly, then smiling knowingly, said, 'The iridium helmet… I should have guessed.'

'It's amazing what you can find hanging around the school, if you search long enough.'

'Yet it will not get you what you want. One slip is all it takes, one forgetful moment and Kuelack will die.' Straining against his chains, Byrak spat, 'Kuelack will pay for the murder of my mentor and my fellow psychics, as will you.'

'It's curious don't you think that there are no psychic swordsmen?' said Kale suddenly.

'We have evolved beyond animal brutality; why would we indulge in Neanderthalic fighting when we can coerce lesser species to do it for us? It's a simple matter of evolution, the superior rule over the inferior.'

'Well, this superior being is at my mercy, his face and clothing covered in excrement and dried blood, mine to do with as I please,' smiled Kale. 'Perhaps for every advantage gained, fate has deemed there must be a disadvantage. Take that helmet, for instance. It's made from a rare element stumbled on quite by chance by a warrior that, according to you, was one of the inferior species fighting against Caberartus. Coincidence? Who's to tell? But apparently, as the mind master and his cerebral army made their bid for power, a handful of fleeing warriors fell into a large sinkhole above an old mine. Looking up at their pursuers and waiting for their brains to be squeezed like giant pimples, they stood amazed as, despite the psychic's efforts, their heads remained in one piece. They all died, of course, killed by archers under their control, all except one. You see, the rock that surrounded the chamber where they stood just happened to be infused with the rare element, which actually blocks psychic abilities. You could say the idea literally fell into their laps. Do you know Caberartus was also looking for the Firebrand shards? I wonder how many minds he destroyed trying to gain their location; being one of this so-called master race, he never comprehended that your kind can never unite the stone.'

'Then Caberartus was a fool.'

'Indeed, so why suffer for a fool? It's pointless. Mass Martin and Caberartus are gone, but you are here, enduring the pain that should be theirs.'

Byrak grinned and began to chuckle, then laugh.

'Something amusing? Funny is it, that you are about to die, that your innards are about to be removed from your body and pickled in a jar?'

'You don't know, do you?'

'Know what?'

'My, we have become sloppy. At every turn he's deceived you all, hanging around outside a certain ironmongery stall, following a certain family of a night-time, breaking and entering, meeting with shadowy figures in the dark.'

'Who has? Answer me!'

Byrak continued to laugh.

Suddenly Kale gestured, and Byrak's head slammed backwards against the post at his back. Then, staring at Byrak with eyes the colour of blood, Kale wrapped his hand around Byrak's throat and began squeezing.

'No need... for... violence,' croaked Byrak, 'I have other information. Call it a gesture of good faith.'

'Is this a pathetic attempt to save your neck, Byrak?'

'Yes,' he gagged.

'Unfortunately for you, you're in no position to negotiate. Now tell me who this person is, and perhaps I'll let you live?' demanded Kale fervently.

His breath coming in short wheezy rattles, Byrak declared, 'It's the school's... groundsman, Micas.'

'Continue?'

'Ahh, you see...., I need some... guarantees before I.... divulge that information.'

'How about I don't kill you?'

'If I'm dead... you'll never get... the information,' he croaked.

Suddenly, the pressure eased. 'Tell me more. A reprieve depends on how useful the information is.'

Trying to clear his damaged windpipe, Byrak croaked, 'He's searching for... something, although I didn't... find out what....' When Kale threw him a threatening glance, he continued quickly, 'when I looked into Micas's mind... I found only darkness and emptiness... a black void, if you will. It left me with a profound sense of desolation and despair, like something not of this world was amongst us.'

'Not good enough.'

'I also have another tipple of information regarding Vara Bruin. She's a Balefire witch.'

'You'll have to do better than that?' said Kale, grasping him around the throat once more.

'She's not any old witch. She's a member of the inner circle.'

'A Magnate? Are you positive?'

'Yes.'

'Very good, Byrak. I will pass it on. You see, if you came to me with this information to begin with, we could have avoided all this unpleasantness. You really are a glutton for punishment, Byrak,' smiled Kale.

Then, without another word, Kale, a distant look on his face, drew his cloak about him and hurried from the chamber.

CHAPTER TWENTY-SEVEN

RASBORA

'Rasbora, concentrate; please recite the rules of progression.'

Closing her eyes, Rasbora began reciting tutor Agost's mantra. 'Incantus, the gesture, the will and the word; the gesture, the will and the word; the will and the word; the will.'

Opening her eyes at the flutter of leathery wings, she looked up, as above her several dragonlets circled.

'Well done, Rasbora, you are progressing nicely.'

'Tutor Agost? If the will is the ultimate in magic, what about mind masters? Where do they fit in?'

'Some mages believe that far from being a breed apart, psychics are the next step in magical evolution. Some even theorise that, given time, mind masters could metamorphose into pure intellect.'

'Legend says that the one-eyes were the first mind masters and could control dragons,' said Rasbora.

'That is a fallacy. Long before man populated Zapata, dragons and one-eyed giants fought over this land.'

'How do we know?' she asked.

'We've found fields full of bones sprawled in and around their old blasted ruins. The majority of them were the bones of giants. We can't be sure but we think the one-eyes, in a desperate bid to survive, began searching for the Firebrand stone.'

'So, what happened?'

'As far as we can tell, they never found it.'

'I wonder if the one-eyes still live?' asked Rasbora.

'It is well known that the giants had a proud and ancient history, but like any species they had their time, just like we will have our time, let us just be grateful that the one-eyes are no longer here.'

'Maybe they live in Calabash,' she had said excitedly. 'Maybe that's the reason we haven't seen them?'

'Well, some say that the surviving giants fled further north, and still live in the mountains beyond the snow line, in fortresses made of ice,' said Agost sceptically. Others say they fled west beyond the Monad Mountains.'

'If that's true, then why hasn't anybody seen them? Calabash have dragons and riders just like us, and range over hundreds of leagues.'

'Calabash is not interested in history, or dragons,' spat Agost passionately. 'We are the only realm to revere dragons. Calabash mages control dragon kind, force them to do their bidding. We, on the other hand, have an alliance; an understanding with them.'

Turning to the class, Agost lectured, 'On a side note, legend tells us that a saviour, born of man and dragon, will free dragon kind. Mark my words, children, it is on that day that Calabash's dragons will turn on their masters and have their revenge.'

'But....'

'Enough questions, Rasbora. OK children, repeat after me the *Mantra of Acquiescence* at the top of the page..., power is not power, knowledge is power, but to wield that power effectively you must have patience, for without patience there is chaos, chaos means stumbling around blindly in the dark without direction, and without purpose...'

'Now turn to page thirty-five of Medeosa's Law...'

Rasbora opened her eyes with a start and stared about her, disoriented. With a grimace across her lips, she remembered where she was. Her childhood memories, those happy times as a child, of dragon filled skies and Zapatian grandeur, had been destroyed, like Zapata's ruling families. Just like her heart, they had been betrayed, cast desolate upon the Zapatian tundra, by the Baron's Protectorate, and she intended to find out why.

She looked around at the open countryside, and the dragons laid about the clearing. She then turned to look up at the black, red and silver dragon staring down at her.

'Why the puzzled expression, Draxlar?'

'You seem distressed, Mistress?'

'I'm fine, thank you, just recalling happier times.'

Rasbora looked around at the remaining twelve dragons that, still free from the baron's grip, had heeded her call. Sat peering into the distance were the two greens and browns, Dronard and Barion, Andiron and Natron. Overhead flew the two reds, brothers, Skered and Smilaxion, as well as the three blues Nimrodian, Nawrath and Tabard. Two more had heeded her call, and they were scouting the surrounding area for patrolling dragons controlled by the enemy, they were the two blacks, Necron Wren and Darkon, who had already voiced his protest, that he should be in charge instead of the mighty flame red Draxlar.

'Is the drove rested, Draxlar?'

'Yes,' nodded the magnificent mountain dragon. 'Are you rested, Mistress?'

'I am.'

'Then climb aboard and let's get to it. My brethren are impatient to erase the baron's scum, and the traitorous squills that follow them, from Zapatian history. We just await your direction.'

'We have to be cautious, Draxlar. I'm puzzled as to why Durbarian forces have not advanced; not all is as it seems.'

Laughing in a deep vibrato voice, Draxlar boomed, 'Isn't it obvious? They have no backbone. The once mighty kingdom of Durbah has grown indolent with conformity.'

'I'm not so sure Draxlar, it's as if they are waiting for something.' Hesitantly, Rasbora climbed up Draxlar's offered leg. 'Be mindful, Draxlar, pride comes before a fall.'

Clinging to the spines along Draxlar's back, Rasbora watched in awe as the drove took to the air; the magnificent creatures filling the sky as they followed Draxlar, who, at her bidding, flew south towards the Durbarian border. It was a sight that never failed to impress. Gliding above the Shan Lowlands where the River Shan joined the mighty River Seddon, Rasbora, letting the cold breeze caress her face, smiled briefly as her thoughts returned to the beginning of her journey and the struggle to reach her homeland...

She had left Pellagrin's in the late autumn and had made good progress through the countryside of the King's hunting lands. But as the horses began to struggle up the incline into the Ural Downs, the carriage had slowed and come to a complete stop.

'What's the hold-up, driver?'

'Soldiers, Mistress.'

Poking her head out from the carriage's window, Rasbora peered into the brisk, cold night. Up ahead, soldiers holding torches and dressed in full Gondarian battle armour blocked the road.

'What is your destination?' asked a soldier, peering into the carriage.

'The capital.'

'What is your business there?'

'I'm to provide company for the Baron Pamir, at a dinner dance in three days' time. These delays mean I will be late.'

'Beg pardon, Ma'am, but I'm only carrying out my orders. The sooner we can ascertain that the carriage contains no outlaws or traitors, the sooner you can be on your way.'

'Can you see anyone else in here, moron?' she snapped. 'May I remind you that the baron has injected a huge number of coins into Kuelack's cause? If the baron's kept waiting, Kuelack will be very displeased.'

Looking her up and down, his eyes narrowing, he waved the carriage forward. 'OK, driver, move on.'

As the carriage resumed its journey northwards, she had assumed her real form.

Patience indeed...

Suddenly, Rasbora awoke as Draxlar bellowed, 'Three of the traitorous fire breathing squills and their riders!'

Draxlar banked suddenly as hot scolding flame passed within inches of them.

'Have they reported back?' she yelled above the whistling of the wind.

'Not yet,' roared Draxlar, tilting his head as if listening.

Just then a large grey and blue dragon and its rider swooped low over her head, and the two reds, Skered and Smilaxion turned in pursuit.

'Here comes the other two,' roared Draxlar.

'Get me closer. We have to take them out before they reveal our presence here!' shouted Rasbora.

Rasbora closed her eyes and the riders' saddles, made of leather, attached to the dragons began decaying rapidly, until the riders no longer supported by their seats and harnesses, fell from the dragon's backs and clattered through the branches of the trees below, causing the dragons to follow their riders.

'Head north Draxlar, towards Lanos Rae, before we are discovered.'

'But what of Smilaxion and Skered? We must support them.'

'Calm yourself, Draxlar, the brothers will be fine.'

'But Mistress, our fallen comrades, we must attack, avenge them...'

'Draxlar, these are your brethren and my countrymen. They attack, not knowing the murderous, power-hungry men they serve, and those,' she said pointing to the horizon, 'are storm clouds controlled by wizards.' She then said savagely, 'Believe me when I say we will bring the traitorous barons and their dragons to justice, but to do that, we have to stay alive. At present we cannot win this battle, we are too few and as the Durbarians say, "To fight another day, we must live."'

CHAPTER TWENTY-EIGHT

WARNING SIGNS

Steering Midge through the streets of Spalding, Perak having picked up some supplies from the village, looked from Selva to the dragonlet sat on Aridain's lap. He then turned to look at his ever-present guardian angels as two of Pellagrin's soldiers trotted along at the rear, having insisted on accompanying him to work.

Army patrols were now everywhere. Having assumed a siege mentality, it was as if the village held its breath, as the populace, hurrying from place to place, spoke little and lingered even less, fearful their very presence would bring the guards' wrath down upon them. Closing his eyes, Perak inhaled deeply of winter's crisp atmosphere. He normally loved this time of year when the warming sun, now rising higher in the sky, filtered through the trees. Snowdrops and aconites pushed their way through the snow all about the village, as did wood anemones. These things reminding him that spring was just around the corner. Normally a time of hope and renewal, the military's presence gave the air a sense of oppressiveness, as if a putrid blanket smothered the village.

'My quiet, contented village has become a military outpost,' complained Perak direly.

'Sentimental twaddle, Perak Bruin. You and your village are under Kuelack's protection now.'

The gruffness of the statement received an angry hiss from Sabra, making the guard recoil in alarm.

'Keep that fire breathing squill under control,' growled the guard, looking disapprovingly towards the dragonlet.

'You don't approve of our fiery companion?' inquired Perak.

'Approval has nothing to do with it. Squills are dangerous creatures. They're only good for one thing, harvesting fruit.'

Rolling his eyes, Perak said stubbornly, 'So, are you going to put us to the sword for revelling in the memory of how the village used to be, before my son's thugs turned it into an army barracks,' admonished Perak.

'Just go about your business. The sooner we reach the school, the sooner someone else can take you off my hands.'

Then Selva began crying.

Leaning close, Aridain muttered, 'Don't worry Selva, Grandpop and me will take care of you.'

'I just want to get home,' snapped Selva tearfully.

'Now see what you've done,' rebuked Perak, looking dagger-like in the guards' direction.

Perak glanced sideways at Aridain, who, unsure how to deal with Selva's grief, copied him as he waved and smiled at the familiar faces tending their shops and businesses, their dour faces reflecting the village's mood. Shaking his head irritably, Perak, urging Midge faster, overtook a pair of wagons loaded with barrels with Pellagrin's insignia burnt into the lids.

Leaving the village proper, they passed the allotments, stretching from either side of the roadway. Perak then drove the gelding onward across Spalding Common and past livestock, munching on fresh haylage. Startling a flock of rooks scratching amongst the snow that flew into the air, cawing raucously, they trundled down the incline. Crossing the stone bridge over the stream, they travelled for another half a league across the snow-covered meadowland in gloomy silence, as all around mist rose from the melting snow in the sun's warming rays. However, Perak didn't see any of this, his thoughts once more focused on their predicament.

The school's residents, apart from their close-knit group of friends, were being slowly coerced by fair means and foul. Thanks to Vara's failed attempt on their son's life, Kuelack had tightened his grip on the school and the surrounding area even more; occupying Spalding and the surrounding villages in an attempt to leave no place to go to ground. Lascana had been right, they should have left the school whilst they had the chance, now it was too late. Having turned the surrounding countryside into one vast military district, he knew that Kuelack's next target was his grandson.

Crossing the stream via a shallow ford, Perak looked sideways at Aridain; the lock without a key, the mystery without a solution. He had run away scared when the creature had threatened him, but reacted violently when he and his family were threatened. Was he unaware or just unwilling to acknowledge anything about his struggle with the creature? His grandson had also changed. A macabre strength now possessed him, and not necessarily for the good. Had Aridain's elemental magic mixed with the creature's primordial power? He then looked intently at the dragonlet as it launched itself across the barley field towards a swarm of winter midges.

Forget prophecy, forget being the guide. Why are you really with my grandson, Sabra? thought Perak.

He received a shock when the dragonlet replied.

To repay a debt.

'Grandpop, I think we're being followed, 'said Aridain abruptly.

'Followed. Are you sure?'

'Uh huh.'

'Who is he? Do you know?'

'It's not a he, Grandpop.'

'A woman then?'

Aridain shook his head. 'It's a nasty.'

'A nasty!' exclaimed Selva, looking around panicked. 'Where?'

Turning to the soldiers, Perak said, 'My grandson says we're being followed by a "Nasty"?'

'Yeh right, do you think we were born yesterday?'

'I'm being serious,' said Perak. 'It's his word for monster.'

'A nasty,' chuckled the soldier, looking at Perak. 'What do you take us for?'

'I always heed my grandson's instincts. I think you should check it out.'

The two men looked at Perak, then at each other, then one soldier, turning his mount, said, 'Very well, I'll check it out.'

Waiting beneath the trees whilst the soldier galloped back towards the stream, a noise behind them convinced Perak to take no chances. Flicking the reins, Perak spurred Midge forwards.

'Hey,' shouted the soldier, 'come back here!'

The cart's suspension working overtime, they were tossed around like grain in a wheat separator as they fled, the guard hot on their heels. Emerging from the wood, Perak encouraged Midge even faster, the trap bouncing over the ruts and troughs, threatening to vibrate the children's lightweight bodies onto the mud-covered track.

Steering them down the incline past the burnt ruins of Aridain's former home, the guard, now caught up, hauled on the reins. 'I ordered you to stop!'

It was only when they reached the bridge over the stream however, that Perak planted his foot firmly on the brake and brought Midge to a stop as the giggling children, having composed themselves once more, sat themselves back down, now that the rough ride had stopped; which suited the gelding, but not the children.

'I'm in charge here! You will do as I command,' shouted the guard, pulling his sword from its holster and pointing it aggressively. 'Do not try to escape again.'

'Escape? As if I would do such a thing.' Seeing the guard's sceptical look, Perak, reinforcing the lie, insisted, 'I was concerned for the children.'

His eyes, the colour of onyx, Aridain turned to the guard. 'I'm sorry, mister, but you won't see your friend again. He's gone.'

'What do you mean, gone?' exclaimed the guard. 'Perak, how does he know that?'

'Don't ask me,' replied Perak.

'We'll wait here!' ordered the guard, watching Aridain curiously.

They waited in the eerie silence on the bridge, bathed in dappled sunlight, the only sound, the trickling of water over the stream's bed. Then they heard a gruff snuffling sound, followed by the breaking of twigs. Drawing his sword, the guard looked back towards the trees.

'Don't do it, it's not worth your life,' advised Perak.

After a moment's thought, the guard announced self-importantly. 'We will carry on towards the school.'

Spurring Midge up the hill, Perak steered the gelding along the road between the topmost fields. As they reached the first of the two gates, Perak, shading his eyes against the sun lancing through the chestnut trees, gave the reins to Aridain.

Perak, jumping down and undoing the first of the two gates, said sarcastically, 'Just sit on your horse and watch; why don't you?'

'I'm not your nursemaid. I'm here to ensure your compliance,' retorted the guard gruffly.

Urging Midge forwards, the trap's wheels crunching through ice covered puddles, Aridain expertly navigated the carriage through the second gate. Taking the reins once more, Perak dropped Selva and Aridain outside the farmhouse, the ever-present shadow of Pellagrin's guard following him. He then spurred Midge along the frozen track towards the farmyard and the ever-demanding animals.

Mira stood and stared out through the kitchen window to the garden beyond the glasshouse, the ominous mist that had shrouded the garden now evaporated in the bright sunshine. As astonishing as it seemed, despite her disbelief at headquarter's claims, the Balefire Taal was her sister's grandson. What had made this rumour even more evident was Aridain's bearing and his mannerisms. It wasn't something physical, but there was something about him, a quality she could not place. Besides, how many children had a dragonlet as a companion...

'So, I'm assuming the dragonlet is the companion to the Taal,' she had asked earlier, as she, together with Perak, had sat at the kitchen table eating breakfast while the children sat quietly reading and drawing.

Perak had looked up, concern written all over his face. 'So, this is the reason why you're here, to gather information, to report back to the coven, to take my grandson away.'

'Perak, wait, I....'

'Because you know I won't let that happen.'

'You would think that of me?'

'You've been away for a long time. A lot can happen, people change.'

'Or some just become more resolute, more determined to do what's right. Regardless of how long I have been gone, I am still my mother's daughter. Taking a long gulp of tea, she had said resolutely, 'Understand Perak, Balefire kind have been awaiting the Balefire prophecy for millennia.'

'The Balefire prophecy is the same as the prophecy, is it not?'

'Balefire prophecy, yes, but this is a Hasp prophecy, a blood prophecy, and they will stop at nothing to see it fulfilled.'

'The worst thing we can do is treat Aridain like a precious flower in winter's chill. Aridain must be allowed to enjoy what remains of his childhood. Wrapping him in cotton wool will only prove detrimental.'

'Perak, the prophecies have been deciphered. The Hasp will take your grandson by fair means or foul. Under their control and subject to their will, he would not destroy the stones. Instead, he would unite the Firebrand shards. It's the reason I need to speak with Vara, Perak. Believe me, if the Hasp knew I warned you of this, they would want me killed.'

'Then, it's a good job we're returning to Pellagrin's school. It's the lesser of two evils, but it's safer than Spalding.' Perak had smiled then and said, 'You really have become the wisest witch, haven't you...?'

A dragon lord centuries dead, and a dragonlet, charged with the Taal's protection. It seemed ridiculous, but there it was. Now, left to deal with whatever was to come, she now faced a host of memories and feelings; feelings akin to the comfort she felt when Perak had protected them from their drunken father. Other memories, however, were not so welcoming, like her and her sisters' Balefire magic coming to the fore as they hit puberty. It wasn't long after that when the coven had come knocking at the door.

With her shoulder, Mira nudged the front door open and carried the buckets hooked to a yoke outside. Setting the buckets down next to the wooden barrels, she filled them with water, then returned to the house. Placing them by the fire ready for the new day, she checked that all was in order. She then put the kettle on for one last cup of tea before she continued on to Leardon.

It was then that an unfamiliar sound issued from outside, an unfamiliar snuffling and grunting sound that just didn't belong.

Wrapping her shawl around her shoulders, she made her way through the kitchen and out into the glasshouse. Unlocking the door, she peered out into the garden, her imagining conjuring shapes that moved just out of eyesight.

Just then the kettle whistled its shrill proclamation, making her jump. Returning to the kitchen, she shook her head and smiled, 'Honestly, Mira, you're supposed to be a Balefire.'

Folding a square of towelling, she wrapped it around the handle and poured the steaming water into a teapot. She then set it down next to a jug of milk and a small jar of honey and a china cup. Carrying the set into the living room, Mira placed the tray and its contents gently down upon a small table in the living room in front of the fire. It was then that she heard a second unfamiliar noise, only this time it had come from the kitchen. Grasping the fire poker, she crept into the hallway.

There it was again, faint but audible, only this time it was things being moved.

'Who is it? Who's there?' she hissed.

Receiving no answer, she pressed herself against the hallway wall. Her heart pounding, she raised the poker and closed her eyes. Appearing suddenly, she ran into the kitchen and looked around desperately for the intruder she was convinced was there, but all was as it should be and everything was in its place. She quickly began opening drawers until she came upon one she knew was filled with a series of small round egg-sized packages, wrapped in dried borage leaves. Putting the packages in her pocket, she then picked up Vara's hefty rolling pin, made of solid beechwood. There it was again, only upstairs this time. About to proceed, she saw movement out of the corner of her eye. Stilling her racing pulse and rapid breathing, Mira opened the front door and peered cautiously out into the garden. Keeping to the shadows, Mira crept out into the lane and came upon a body. She leant close and watched as blood slowly stained the snowy ground. Turning the body onto its back, she realised it was a soldier that had been guarding the house, and his throat was cut. She looked up then and saw a stooped, cloaked figure stood in the lane. Stilling her racing pulse and rapid breathing, Mira grasped the wooden rolling pin tightly and then crept slowly beside the hedge until she was level with a tall figure; it seemed totally oblivious to her presence.

With a hiss, the stooped figure turned and looked at her, the cowl falling from its head. 'Who dares?'

Mira stared at the craggy, gnarly face. 'What are you doing here, hag?' she hissed. She knew exactly why the yellow hag was here, so why had she asked that question? Perhaps it was an attempt to hide her fear?

Gritting her teeth, she bellowed, 'You will not have him.' Putting her fear to one side, Mira ran and tackled the hag to the floor. Then, with one quick movement, Mira hit the hag over the head with the solid rolling pin. Sat upon its chest, she began raining blows upon the creature now squirming in the snow. Only the hag seemed not to feel the impacts at all. The creature then grasped the rolling pin, and wrenching it from Mira's hand, threw it aside. Grasped by the throat, Mira gagged as the yellow hag squeezed.

'He will make a fine Balefire Taal. It's just a pity you won't be alive to see him on the throne after I ingest your flesh and consume your power...'

The hag then opened its mouth, and with unworldly strength, drew her inexorably towards two rows of sharp gnashing teeth. But before the hasp could bite down on her flesh, Mira reached into her pocket, and producing one of the golf-ball sized spheres, wrapped in borage leaves, rammed it into the hag's gaping maw. She then clamped the hasp's jaws together with her hand, crushing the sphere within. With a look of surprise, the hasp tried desperately to expel the object, but Mira held on with all her might as the ball of phosphorous, mixing with the moisture in the hag's mouth, ignited. Mira covered her face, and leapt sideways as the scorching, purple fiery jumping-jack began melting the inside of the hasp's mouth. The substance contracting the muscles in its face, the yellow hag began screeching like an insane hyena from an emaciated mouth.

Climbing to her feet and dousing her smoking robes, Mira looked towards the hag that had spat out the volatile substance. To her chagrin, the hag, now burning fiercely, sat upright and tried to climb to its feet once more. Loath to see any creature suffer, Mira grasping a second borage wrapped bomb, thrust it into the hag's open mouth. She watched in morbid fascination as the bomb, ignited by the first, began burning, only this time with an intense yellow flame. The second bomb that she recognised as sodium, and the opposite of phosphorous, undertook its morbid task, and the hag's face began to bloat. Unable to turn away, Mira watched entranced as, with an astonished look engrained on its face, the yellow hag screamed one final time. The hag's skin, unable to contain the swollen muscles within, expanded to bursting point, and with a dull pop, the hag's skull disintegrated. The headless creature then flopped forward onto the frozen snow, surrounded by a blood-red star halo.

She looked up suddenly at another sound, and reaching for the rolling pin, crawled along the hedge, and watched as a second cloaked figure emerged from the garden.

The second figure looking around said, 'Clever! But you are not clever enough, Vara Bruin. Acumen Monssssstera will have your grandsssson. It is his destiny. Then, convinced it was alone, the creature, crouching down, began exploring the dead hag's body.

Mira watched with a look of revulsion as the yellow hag took out a sharp instrument and stabbed it into the dead hag's arm. Chanting softly then, the hag, like a perverted vampire, began sucking on what Mira realised was the stem from a clay pipe. She watched in silence as, having had its fill, the hag wiped the flecks of blood from its thin bleached lips.

Were there more? Were there only two? Fearful now that the creature would travel to the school and seek Perak's grandson, she leapt over the hedge.

Racing down the path, she dashed into the kitchen. She then stopped and looked around frantically. It wasn't until she turned towards the stairs that she saw an opening in the wall that had not been there before. It was obviously a place Vara stored dangerous ingredients. Searching the tall narrow cupboard, everything seemed in order, and many of the ingredients remained, monkshood for example, woad, foxglove and Navarian orchid, to name a few. However, the very bottom shelf looked suspiciously empty. Had the hasp found what it was looking for? Picking up some choice items and placing them in her travelling bag, Mira, checking the house was secure, ran out into the lane after the remaining hag.

Having made good time across the common and the meadow, Mira, reaching Farend Wood, walked cautiously through the trees, alert for any movement or deception; a grenade wrapped in borage leaves clasped tightly in her hand. But as thoroughly as she searched for the yellow hag, there was no sign. It had disappeared like smoke into a foggy morning. Abruptly she heard the snorting of horses followed by feeble groaning further along the path. Ducking down in between a series of small earthy hummocks that she discovered was a badger set, Mira emerged warily from her hiding place, and keeping her bag of Balefire weapons handy, crept down the path. Scanning the woods, the path took a sharp turn. On the path, two horses, tethered to a supply wagon, were serenely cropping on what foliage they could find under the snow. Using the wagon as cover, she saw two bodies laid on the woodland floor. Creeping closer, nervously, she discovered one was a soldier, and checking for a pulse, she realised he was dead. The other, moaning quietly, she assumed, was the driver. Approaching the horses, she calmed them with a word, then scanning her surroundings once more, attended to the comatose figure. He was alive and had no apparent injuries, but no matter how hard she tried, she could not revive him. Suspicious now, she scanned the load that was all there and intact, so this wasn't bandits?

Then the wood became shrouded in an inky black mist so substantial that it was almost solid, that clung to her skin like clammy fingers. Immediately Mira realised the dominion of a goshen. Suddenly, an intense point of blackness formed over the driver's prone, ashen, lifeless body, and from it emerged a wrath like creature. Sheathed in a long dirty-white ragged shroud, cursing and spewing obscenities in a crow-like voice, the goshen leered at Mira, gesturing and threatening dramatically with its skeletal arms and its elongated skull-like head.

'Mira Scosa! Oh yes, I know you followed me. I have conjured this goshen as a reminder to stay out of the Hasp's way.'

'I will not renounce my duty as a Balefire, because you conjure an undead spirit.' Encountering only silence, Mira addressed the goshen. 'Return to your realm, wretched plaything of the Hasp,' commanded Mira, 'or I will banish you from this world and the next.'

'Why would I do that? Human kind is so vibrant and full of life, and I am strong with this human's suffering, his immorality. Be gone whilst you still have yours.'

Suddenly, Mira threw a handful of sparkling powdered silver into the air, and everything happened at once; the horses panicked, as the goshen issuing an unholy howl, disappeared with a pain-wracked shriek. Wrapping her arms and legs around the wagon master's comatose body, she rolled the driver who was a third heavier than her, into the undergrowth, as the horses, their eyes wild and their ears pinned back, galloped past, causing the wagon now slewing out of control, to spew its load across the track. This caused the horses to panic even further, and the whole ensemble disappeared into the woods.

Mira knew the silver powder would not stop the goshen, but it would give her the vital time needed to do what she must. Taking a pearl of moonstone, she placed it around the man's neck. Then she drank a hastily mixed herbal infusion to help her fight the goshen, should it try to possess her. Next, she collected together some ingredients found in her bag, then began quickly blending them together in her portable mortar and pestle that every witch carried as standard.

A goshen, she knew, could not exist without negative energy. A criminal, a serial killer, she knew not what this man was, but not only did they feed off of their foul behaviours, but actively encouraged more.

I just hope what I have will be enough, she thought.

Without warning, the goshen returned, howling its displeasure, and when the spectre realised it could no longer access the link with its victim, it panicked, throwing bits of smashed crates and their spilled contents in her direction. Ignoring the flying debris and the goshen's baleful howling and suggestive taunts, Mira, chanting, sat down next to the man's inert form.

By the power of the full moon and the power invested in me,
I command you. Be gone from this place, to infest no more,
the fabrics of this world, its occupants, and this realm.
I am a Balefire witch of the Coven Select, and I banish you
to the dark realm from whence you came. I banish you from
this world and the next.

As the barrier slowly strengthened and the flying fragments ceased, Mira placed a small quantity of ground diamond together with mineral labrodite in a small earthenware bowl, and hung it over a burning candle along with ground up amethyst, garnet and pyrite. When the powder gave off a vapour, Mira placed the evaporating liquid next to the sleeping figure, and whilst repeating the chant, she wafted the mist over his face with a fan. There was a minute clap of thunder as a vortex of air appeared, that sucked all that was the goshen and its realm into its small, undulating core, and with one last futile scream, the goshen disappeared along with the remnants of its domain.

Heaving a silent sigh of relief, Mira slumped tiredly over the body. Her task unfinished, she raised the man's head and produced a funnel. Rousing the man sufficiently to swallow, Mira poured in a cure-all infusion of burdock, hawthorn berries and fennel.

Wearily, Mira then searched the air for any sign of the dark matter that might signal the creature's return, and finding nothing, smiled thankfully. She then turned to the stranger and felt his pulse. His breathing, she noted, was less sporadic and his skin had lost its ashen hue. Nodding and grunting satisfactorily, she then took a small mouthful of the cure-all herself.

'Where am I? What the hell happened,' exclaimed the driver, opening his eyes suddenly and peering about nervously, 'Who are you?'

'A Balefire. Do you remember what happened?'

His eyes searching but not seeing, he said, 'I remember urging the horses forward; then the woodland went dark, and the creature attacked. It was horrific,' he said, 'like something from a nightmare.' Looking around fearfully, he asked, 'Is it gone?'

'Yes,' placated Mira.

'Where's Stones?'

'Your companion?'

The man nodded.

'I fear he's dead.'

'Where's my load, my horses?'

'Follow the debris trail. Hopefully, there are soldiers patrolling the fields, they should find it, if it's still in one piece?'

'One piece! Do you know how much money's tied up in that load?'

'If I were you, I'd just be thankful you're alive.'

Preying on evil and wickedness, perhaps Goshen weren't such a bad idea after all, she thought, glancing distrustfully at the thickset man. *They could do with releasing them at the school and save us all a job. At least there, they'd have plenty to feed on.*

CHAPTER TWENTY-NINE

FRIEND OR FOE

Aridain was sad because Selva had run away in a storm, accusing him of taking Duran's side. Even more annoying, Duran played alongside him in the sand pit as if nothing was amiss.

'Come on Aridain, this is fun,' Duran shouted, throwing himself from a large wooden barrel that stood close by, spraying sand across the path as he landed and slid down the sand heap.

'But what about Selva?' worried Aridain.

'She ran away, didn't she?' said Duran angrily. 'She never wants to play boys' games and always tries to boss us around,' complained Duran, his face taking on that petulant look that always infuriated Aridain. 'You're always trying to please Selva. You're so sissy sometimes, just tell her to go away and that you want to play boys' games.'

Aridain looked at Duran sympathetically. 'My mum says I've got to be understanding, she said to put myself in your shoes. Selva's sad. I know I would be if my dad was killed. We can all play together, Duran. Selva wants to!'

'Well, I don't want to,' Duran said, staring moodily at the sand whilst sifting it through his fingers.

'I'll play with you, but you'll have to put up with Sabra.'

'OK,' he smiled. 'I'll play with you and the dragonlet if you don't play with Selva,' Duran said deviously.

Aridain sighed; He couldn't win. If he promised to play with Selva, Duran got nasty, and if he played with Duran, Duran wanted to exclude Selva, Duran had even conveniently forgotten about his dislike for Sabra. All he tried to do was play with the twins equally, but no matter what he said, or as hard as he tried, he couldn't make them happy.

Just then, their bone of contention appeared overhead, and settling upon the apex of a slated roof opposite the sand pit, Sabra began licking his scaly lips and cleaning his leathery body.

Abruptly, there was a loud anger filled hiss and Aridain, looking up in fright, saw Sabra encased in a dark transparent bubble, tumbling helplessly through the air. To Aridain's horror, Kale, with intricate gestures of his hands, stood drawing the bubble toward him, then with an almost evil grin, he brought his hands together. To Aridain's consternation, the bubble slowly began to contract.

'Kale, what are you doing?' Aridain screamed. 'You're hurting Sabra!'

'Aridain!' blurted Kale, looking down at him with an annoyed frown. Releasing the struggling dragonlet, Kale looked at the grinning Duran and said impassively, 'I thought Duran here was in danger.'

With a loud hiss the enraged dragonlet, its body now the colour of a shimmering red flame, spat fire at Kale, who threw up his cloak protectively.

'Sabra no!' shouted Aridain, stepping between them.

Veering away, albeit reluctantly, Sabra hissed, *The man with the name like a vegetable tried to kill me, youngling.*

'Mr Kale, why did you do that?' insisted Aridain angrily.

Pausing for a moment, Kale, watching the flame-red, pint-sized dragonlet that stared back at him balefully from its perch upon the equipment shed's roof, said apologetically, 'I'm sorry, is, umm, Sabra all right?'

'The dragonlet's not very friendly,' complained Duran. 'It attacked me too.'

'You threw a log at me,' Aridain said accusingly.

'So why don't you like the dragonlet, Duran?' Kale asked, squatting down in between them. 'Oh, I get it. You're jealous, jealous that Aridain prefers the dragonlet to you.'

'No!' Duran exclaimed hastily. 'Why would I be jealous of that thing? Wild animals don't belong here; it should be killed. Were you going to kill it, Mr Kale?' said Duran hopefully.

'No, of course not, just remove it from the grounds.'

'Pity, you should have had it killed,' said Duran smugly.

You call this pouchling your friend? interrupted the dragonlet angrily.

Not anymore, stated Aridain as he listened to Duran, who was busy listing things wrong with Sabra and wild animals in general.

'Right Duran, that's it. I was told to feel sorry for you and to try to be your friend, but you're not sorry at all that your father's dead, shouted Aridain angrily, 'You're just a nasty bully who only cares about himself. From now on, I will be playing with Selva.' Aridain then stomped angrily across the yard, between the workers busily repairing the fire-damaged glasshouse, and out onto the playing field through the snow.

"Aridain, wait!' shouted Kale. 'I need to discuss something important with you.'

As Kale hurried after the youngling, Treerinks watched the Corvus boy, who with fists curled, stared balefully towards Aridain, whilst poking out his tongue spitefully. Deciding that from now on he would keep a watchful eye on Duran, Treerinks turned his attention to the Animistic.

Flying in close attendance, Treerinks studied the human called Kale, experiencing the same feeling of distrust he always felt when dealing with adult humans. Something was not quite right. It was Kale; but it wasn't. Something was different about him.

You know Kale's lying, youngling! Sabra insisted. *And you know that he was trying to kill me.* Staying very close now, Treerinks followed and listened.

'You're acting very strangely, Mr Kale?' said Aridain suddenly.

'So would you, if you'd tried to communicate with a Zircon worm,' laughed Kale. Realising his joke had fallen on deaf ears, he elaborated. 'They spew an obnoxious gas, muddles the brain,' indicated Kale with a twirl of his fingers against his forehead. Then, with a puzzled frown, he asked, 'So Aridain, how come you befriended the dragonlet?'

'Didn't my dad tell you?'

Kale shook his head.

'I'm not surprised. He doesn't like Sabra very much either,' said Aridain miserably. 'I saved Sabra from a cruel man at the fair. He was a bad Animistic like you; well, not exactly like you, and he was keeping Sabra and the other creatures in dirty cages. They were all starving.'

'Did you and Duran let them go?' asked Kale, concentrating and watching Aridain carefully.

'No! Duran's a scaredy cat, besides he was at home being punished for throwing an apple at my head,' growled Aridain. 'Duran's always angry and always throwing things at me; he's mean.'

Youngling, does this Kale always try to look into your mind when he meets you?

I don't remember, but don't worry, I won't let him, thought Aridain innocently.

'I fancy a walk in the woods. Care to join me?' smiled Kale.

'I want to, but mum and dad have told me not to.'

'Your mum and dad trust me, don't they?'

'Well...' replied Aridain hesitantly.

'Do you trust me?'

'I guess?'

'Then, let's go.'

Soaring above the fields, the air was cold on his hot skin. It was the reason dragon kind loved northern and temperate climes. It was so much more comfortable; the cold made him and his kind feel more alert, more alive. Revelling in the freedom of flight, Treerinks dropped lower, skimming the earth towards a swarm of echo bugs. With a jet of flame, he opened his crocodilian jaws, scooping the incinerated insects into his mouth, startling deer and rabbits cropping on the grass, and scattering a flock of panicked wood pigeons into the air.

Licking his lips, Treerinks followed Aridain as he led Kale eagerly through the trees, the rays of the noon-day sun causing the blanket of snow on the woodland floor to shimmer like diamonds. Settling in the branches above, Treerinks, realising a worrying fact, warned, *If he is an Animistic, youngling, then why can't he hear us?*

Sabra, now you're just being silly. Perhaps he's just not listening?

Gazing around the canopy, Kale said, 'There's an ancient magic here. It's in the ground, the trees and in the very air we are breathing. Can you not feel it, Aridain? I don't suppose you know the reason for these changes?'

'Of course I do, so do you?'

After a few moments of silence, Kale declared, 'Of course, the sapphire sprites, I was there in the grove when you and the creature joined. Tell me, what does pure evil feel like, Aridain?'

'What do you mean, Mr Kale?'

'You know, when you and the creature merged, how did it feel?'

'I don't want to talk about it.'

'That's a shame. Joined, you must have felt powerful and unstoppable.'

'Where's the fun in that?' said Aridain, looking up at Kale innocently. 'The nasty died sad and lonely.' Then more upbeat, Aridain said, 'Come on Mr Kale, I haven't seen my friends in a while. You can meet them if you like?'

Treerinks gazed balefully at Kale. It seemed to the dragonlet, almost as if Kale were convincing himself of his own words, as if he was listening to a separate voice in his head.

All too soon, they reached the grove and Treerinks flew through the branches, watching. Closing his eyes and reaching out as he always did, Aridain stood confidently beside the cherry tree sapling. However, his smile soon turned to a frown and, with a perplexed look on his face, shouted, 'They won't come down. I told them who you are, but they're scared. They say you are different now.'

'Different! That's ridiculous,' chuckled Kale.

Now more than ever, Treerinks, convinced that something was amiss, shouted into the youngling's mind, *They don't trust him, youngling. If you won't listen to me, listen to them!*

Ignoring Sabra, and mistaking Kale's caution for disappointment, Aridain said, 'Don't be sad, Mr Kale. Grownups locked them away, and they were treated badly for a long time.'

'Can't you talk to them? Tell them I mean them no harm.'

'It might be to do with my recent struggles with the creature, but I'll try again if you like?' said Aridain helpfully.

And I'm the spawn of a scarrion lizard, youngling! retorted Sabra.

'It's all right. This is my friend, Kale. He won't hurt you!' shouted Aridain into the surrounding trees.

When the sprites still failed to appear, Aridain looked disappointed. 'My dad says I shouldn't choose creatures over humans. He says sprites are scarce because their magic causes confusion and disorder, that they disrupt the natural order of things,' said Aridain, carefully mouthing the complicated words. 'But my grandpop says they are part of nature and that they make the world a better place.'

'And what do you think?' asked Kale.

'I think my dad is very angry at the moment. He has a bad man inside his head.'

'A bad man? What do you mean?'

Youngling, I implore you, don't tell him another thing.

Be quiet, Sabra. Everyone keeps telling me what not to do, but Kale is my friend and he listens to me.

'A bad man that won't leave him alone,' continued Aridain, juggling the two conversations simultaneously.

'Remarkable,' nodded Kale. 'Have you done any other remarkable things recently, Aridain?' asked Kale, following the youngster along the well-defined path.

'Well, I found out I can fly with sparrow hawks and buzzards. Grandpop called it Trans... trans.. habit..'

'Transhabitation.'

That's right, and when I climbed Pellagrin's oak tree with Duran, a strange woman talked to me.'

'Strange woman?'

'Yes, in a dream. She wore a mask and was dressed in long dark red robes and was in a large, round, blue and green room, but it wasn't scary.'

'Can you tell me more about this woman?'

Alighting on a branch above their heads, Treerinks hissed menacingly.

'Stop hissing Sabra, you're being rude,' admonished Aridain.

Your so-called friend is not to be trusted, Treerinks hissed.

'Ignore him, Mr Kale. He's always grumpy. He is over a hundred years old after all.'

'Who is?'

'Sabra.'

'Is he really, although I am intrigued as to how he talks to us? They've never been known to obey humans,' said Kale.

Did you hear that, youngling? What do I have to do to convince you?

'Oh no, Sabra's with me because he wants to be.'

His skin now a strange mottled greeny-red, Treerinks demanded, *As your guardian, I order you to stop talking to this human.*

'Intriguing,' said Kale. 'I'll tell you what? When you're old enough, you could help me learn about the creatures I keep and I could teach you magic. Would you like that?'

Sabra, his skin now a flame-red, indicating his level of frustration, watched as Aridain continued to ignore him. 'Oh yes,' Aridain said, nodding vigorously, 'as long as they're not in cages.'

'Then it will be done,' said Kale resolutely.

'So where do you keep your animals?' asked Aridain. 'You don't work at the school anymore.'

'A secret place.'

'What kind of animals do you have, Mr Kale?'

'Unusual ones. I have piranha bats, Zircon worms and a woad spider.'

'They're strange things to have as pets.'

'Beauty is in the eye of the beholder, Aridain. We like what we like. All animals, regardless of their tendencies, deserve to live.'

'My dad says that some animals should be killed because they cause nothing but harm.'

'We tend to attach human values to the creatures of the wild, when in fact we should see them for the way they truly are, wild and instinctive. Who's to say what is good and what is evil? It's all a matter of perspective.'

Sabra followed the pair to the stream, but no matter how many times Aridain asked, no sprites replied or appeared, apart from the occasional echo bug or mischievous woodland imp.

Turning abruptly towards Aridain, Kale squatted down in front of him, and searching his face, said, 'We're friend's, right, and friend's don't lie to each other.'

Aridain nodded.

'As you know, I was searching for the dark creature and now that creature is destroyed.'

'Yes, I know,' replied Aridain darkly.

'It's my belief that the creature pursued you for a reason. Do you know why?'

Aridain began to cry. 'Yes,' he said.

Sensing Aridain's uneasiness talking about an experience he was trying desperately to forget, Sabra said urgently, *youngling, no, he cannot see the shards, no one can.*

He won't steal them, Sabra. He's my friend.

Smiling, Kale continued, a wistful look upon his face. 'Lord Pellagrin himself entrusted me with your safety; if I'm to help you further, I need to know what the creature was after. Only then can I teach you how to protect yourself. Do you understand?'

Reaching into his inside pocket, Aridain said, 'I would like that, because I don't trust Auntie Magen.'

He then took out the silk bag.

Youngling, no!

Aridain looked up then as Kale reached for the bag. But Kale wasn't quick enough as suddenly Treerinks darted from the branch, snatching the silken bag from Aridain's hand, before disappearing into the trees.

'Sabra, what are you doing?' shrieked Aridain.

What I must. He cannot have them, nobody can.

'Sabra, give them back,' demanded Aridain. When there was no reply, he screamed, 'YOU NASTY DRAGONLET, COME BACK HERE!'

Finding a place to cross the stream, Aridain waded through the freezing water to a shallow gravel bank. Then, with the aid of some roots, he frantically pulled his small but wiry body up the opposite bank into the woodland on the far side. Calling the dragonlet's name, Aridain sprinted up the rise through the snow-covered undergrowth, the woods now dominated by beech, oak and sweet chestnut trees.

Immerging into a large diffusely lit clearing, Kale's voice calling after him in the distance, Aridain began searching the trees.

'I know you're here, Sabra! That wasn't very nice; what you did. They are mine to keep,' despaired Aridain.

Taking notice of me now, are you? intruded the dragonlet's exasperated thoughts. *If I hadn't done what I did, that man, whoever he is, would now have the shards.*

Kale is not a 'whoever'; he is my friend, lectured Aridain, walking towards a medium-sized beech tree and gazing up into the many branches growing at regular intervals from the trunk.

Then why didn't he know that we talked? I am your guardian, and I will not apologise for keeping you or the Siamang safe and out of the hands of men. Now what are you doing?

Climbing, Aridain declared moodily.

Why?

Because I want my shiny stones back.

Why go to all that effort? I could just as easily fly down to you.

Because I like climbing.

Joining the dragonlet, Aridain held out his hand. 'Give me my shiny stones,' commanded Aridain in a voice filled with menace.

Droping the silken bag into Aridain's outstretched hand, Sabra said compliantly, *You are the keeper of the shards and I cannot disobey you if you wish it, but you have to keep the shards safe, youngling, don't give them to anyone.*

Just then, Kale entered the clearing and demanded, 'Aridain, where are you?'

About to respond, Aridain looked at Sabra, but the dragonlet shook its head resolutely. *Don't answer, youngling!*

'I'm your friend, remember?' shouted Kale. 'You have nothing to fear from me.'

Looking at Sabra's wise and wisdom-filled eyes, Aridain decided to stay quiet and watch, as Kale began desperately searching the clearing, kicking frustratedly at dead logs and branches.

'Aridain, I know you're here. Come out now, this game has gone on for long enough.'

Silently they watched as a darkness formed around Kale's hands as he curled them into fists, and with a shout of rage he swore, 'Curse that fire breathing squill.' With an effort, Kale calmed himself. 'Oh well, it matters not. Now that I know the shards' location, they will soon be ours…'

Waiting until Kale had left, Aridain a tear in his eye turned to Sabra, 'You were right. Kale is a bad man.'

Of course I was, now, being right all the time has made me hungry. Is there food here?

'No, not unless you like old beech nuts. Sabra, I've decided your life must be horrible. You don't trust anyone, and you're grumpy all the time. There must be something you like doing?'

I like stalking and killing my prey.

'And how does that make you feel?'

Exhilarated.

'Well, that's sort of like fun. Some people find killing fun, but they're not very nice, though.'

Yes, I've noticed, mainly we keep away from humans if we can; most have no honour. In all the lands, you are the only species who kill your own kind for pleasure.

'Yes, my dad says, "We should learn to live together, then the world would be a much better place, and that hardship forges bonds of friendship",' said Aridain, trying to remember his father's words, ' "It galvanises people to fight against a common enemy".' Ooowwwww.'

Nearly falling from the branch, Aridain held on tightly as he searched frantically for the source of the pain.

A bees' nest, youngling; and you said there was no food up here! thought Sabra happily, as with a lick of flame and a flick of his leathery wings, he gathered the bees efficiently into his mouth, as the insects dozy in the cold winter air, spilled from a small recess in the trunk of the beech tree, beneath the branch Aridain had been sat upon.

Swiping at the remaining insects that continued to attack, despite Sabra's attentions, Aridain, now very scared, scrambled down the tree as fast as he could. His frantic waving, however, combined with the slick branches, resulted in him losing his grip, and with his arms windmilling wildly, Aridain plummeted to the ground.

CHAPTER THIRTY

THE DREAM

Sat upon a cushioned and padded litter, and carried by four shrouded figures, one on each corner, Aridain, looked around through a syrupy turquoise light. He was in a vaulted chamber, supported by luxuriant columns that arched above ornate balconies and cloistered alcoves. Interspersed with the balconies and alcoves were murals and frescos that looked down upon a raised dais, above a large circular star design on a turquoise and white inlaid floor. Around this dais, and the cauldron-shaped throne at its centre, were eight hooded figures sat upon silk embroidered cushions.

Recognising the figure wearing the ornate mask from his previous dream, Aridain took the offered hand and stepped from the litter. The figure then led him up a series of steps towards a chair embellished with silk cushions and embroidered covers.

'At last, the mind that hides inside the body returns to the star circle within the sanctum,' said the figure. 'We rejoice in your triumph, as prophecy foretold. You have defeated the Dark creature, now you must take your rightful place amongst the sisterhood.'

In this syrupy dream world, Aridain, from his seated position, looked up at the masked figure stood beside him to the chanting figures laid prostrate at the base of the dais. Pulling back their hoods, they revealed emaciated faces that reflected longing and a debased craving. That was all except two. Feeling keenly their unhappy desperation and peril, he gazed toward them. As the emaciated figures began climbing the steps towards him, the two figures, in a silent plea for help, uttered his grandmother's name. Distressed now, Aridain began to cry, as skeletal fingers began removing his clothing. Then, with hands slick with oil, the creatures caressed his face and explored his skin. They then began chanting over and over again…

'You are the fated Balefire. You will purge the world of the unclean and the unworthy…'

Pushing and clawing frantically at the emaciated hands, Aridain's focus shifted. Suddenly, he was running through the woods, his mother leading him by the hand. His blood burned and his skin crawled, and when he glanced sideways, he saw the creature, its eyes aflame and its teeth bared.

Water engulfed him then, and from a faraway place he heard his mother shouting for him to act. Desperate for the creature to leave him alone, he instead grabbed hold and didn't let go, no matter how hard it struggled. He felt sorry for the creature as he saw it for what it was; his abandoned brother. It was also his opposite and his enemy. His world then filled with a blue ephemeral light as the sapphire sprites appeared. Then, he began sneezing. Abruptly his eyes snapped open, and he rubbed at his itchy nose.

Ah, it lives! hissed Sabra, staring down intently from his position on Aridain's chest, his serpentine tongue brushing his nose.

Aridain stared up at the bare branches of the beech trees, then sat up, trying not to cry from the painful throbbing of the bee stings on his hands and face, and the pain in his back.

'Are they all gone?'

Delicious, the dragonlet nodded, licking his lips. *Good job I was here,* thought Sabra. *Luckily, you fell from the tree into this shallow pit.*

Aridain got painfully to his feet, and heard a strange noise from beneath him, a noise that frosted snow or dead leaves shouldn't make. His curiosity aroused, he began sweeping away the thick leafy covering to reveal a large skin of leather. Pulling the skin aside, he found a hessian sheet plastered in grease, and pulling that away, he found several leather-wrapped packages.

'Look at this, Sabra?' said Aridain, opening up a package.

Weapons; leave them here, youngling. They will only cause you unnecessary trouble.

'But what are they doing here, Sabra?'

I don't care, youngling, and neither should you?

Unwrapping one of the bundles tied with string, Aridain exclaimed, 'Swords and bows and arrows!' Examining the weapons, he said, 'They belong to the school, Sabra, I know because Karnack gave one to me with that exact same mark on it.' Deciding, Aridain said resolutely, 'We have to tell somebody.'

Following the path to the road, Aridain's thoughts were as heavy as the sword he dragged behind him. Not only was his father angry with him all the time, but now Kale was not who he thought he was. He couldn't show the sword to his father, it would just make him mad. He had to find his grandfather or his mother and tell them what he had discovered; they at least would think well of him. Suddenly, a noise up ahead made him stop in his tracks.

'It's OK, Aridain, it's me!' announced Keegan suddenly, appearing from the undergrowth. 'What happened to you? Your clothes are all ripped, you're covered in mud and grime and are those bee stings? Is that blood, and what are you doing with that sword? 'Why are you looking at me like that? What's the matter.' asked Keegan?

'Everyone is turning into people they're not. How do I know you are who you say you are? You could be an evil person, too?'

'Too, what do you mean...' Keegan, in sudden understanding, smiled, then said.... 'Remember last year, when your mother chastised you for reading my mind, you found out about your birthday present? Do you remember?'

Aridain nodded that he did.

'How would I know that, if I wasn't who I say I am, if you're still unsure...'

Dropping the sword, Aridain suddenly ran into Keegan's arms and burst into tears.

'There, there, that's enough now. So, do you want to tell me what happened?'

'Not only is there a bad man in Daddy's head, but now there's something wrong with Kale,' said Aridain miserably, 'and the bee stings hurt.'

'Why do you think there's something wrong with Kale?'

Explain to him, youngling, why the sprites wouldn't come out of the trees, encouraged the dragonlet.

'Sabra says it's because the sprites were scared of him, and when I wouldn't let Kale look into my head, he got furious. He also attacked Sabra. Why would he do that?'

'Did he say anything else?'

'Yes, that he has woad spiders and piranha bats.'

'Woad spiders and piranha bats?' considered Keegan thoughtfully; 'these are not creatures you'd normally associate with Kale!'

'He then asked me lots of questions. He asked me about magic, about Sabra, and if anything strange had happened to me. Then he asked me if I would like to learn all about his magic.'

'And did you agree to help him?'

'Yes, I thought Kale was my friend,' said Aridain, suddenly angry. 'Then he wanted to see my shiny stones.'

'Shiny stones?' queried Keegan.

'Yes, but Sabra stole them. I chased Sabra, and Kale chased me, and I escaped up a tree, but then I fell into a pit, where there were lots of swords and....'

'Whoa, hold on, swords?' said Keegan, confused.

'Yes, and bows and arrows as well,' Aridain said, tearfully rubbing at his arm.

'Is that one of them?'

'Uh huh,' nodded Aridain.

Taking the sword and studying the school's mark etched clearly into the steel, Keegan smiled. 'What is it with you always finding mischief?'

'I don't mean to Uncle Keegan.'

Deep in thought, Keegan wiped at the blood and grime on Aridain's face. Then, taking the sword, he said, 'Come on, let's get you back to the school.'

Dodging several leather clad soldiers, Keegan escorted Aridain as far as he dare.

'OK Aridain, give me the sword.'

'You won't tell Dad I found it, will you?'

'No, and don't worry, I will deal with this. Now run along.'

Planting the point of the sword into the ground, Keegan, rubbing at the wound, inflicted by the Scarrion Lizard, watched the young mite, the dragonlet in tow, run back towards the old fortress, and couldn't help but wonder how, knowing the weight of expectation on his shoulders, he would have coped at that age.

Using the lengthening shadows created by the setting sun, to avoid the many patrols and students hurrying about in the cold, he covertly made his way to the woodworking shed. Then, slipping quietly through the door, he dropped into the tunnel. Feeling for the false wall that allowed only him and his friends to pass, Keegan entered and threw the sword to an astonished Mace.

'I just met with Aridain. He says he found this in a pit in the woods, it was made at the school.'

'The young mite found this in the woods, you say?'

'Yes. He fell into a pit, apparently, and found this, together with many more. Intriguing, isn't it?' said Keegan.

'He is full of surprises, isn't he?' said Mace fondly, dabbing at his sweating forehead. Turning the sword this way and that, Mace studied the workmanship, the tang, the lines of the blade, and the simple but precise cross guard. 'This is Gable's work!'

Removing his thick padded helmet and clearing his long blond hair from his sweating face, Vanir said, 'Can I look at that?'

Handing the weapon to Vanir, Mace, running a hand through his hair, and depositing long streaks of dirt upon his forehead, confirmed, 'Thanks to the young mite, this sword verifies what Gable told Alfic, that weapons were going missing. Now we know where. But why are they ending up in a pit in the woods? Who are they for?'

'There's also Kale?' offered Keegan.

'What about him?'

'Aridain confirmed what I suspected, that Kale's working for Kuelack.'

'How do you know that?' said Mace, aggressively.

'Mace I know you're fond of Kale, but from what Aridain told me, Kale was fishing for information. He also mentioned Kale attacked Sabra, and that he kept woad spiders and piranha bats as pets. According to the little mite, it seems that he also struggled when remembering certain events, this was something I noticed when I brought Kale here, like when I asked him about Molly and Mo, it was as if he didn't know the ferrets either? All of this together with his insistence on keeping Lascana and Alfic in the dark, plus falling ill when he was here…'

'Perhaps it's because like us, he's fatigued and exhausted.'

'No, that's not it. Perak had also aired his concerns regarding the Animistic. Mace, this is more than mere coincidence. Something's going on.'

'It's conceivable he's being coerced, like Magen, to act against his better judgement,' pondered Vanir.

'I too thought that. However, for a while now, I've had this nagging doubt in the back of my mind,' insisted Keegan.

'Whatever's going on, we can't just give up on him,' said Mace angrily. 'There's something else we haven't considered, if Kale is now working for Kuelack and Aridain saw through his deception...., if he feels his cover's blown...'

They looked at each other in realisation.

'We have to go now!' said Mace, voicing what they were all thinking.

Strapping on their armour and weaponry, they threw what supplies remained into a satchel. Strapping the satchel across his back, Keegan looked one more time around the chamber. Silently thanking the dragon lord for this haven, Keegan followed the two greyswords through the ephemeral wall out into the tunnel.

CHAPTER THIRTY-ONE

SAVARIN

Snow fell all around, creating a soft feathery down, the leaden sky once more shrouding the school and its grounds in a duvet of silence. Perceiving none of this, the belligerent weather wizard, enraged, had come for a walk in the late afternoon gloom, having vented his fury with daggers of lightning that had destroyed part of his apartment. Everything he had been told, everything he suspected, had come true. Friends had turned to enemies, people he thought he could rely on had deserted him, and the people he loved were being forced to make a choice, join Kuelack or die. He also had to face the fact that his life was now forfeit; to think otherwise was stupidity. He knew he could no longer stay neutral. To stay neutral was to be alone, and to face Kuelack and his associates alone would be foolish.

The problem always was his brusque manner. It was a defence he had nurtured from his time as a child living in The Wilds, and the bullying he had endured. Now, because of this, people steered clear of him, all except a certain few.

He never intended to come across as a thorny individual, but the years growing up in the brutal frontier town of Elohim in the Southern Wilds had simply never left him.

Elohim was a place where you quickly learnt to survive, or you perished, and it wasn't only the people that were wild and untamed, so were the beasts and the terrain they roamed.

Shaking the snow from his plain brown and red cloak irritably, he stared grimly with grey smouldering eyes from beneath black bushy eyebrows towards the farmhands, as they systematically cleared the paths of snow. He then looked towards the school beyond, and the line of leafless cherry trees that lined the path. The fruiting plants reminded him of his efforts as a child to reach the wild crab apples hanging just out of reach on a neighbouring Elohim croft, whilst children twice his height and age plucked the juicy crop from the branches...

Orphaned, his mother and father killed whilst out foraging, by the creatures of the wilds, he had refused to become a victim of the villager's constant persecution. Although he made few friends, he had earned a healthy respect from villagers, old and young alike, for his tenacity. His extraordinary talent for weather magic surfaced during puberty, as was common, manifesting itself during yet another attempt to assert himself, his raw power badly injuring the other children around him. Deemed too dangerous to remain amongst his fellow Elohim's, they banished him to face The Wilds alone, like the thieves and murderers he'd watched being expelled so many times before. Frightened and alone, he soon discovered why the region was called The Southern Wilds.

Luck, combined with toughness and resilience built up during his youth, enabled Savarin to survive the attentions of the many beasts that roamed the mountainous region, which included firedrakes, darklings, wood trolls and furies as well as the brutal sparlings; bird-like creatures with rakish feathered heads and sharp beaks that walked upright on feathered legs and clawed feet. But creatures weren't the only things living in The Wilds. There were also bands of wild men called The Outcast, a resilient species that had, over the centuries, interbred with the snake-headed Gorgons. The merger had made a formidable combination. Exploiting the weak and injured, these freaks of nature had, over time, ranged northwards until they encountered mankind, this resulted in the Gorgon Wars. These so-called killers of men now roaming The Wilds wouldn't hesitate to take and torture a bewildered, inexperienced teenager, lost in the rugged scrubland, for their own personal pleasure.

Having survived The Wilds many perils, he had made his way to Gonda, but with no understanding of how to act in a civilised society, he decided to use his talents for his own gain... He chuckled unashamedly as he recalled Gonda's inhabitants running in panic, thinking the gods themselves had descended, as he, under instruction from the Baron Pamir, whose crops hadn't seen rain for weeks, created a thunderstorm that spiralled out of control and deluged the city for four days. Sent to Pellagrin's School, with the understanding that the armed forces acquire his prodigious skills as a weather wizard, he was taught to control his anger and channel his gift. Choosing not to stay in the army, however, he returned to Pellagrin's after serving his time...

Electing to keep to himself, the only people that saw through his gruff exterior to the man beneath, was Almagest, Perak, Alfic and Rasbora. These four individuals never seemed fazed by his irate outbursts or gruff manner. Almagest he had known the longest, his sheer will and forcefulness matching his own. Perak and Alfic were totally the opposite, being so laid back in his presence that he could do nothing but be relaxed in their company. The Bruins simply taking his crotchety manner with a pinch of salt. Rasbora, on the other hand, always in control, was an enigma. Her power and ice-cold intellect always commanded respect and caution, and as strange as it seemed, that distance always made him feel relaxed in her presence.

Then, like a bolt from the blue, it struck him. Rasbora leaving the school was no accident. He already knew that Kuelack's ambitions extended further afield, so it only stood to reason that to prevent Rasbora's opposition here at the school, Kuelack had caused trouble on the Zapatian border to lure her away. It all made perfect sense. After all, if anyone at the school could go toe to toe with Kuelack and Magen, it was her.

He thought of Exedra then. He had gazed at her saintly figure from afar, never having the courage to approach her for fear of rejection. Now he would never know, as she was dead.

'She was not worthy of your love, Savarin. She didn't even notice you!'

Wiping the freezing snow from his face and running his hands through his wet head of hair, Savarin focused on the imp-like face of the astral magic teacher coalescing beside his right shoulder.

'She was weak. Exedra's fate was sealed even before they voted her onto the Sivan. Fought over by Magen and Mass Martin, her mind was a battleground, even before the mind master used her to kill Kuelack.'

'Consider your next words, Iona. They may be your last.'

'Forgive me, Savarin, but she was killed by Magen who was protecting her brother.'

'Magen explained her death was an accident.'

'I'm sorry Savarin, Magen lied to you.'

'What else have you discovered?' snapped Savarin crossly.

'It is indeed as you believed. Kuelack commissioned Hogan to kill Almagest.'

'And for all we know,' continued Savarin, 'Mass ordered Hogan and Tallus to attack the Bruins? What of Cardia and Torsk?'

'Kuelack had them killed, to be replaced with someone they could control.'

'Exedra...' growled Savarin.

'I know it's small comfort, but you are not alone. There are those who would stand by you, support you, comfort you even.'

'Anything else?' asked Savarin, staring grimly at nothing in particular.

'Yes, curious of the rumours regarding Kale's strange behaviour, I decided to follow him. He met up with Keegan, and the two of them descended into a tunnel under the school!'

'A tunnel!' exclaimed Savarin.

'Yes, there are tunnels under the school. Anyway, Keegan led Kale to a section of wall that melted at their approach, allowing them access to a large underground chamber. Inside were Mace and Vanir. There was also a large sarcophagus sat upon a plinth, and above on the ceiling was a network of roots. I believe this was Pellagrin's chamber.'

'Pellagrin's chamber is a myth,' said Savarin with certainty.

'So I thought. Nevertheless, it's real.'

'Well, I'll be..., the perfect hiding place,' surmised Savarin.

'Not anymore. You see, Kale is not who we thought he was. He has been working for Kuelack all along.'

'How do you know this?'

'He left the chamber on a premise that he needed some fresh air, so I followed him. He went to the dungeons. Locked up were all the people who have gone missing. He even has Byrak strapped to a torture device.'

Trying to keep his anger in check, sparks appeared at his fingertips. 'Then Kale will pay for this betrayal,' spat Savarin, 'as will Magen and that piece of troll dung, her brother.'

His hair standing on end, the snow at his feet now swirling faster and faster; he turned towards the school, a deathly intent etched on his face.

'Calm yourself Savarin, Kale knows the whereabouts of the greysword's hideout, and their plans. Gradine has set a trap. She means to destroy them.'

'Get out of my head, Iona. Kuelack and Magen started this; they have this coming to them.'

'No, I cannot let you sacrifice your life. You have friends that rely upon you, I rely upon you, the reason I do this is…. something is amiss,' exclaimed Iona, 'I am discovered!'

His senses alerting him to the murmurings of a spell, Savarin turned inquisitively in the silence as an ill breeze stirred the snow beneath his feet.

'I suggest you leave now, Iona, before it's too late.'

'Very well.' Caressing his face with an ephemeral hand, Iona said, 'One more thing; Kuelack has an army of followers and accomplices that are growing daily. This includes many that were presumed dead. However, one is not as loyal as he thinks…' and then, like a transient spirit, she faded into nothing.

Closing his eyes, Savarin cast about the surrounding area, probing the aether for anything out of the ordinary, and there it was, a dark remnant that persisted in the air despite its caster's efforts to prevent Iona communicating with him.

'Magen,' he hissed, 'a dark heart indeed.'

Plots, deaths and citizens imprisoned simply for not agreeing with Kuelack's vision. The situation was far worse than he had imagined.

CHAPTER THIRTY-TWO

SWORDS & FORGES

Mace, with Keegan ranging in front, and Vanir at his back, listened intently for anything that might show an ambush or a trap as they made their way silently along the dusty corridor. Proceeding silently to the dangling, knotted rope, they hauled themselves up into the woodworking shed, not bothering to conceal the dry rot infested hole. Creeping silently across the darkened room, they opened the door and peered left and right down the frozen track. Keegan, gazing up into the dull late evening sky, warned, 'Our chances of being seen are highly likely. There's no cover.'

'I agree with the gamekeeper,' said Vanir grimly.

'We all came to the same conclusion, that we have no choice. I know if I were Kale and my cover had been blown, I'd be rounding up the soldiers right now. He *will* come for us.'

'So, where are they?' hissed Vanir severely.

'Overconfidence,' said Keegan simply, 'They think we don't know, therefore they think time's on their side.'

Satisfied the coast was clear, they crept beside the shed. With hands poised upon the hilts of their weapons, they turned the corner and crept quickly around the barracks, built into the end of the old wall, and melted into the shadows. Certain the coast was clear, they continued as the busy sounds of hammers on anvils sounded loudly in the night's silence.

At the murmuring of voices, Keegan whispered harshly, 'Guards!'

Then, backing towards the two greyswords, Keegan led them quickly up the bank where they hid beside the beech hedge, beneath the row of grey pines. Suddenly four soldiers led by Cordovan Harker appeared. Pausing by their position, Cordovan ordered two members of the patrol to remain where they were. He then continued on with the remaining two.

Crouched in the dying light, his breathing visible in the cold, his teeth chattering, Mace pondered the circumstances that had led to now.

It seemed inconceivable, even knowing of his betrayal, that Kale was capable of treachery, that he would capitulate, and just like the luckless Janus Loker, become yet another victim of Kuelack's ambitions. Their instincts had all pointed to an honest individual, even though the warning signs were staring them right in the face; Kale's sickness in the cavern, Crystal's concerns. He shook his head in annoyance. Beria, too, had disappeared, as had Tance and Albain. For all they knew, their friends were dead.

'Those guards aren't going anywhere soon,' suggested Vanir, voicing their concerns.

'We have to move,' hissed Keegan. 'The longer we wait, the more chance there is we'll be discovered.'

'Yes, I know!' snapped Mace irritably.

Leaving the soldiers to their frozen vigil, Keegan led them along the grassy bank atop the wall. Treading carefully, Mace, his expression taking on a look of foreboding, watched, as below, Francis, one of the school's apprentice farriers, re-shoed teacher Konya's charger, under her watchful eyes and that of two more guards.

Holding up his hand abruptly, Keegan hissed, 'Karnack!'

Melting back into the shadows, the three friends watched from their position overlooking the blacksmiths, as soldiers under Karnack's instruction entered the forge. The incessant clanging from the hammers suddenly ending; they watched in the deafening silence as the guards emerged from the forge, pushing a manacled Gable Bagley before them.

'Gable Bagley, you are under arrest for sedition and forging illegal weapons,' announced the elder greysword loudly across the courtyard.

'I knew Gable would never willingly work for Kuelack,' hissed Keegan confidently.

'Not so long ago, I remember you saying that your famous instincts told you he was guilty,' whispered Vanir tersely.

'I never did!' replied Keegan, feigning incredulity.

'Will you two knock it off?' hissed Mace, 'there are more important issues than who's said what.' He then turned and listened to the conversation playing out below.

... 'Sedition, weapons, I don't know what you're talking about...,' Gable pleaded innocently.

'You have been aiding and supplying weapons to the resistance,' accused Karnack grimly. 'You've been seen talking to Alfic and his little cabal on several occasions.'

'I've been commissioned to forge weapons for our forces. I have the manifest to prove it.'

'We have no record that the swords you produced reached their destination, only those of your apprentices.'

'That's preposterous. I signed for those weapons myself.'

'You hulking ignoramus, are you that naïve?' spat Delran.

The three watching men glanced at each other and shook their heads. Gable had walked right into Karnack's trap.

'Is this the document, and is this your signature, Gable?' announced Karnack loudly.

'Yes, but I would never....'

'As you can see, the numbers do not tally.'

Gable, nodding sadly, fixed Karnack with a withering stare. 'After all the years we've known each other, this is how you would treat me? This has nothing to do with swords or forges, does it? Are you so entwined in Kuelack's web of deception that....'

'Silence blacksmith!' roared Delran. 'Despite Kuelack treating you with clemency, you and your friends still insist on disrupting life here.'

'You know as well as I that this is a lie. I have experienced the sham that is Kuelack's clemency.'

'Silence,' interrupted Karnack.

Glancing sadly towards the silent forge then, Gable said, 'We both know what's happening here. I never took you for a turncoat, Karnack.'

'Protest all you like, blacksmith, the days of you and your resistance friends poking your noses into things that don't concern you are over,' smiled Delran.

Karnack backhanded Delran across the jaw. 'Hold your tongue. Speak only when asked.'

Mace gripped his sword tighter, watching the grizzled old warrior intently from the shadows, studying Karnack's weathered, pockmarked face for any signs, any hint, that might attest to his intentions regarding the increasingly volatile situation.

... 'As chief blacksmith and armourer, you are responsible for the weapons made at this forge,' accused Karnack. 'I have been ordered to find out the truth, nothing more, nothing less.'

At Mace's back, Keegan growled, 'Don't say it Gable, don't...'

'You can all burn in Fornax's fires for all I care,' bellowed Gable, 'and Kuelack can shove his laws where the sun don't shine.'

'He said it!' finished Vanir.

They then watched helplessly as Karnack levelled his sword at Gable's head.

'Mace!' hissed Keegan, 'We have to do something!'

'Like what?' said Mace, looking on dourly.

'Do it, Karnack,' roared Gable as he was dragged away, 'take my head off, if it's Kuelack's will, for I want no part of his new order,' spat Gable, struggling violently. 'One day, all of you will get their comeuppance.'

His steely countenance demanding instant compliance, Karnack, casting a quick glance in their direction, ordered, 'Gag him before I do something we both regret.'

Slowly, like a coiled Brean lion that had lost the opportunity for a kill, Mace relaxed. Exhaling slowly, Mace looking down thankfully, said quietly, 'Thank you, Karnack.' Like swallowing a bitter pill, Mace watched as Gable, bound and gagged, was led from the courtyard flanked by guards towards the fortress. They were led by Karnack, the man who had inspired him, a man of courage, a man who he had called a friend, who he now presumed had thrown his lot in with Kuelack. Presumed? Now why had that word suddenly come to mind? Mace relaxed his grip on his sword in an effort to ignore his growing sense of confusion at Karnack's actions.

'You knew he wouldn't do it, didn't you?' exclaimed Vanir knowingly.

'Yes, although for a split second there...'

'Well, thanks for the heads up. So now what? Do we rescue Gable?' exclaimed Keegan hopefully.

'No.'

'Why?'

'So that we can live to fight another day. Oh, we could take them on, maybe kill a couple of dozen, but in the end we'll be captured or killed, then what use will we be? Besides, Karnack knows we're up here, Gables arrest is a trap intended to lure us out.'

'Does Mace remind you of anyone?' hissed Keegan.

'Uh huh, Alfic!' agreed Vanir.

'I'll take that as a compliment, gentlemen.' Smiling grimly, Mace continued, 'Discretion is the better part of valour; it is one of the many things Alfic taught us. When you and me both blundered into impossible situations, how many times did Alfic save our necks? Right now, Karnack's waiting for us to blunder gormlessly into his trap.'

'But, if we can't act, what are we doing here at the school?' countered Vanir.

'Patience, Vanir, our time will come. Not right now, but it will come.'

'Well, one thing's for sure, with Gable locked up, our armour will suffer.'

They waited in the dark as the hammering, and shaping of metal echoed across the school grounds once more.

'How long does it take to shoe a horse? We have to move,' hissed Vanir irritably, blowing into his hands.

The adrenalin having left his system and his teeth chattering loudly once more, Mace, studying the row of stately cedar trees being swept this way and that in the cold swirling wind above their heads, said grimly, 'It's done when it's done?'

'Just like us,' hissed Keegan.

Loath to quit a fight; he was about to respond, but thought better of it. The ironic truth was that Keegan was right.

It was another fifteen minutes before Konya finally led her horse from the stable block. Standing and stretching their legs, now stiff with the cold, they noticed a figure exiting the forge wheeling a barrow filled with a large leather bundle.

'So, where's he going, do you think?' enquired Keegan.

'You wanted to know who's responsible for forging the swords, Mace,' said Vanir. 'Now's our chance to find out.'

Personally, Vanir hated inactivity, preferring a straight fight to skulking in corners. He could never understand Keegan's love of sitting still for hours on end, gathering intelligence, and following people covertly. Looking out across the courtyard and the darkened buildings, Vanir couldn't help but grind his teeth in anger when he pictured Kuelack's hate filled face, ruling supreme over the school's gleaming spires and domes he knew and loved, as his lust for control grew.

'Mace,' insisted Vanir, 'we can skulk around in the shadows, attempting not to upset the apple cart until we're blue in the face. We have to do something?'

Having decided, Mace said, 'Very well, go, but be quick. I will not risk all our necks for this.'

Buoyed by a renewed sense of purpose and a ruthless conviction, Vanir, with the grace of a mantra cat, disappeared through the main entrance. Followed covertly by his two friends through the falling snow, he overtook the cloaked, straining figure, slipping and sliding, as he strove to push the wheelbarrow across the courtyard. Waiting silently beside one of the ornate pillars that marked the entrance, he waited until the squeaking wheelbarrow and the young blacksmith drew level, then stepped out and thrust his knife's point into the small of the apprentice's back.

'Evening, Jack.'

'Vanir. Lovely evening, isn't it?' said Jack smugly.

'These weapons. Who are they for?'

'The army, we're at war, remember?'

'You wouldn't be taking them to Higher Woods by any chance and burying them in a pit?'

A fleeting look of surprise replaced Jack's look of smugness. Then, regaining his confidence quickly, Jack said, 'These weapons are destined for the army, not the resistance.'

'We both now know that pit has nothing to do with Gable or the resistance. So I want you to tell me which one of you squealed? Who betrayed him?'

'He betrayed himself!' spat Jack vehemently.

Grabbing his shirt collar roughly at the base of his neck, Vanir thrust his knife up against Jack's groin. 'Tell me what I want to know. I will not ask again.'

'OK, OK,' squeaked Jack, 'Keep your hair on.'

Noticing Jack's glance over his shoulder, Vanir, in one fluid movement, span around and drew his sword. 'Jackamar!' he hissed.

With the point of his sword in the snow and his hands placed upon its pommel, the youngest of the four greyswords stood confidently with a smile upon his face. 'Hello, Vanir, you should have kept going. You might even have made it, now however, I am going to rid the school of your incessant interfering. Then when I'm done with you, I'm going to kill Mace and that irritating gamekeeper. You have been an irksome thorn in our side for long enough.'

'To get to them you will have to kill me first, and as you never could best me...?'

Grasping his sword in two hands, Jackamar brought it to guard, then pointed it at Vanir. Circling, he suddenly attacked with quick, precise cuts and thrusts. Forcing Vanir backwards towards the perimeter wall, Jackamar sneered, 'You should never have left your rat hole, now you're going to regret it.'

Bright sparks filled the darkness as Jackamar attacked again, but parrying and counter thrusting with his sword, Vanir stabbed with his knife. Neither besting the other, the pair drew apart and circled warily.

'And what of your oath? Does that count for nothing?' spat Vanir, planting his feet and attacking with a flurry of blows.

'Outmoded notions for old men. Both have no place in this world anymore. Once I'm done, there will be no one left to quote outmoded greysword doctrine.' Advancing steadily, Jackamar attacked once more.

Parrying Jackamar's attack, Vanir thrust with the knife, but before Vanir could react, Jackamar grasped his wrist.

'Impressive. That thrust would have found my solar plexus, and I'd be on the floor gasping for breath. However, since then, I've had some enhancements.'

'You talk too much,' spat Vanir, who, with intricate footwork, lunged one way and then the other.

Once again, Jackamar parried, then deflected Vanir's blade sideways. Stepping inside Vanir's kill-zone adeptly, Jackamar smashed

Vanir's nose with his forehead, then drove his foot up into his exposed groin.

Gasping, Vanir fell to his knees. Wiping at the blood pouring from his broken nose, he smiled and looked up at Jackamar determinedly, as the ginger-haired Greysword, smiling demonically, backed away confidently.

'Oh dear, what will those whores you bed think of you now?' Presenting his sword once more, Jackamar then began to chant, whilst at the same time rotating his weapon in ever-increasing circles. 'You think you know what power is? Let me show you real power.'

Vanir felt the air thicken with tendrils of magic as Jackamar swung his sword in ever decreasing arcs, left and right, faster and faster; abruptly Jackamar brought his sword to bare. Holding his own sword out in order to ward off the unknown magic, Vanir felt himself lifted from the ground and hurled through the air, impacting with the old perimeter wall. Winded, his whole being shuddering from the strange greysword magic, Vanir lay on the path gasping for breath, watching helplessly as Jackamar strode purposefully towards him.

'What is this? This is not the greysword way, that is not greysword magic.'

Stamping down hard upon Vanir's wrist, Jackamar sneered, 'Hogwash, old wives' tales, our swords were forged with magic, and what magic it is. If only you had the courage to embrace it, to enhance it!'

'Greysword magic is only used for defence,' gasped Vanir.

'But when you needed it most, your famed greysword magic has proved ineffective.'

'You are tied to Vehemence, Jackamar. You know the rule. Betray your oath, betray your sword, and they will betray you, there will be a reckoning, a price to pay,' hissed Vanir.

Again, Jackamar slashed his sword back and forth, and like a rag doll, Vanir was once more smashed up against the wall. 'Join me, Vanir. Just think what we could achieve, we could take what we want, do what we want.'

'Never!' spat Vanir. 'These swords were entrusted to us, to be used with honour.'

'I don't understand why the playboy greysword, seducer of women and consumer of alcohol, will not take advantage of this offer?' said Jackamar. 'Under Kuelack's banner, we could drape ourselves in women and drown ourselves in wine.'

'You spoke the words, but that's all they were, words. You never truly believed them.'

'Oh please, spare me the noble rhetoric.'

'An oath of fealty has nothing to do with having fun,' said Vanir. 'I would rather die fighting for a just cause than for darkness and despair.'

'Then I will grant you your wish. Goodbye, Vanir, it hasn't been fun.'

Feeling Jackamar's fingers around his throat, Vanir felt himself lifted up the face of the wall. Straining against Jackamar's vice-like grip, his feet dangling, Vanir kicked and beat futilely against the tall, lean, inhumanly powerful figure of Jackamar. The world around him turning grey, Vanir remembered the knife in his hand. Gripping the hilt tightly, he slashed at Jackamar's face, opening a cut across the young greysword's cheek.

Suddenly released, Vanir rubbing at his throat, dropped to the ground as Jackamar cursed and felt at the deep laceration.

The young greysword smiled then. 'Is that your best?'

Vanir looked up and watched in astonishment as the wound, bleeding so profusely moments before, began to close.

'Turn and face me, traitorous oath breaker.'

Turning, Jackamar smiled. 'Mace, you old has been, I wondered when you would appear?'

Ducking beneath Jackamar's swing, Mace rolled and slashed at his calf. Gasping in pain, Jackamar collapsed to one knee, then almost immediately got to his feet.

'When will you get it into your thick heads that you cannot beat me?' cackled Jackamar. He then charged towards Mace with a series of strikes, forcing the captain of the guard backwards.

'Admit it old man, this is a young man's game, your outmatched. You're *both* outmatched.'

'Saying it doesn't make it so,' said Mace assuredly.

As Jackamar began chanting once more, Vanir, gritting his teeth, bellowed, 'Mace, no! Be careful! Jackamar... his sword, together they've been..., presenting your sword doesn't work...'

Vanir's concerns were unfounded, however, as Mace rolled sideways and came to his feet.

Reaching for his sword, Vanir climbed shakily to his feet. Stealing himself, he pronounced, 'It will take more than a sword compromised by dark magic to destroy the brotherhood. Vehemence will not save you from greysword justice,' grunted Vanir, driving Jackamar backwards with a series of hefty blows.

'Your words and your efforts are meaningless,' cursed Jackamar, swinging his sword and causing Vanir to duck.

Then, placing the guard of his sword across his forehead, Jackamar stared at him with cruel, slitted eyes. 'Both of you are beaten; the more you attack, the stronger I become,' cackled Jackamar. He then began mumbling under his breath.

'Don't let him finish the incantation!' yelled Vanir.

Bellowing insanely, Vanir, followed closely by Mace, charged. However, they were thrown from their feet once more.

Twirling his sword confidently, Jackamar said. 'This is too easy. I expected more from you.'

Sitting upright from the hard-packed gravel floor painfully, and rubbing at his backside, Vanir, looking over at Mace, groaned, 'This is becoming a mite tedious.'

At first it was only tenuous, but to Vanir's surprise, fog, increasing in thickness, quickly filled the air, a thick soup like fog that obscured everything, turning the evening gloom even darker. Getting slowly to his feet, Vanir peered into the murk, then started towards where he had last seen Mace. Then, through a haze of pain, he thought he saw a tunnel in the fog, and stood at its centre, beckoning to him, Keegan. Vanir then looked around as many urgent voices, whom he assumed were Pellagrin's soldiers, called to each other through the murk. Then someone close by called his name and Mace appeared, grasping him under the arm and hauling him to his feet. The pair then staggered towards the strange tunnel with Keegan beckoning frantically at its centre.

Keegan looked nervously through the thick falling snow, as if expecting soldiers, to suddenly appear like ephemeral snowmen. Crouching abruptly, he signalled for Mace to stop as he scrutinised the ground.

They then both looked up at a noise and came to the same conclusion. 'These footprints are fresh. They weren't supposed to follow us?' confirmed Keegan. 'So much for that plan.' Peering into the darkness, he hissed, 'Go, help Vanir. I'll lead our bloodhounds a merry chase.'

Looking at Keegan in understanding, Mace said, 'Don't get yourself killed; you sad excuse for a tracker.'

'Hey, it's me?'

Retracing his course noisily, Keegan blundered slowly through the snow, allowing Pellagrin's soldiers to catch him up. Listening to the confused voices as they struggled to make sense of his blatant tracks, he sat in between the impressive buttresses of Pellagrin's oak.

He chuckled to himself quietly, '*Morons!*'

Allowing his eyes to close for a second, the sound of soldiers' voices combined with jingling armour snapped him back to reality. Peering around the tree's trunk, he waited until the soldiers blundered past in the dark and then followed them. His task performed, Keegan reverted to kind, making his way in silence, back towards the sheds. Covertly, producing no sound or reverberations, he opened the door to the woodworking shed and slipped quietly inside. Creeping cautiously towards the corner of the room, he found the hole hidden by the barrels. However, it was then that he heard someone scrabbling up the rope.

Hurrying along the corridor, Savarin came upon the knotted rope dangling from the hole in the woodwork shed floor. Grasping it firmly, he then began pulling himself upwards. However, when he pulled himself level with the hole, he came face to face with a knife blade.

'Teacher Savarin?'

'Keegan, am I glad to see you!'

'What are you doing?'

'What? Because I'm a teacher, I shouldn't be able to climb!' said Savarin irritably. 'Now, if you please, could you withdraw your knife so I can climb out of here? Soldiers are right behind me!'

'Yeh, of course, but you still haven't answered my question?'

Noticing that Keegan hadn't holstered his knife, Savarin said more urgently, 'I came to warn you that the school knows where you're hiding. Now please, put away your knife. You have nothing to fear from me.'

'I don't understand. How do you know about all of this?' said Keegan, holstering his knife, and offering Savarin a hand up.

'Knowing where you've been hiding is a long story. What's important is that this is all a trap set to capture you and your friends.'

'I know you're friends with Perak and Alfic, but why would you help us? I mean, you're on the council.'

'Because the Sivan is corrupt, and I will *not* serve a corrupt council.'

'You know that if you're seen helping us, Savarin, your teaching days here are done.'

'Better to fight for something than live for nothing, is what I say. Besides, I've had enough of standing idly by whilst Kuelack turns this school into his own personal recruitment camp for the gifted.'

'I agree with you there. Even when you avoid trouble, trouble always seems to find you.'

'Hey, stay right there!' issued an order from the tunnel below.

'Gavin Torn, how nice to see you. You look like a rat, in a rat hole. I'd stand back if I were you, Savarin, as I'm not sure if this is going to fit,' said Keegan, rolling one of the barrels towards the hole.

Avoiding a crossbow bolt that flew past his ear and stuck into the roof above his head, Keegan dropped the barrel into the hole. Satisfied that the barrel was wedged tightly, the pair exited the shed and skulked quietly through the dark evening, the sounds of muffled urgent voices all around, calling through the night.

'Curses,' Keegan exclaimed, crouching down and examining the ground. Shaking his head, he said, perplexed, 'Snow has covered everything. I can't tell anything anymore.'

'Stop panicking and tell me where you saw them last?' demanded Savarin.

'When I left Mace, we were following Vanir towards the student block in the hope we could capture some soldiers loyal to Kuelack, gather some information. All I can hope for now is that they're still alive.'

'Hope, ifs and buts, is this your resistances mantra?' Savarin said gruffly, 'Keep an eye out while I deal with this.'

His head bowed, Savarin closed his eyes. Reaching out through the snow, Savarin delivered fingers of magic out through the storm, caressing the snowflakes until in his mind he had a 3D profile of the landscape and everything the snowflakes touched.

'There are three combatants outside the student dorm. But what I don't understand is... Jackamar's attacking Mace and Vanir; but they're all greyswords,' said Savarin in astonishment.

'It seems you were right when you said Pellagrin's is riddled with corruption,' said Keegan grimly, 'Although Jackamar rallying behind Kuelack doesn't come as a shock.'

'We don't have much time; soldiers are converging on them as we speak.'

'Then we need to hurry, don't we?' said Keegan.

Hearing movement all around them, Keegan, gripping his knife firmly but loosely, growled resolutely, 'Soldiers! Well, if I'm to die, at least I can take a few with me.'

'Or you could make use of a weather wizard?'

'Or I could make use of a weather wizard,' said Keegan sheepishly.

'Now, I'll need a little time for this, so keep an eye out.'

Sitting himself down on the snowy ground, Savarin concentrated again. Reaching out through the air, he sent tendrils of magic out through the snow. Melting the millions of individual flakes turning them to rain, he then began rapidly evaporating the moisture to form fog. The effect was slow at first, but the accumulative effect began rapidly obscuring their surroundings and the buildings in a thickening miasma.

'This should suffice for now,' gasped Savarin, holding out his hand, 'now help me up here.'

Helped up by Keegan, Savarin, rocking unsteadily on his feet, said, 'I haven't done that in a while, but I'll be fine now. Go on ahead.'

Savarin, attempting to control his laboured breathing as best he could, followed Keegan across the yard and out of the main gate. Slowing their pace but not stopping, the pair heard, before they saw, two soldiers as they emerged from the smog, swords raised. Undaunted, Keegan dropped and slashed the lead soldier across the thigh with his knife, then planted the vicious weapon into the soldier's back as he fell to his knee. Wrenching his Korda knife from the soldier's back, he spun and ducked as a second sword whistled overhead. Thrusting his knife up into the soldier's chest, Keegan ripping upwards, opened up the soldier's chest plate like a tin can. Not waiting for his victim to fall lifeless onto the ground, Keegan beckoned Savarin onward. As he passed, however, Savarin couldn't help but despair at the loss as he watched the soldier's lifeblood staining the surrounding snow.

With the perimeter wall at their back, the friends united once more, heard soldiers slowly approaching through the dense fog, threatening to cut them off.

'Spread out across the road,' they heard Karnack bellow. 'Don't let them double back; drive them towards Jackamar.'

'So now what?' hissed Vanir. 'Savarin, can't you do something?'

'Whatever I do now, it will only pinpoint our position. We have to use this cover to our best advantage.'

Deciding, Keegan said, 'Keep quiet and follow me quickly now!' Hurrying across the road, Keegan led them to the dormitory that backed into the fields beyond. 'Curses, back up!'

'Now what?' questioned Vanir.

'Soldiers. Shit!'

Seeking cover, they found the locked rear entrance to the young wizards' quarters, and Mace began hacking at the door.

'There! They're over there!' shouted a voice in the dark.

'Hurry, you pitiful excuse for a greysword,' bellowed Keegan.

'Keep your hair on, I'm nearly through!'

Suddenly, with a splintering of wood, the thick oak door gave way and with Savarin covering their retreat by creating intense vortices of wind, they ran onto the building's ground floor corridor to the astonishment of incredulous students. They immediately began searching for a way out, as from the far end of the corridor, soldiers marched confidently towards them, led by a grinning Jackamar.

Presenting his sword, Vanir yelled frustratedly, 'Brilliant plan, Keegan, now there's nowhere to go. I can see now why Alfic made all the decisions.'

'Stop complaining and keep looking!' said Mace savagely.

Struggling now to maintain his two swirling vortices, Savarin shouted angrily, 'Do something! I can't hold them forever.'

'Have you found anything?'

Keegan, shaking his head and shouting above the wind and noise, said, 'These rooms are all dead ends.'

Mace, drawing his sword and planting his feet, bellowed, 'Then this is where we make our stand.'

'Quickly, in here! This way!'

Mace turned to see a young female student gesturing from a doorway, about a third of the way down the corridor, urging them to follow her.

'Erica! Erica Markeson? What are you doing?' said Mace. 'Get back inside.'

'Do you want to get out of here or not?'

Conceding, albeit reluctantly, Mace ordered, 'Vanir, cover Savarin's back. Keegan, hold on to Savarin. It will be tight once Jackamar realises what we're doing, but I think we can make that doorway.'

In a tight-knit group they hurried down the corridor in cover-formation, Savarin's weakening vortices tracking their progress like demented, whirling dervishes. Bowmen fired arrows towards them but in the swirling wind they went awry, some impaling the walls and door, some lancing back towards the archers.

Diving through the doorway, they slammed the door shut. Now in a storeroom filled with furniture, they grasped an old chest of drawers and thrust it against the door, just as Jackamar and Karnack, backed by a knot of soldiers, reached the entrance.

Pulling an old rug from the floor, Erica said, 'This trap door leads to the tunnels. They've been using this for months now.'

'Now we know how the weapons were reaching the woods without anyone noticing,' said Keegan, over the deafening impacts. 'And right under our noses, too.'

'Whatever you're going to do, do it now,' shouted Mace over his shoulder. 'This door won't hold.'

Dropping into the hole one by one, their excited breathing loud in the tunnel, they followed Mace along the passageway until they came to an intersection.

'What are you waiting for, what's wrong with turning right?' insisted Vanir.

Suddenly, appearing from the darkness, Keegan announced, 'This tunnel's blocked.'

'Forget I asked,' said Vanir dryly.

Running as fast as their legs would carry them, they retraced their steps, their only hope was that they could, by some miracle, outrun the soldiers that were no doubt tracking them from behind and above. Reaching the intersection leading to Pellagrin's chamber once more, they could see figures illuminated in the chamber's lights, drawing inexorably closer, accompanied by harsh, urgent voices.

'Why are we stopping?' complained Vanir. 'Keep going!'

'We can't go forward. Look,' said Keegan, indicating the flickering lights coming towards them, 'and we definitely can't go back. So, unless anyone has a better idea, we get to the chamber.'

'No,' despaired Vanir, 'not the chamber again. I'd rather fight. We could find out where this branch of the tunnel leads?' proposed Savarin.

'It's no good; I looked,' said Keegan. 'There are steps leading upwards, but they're riddled with rot.'

'How do you know?' exclaimed Savarin.

'Because I tried climbing them!' said Keegan.

With no other ideas forthcoming, Mace led them back towards the chamber.

Their laboured breathing reverberating around the cavernous chamber. Keegan, shaking his head, hissed, 'Well, that was fun!'

Breathing heavily from the adrenalin powered flight, Vanir slumped wearily against the stone sarcophagus, and then looked down at his scratched and torn leather tunic, trousers and grieves. Wiping the dried blood from his knife with a piece of cloth, he said contemptuously, 'I didn't think we'd be coming back here again.'

'I don't believe it! Karnack and Jackamar both working for Kuelack! Just how deep does this conspiracy go?'

'Conspiracy! It's a full-blown military coup, Savarin!' spat Mace.

Each caught up in their own thoughts; it was Keegan who broke the silence. 'I thought my days of avoiding enemy soldiers were done.'

'Hey, we're all still alive,' smiled Mace proudly, 'and where there's life, there's hope. Now, let's have something to eat and drink, then discuss our options.'

Having rested, Vanir hissed in discomfort as he reached for the satchel containing their rations.

With concern in her kind, hazel eyes, Erica said, 'You're in pain, Vanir. Let me tend to your injuries.'

'I'll be fine,' insisted Vanir grumpily.

'No, you won't,' she insisted. Rolling her eyes, Erica said, 'What is it with you men? Always in denial. Injured, you're no good to anyone, besides we're not going anywhere just yet. Now take off your armour, lift up your shirt and hold still,' commanded Erica.

Vanir, looking down cautiously at the diminutive, dark-haired, attractive student, did as he was told.

'With attention from a good-looking woman like that, I'd gladly lift up my shirt,' smiled Keegan, nudging Mace's arm.

'Imprisoned in a chamber under the school, with no escape, the school baying for our blood, and all you can do is joke?' fumed Savarin.

'Steady Savarin, it's just our way.'

'At least we have food and water?' smiled Keegan, offering Savarin a dried fillet of fish from his satchel.

Tearing forlornly at the dried fish, Savarin, shaking his head, grumbled, 'All of my efforts, all my struggles, have come to naught. What a fool I've been?'

'Savarin, you're not the only one taken for a fool. We all have,' confirmed Mace.

'Yeh, don't be so hard on yourself, Savarin. If it wasn't for you, we'd be prisoners now,' smiled Keegan, 'or dead. You did good. In fact, it was a shame you weren't with me during my attempt to save Mace; we would have escaped a lot quicker.'

'Your ingenious plan!' exclaimed Mace sardonically.

Mystified at their puzzled looks, Keegan, with a hurt expression, turned to Savarin and said, 'To save Mace from the dungeon, I let myself be deliberately captured, but Captain grey pants here, doesn't believe me.'

'And did you?' asked Savarin indifferently.

Seeing Savarin's and Vanir's look of scepticism Keegan, feigning outrage, said, 'Are you questioning my integrity?'

'Absolutely,' said Vanir, 'the thought of you getting yourself deliberately caught is, to quote a well-known phrase, "Bullshit". On the other hand, a greysword breaking in, to break you out; now that is entirely feasible.'

'Believe what you will. We escaped. That's all the proof you need,' insisted Keegan, smiling meekly, picking at a piece of beef that had stuck in his gold tooth with his knife.

Looking towards Keegan and Vanir, and shaking his head severely, Mace, failing to see the funny side of the conversation announced, 'Jackamar's enchantments!'

'What of them?' said Vanir, his mood turning darker.

'A worrying development, don't you think?'

'But it confirms what we already suspected,' continued Vanir, 'that weapons forged at the school, together with students, are being enhanced, presumedly by Arhass.'

'I too thought to uncover these schemes and a lot more,' said Savarin darkly, 'But, with the school's residents firmly behind Kuelack, I might as well have been beating my head against the fortress walls.'

'But why? Why would students choose to stay at a school that practices evil, dark ways?' said Erica, looking around at them, puzzled. 'It's not as though it's any more powerful than the powers of light?'

'It promises a quick path to power, glory and fame,' stated Savarin, as if that explained everything. 'But, like everything, the quick path isn't always better. The dark path is riddled with risk, and can exact a high price; take Serac, for instance. Study is the key, and diligence, it is why practitioners of good magic are so revered, and attain so much status and prominent positions in society. It's also the reason why more evil mages abound.'

'Better to go along with the crowd than be crushed beneath it,' agreed Vanir. 'Look at Karnack and Jackamar. Quantity over quality.'

'Many students, with a promise of an easy route to greatness, power and authority, jump at the chance, Erica, especially if they hark from nothing,' continued Savarin solemnly.

'Like Hogan and Tallus, for instance,' said Mace. 'So drunk with dark magic were they, that when Perak and I fought them, they thought themselves invincible and beyond harm. Dark magic warped their minds and, in the end, lack of knowledge killed them.'

Cleaning the Korda knife diligently on his leather trousers, Keegan, studying the blade critically, said darkly, 'And now Jackamar and Karnack are being consumed by that same darkness.'

Lost in their own thoughts, the food in their bellies imparting a more reassuring feeling, the comrades began tending to their numerous cuts and scrapes.

'Ahh, easy, woman!' hissed Vanir in the sudden silence.

'Oh, don't be such a sissy. I hardly touched your nose,' said Erica. Then, closing her eyes and concentrating, she stated calmly, 'I noticed the sarcophagus. Are we where I think we are?'

'Yes, this is Pellagrin's chamber, and those are the roots of Pellagrin's oak spreading across the roof,' said Vanir, pointing at various details around the chamber.

'I suspected as much when we entered. Can you not feel it? The chamber has a certain magical quality.

'You're right, it does have a certain feel about it,' agreed Vanir, staring at her strangely. 'So, mind telling us why you helped us escape? I mean, you're a healer, not a fighter. Why sacrifice your place here at the school?'

'Why did you?'

'That's not a valid answer. Our circumstances are completely different.'

'Do you not feel aggrieved at the injustice here?' pressed Erica.

'Well, of course, but...'

'Did you not feel wronged that they expected you to carry on your duties as normal, knowing that certain residents at the school are under lock and key, or in hiding?'

'Well, I guess I felt I had to do something to....'

'Then, you have your answer!' Examining Vanir's wounds, now healed, she announced wearily, 'OK, you're done. Now, is there anything to eat?'

Pointing to an old table, Vanir said, 'There's some dried beef and fish and a skin of cider in my satchel....'

'Savarin, when I asked you how you knew we were about to fall into a trap, you said it was a long story, mind sharing, now that we have time on our hands?' asked Keegan.

'My source has, shall we say, been following certain individuals, but mainly Kale.'

'Kale!' exclaimed Keegan.

'I know you don't want to hear this,' announced Savarin dourly, 'But my source was in no doubt as to Kale's complicity, and that he provided the intel leading to our current predicament.'

Mace shook his head vigorously.

'I don't want to believe it either, Mace, but all the evidence is against him. It may be time to accept that Kale is working for Kuelack,' said Vanir.

'I don't care what the evidence says,' proclaimed Keegan, 'that person is not Kale. It's something else, a changeling perhaps?'

'Changelings are a thing of myth, told to frighten children,' retorted Vanir.

Abruptly, there was a loud crack against the cavern wall.

'MACE, VANIR, CAN YOU HEAR ME? I HAVE TEACHER PALMER WITH ME.'

'It's Karnack, together with the teacher of stone magic,' hissed Keegan, testing his knife's edge. 'Well, they certainly took their time!'

'I KNOW YOU CAN HEAR ME. HOW MANY MORE STUDENTS ARE YOU GOING TO CONDEMN TO A LIFE OF IGNOMINITY?'

Standing, Vanir drew his sword, as did Mace, and static crackled at Savarin's fingertips.

'What do you think you're doing?' chastised Erica.

'We're going to fight!' shouted Vanir defiantly. 'I, FOR ONE, AM SICK AND TIRED OF RUNNING!' 'Besides, we've nowhere to go.'

'No, you can't,' cried Erica. 'There are too many of them. There must be another way.'

'Do you see another entrance, woman? An alternative?' spat Vanir. 'All our options are exhausted; the only way out is through that wall.'

'Vanir's right. Sooner or later, they will gain entry,' said Mace determinedly.

'IF YOU DO NOT SURRENDER QUIETLY, PALMER HERE WILL TEAR DOWN THIS WALL AND YOU WITH IT.'

'But it doesn't make sense to allow certain people entry, just to trap them here?' despaired Erica.

'FOOLS,' raged Karnack, 'YOU HAVE LEFT ME NO CHOICE BUT TO DESTROY YOU.'

Just then, the atmosphere filled with a soft blue-white light, and in the centre of the chamber, a figure appeared. *Rest easy. You are in no immediate danger.*

'Pellagrin!' proclaimed Savarin reverently.

Don't be in such a hurry to die, announced Pellagrin. *Those men trying desperately to gain access to this place will not succeed, not for a good while, at least. The time will come when your skills are needed, but that time is not yet upon you.*

'So Kale wasn't exaggerating when he said you revealed your presence to him,' said Keegan incredulously, 'and told him he was one of Aridain's protectors.'

That is correct.

'In that case, perhaps you can answer a question for me?'

Ask away gamekeeper, but whether I answer or not, depends on your question.

'Keegan, what are you doing?' said Erica, her head bowed. 'Pellagrin is not at our beck and call.'

Ignoring Erica's concerns, Keegan asked, 'If you chose Kale as Aridain's protector, what happened?'

The man in this chamber? Was an imposter. But Rest assured; Kale is alive. His mind, though, is in a darker place.

'What? What sort of answer is that?' despaired Keegan.

Abruptly, a loud grating of stone grinding upon stone issued from the far end of the chamber. Then an opening appeared in the rock face at the far end of the cavern, and the companions were saturated in an eery pulsating yellowy-white light.

Enhanced by the power of the past, sanctuary and harmony can be of great value, but we must also learn that gaining the advantage isn't everything. There are more important things in the world, lectured Pellagrin.

Cautiously approaching the strange chamber, they saw a humming, clicking, cigar-shaped object sat upon a strange polished pedestal which stood in the centre of the small chamber. Hard to look at directly, and covered in small multi-coloured lights that flickered and faded, the transparent object shone like a full moon.

'What is it?' Erica gasped.

A remnant of an era long past, said Pellagrin sadly. *Tied to my power, this creation has served the school for centuries. With its exotic power, I installed many of the safeguards at the school. But now its power is waning, and with it, many of the school's defences.*

'That's fine Pellagrin,' said Vanir sceptically. 'But it doesn't help us in the here and now.'

Observe greysword! announced Pellagrin. *The young healer was correct when she assumed there must be another way out. Beyond this otherworldly apparatus, at the far end of the chamber, is a door to the entrance that led me here. It has remained hidden ever since.*

'Why show us?' asked Keegan.

I would have thought the answer, obvious.

'Where does it lead?' asked Mace, testing his movement by flexing and bending.

To the courtyard.

'So, out of the frying pan and into the fire,' announced Keegan.

'I can't see as we have any other choice,' said Mace. 'It's just the cards we've been dealt.'

Keegan, securing his knife to his left upper arm, grinned. 'You're sounding more and more like Alfic every day, Mace. Do you know that?'

'Why thank you, you washed up old excuse for a gamekeeper. Now, where are you going?'

'I just need to get the rucksack,' declared Keegan. 'I'll catch you up.'

Followed by the sounds of shuddering and vibrating rock receding into the distance, the friends, passing the strange pulsating machine, scrambled through the ancient opening beyond.

CHAPTER THIRTY-THREE

FORTUNE AND BRAVERY

'So anymore flashbacks?' enquired Perak.

'Yes, it seems I'm an excellent horse rider,' replied Drench.

'And this has to do with your flashbacks; how?'

'I was feeding Mistress Konya's grey charger, Plunderer, and suddenly had a sensation of galloping through fields on the back of a large grey horse. Then, for no apparent reason, I mounted him, and to Konya's consternation and my surprise I rode him around the field, without a saddle; you understand. Despite her anger, Konya said my level of equine skills was impressive. I've always felt at ease around horses, Perak, but never dreamt I could ride one.' Drench's look of perplexity then turned to frustration. 'I hate not knowing, Perak, waiting for the next revelation; I just want to know who I really am, where I came from?'

'Don't worry,' Perak said encouragingly, 'I'm sure it's only a matter of time.'

With a squealing and a flurry of activity, one of the nets suddenly bulged as a rabbit, flushed from its burrow, struggled to break free. Drench rushed over and grasping the animal firmly, twisted its neck quickly and neatly; it was followed by one of the ferrets that popped its head above ground and, seeing that its meal had escaped, quickly ducked back underground.

'Blast. Well, we're not going to see them for a while. Oh well, whilst they're chasing their lunch, I'm going to have mine.'

'I'll join you,' smiled Drench.

Despite the cold snowy weather, the pair had had a satisfying afternoon, bagging twenty rabbits already as they moved steadily along the warrens dug into the earth between the orchard and the horse chestnut trees.

Perak studied Keegan's understudy as the youth efficiently tied the rabbits together and hung them over a branch. Square-jawed and handsome with short, light brown hair and alert brown eyes, Drench sported a nose reset badly after it had been broken during one of Crystal's self-defence lessons. A mystery wrapped up in an enigma, Drench, had settled in to a fulfilling life at the school. It wasn't until recently in his middle teens that he'd started suffering from flashbacks. He had been searching for answers ever since.

'So, how are you finding it, being the school's replacement game warden?'

'It's not too bad. Keegan's already taught me most of what he knows, but I do miss him being around. It's such a shame he's living a life in the shadows. Living in his hut feels weird, though.' He then looked over to the soldier leant against the tree, picking at his nails, and said quietly, 'I still feel like an intruder, like I'm a temporary lodger, I guess because he still visits, it just doesn't feel like mine.'

'Remember, Drench, the one thing that's constant in life is change. Without change, we don't grow, we don't undergo new experiences, sensations, or discover new horizons,' said Perak with certainty whilst looking searchingly at Drench's face.

Looking away deliberately, Drench said, 'Thank you, Perak, for convincing Teacher Crystal to take me on, although I can't imagine why she would want to teach me again, especially after the problems my anger caused.'

'She didn't take a lot of convincing, and yes, Crystal told me that because of you, your fellow students were some of the most bruised and broken she had ever taught. She also told me that despite your lack of discipline and control, you were her most gifted student; but I didn't tell you that, OK?' Seeing Drench's' sadness turn to self-satisfaction, and then pride, Perak, grinning absent-mindedly, said, 'That's more like it. You look like a pig that's found a truffle.'

Sat in silence, Perak, tucking into his lunch of ham, bread and cheese, lifted his face towards the light drizzle of snow. Closing his eyes in the fading light, and allowing the thick snowflakes to caress his face, he was distracted by a pair of raucous jackdaws, squabbling over something buried amongst the roots of one of the chestnut trees.

Abruptly, a memory of happier times flashed into focus, of him together with Alfic, Aridain and Chipper, performing this exact same task. It was the day that Aridain had learnt that to eat; you had to kill.

'.... Corvins are a pain in the ass;' had said Alfic during that cold, crisp morning two years ago. 'Blasted things will eat anything. I swear that if I get the chance....'

'Then you'll have to kill everything, Daddy. Life preys on life.' Aridain had sermonised.

'Are you lecturing *me* on how the world works?'

'It's the way things are, Daddy,' Aridain had said self-assuredly.

'Exactly, which is why we do this. By controlling the pests, it helps feed everything else. It maintains balance.'

'But Daddy, the animals don't know we grow food just for us. All they know is that there is there's lots of food here...'

Perak remembered his grandson's look of total confusion, which at the time was understandable ...

'Look at it this way,' Alfic had continued, 'say we never culled the rabbits or the pheasants, they would continue to breed out of control, consume more of the school's vegetables, then once they'd consumed all the produce, they would turn elsewhere for their food and the rabbits would start gnawing at the bark of the fruit trees, killing them. That would mean no more fruit and nowhere for the finches to nest. They, in turn, would leave, meaning there would be no more birds to eat the insect pests that would, in turn, devastate the trees. Culling also prevents suffering. It prevents disease from spreading amongst the rabbit population, which would be counter-productive. Also, an overabundance of prey would attract bigger predators; predators we've spent decades driving from the region, like firedrakes and Ardent wolves. Do you understand?'

Perak remembered as Aridain had looked up at him and nodded with wisdom, far in advanced of his years. His grandson may not have liked the truth, but Alfic made sure he understood, anyway...

Washing down his lunch with some cold tea, Perak was shaken from his thoughts by the chittering of ferrets.

Jumping up as the illusive creatures poked their heads above ground, Drench collected the now compliant creatures that, judging by their full bellies, had found another victim.

'Been enjoying yourselves down there, fellas? The plan is, you chase them to us, not catch and eat them. Now, in you go, time for bed. Seline preserve us! I'm turning into Keegan,' he chuckled whilst placing the ferrets back into their cage. Drench, turning towards him, then said, 'Regarding Alfic, is there nothing to be done? I mean, when in all of history has a mind master ever cared about humans?'

'Unless we can find that gutter worm, and persuade him to relinquish his hold on Alfic's mind, I fear for my son's sanity.' Standing and peering intrigued through the branches towards the school, Perak exclaimed, 'What's going on over there?'

'Never you mind, Perak Bruin,' ordered his ever-present guard gruffly, 'just attend to your own business.

Talking of Alfic, 'Where has he and his nursemaid soldier got to?' announced Perak.

Perak and Drench suddenly looked at each other in understanding.

'You don't think?' said Drench.

Perak turned to the guard. 'We need to find Alfic, now!'

'We'll do no such thing!' replied the guard.

'We think he's going to kill Kuelack.'

'Kill, Kuelack, pah, he wouldn't get close, especially tonight!'

'Why? What aren't you telling us?'

'None of your concern. Now get back to trapping rabbits; or whatever you're doing?'

'Alfic has no choice!' insisted Perak.

'Say for one minute, I believe you. How's he going to do it? we have men everywhere.'

'Alfic's been very clever, don't you see? He's using whatever's going on over there, to his advantage. As far as the soldiers are concerned, Alfic's one man amongst many.'

The guard turned his back on them, unconvinced.

'You're not listening to me. This is my son we're talking about; he's ex-army. OK, tell me this then, why haven't they returned? Where are they?'

Staring mutely, the guard's face suddenly expressed indecision.

'We're wasting time. Kuelack could be dead for all we know. Do you want your head adorning the school gates?'

'You're right. We have to go right now,' said the guard, changing his mind abruptly.

Hastily packing their equipment into a rucksack, Perak tossed it over his shoulders together with the rabbits, then helped Drench do the same with the ferrets' cage. They then made their way along the bank beside the orchard before crossing the combat field.

Spinning him around, Perak looked at Drench seriously. 'Take the catch to the kitchens. I need to stop my son before he makes a terrible mistake.'

Throwing the rabbits to the ground, Drench replied, 'Not on your nelly, I'm coming with you!'

Leaving the lighted chamber behind, Keegan led the party quickly through the tunnel, the air becoming increasingly damp with moisture the further they ventured. Revealed by the strange, intermittent lighting on the walls was a surface made from a strange, smooth, shiny metal, that had resisted any attempt by foreign plant invaders to tarnish its surface. However, venturing further, sections of the shiny walls and ceiling, together with the magical lights, now littered the floor and gave way to roughhewn rock.

Holding up his hand for them to stop, Keegan said, 'Listen, that's water up ahead. Must be the stream that feeds the well.'

However, as they resumed their progress forwards, some of the remaining magical lights had failed, whilst others, like a sputtering candle, flickered and dimmed, until eventually none remained, leaving them in darkness.

'So, did anyone think to bring torches?' said Vanir anxiously.

They all shook their heads.

'I know! Savarin, you can make some lightning,' said Keegan, waving his arms around wizard-like.

'Yes, I can, but in this confined space, I would kill us all.'

Fishing around in his rucksack, Keegan, producing some dried moss and a firelighter, said, 'Mace, I need your sword, and Savarin, your cloak.'

'What for?' asked Savarin suspiciously.

'It's OK Savarin, it's for a torch,' reassured Mace.

Tearing strips from the robe, Keegan lit the moss, then placed it upon the strips of cloth that crackled and spat noisily into life. Wrapping the cloth around the sword with his knife, the light revealed ground-water ahead. Water emanating from a hole in one wall ran across an algae-covered floor in wide fan shaped waves, then deliberately diverted to flow parallel with the opposite wall. Quickly reaching the end of the tunnel, Keegan, adding more strips of cloth to the fiercely burning torch, revealed an old set of wooden steps leading upward to a trapdoor in the roof.

'These stairs seem awfully fragile,' commented Keegan, caressing the crumbling wood.

'There's only one way to find out. Erica, are you up for it?'

'Why Erica?'

'Because she's the lightest!' exclaimed Vanir indignantly.

'I'm the obvious choice Vanir,' concluded Erica, standing on the bottom step.

'Then be careful,' said Vanir, 'and take your time.'

With the stairs creaking and groaning, Erica, stepping as gingerly as she dared, reached the top step and, reaching up to the ceiling, began feeling gingerly around the trapdoor's edges.

'Can you open it?'

Grasping the old metal bolt, she tried to slide it free but with no success; the stairway rocking and shuddering as Erica tried a little harder. Suddenly, the entire assembly came away in her hand, together with the old door, showering the group below in rotten wood and dust.

'Sorry?' said Erica sheepishly.

'Don't worry. What can you see, Erica? Is that….'

'Yes, it's been sealed with lime mortar.'

Looking sideways at Vanir, Keegan smiled. 'She's a clever girl, that one.'

'I knew it. We should have stayed and fought?' growled Vanir irritably, wiping at sweat that had run into his eyes.

'Calm yourself, Vanir,' barked Mace. 'We'll be out of here soon enough.'

'Why are you all looking at me like that?' said Vanir apprehensively. 'I'm just concerned about Erica's welfare, that's all.'

'You're claustrophobic!' announced Keegan.

'Claustrophobic, don't be ridiculous, greyswords don't get claustrophobia.'

'Hey, I'm not judging. We all have our foibles,' smiled Keegan.

'Like Keegan's fear of anything covered in slime,' smiled Mace.

'Or Mace's fear of spiders,' countered Keegan.

'You're scared of spiders?' said Vanir.

'Hey, lots of people are scared of spiders,' emphasized Mace, shuddering involuntarily. 'They are all "leggy" when they scuttle across the floor.'

'Can we please concentrate on getting out of here and not on this boyish rhetoric?' growled Savarin angrily.

Just then, the torch began to sputter and Keegan quickly added some more cloth.

'So, now what do we do?' urged Keegan.

'We could hack our way through,' said Vanir, 'but it would take too much time, and we'd be discovered.'

'Savarin, can you blast a hole through the ceiling?' suggested Mace.

'I can, but not knowing what's above, I can't guarantee the outcome,' exclaimed Savarin anxiously, 'and it won't be subtle.'

'It's the middle of the night, most people should be in bed, that should minimise any casualties and give us more time,' said Mace. 'Before we do this, has anyone else got a better plan…?'

'I'm really tired of hearing that sentence,' said Vanir.

'Hey guys, what do I do?' echoed Erica's voice from above.

'Come back down, slowly,' ordered Mace.

With no ideas forthcoming, and Erica back on firm ground, Savarin warned, 'In the confines of the tunnel you might find yourself short of breath for a spell. Now stand back and cover your eyes and ears.'

A breeze had sprung up as Drench, led by Perak and accompanied by the soldier, ran purposefully around the healing centre, the icy snowflakes prickling his skin like cold needles. Coming up short as Perak suddenly stopped, Drench watched as the gardener, through slitted eyes, peered into the night.

'What is it?'

'Something's amiss,' said Perak abruptly.

'Is it Alfic? He's not...?'

'...dead. No, this is something else. Something's happening now, tonight. I can feel it. The guard knew it, but wouldn't say.'

'You've mentioned that Byrak seeks revenge. For what?'

Perak hissed knowingly, 'Byrak seeks revenge for the death of his classmates, Drench, and his mentor.'

'If that's true, Byrak must know it's a suicide mission?'

Grasping Drench abruptly by the shoulders, Perak stared into his eyes, 'Byrak doesn't care if Alfic's attempt to kill Kuelack fails!' Perak then shook his head. 'Don't you see, as well as being my son, he's also the leader we need to challenge, Kuelack? Without him, our opposition here at the school will be in vain.'

After a few moment's silence, Drench, looking at him strangely, announced, 'Then what are we waiting for? We have to stop him?'

Together, they turned and ran after the guard, past the old guardhouse and around the edge of the fortress wall.

'Hey there's Alfic!' exclaimed Drench. 'Stop that man, don't let him through!' he bellowed, gesticulating to the guard who had reached the base of the steps.

Alfic, who was about to enter the fortress, turned at the mention of his name, then hastily began exchanging words with the two soldiers guarding the entrance.

Cursing when Alfic was allowed to precede inside, Drench watched as their guard reached the top step. Then, a heated exchange involving pushing and shoving ensued, together with angry gesticulations.

Catching sight of Perak and Drench striding determinedly up the steps, one of the guards suddenly announced, 'Perak Bruin, Drench, stay where you are! You are under arrest for attempting to murder Head Wizard, Kuelack.'

'Don't be a fool; let us through before it's too late,' their guard said angrily, forcing the soldier's hastily drawn sword towards the floor.

'Let us through, you idiots, Alfic's going to kill Kuelack,' announced Drench angrily, bounding up the steps and trying to force his way past the two guards that stubbornly refused to move from the entrance.

'Hey...? Get those things back in their cage!'

'I'm sorry,' shouted Perak. 'I must have left their cage door unlocked.'

Drench looked in horror as Molly and Mo, having somehow undone their cage door, were now scampering across the entrance hallway floor after Alfic.

The guards looked at each other, indecision on their faces.

'Now do you see? Alfic's headed towards the stairway.'

'Hey you, you're not allowed up there; you're staff!'

'Morons, follow me!' exclaimed their guard angrily.

Together with Perak, Drench and the soldiers sprinted after Alfic, who was performing a strange, perverted and stunted dance. It wasn't until they approached more closely that they saw, beneath his clothing, two undulating lumps moving about his person, biting and clawing.

'Alfic, stop right there,' shouted the guard.

'He won't stop, because he can't hear you,' despaired Perak. 'He's focused now, enchanted.'

The groundsman turned towards them abruptly, an almost feral look on his face. He then reached beneath his shirt and pulled out one of the ferrets. Despite Molly's aggressive attentions, he threw Mo across the floor, then withdrew a vicious-looking hatchet he'd concealed under his clothes. Locating the second ferret clawing its way to his groin, Alfic reached in and threw the biting, clawing creature to the floor.

'Alfic!' shouted Drench desperately. 'This is madness. Think what you're doing. You'll spend the rest of your life in a cell or worse. Think of Lascana and your son.'

Alfic paused and turned towards them in confusion. Then, his face a picture of determination, he turned around and sprinted towards the stairway.

'Wait,' warned Perak, suddenly standing still and grabbing Drench's arm. What's that noise?'

'What noise?'

Suddenly, the floor beside the grand stairway exploded upwards with an ear-shattering rending of stone and concrete that sent Alfic and the pursuing guards, tumbling through the air, peppering Drench and Perak and their surroundings in fragments of wood and concrete. Through a haze of confusion, Drench glanced at Perak, then peered through the swirling mass of dust and debris to see a twisting column of air as it spiralled across the atrium's stone floor. Pulling Perak to safety, beneath one of the heavy, robust administrative desks, Drench noticed Alfic lying prostrate and unmoving on the bottom step of the polished stairway, whilst the guards, their limbs contorted into strange, unnatural positions, lay dead next to the crater.

'This is Savarin's work!' hissed Perak.

As the dust and debris filled wind began to subside, Drench stared astonished, as a woman's head appeared from the newly formed crater.

'I know that face; that's Erica Markeson!' exclaimed Perak, 'She's a student of the healing arts.'

Drench then watched astonished, as Erica, looking around covertly, quickly tied a knotted rope to the marble embellished banister then dropped the other end down the hole.

A guard appearing through the main entrance, sprinted towards the gaping hole, ordering Erica to stay where she was. Thrusting his pike into the darkness repeatedly, he peered into the ragged hole, then suddenly disappeared from view. The soldier was replaced by the ragged, unkempt hair and face of Keegan, peering around dramatically, looking like an inquisitive meerkat. Wielding his favoured, serrated Korda blade, Keegan pulled himself from the hole and, scanning the courtyard, looked in his direction.

'Don't just stand there, Drench, Alfic's beginning to stir. We have to get him away from here.'

Shaken from his stunned confusion, Drench joined Perak, and they sprinted across the hallway. Acting instinctively, Drench leapt upon an increasingly agitated Alfic.

'It's like wrestling with a Brean lion,' bellowed Drench. 'We'll never get him to safety struggling like this.'

'You're right.' Perak turned to his irate son and said, I'm sorry Alfic.' Perak then delivered a solid punch to Alfic's jaw.

Drench glanced over his shoulder once more to see Keegan and Mace standing ready as soldiers began filing into the enclosed courtyard.

'Help me here, Drench. DRENCH!'

He turned savagely towards Perak. 'What sort of man are you that you would just abandon them?'

'We can't help them, but we can save Alfic! I understand your frustration, Drench, but as much as we want to help, we must disassociate ourselves. Trust me, Keegan and Mace can take care of themselves. They also have Vanir with them, and the finest weather wizard in the land fighting by their side.'

Drench, tears of anger stinging his eyes, grasped Alfic's legs. With one last forlorn look behind, he let Perak lead him blindly towards a thick oak door, the fading sounds of clashing swords and aggressive cursing and shouting, reverberating intensely through the fortress.

CHAPTER THIRTY-FOUR

ALFIC'S MADNESS

Stroking the head and snout of the Dragonlet sat contented upon her lap, Lascana, together with Vara's sister Mira, sat and watched the glowing embers of the wood burner, whilst listening to the sputter of candles in the silence of the small claustrophobic apartment.

It must be nice, she thought to herself, looking down at the dragonlet, *to be able to disassociate yourself, and prioritise your feelings regarding the situations you found yourself in, instead of constantly questioning your actions.* She then looked over to Aridain laid asleep on his cot.

After all, they'd been through, she trusted her son's instincts implicitly. So, when he had told her of the bad man in Alfic's head, she had believed him. His instincts had been confirmed earlier that day when she had discovered Alfic searching through Aridain's possessions. Asking what he was doing, Alfic had become angry and defensive, demanding she tell him where Aridain was. The very question had raised suspicions, as they never knew where their son was, and he could literally be anywhere. His mood, however, had suddenly flipped when she had mentioned the man in his head. The hurt in his eyes had nearly broken her as, apologising profusely for his behaviour, he had pleaded that he didn't know what was happening to him. Then, reassuring her of his sanity, he had, as far as she was concerned, returned to work. It was later that day that Vara's sister, Mira, had arrived on her doorstep. The story she had told of the Hasps' intentions toward her son had been impactful, to say the least. It was one more problem they didn't need.

Looking up at what she thought was an explosion, Lascana crept towards the door. Looking to Aridain one more time to confirm he remained asleep, Lascana, together with Mira, slipped out into the corridor.

'Out of the way, woman!'

Retreating into the doorway, they waited as several guards hurried past. Following, she pressed herself against the open oak door and stared flabbergasted into the administration hall. Hit by a wave of pressure that threatened to knock them from their feet, they stared in dismay as Keegan, Mace and Vanir, battled their way towards the main entrance, leaving a trail of dead and dying soldiers in their wake.

Lascana then looked down and closed her eyes, caressing her swollen belly, recalling Alfic's dismay when he had discovered her continued involvement, despite her being heavy with child. *Is this the future her child had to look forward to?* she thought.

'Hold the door!'

Lascana baulked as Perak, together with Keegan's apprentice Drench, hurried towards them carrying a comatose Alfic.

Closing the thick oak door as if the act would close a curtain on the violent events, Lascana, ushering them into the small apartment, instructed, 'Lay him down over here on the bed.'

Seeing the trauma etched upon Alfic's twitching features, Mira said reassuringly, 'I'll give him something to make him sleep.'

'Mum, what's the matter with Daddy?' asked Aridain, sitting up and rubbing at his sleep befuddled eyes.

'Your father's just a little tired, dear.'

'This is about the bad man in his head, isn't it?'

'Go back to sleep Aridain, there's nothing to see here?' snapped Lascana irritably.

'It's not fair,' said Aridain, laying back down upon the bed and turning over grumpily, 'no one tells me anything.'

Instantly regretting her outburst, she turned to Perak. Throwing her arms around him, then straightening up and punching him on the arm, she asked, 'What happened, Father? Are you both all right?' worried Lascana. 'Where did you find him?' she snapped. 'I was going out of my mind.'

'He's....'

'If it wasn't for Mira here, I don't know what I would have done.'

'Lascana, if you'd let me....'

'Alfic's accusing people of conspiring behind his back, and no one's talking to me because of Alfic's fearsome reputation,' cried Lascana, 'he's even accused me of....' Lascana, looked up, and noticing Drench's knowing glance towards Perak, said... 'What is it? What aren't you telling me? You know who's inside my husband's head, don't you?' said Lascana irately.

'The reason why Alfic's not been himself is Byrak,' said Perak miserably.

'Byrak? But he's a....'

'....yes, a psychic, and until Byrak decides otherwise, Alfic will continue with his task until either he or his target is dead, and no Lascana, killing Byrak will make no difference,' said Perak, pre-empting the question he knew was coming.

'But there must be a way?'

Just then, there was an insistent banging on the door. 'Lascana. Open up!'

'It's Karnack,' hissed Perak.

'What do you want?' said Lascana, now all serenity and calmness.

'You know why I'm here.'

'I can assure you I don't.'

'Mummy, what's going on?' said Aridain, grasping her leg fearfully, having appeared without a sound.

'It's all right Munch Kin, everything is all right.'

'Open this door Lascana, before we break it down.'

Looking at them all Lascana said, 'Hold your horses, Karnack, I have to find the key.' Approaching Aridain's bed, Lascana said, 'I don't know if you can understand me Sabra, but I need you to hide, just until these people leave.'

To Lascana's surprise, the dragonlet replied in her head, *Perfectly, Aridain's birth mother.*

Lascana smiled then and nodded in understanding.

When Sabra had disappeared into the night, Lascana closing the window, straightened her clothes, then walked serenely across the room, and opened the door.

Barged aside by soldiers wielding heavy wooden clubs and flaming torches, Lascana squaring her shoulders, said, 'They're not here, if that's what you're thinking?'

'Oh, we know. Jackamar is in pursuit of the outlaws as we speak. When we arrest them, we will wring a confession out of them. Then we'll see how cocky you are when Alfic, you, and your pathetic resistance are rotting in the dungeons.'

'This is insane,' said Lascana 'You're acting like the leader of an angry mob on a witch hunt.'

'And you said the door was locked,' hissed Karnack aggressively.

'No, I didn't. I said I had to find the key.'

The greysword then raised his hand to Lascana, then thought better of it. 'You think me a fool?'

'No, just someone who has lost his direction, his purpose in life,' replied Lascana.

'So, you have come to arrest your friend, laid comatose upon a bed, and accuse him of aiding his friends' escape,' charged Perak dourly.

'I am a greysword charged with defending the school.'

'Don't make me laugh, Karnack. Using your position to bully your friends was never your mandate.'

Turning to the soldiers, Karnack ordered angrily, 'Wake him up.'

'What are you doing? He's in no condition to be moved, let alone harm anyone!' said Perak angrily.

'As you well know, he attacked one of the two soldiers assigned to him. This cannot go unpunished.'

'He wasn't in his right mind,' pleaded Perak.

'More excuses and apologies!'

'Please Karnack, don't do this. You've been a friend for as long as I can remember,' pleaded Lascana.

'Yes, what happened to the man I knew, who would never have raised his hand to a pregnant woman, let alone Lascana?' said Perak. 'What happened to the honourable man who would stand against injustice, fight for his friends?'

Karnack, reaching subconsciously for his eye patch, replied, 'Reality happened.'

Turning angrily towards the soldiers, Karnack barked, 'I told you to wake him up.'

'We've made enough noise to wake the dead. He won't wake up.'

'Don't blame them,' said Mira. 'To help his mind cope, I've given him something to help him sleep.'

'With the workload his brother, your boss, has heaped upon him, together with Byrak creeping around in his head… my husband is at breaking point,' beseeched Lascana.

'The psychic, Byrak?'

'Yes. You didn't know? I'd be amazed if Alfic hasn't sustained permanent damage,' said Perak, pointing to his forehead.

Turning towards the guards, Karnack said, 'Assign guards to the door and window. Don't let anyone else in or out. I'll handle this.'

Waiting until the guards had left, Lascana, with tears in her eyes, said, 'Bless you Karnack.'

'I do this for the friendship we once had, but understand that this is the last time I will grant you leniency. The next time you slip up, I cannot help you.'

When Karnack had left, Lascana, feeling that not just the school but the gods themselves were conspiring against her and her family, looked around at Perak accusingly.

'Permanent damage! What did you mean, permanent damage?'

Perak, taking Lascana's hands in his, urged her to sit down. 'I thought the statement would add weight to our cause. Don't fret, Alfic's strong. I'm pretty sure he'll be all right.'

'Very reassuring, I don't think!' she worried.

'I'll put the kettle on and make us all a drink,' said Mira softly. 'I know I could do with one.'

Lascana stared over at her husband asleep on the bed. It was hard to imagine two personalities vying for domination in his head, one willing to do whatever it took to complete Byrak's instructions; the other… well, that worried her. Alfic already nurtured an inbred hatred for his brother, so would he put up that much of a fight?

Lascana watched Mira from her position sat wearily in front of the fire, filling the copper kettle with water from the water barrel in the corner, then placed it upon the stove. Filling the teapot with tea, she located some ground hops wrapped in a paper bag sat upon one of the shelves, and then emptied the contents together with skullcap root, pennyroyal, chamomile and mustard powder into a pestle.

'So, Alfic is to remain asleep indefinitely?'

'Drench, we've only just saved him from a suicide mission. Until we can find a way to cure him, he has to remain sedated,' insisted Perak.

Lascana watched miserably, as Mira then began busily grinding the ingredients into a powder, then empty them into the earthenware pot. When the kettle whistled, indicating the water had boiled, Mira poured the water into the teapot and the rest over the ingredients. When it had infused, she sifted out the contents, adding two tablespoons of honey into the mixture. She then emptied a mineral powder the colour of raspberry into the infusion.

'What was that?' asked Aridain, peering up at Mira, as she busily stirred the water infused contents.

'Raspberry garnet. It's a mineral that imparts health, self-discovery and balance. Hand me that large China container, will you, Perak?' requested Mira. 'It should be big enough.'

Draping another muslin cloth over the container, Mira poured in the ingredients. She then transferred the mixture into small stoneware jars.

'This is all I can do. If I increase the dosages any higher, I'll do more harm than good. Alfic's destiny is in the hands of the gods now.'

Troubled, and watching sympathetically as Aridain settled beside his father, now laid upon the bed, Drench said, 'But surely there's something more we can do? It's like we're just giving up.'

Approaching his son and grandson affectionately, Perak said solemnly, 'We're not giving up, just sparing my son unnecessary torment.'

'I say we get Alfic away from the school; away from Byrak,' said Drench dramatically.

'If it were only that simple,' contended Perak. 'Imagine an itch you can never scratch, an itch just out of reach. Then imagine that itch is a person in your head, urging and compelling, on and on until that itch is sated. Mind masters are the pinnacle of magic. For all we know, they transcend magic. A mind master can sense you coming, and before your even aware, your conscious and unconscious mind is theirs to command. If you imagine the damage just one psychic could do in control of one wizard, then imagine the damage a group of mind masters could do in control of an army of the greatest wizards in Aymara.'

The realisation and despair in Drench's eyes were all Perak needed to know to confirm that his message had hit home. Then more sympathetically, Perak said, 'Now you understand that until we can convince the novice psychic to reconsider his foolishness, this is the only way.'

'That's enough, the both of you. It's time to sedate my husband before Byrak realises what we are doing and wakes him up.'

With Lascana looking on forlornly, Mira, approaching with a bottle of the herb infused liquid and a small copper funnel, instructed, 'Place the funnel into his mouth, Lascana.'

With a silent sigh of acceptance, Lascana opened Alfic's mouth and placed the copper funnel between his lips, allowing Mira to slowly pour the liquid down Alfic's throat.

'Now your husband cannot harm anyone, as hard as Byrak tries,' confirmed Mira. 'Best we feed him whilst we're at it.'

Perak then appeared beside Lascana, and wrapping his arm around her waist, stood looking down at his son. 'So, this is how it is. This is how the gods reward the great and the good. I don't believe I'm going to say this, but we could do with Vara's skills right now.'

Joining them, Mira said guardedly. 'We're lucky Byrak's only an apprentice psychic. If he was fully fledged, like Mass Martin, there's a good chance he would wake up, regardless of the dispenser.'

'Will Daddy be all right?' worried Aridain.

'Yes, Munch kin, this is your father we're talking about,' she smiled.

Lascana began dishing a meat pie and vegetables into wooden bowls and they sat around the cramped quarters in silence, whilst Lascana scraped the remains into a small wooden dish for Sabra who had, not surprisingly, appeared at the window.

'This pie is really good, Mrs Bruin,' said Drench.

Licking at a glob of gravy that had dribbled down his chin, Aridain nodded in agreement. 'Mummy's pies are always yummy.'

'Glad you like it,' smiled Lascana serenely.

Having put Aridain to bed, Lascana poured the tea and then settled next to the fire. Sipping at her stewed, piping-hot tea, Lascana said resolutely, 'Now, it's about time you all catch me up on the day's events.'

With Perak and Drench looking on expectantly, Mira began…

'Well, the reason I'm here is that the Hasp have targeted Lascana's son, the Balefire Taal…'

Sat alone in the food hall, Karnack swallowed yet another tankard of ale. Signalling to the serving girl, he sat and stared morosely at the tabletop.

'Another?'

'Yes Aimee, another?'

'Mr Karnack, are you OK?' she said, looking down at him concernedly.

'I will be when you serve me my beer girl,' snapped Karnack angrily.

Don't take your frustrations out on others, he thought. *It's not their fault, you pathetic excuse for a greysword.*

Without turning his head, Karnack perceived Jackamar as he entered the room and made a beeline for his table.

Jackamar, the youngest of the four of them, had never embraced the Greysword responsibility. To him, the obligation seemed otherworldly, someone else's burden. To him, it was a tool, something to be used to his advantage, something to exploit, so when the offer came to enhance the magic and ability already bestowed upon him, Jackamar had jumped at the chance.

Waiting in silence until the young, brash greysword had sat down opposite and ordered a beer, he looked up and said grimly, 'Report!'

'They escaped!'

'Prey, tell me how this happened. You had plenty of men.'

'It was impossible to get close. When we thought we had them boxed in, and were ready to pounce, they would disappear, it was like chasing ghosts,' spat Jackamar angrily.

'Is there no one I can trust, no one to carry out my orders,' rumbled Karnack, eyeing the young greysword dangerously. 'As a result of your feeble efforts, I have to explain to Kuelack why two of the best swordsmen in the land escaped, together with the most powerful weather wizard in the land.'

'Which reminds me Karnack, why isn't Alfic locked up in the dungeons?'

'When I confronted the Bruins, he was laid comatose. He posed no threat.'

'Or it could be your former association with the Bruins? To the uneducated, it's almost like you're conspiring to help the traitors.'

Karnack watched, satisfied, as Jackamar squirmed under his baleful stare. 'Are you accusing me of something?' growled Karnack, reaching over his shoulder and grasping his sword's hilt. 'You're not the only one with enhancements here, remember, and I'd prefer not to have to explain why I severed your head from your body.'

Retreating only slightly but not backing down, Jackamar, through clamped jaw and pursed lips, said cautiously, 'I'm saying that only those who embrace the future, who believe in Kuelack's new utopia, deserve a place in it.'

'Those so-called traitors are more deserving of a place here than you or me. They have more honour and integrity in their little finger than we will ever have.'

'So, according to your code of honour, the Bruins and their friends go free. And what about the traitorous greyswords? Do they also deserve your reverence?'

'I'm more concerned with Savarin's whereabouts.'

'He's just one weather wizard,' said Jackamar brazenly. 'What's the problem?'

'Savarin is the most senior weather wizard in Durbah, and Kuelack has pissed him off. Savarin has the power to destroy the school and everything Kuelack has built here. We'd be fools to underestimate him.'

'You're afraid! Afraid of people who are nothing more than fugitives and peasants.'

'Remember Jackamar, pride comes before a fall. Jailing the Bruins or killing Alfic will not solve our problems. Kuelack agrees and has decreed that the Bruins must live.'

'Or perhaps your affection for the Bruins is blinding you to our cause?'

Karnack stood and drew his sword from its scabbard on his back, causing Jackamar to step back and do the same. Pointing it at the young greysword, Karnack warned, 'One more word...'

They stared at each other for a time, neither willing to back down or make the first move. Looking around at the staff and the concern upon their faces, Karnack turned his back on the young greysword, holstered his sword and sat back down.

'Kuelack's demands will be carried out,' stated Karnack imperiously. 'And without support, the resistance will fail. Then, when their guard is down, we will bring their friends to justice. Now, if you need to vent your anger, I suggest you teach those pathetic students you call swordsmen a lesson,' said Karnack unsympathetically. 'Enhanced they may be, but there is nothing like good old school combat. Now, sit down, we have plans to refine.'

CHAPTER THIRTY-FIVE

THE PRECIPICE

It was nearly lunchtime of the following day. Drench had left early that morning, as had Perak, followed soon afterwards by Lascana, in order to fulfil her duties in the fortress. The snow clouds having cleared away overnight, Mira, humming a melodic tune, set down the wooden buckets having filled them with water. Assured, knowing that Aridain was safe in the dragonlet's care, Mira held her hand in front of her face to shield her eyes from the sun's weak, but none-the-less uplifting light. She marvelled at its sparkling halo that, according to Perak, was formed by minute crystals of ice suspended in the air. Basking for a moment longer, she squatted beneath the yoke, then hefted the full buckets clear of the ground. With the yoke balanced upon her shoulders, she approached the Betrayer's door, located in the fortress's outer wall. At a word from the guard, the door slowly opened, allowing her inside. Scuttling through the arched tunnel beneath the fortress's wall, trying not to spill any water, she then made her way across the snow-covered open courtyard, and its attendant-like workers milling around, gesturing here and pointing there. Entering through the rear of the fortress, she then reached Lascana's small apartment, closing the door behind her. She was greeted by the boisterous Aridain and the ever-attendant dragonlet.

'All present and correct, Ma'am,' saluted Aridain.

Setting the buckets down and returning his closed fisted salute, she replied, 'As you were private.'

She smiled as Aridain sat down once more and devoured a book containing Balefire enchantments, given to him apparently by Vara. Yes, he would make a good Taal, that was provided he stayed alive long enough. Massaging her throat, Mira thought about what the yellow hag had said;

"Acumen Monstera will have your grandson. It is his destiny."

The Taal needed her protection, but she also needed to know what the hag had taken from the bottom shelf of Vara's cupboard, and the only person who could tell her was Vara.

Turning abruptly, she relaxed as Lascana, her face like thunder, entered the small apartment.

'My shop has been seized?' said Lascana, aghast, banging her hands on the counter aggressively. 'The shop owners are nowhere to be seen, either. In fact, anyone opposed to Kuelack has now been "disappeared". When I protested, I was told that all the stores had been commandeered for the war effort, and that my duty should be to the school, not my own self-serving interests.'

'Ingrates, it is the way of the uneducated, the unenlightened,' said Mira darkly.

'All of my friends, gone,' continued Lascana, angrily, 'and where are they? In the dungeons, or worse. Catherine Galfonsen is now serving in Bern's greengrocers, and the obnoxious father of the apprentice blacksmith, Jack Inware, is now the butcher. Only the apothecary and the morgue still belong to their owners. I don't have a clue who's tending the other stalls.'

'It's the way of the paranoid, Lascana, the bully. They fear the unknown, and what they fear and don't understand, they control and oppress. Your husband's brother is just being systematic. Take the stalls, for instance; these are all services vital to Kuelack's efforts, and now, consequently, he has eyes and ears everywhere, belonging to people under his control.'

'People like Milvus Block, who are on board of their own free will,' said Lascana, heatedly.

Helping unpack the bacon, eggs, black pudding and sausages from Lascana's wicker basket onto the table-top, Mira couldn't help but notice Lascana's forlorn glances towards her husband laid on the bed, as if in a dreamless sleep.

'This is all part of Kuelack's plan, you know, to demoralise us, but it will only succeed if we give up,' growled Lascana angrily. 'We always thought that as Aridain's parents we were relatively safe, however, this stalemate will not last. Eventually, Kuelack will want us either to concede or he'll want us gone.'

Having eaten, they sat down next to the wood burner, drinking tea. Then, looking up in thought, Lascana said, 'Talking of misfortune, you mentioned, Mira, that a goshen attacked you. Care to elaborate?' said Lascana.

'Well, a Goshen is an undead spirit, conjured from another plain. Drawn here to cause chaos, they feast on the spirits of the living.'

'Like a ghost?' asked Aridain, intrigued.

'Yes, Aridain, but these are more substantial, more like a half ghost.'

'Aridain, be quiet now.'

'It's not fair, I....'

'Aridain, if you say, I never get told anything, one more time, so help me, I'll....'

'Don't be hard on the boy, Lascana. This is something he needs to learn.'

Squatting in front of Aridain, Mira explained, 'Goshen are discontented. They crave life. Once summoned to this world, they are drawn to anything living. But what they really crave is iniquity and sin. They consume these souls in a failed attempt to obtain mortality. The more they consume, the more substantial they become, so the more souls they want. But they can never achieve life.'

'Did the goshen get away?' asked Aridain, now wide-eyed.

'No, I banished it back to its realm, wherever that may be.'

'You said that when you returned to the house, you found Vara's private store open and an entire shelf empty. What aren't you telling me, Mira?' said Lascana.

'We need to know what those missing ingredients are. It will determine how we counter this new threat. I know, these are uncertain times and you're scared; we all are. I believe that this entire episode was orchestrated to one end only, to gain access to your son.'

'So, what you're saying is that Aridain is some kind of messiah to The Hasp.'

'Correct. They believe he belongs with them, in the capital.'

'I've never been to Gonda before,' said Aridain, intrigued.

'Barring my death, you never will either,' said Lascana, outraged. 'You are to stay away from that chaotic melting pot of debauchery and corruption, do you hear?'

Hissing loudly, the dragonlet matching Lascana's determination, nodded in agreement.

'As if we didn't have enough on our plates, with Alfic, and the threat from within the school....'

'I'm so sorry that you had to hear it from me. But no matter what the odds, and despite the destruction and chaos, you and your family will adapt. You will prevail; it's in you, it's a part of your family's makeup and why you and Alfic, as Aridain's parents, were chosen.'

Holding Mira close, Lascana whispered in her ear, 'Bless you, and thank you for that.' Holding her at arm's length, Lascana looked at her strangely.

'What is it?' enquired Mira.

'I'm just trying to fathom how two sisters can be so different.'

'Different; in what way?'

'Vara is so hard and unreachable, whereas I feel I've known you for years.'

'Don't be so hard on my sister. When our father left, it hit our mother hard, Vara harder still. Being the eldest, she also took on a lot of responsibility.'

'If you're willing, I'd like to hear that story.'

Mira said forlornly. 'Another day, perhaps?'

Looking at Mira intently, Lascana said, 'Thank you for your kindness and support. All I can offer you is my heartfelt thanks.'

Mira, a genuine smile upon her face, said, 'It's the only reward I require.'

Washing the plates and mugs, Mira turned to Aridain and said, 'Come on. Tell me everything you've done recently.'

'What, everything?' exclaimed Aridain.

'Yes, everything,' encouraged Mira, following him as he ran and leapt onto his small bed. Then, pointing to her head, Mira said, 'If I'm to help you, I need you to tell me how you feel, what's going on up here.'

Suddenly, his face creasing up in thought, Aridain said, 'Mummy, soldiers are outside the door.'

Lascana, looking towards Mira and shrugging her shoulders, in a way that said, "This is what my son does", approached the door, then opened it.

Poised to knock, with two soldiers at his back, and attired in the crimson leather armour of Pellagrin's school, a tall, handsome youth, announced self-importantly, 'There's work to do. Alfic's presence is required.'

'Why, it's Kuelack's errand boy, Gavin Torn,' sneered Lascana. 'Karnack has decreed he be left to rest,' said Lascana confidently.

'This decree is from Kuelack himself,' said Gavin Torn. 'Alfic must return to work.'

'In other words, you're here to torment my family further on Kuelack's behalf...' protested Lascana. 'Well, thanks to your boss, Alfic is unavailable.'

Pushing past, and ignoring the dragonlet's menacing hissing, Gavin Torn strode over to the bed and began shaking Alfic vigorously.

'You won't wake him up! He's asleep for a reason,' insisted Mira.

'Wake him up!' ordered Gavin aggressively.

'Kuelack does understand that with Byrak's compulsion embedded in Alfic's mind, my husband *will* try to kill him again.'

'We have contingencies in place for that. Right now, we need his construction skills.'

'So, my husband must suffer even more at Kuelack's whim?'

'I call it poetic justice,' sneered Gavin, the two soldiers nodding and smiling in agreement. 'When I return, I want him awake and ready to work.'

When Gavin and the soldiers left, Lascana hissed, 'Snotty nosed little shit, he's got his nose so far up Kuelack's corrupt arse that the smell of decency is a distant memory.'

'But Mum, the bad man is still in Daddy's head!'

Her blood boiling, Lascana, with barely contained anger, said, 'I know, Munch kin. It seems the gods, in their infinite wisdom, have decreed that we haven't suffered enough.'

'In order to wake your husband, I need to ingest the sleeping draft,' said Mira, smiling purposefully. 'I then need to mix it with my "essence", shall we say?'

Handed another small bottle of the sleeping draught, Mira emptied it into her mouth. Concentrating, Mira, her face now a mask of pain, swilled the concoction around her mouth. Leaning over Alfic, she opened his mouth, then placing her lips against his, she allowed the liquid to dribble into his mouth.

A short time later, Aridain, staring at his father forlornly, said warily. 'Mummy, Mira, Daddy's waking up.'

Walking over to Alfic, Lascana asked cautiously, 'How are you feeling, Alfic?'

Alfic peered about him, a look of confusion on his face. 'I don't understand? I was ferreting with Father and Drench, and now I'm here?'

'Alfic. Perak and Drench stopped you killing Kuelack, don't you remember?'

'I tried to kill Kuelack? I have no memory of this! What's the matter? Why are you stood so distant?' growled Alfic, looking around in confusion.

Stood together with Aridain and Mira, the dragonlet perched upon her son's shoulder, Lascana, her heart breaking, watched as Alfic tried and failed to rise from the chair. Gripping the hand offered her by Mira, she watched Alfic's increased agitation as he stared down in disbelief at the straps tied around his ankles and wrists.

Testing the restraints, his persona taking on a deadly calm, Alfic said, 'Ahh, I see, you think Byrak's still controlling me, don't you?'

'The very fact that Alfic mentioned Byrak, Lascana, confirms that he is still the psychic's pawn,' whispered Mira stoically.

Pleasantly Alfic said, 'OK, now this is getting ridiculous. This woman, Lascana, whoever she is, obviously has you under some kind of spell.'

'Alfic, please try to understand. You are a danger to yourself, the school, and our family. It's the reason for these precautions.'

'This is ridiculous,' said Alfic incredulously. 'Release me, let me prove to you who I really am. Aridain, son, come here, there's no need to be afraid, I'm your father,' said Alfic, smiling at him kindly.

Lascana watched as Aridain stared intently at Alfic, then at Sabra.

When Aridain refused to obey, Alfic said, 'Don't look to the dragonlet, Aridain, listen to me. I'm your father. Do as you're told!'

'No!' cried Aridain.

Alfic's head dropped to his chest, and he began shaking as if he was sobbing.

Lascana started forwards, but was stopped by Mira.

'Lascana, no!' exclaimed Mira. 'Remember that your son is the Balefire Taal,' as if that statement explained everything.

Suddenly Alfic looked up. Then, as if a shutter had been firmly closed, he said, 'Stay out of this witch. This is about a father's authority over his family.'

'This is about reality and your absence from it,' alleged Lascana angrily.

Gazing upon Aridain as a firedrake gazes upon a jackrabbit, Alfic said, 'Aridain, I want you to show me your pretty stones.'

'You can't have them!' cried Aridain wretchedly.

His face mad with blood lust, Alfic, like a wildling outcast, began thrashing about uncontrollably.

Thrusting Aridain and Lascana behind her, Mira reached into her pocket just too late. As, with an almighty effort Alfic wrenched the weakened chair apart. With remnants of the chair still firmly tied to his forearms and calves, Alfic laid about him, striking Mira to the ground and advancing upon Aridain. This prompted the dragonlet, its skin now the colour of lava, to rise to Aridain's defence.

'Sabra! No!' screamed Lascana. 'He's not himself, and you might hurt Aridain.'

'I don't want to hurt him, Aridain's birth mother, but I will do all in my power to prevent his birth father from hurting the youngling and taking the shards.'

'Sabra,' instructed Mira confidently, 'trust the Taal'.

Alfic, thrusting Lascana aside, grasped Aridain by the hair. Then, holding him close, Alfic said, 'Yes, Treerinks, how deep is your affection for this child?' Spinning the youth around, Alfic, caressing Aridain roughly, said, 'No more games son, give the shards to me now.'

'They're mine to keep. Nobody else can have them,' shrieked Aridain, staring determinedly into eyes that were not his father's.

Alfic, searching Aridain's clothing, bellowed, 'I order you, give them to me, now!'

Unable to prevent Alfic, Aridain screamed, 'No!!!'

But before Mira or the dragonlet could react, Aridain, with determination and grit, grasped Alfic's ears. Then, with tear-filled eyes, Aridain, with strength born of desperation, began shaking Alfic violently. 'Leave my daddy alone,' he screamed, 'Get out, get out!'

Then Aridain's tirade abruptly ceased, and a hush descended upon the small room. Lascana started forwards as the pair sat staring at each other, then felt a solid hand upon her arm.

'Wait Lascana,' said Mira, 'something's happening here?'

Aridain opened his eyes and looked around; he was in a strange irregular world that wavered and shifted.

With a feeling of nausea threatening to overwhelm him, his voice resonating loudly, Aridain said fearfully, 'Mum? Mira?'

People he did and did not know came into focus, then disappeared, accompanied by familiar smells and familiar landscapes. Remembering the lessons Auntie Magen had taught him, Aridain closed his eyes and focused on his racing heartbeat. Having calmed his fear to an extent, he opened his eyes and found himself in the dead and diseased rear garden, at the rear of the ruined cottage. Black sludge covered everything, and in front of him, decaying trees lay dead and dying.

Looking around in despair, his voice echoing in this lifeless place, Aridain, struggling to make sense as to where he was, shouted, 'Hello, is anybody here?'

It was then that a familiar friend appeared, bounding towards him from out of the trees.

'Chipper,' he smiled, 'Hello boy, it's so good to see you again!'

Leaping towards him, the spirit of his chocolate doberman flattened him to the ground and began licking his face enthusiastically. Chipper then looked down at him with intelligent forethought.

Looking into the Doberman's eyes, Aridain said, 'Daddy, is that you?'

His tongue lolling, Chipper looked at him in understanding. Disengaging and barking enthusiastically, Chipper turned towards the trees. It was a gesture to follow that Aridain instantly recognised from so many times before.

Accompanying the doberman into the withered woodland, his canine companion led him through the decay and putrefaction to the cherry tree grove. At its centre, amongst what seemed to be the only vestiges of life left, tethered by branches to the old gnarly, withered cherry tree, was his father. Through fresh tears, Aridain studied his father's torn and tattered clothing, his emaciated body and skin now the colour of ash.

'Daddy, we found you. But why are you tied to the old cherry tree?'

His father looked up wearily at his approach with deathly sunken eyes, ravaged with pain. 'Do you... not know... where you are... my son?'

'The cherry grove, but it isn't?'

His face creasing in pain, his father, struggling to get the words out, said, 'You must... comprehend where you are... you must... work it out.'

Aridain looked around. The Dark creature was dead, so why were the woods in darkness and covered in the slime? Why was everything dying, and why did his father look like that?

Aridain started towards the cherry tree, but before he could reach his father, a dark swirling mass appeared between them, menacing and intimidating. Coalescing into the shape of a face, it boomed, 'Leave this place boy, I am the master here. Your father is mine.'

Suddenly, the truth dawned. Scared, but angry, Aridain looked up at the scary face and said resolutely, 'Leave my daddy alone, nasty man. Get out of my daddy's head.'

'Son... leave this place... before he takes you too,' gasped his father.

'No, never, me and Chipper will save you!'

'Foolish boy, you are no match for me.'

Suddenly, everything turned upside down, as the darkness, in an effort to overwhelm him, began flooding his mind.

With every instinct telling him to heed the evil face's warning and run, a maxim that his father, Keegan and Mace used to recite suddenly popped into his head.

Calming his mind, Aridain began reciting ...

You can tighten your fist, take away people's choices; but
you can never still the people's voices.
The tighter you increase your grip, so hardship forges bonds
of lasting comradeship.
As the thirst for freedom fuels the hunger for vengeance, the
more the people will endeavour to escape from the shackles
of a lasting sentence…

His father then took up the words, and together they began reciting
over and over. It was then that Aridain saw the first signs of panic in
the dark face.

'What! What are you doing?' boomed the entity.

'You will leave my daddy alone, now!'

The attack suddenly intensified. 'You are but a child, mind masters
do not bow to children!'

Buoyed by Chipper's loving companionship, he was suddenly
reminded of the nasty psychic at the fair, and his attempts to travel
through his mind, whose attack he had hardly registered. Reinforced by
the thought of Chipper by his side, and buoyed by the mantra, Aridain
forged a path towards his father. Pressing his outstretched hands to the
evil mind, represented by the dying cherry tree, Aridain murmured
loudly, 'Time for you to go. Time to rid my father of your nastiness.'
His eyes sparking, his father's life-force, reinforcing his own. Aridain
shaped a barrier of light, that slowly but surely pushed the darkness
outwards until not one iota of it remained.

Looking down at Chipper fondly, Aridain said, 'We have to go
now. You may be a figment of my father's imagination sent to help me,
but you are real to me.' Grasping Chipper around the neck, he gave the
doberman a big hug. 'You will always be my friend.'

Then, as the strange, convoluted world faded, Aridain reached for
his father's outstretched hand…

'Are you better now, Daddy?' Aridain asked tearfully.

'Yes… I think… so,' said Alfic, looking around the room in
bewilderment. Then, gazing in wonder into his son's eyes, he said
emotionally. 'I'm so proud of you, Son. How can you ever forgive me?'
said Alfic apologetically. With fresh eyes then, he saw Lascana.

Hurrying forward, Lascana wrapped her arms around them both, and cried hesitantly. 'Alfic, you're awake, is this the real you?'

'Yes, yes it is, thanks to our young hero here,' he smiled, hugging Lascana fiercely. 'What happened to me?'

'The nasty man tried to make you take my shiny stones, do nasty things,' accused Aridain.

'If I'd have known that reciting an ancient oath was all it took... truly inspirational. And when did you discover that words contain power?'

'Auntie Magen taught me?' said Aridain, hugging his mother and father. 'Oh, by the way Daddy, Chipper says he doesn't blame you for his death.'

'Chipper! Oh, I'm so sorry Aridain.' Alfic began to sob then uncontrollably.

'Chipper? Oaths? What are you talking about?' asked Mira.

'Welcome to our world.'

'Mira?' sniffed Alfic, wiping at his eyes.

'Alfic, meet Vara's long-lost sister.'

'Mira?... How long has it been...?'

'It's been a while, Alfic. Last time I saw you, you were a child.'

Turning to Lascana, Alfic, grasping her shoulders, looked deeply into her eyes. 'I'm so sorry. I could see and feel everything, but no matter how hard I tried, I couldn't stop what was happening. It was like a giant fist was squeezing my head. I felt like a prisoner in my own mind. Byrak,' he cursed vehemently. 'If I ever get my hands on him? So, what's your story, Mira?' asked Alfic.

'There's not much to tell, only that after what I just witnessed, I can totally sympathise with your fight against a leader who's provoked this misjustice. Now, enough talk; a student called Gavin Torn will be here soon,' said Mira, searching the cupboards, 'and I need to mix something together to make you fit for work.'

Kissing the top of her son's head, Lascana whispered, 'I don't know how you did it, but I'm really proud of you. You too, Sabra,' she smiled, stroking the dragonlet tenderly. 'So, care to enlighten us on what happened up here, husband?' she said, pointing to his head.

His brow creasing in puzzlement Alfic said, 'Byrak used my guilt, my failings, to imprison me in my own mind. How ironic is that? Before

Aridain appeared, everything was fuzzy and indistinct. Chipper was there also, I think as a manifestation of me, sent by me, a redemption if you will, for killing our dog. The world Aridain imagined, the black sludge, was his way of making sense of the decay in my mind. Then, when he appeared, he brought with him clarity.

'You were mumbling something repeatedly just before Aridain freed you. Do you know what those words meant?' asked Lascana.

'Yes,' said Alfic searchingly. 'It's part of an oath you take as a serving soldier. We just adapted it.' Scuffing his son's hair, Alfic smiled genuinely. 'A little sod he may be, but I could not have survived without him.'

CHAPTER THIRTY-SIX

BLOOD AND INCANTATION

Distant agonised screams, like obscure footsteps echoing through empty tunnels, sliced through his cacophony of drug induced dreams and nightmares. The sounds of metal grating upon metal clawed its way through his head, and he swam up through indistinct hallucinations to consciousness. His head unclear, he became aware of a painful void in the pit of his stomach, and when he tried to swallow, his throat felt as though it was coated in sand.

The fingers of his left hand felt at iron bars, whilst his right brushed against the edge of a mould ridden wooden pallet, and a floor covered in damp straw. Concluding he was in a cell, Kale tried to open his eyes, welded shut with encrusted mucus. At the second time of asking, he prised them open and looked up to a domed brick-built ceiling. Hauling himself into a sitting position, Kale grunted in pain. Cramp exploded in his calves and thigh muscles as he swung his legs over the edge of the straw covered pallet. He sniffed at the foul air and identified it as a combination of urine, faeces and rotting cabbage, and somewhere, someone was snoring loudly. Peering desperately about the cell, he saw, reflected in the torches' flickering light, a small puddle. Feeding this was a small rivulet of water that ran freely across the floor, and disappeared into the wall opposite through a crack in the masonry. Weak, his head swimming, his body screaming in pain, he crawled across the floor to soothe his thirst. Ignoring the foul taste and the razor-sharp pain as it touched his sore, split lips, he sucked the foul liquid into his mouth, his desire for water overriding all caution.

Where am I? thought Kale. *What happened to me? I remember meeting that carpenter Gillion, then... nothing.*

Ignoring his pounding head, he stared in consternation at his blood covered forearms, then at the arcane symbols covering his body.

'Dark arts,' he hissed savagely? Concluding he had been injected with mind-altering drugs, he gathered handfuls of water, and wiping frantically at the blood and arcane symbols like a man possessed, revealed several puncture marks. Taking another mouthful of water, he tried to stand and stretch out his cramping muscles, but fell back onto the rotting pallet that shattered into large splinters.

Understanding that his user would know he was awake, and that the connection had been severed, he tried to clear his head. Climbing to his feet once more, he hobbled up to the rusty bars, then peered out into a large room filled with implements of torture and pain. Intent on locating the snoring, he discerned a soldier, sat with his feet on a small table in the corner of the vaulted room, and dangling from his belt was a set of keys, but he wasn't the only inmate. Another figure wearing a strange metal helmet slumped lifelessly, strapped to a chair. Ignoring his protesting body and despite his weakened state, Kale pressed his palm to the lock and concentrated. When nothing happened, he tried again, with the same result. Strangely then, Perak Bruin came to mind...,

You must learn to overcome your physical shortcomings. Commanding creatures is only the first step on the road to becoming a master of minds. Remember, focus on only what you want to do, then everything else will fall into place...'

With the last of his waning strength, Kale, listening to the dripping of water in the silence, sat cross-legged on the floor, and closing his eyes, sought a memory, a place of serenity. He could have chosen his childhood, climbing trees or running with his friends through the woods that covered the hills around his home village of Pheton. Instead, he thought of Crystal, her dark inviting eyes and her surreptitious smile, alluring and appealing, enticing him like a secret waiting to be uncovered, a new land waiting to be explored. Smiling then, his mind unburdened, he roamed the chamber until he stood looking down at the guard. Planting a suggestion with what remained of his strength, like he would a seed in soil, Kale returned to his body and fell backwards on the damp floor, utterly spent. Closing his eyes for a moment, a memory of Aridain, playing in the garden with his dog, popped into his head, his innocence and happy abandon infusing all around him as did his boundless energy.... Images of his good friend Keegan entered his mind also, teasing him over his awkwardness with the opposite sex, and his reluctance to rock the boat. Then the pair were there together, beckoning and urging. Then, grasping his face roughly, they bellowed,

Mr Kale, get up.

It's all right, I will die in the knowledge that I gave my all. I am content now, knowing that you both will live.

Don't be so melodramatic, Kale Simm, your time is not yet done, assured Keegan, *Besides, you and Crystal still have a chance of life together.*

You certainly know how to kick a man when he's down, Keegan Fold.

Reaching for their outstretched hands; Kale looked up to see the soldier dressed in the school's battle armour, the key in the lock, looking in at him with a puzzled look on his face.

Blinking as if waking from a dream, the soldier looked around in confusion. 'You, you're awake! You're not supposed to be awake!'

Opening the cell door and drawing his sword, the guard entered the iron cage.

'Hey, now wait a minute,' exclaimed Kale.

'My orders are specific.'

Recalling the smashed pallet, Kale grasped one of the shattered planks, and with an agonised bellow, swung the improvised weapon at the guard's legs.

Taken by surprise, the guard, grasping at his shins, collapsed to the floor.

'Why, you pathetic excuse for an Animistic! I'm going to enjoy this,' cursed the guard.

As the guard attempted to get to his feet, Kale, grasping the thick end of the shattered plank with both hands, and with a scream of desperation, thrust the thin end of the improvised weapon into the guard's chest. However, the weapon failed to penetrate.

'I'm wearing body armour, you imbecile,' said the guard confidently.

Realising that if he didn't act quickly, he was going to die. Kale pulled the splinter shaped piece of wood free of the leather armour, and before the guard could react, thrust it like a dagger into his eye socket.

With a look of utter surprise, the guard gasped then lay still.

Pitching forward, Kale lay on top of the guard, gasping for air, and countered exhaustedly, 'But you forgot to put your helmet on.'

After a short time, however, buoyed by the hope of escape, Kale, undressing the dead guard, donned his armour. Then, hefting the guard's sword, he staggered from the cell.

Ever since the altercation in the food hall, Perak's words, "Now is not the time for procrastination, now is the time to act," had haunted her. She had also pondered on Perak's concerns that had mimicked her own, like Kale's continued erratic behaviour, and the school's continued persecution of Perak, his family and friends. Her world in turmoil, she had conducted her own enquiries. Following the Animistic during his daily routine, she had at first refused to believe Kale would ally himself with Kuelack. However, her diligence had revealed Kale's illicit meetings with the likes of Arhass, Ryan Delran, and Gavin Torn. She had also observed, in secret, as Kale conversed with Alfic and Sorin's children by the work sheds. Unable to follow, for fear of being discovered, she had nonetheless uncovered a truth she was unprepared for.

Convinced that the man she loved was in league with Kuelack, Crystal, after finishing her classes for the day, was determined to confront her traitorous partner. Enraged, she had collected her staff, and donning her deep blue leather battle suit, had disappeared into the night, determined to end his secular alliance once and for all. These strange chain-of-events, however, had taken on yet another bizarre twist. Whilst tracking Kale to the young wizards' dorms, she had watched astonished as his form abruptly shimmered and morphed, until in his place stood the dark arts teacher Serac, apparently risen from the dead. Moments later, a deep-seated scream in her mind had sent her to her knees.

Filled suddenly with a deep sense of despair and helplessness, and not knowing why, she whispered harshly, 'Kale!'

Utterly baffled by the strange turn of events, Crystal, unsure what had just happened, now sat and watched from the shadows as

Serac, with a sudden sense of urgency, turned and hurried towards the fortress. In the gathering gloom, she gripped her trusty hornbeam staff tightly and, suddenly scared for Kale's wellbeing, followed the dark arts teacher who, gathering soldiers along the way, entered through the fortress's sturdy entrance doors.

Composing herself, Crystal, with head held high, nodded to the guards. 'Serac has requested my assistance. Don't let anybody in or out,' she ordered. Students and administration staff ran around in panic as she rushed into the grand hall. Grasping a serving girl by the arm, Crystal span her around. 'What's happening?' she demanded.

'The prisoners, they've escaped!'

'Where are they now?'

'There!' shrieked the serving girl, pointing towards the entrance beside the grand stairway.

Crystal looked up just in time to see Serac and several soldiers disappear through the accommodation wing door. Avoiding retainers and maintenance staff now milling about aimlessly, Crystal ran across the atrium towards the open door leading to the guest quarters. Hurrying through the sturdy oak door and pressing herself to the wall, she heard the sounds of combat, together with agonising screams from within. Gripping her staff tightly, Crystal took a deep, calming breath.

CHAPTER THIRTY-SEVEN

THE FRIEND OF MY ENEMY
IS STILL MY ENEMY

Stuffing what remained of the dead guard's meal into his mouth, and taking a long draft of what tasted like cider, Kale scanned the semi-darkened surroundings. He then looked towards the far corner, and the figure tied by leather bonds to the spiteful looking chair.

Making his way between the grisly implements and apparatus, Kale approached the figure. Blood had spilled down the front of his ripped and torn clothing and from his maimed hands and feet. Removing the dull metal helmet from the man's head, Kale recognised instantly who it was. Compared to his body, Byrak's face, a thick gag thrust into his mouth, was relatively untouched.

'Well, well, well,' murmured Kale wearily, 'Who'd have thought it Byrak, the master of minds, who thought to go it alone, and thought to pull the wool over all our eyes, resides beaten and broken in the school's dungeons.'

Removing the gag from Byrak's mouth, Kale recoiled when Byrak murmured resignedly, 'Here to give me another beating, are you, Kale?'

'Beat you!'

Opening his eyes, Byrak looked up at him. 'Just leave me alone, so I can die in peace.'

'What's the matter Byrak,' rasped Kale, 'things not going as you predicted, feeling sorry for ourself, are we?'

'Revenge is all I asked for. Make you cursed humans pay. Now, even that pleasure has been taken from me.'

'Coercion and using others to do your dirty work, you deserve nothing less than being strapped to a torture device.'

'Kuelack and Serac killed my mentor.... my friends...' he said bleakly. 'And now you're helping them. Now I have nothing more to live for, so grant me my death, put me out of my and everyone else's misery.'

'Killed your friends? What are you talking about?' He pointed back the way he came. 'I've been a prisoner in that metal cage for, well, it could be months for all I know.'

Byrak looked up at him then. 'Torture, not working, so you're trying to trick me with riddles now?'

Suddenly, everything became clear. 'I don't know who was torturing you, Byrak,' said Kale, 'probably the same person who tricked me. What I do know is that strapped to this contraption, you have no chance of exacting your revenge. Help me. Help the resistance and I will help you exact your revenge. Once done, I will, if you wish it, relieve you of the burden of life.'

'I neither care nor worry over the opinions of lesser beings.'

'And you wonder why people mistrust psychics,' sneered Kale. Fumbling wearily for the right key, Kale unlocked Byrak's shackles and insisted, 'Now get up and fight, damn you!'

Helped to his feet, Byrak stretching his cramped muscles and testing his stiff limbs, grasped a torch from a holder upon the wall.

'Remember Byrak,' said Kale guardedly. I help you so you can help me.'

'Don't fret Animistic, I'll uphold my end of the bargain.'

Then, arm in arm, and holding each other up, they made their way painfully past the instruments of torture, and using the stolen keys, they opened the door to the dungeon. They then staggered along the torch lit corridor, emerging into an open area.

Indicating a door at the top of the stone stairway, Byrak insisted, 'Hurry, we have to get out before the school realises what's happening.'

About to ascend the stairway, a voice issued from an open doorway to their left, 'Get in there, troll dung....' The voice then paused and said, 'Is that you Fitler, you know you can't just leave the dungeon like…'

Kale and Byrak looked up as a tall man dressed in dirty, grey trousers, old leather boots and a thick, grey shirt appeared in the doorway. They stood and stared at the dirt-stained jailor for what seemed an age before Kale, with what remained of his strength, charged. Forcing the jailor backwards, the pair slammed hard against the metal bars of a cell. Rolling around on the floor, Kale pulling the sword from the guard's belt, thrust it into his belly. Stunned, the jailor clawed at Kale's throat and face with an agonised groan. 'Got you, you bastard!' growled Kale.

'Kale?'

'Beria, is that you?'

'Yes. Yes it is!'

'Hand me your torch, Byrak,' ordered Kale.

The torch held aloft, Kale followed by Byrak, peered into the barred chambers to see eyes peering back at him from the darkness. In the first of the iron-cages, was the solid figure of Gable, together with Beria and Keen. Also, lying upon a wooden pallet, a crude bandage around his face, was the greengrocer Bern.

'Beria, what happened? What are you all doing here?' wheezed Kale.

'Kuelack! That's what happened,' replied Beria.

Unlocking the cell door, Kale, fumbling for the right keys, began unlocking the cells arranged down either side of a narrow corridor, the torch's flame revealing the faces of people he knew and loved. Some were bloodied, others were weeping openly at the sight of him unlocking the doors to their dark, dank cells.

'Kale, we have to go.'

'Byrak, you said you would help me. Are you rescinding on that promise already?'

'No, but if we stay to help, we'll be trapped here too,' insisted Byrak.

Suddenly rushing from the open cell and wrapping his hands around Kale's throat, Bern spat, 'Traitorous bastard.'

'I'm not… your enemy. If I was… why would I… be trying to release you!' gagged Kale.

'Your words mean nothing, traitor,' spat Bern.

His face pressed against the bars, Kale groaned, 'Beria, please, what can I do to prove that wasn't me?'

'Eat shit and die, traitor,' scoffed someone in the dark. 'You've done enough damage.'

Staring at Kale's emaciated body and studying his pain wracked eyes, Beria's expression softened, and she said calmly, 'Let him go, Bern.'

'But mistress Beria, look at what he's done?'

'Can't you see, Bern, that this man has also tasted the dungeon's hospitality? Let him go, don't be blinded by hate. That's Kuelack's way, his follower's way. This is not the man you should be directing your anger towards.'

Released by Bern, Kale fell to his knees like a rag doll.

Holding onto the bars of the cell, Kale said, 'Here Byrak, take the keys, release the rest!'

Now free, the prisoners began milling around noisily, unsure of what to do next.

'QUIET,' shouted Beria, 'if you want to be free, be quiet all of you. Byrak, hold your torch up. You two, help Kale out of his armour, so as I can attend to him,' she ordered. 'Who's our best swordsman?'

'Well, Bern, but he's in no condition to fight, but I've had some experience using a sword,' said Gable.

'That armour's too small for you, Gable, give it to Keen,' said Beria.

'So, is there a plan?' enquired Gable.

'A plan, look at us; do we look like we have a plan?' said Byrak desperately.

'One thing is for sure; we can't stay here?' Taking Byrak's youthful face in her hands, Beria said steadily, 'I know you're tired, but I need you to focus. You're our best chance of escape. I need you to find out who's around, OK?'

The party consisting of nearly fifty, in various states of health, quietly exited the cell block, but when they began climbing the stone steps, Byrak stopped abruptly and announced, 'Soldiers! Coming this way, and they're being led by Serac!'

Smashing the table and the two chairs, several of the imprisoned men, salvaging what weaponry they could, stood together with Gable and Keen, as with a rusty squeal, the door to the cell wing opened.

Serac, together with a knot of guards, appeared at the top of the steps, and announced, 'STAY WHERE YOU ARE!'

'If you have any suggestions, now would be a good time?' hissed Keen nervously, as the soldiers, their swords drawn, bounded down the steps towards them.

'Follow me!' bellowed Gable. Then, the man-mountain, followed by the rest of the men and their improvised weapons, began laying about him with the stolen sword.

Stood together with Beria, Kale watched as the soldiers began forcing the prisoners back down the stairs. He looked up then to see Serac striding down the steps towards them.

Pausing, the dark arts teacher stood looking at them with cold, blue eyes from a cruel, grime-streaked face. 'I'm impressed at you, Kale, standing and talking despite my potions and my conjurings.'

'You did this to me!' croaked Kale, staring at Serac's slight, anaemic figure.

'Yes, and now, having served your purpose, you will be killed.' His demeanour taking on the dispassionate bearing of a feeding vulture, Serac, indicating the fight and the dead and dying prisoners, announced dispassionately, 'As you can see, the fight doesn't go well. None of you will live long enough to tell anyone the tale of your valiant last stand!'

'And we will not surrender, so do your worst, demon,' wheezed Bern.

With an insane cackle, two scorching globes of fire formed in Serac's outstretched hands.

CHAPTER THIRTY-EIGHT

CRYSTAL

Entering the dungeon, Crystal, looking down upon a scene of chaos, saw the stallholders fighting and dying beneath the soldiers' blades. Rushing down the steps with a cry of defiance, Crystal watched as Serac, two globes of fire in his upturned hands, approached and stood before the greengrocer Bern, and the man she loved, both seemingly on the verge of death, Kale's head propped upon Beria's lap.

She then stopped, amazed, as Serac turned, his face ashen, as Byrak suddenly appeared and glared at Serac with unbridled anger, then closed his eyes.

Now under Byrak's control, Serac turned and sent the fiery balls hurtling through the air, to explode amongst the combatants with a thunderous hiss.

Then, like puppets with their strings cut, the remaining soldiers simply dropped and lay unmoving on the dungeon's straw-covered floor.

'Crystal, how nice of you to join us,' said Byrak, as if he hadn't a care in the world.

Looking around at the dead and dying, Crystal turned towards the psychic and spat, 'What the hell were you thinking, Byrak?'

'I'm thinking I just saved your necks.'

Crystal then looked to the dark arts teacher, Serac, stood upright, shaking and convulsing. 'What are you doing?'

'I thought that was obvious. I'm making this piece of horseshit suffer, before I kill him.'

'No Byrak..., we had an agreement,' muttered Kale weakly.

'Still conscious, Kale?' said Byrak. 'Impressive.'

His words slurring significantly now, Kale said, 'Don't... sacrifice... your honour... for... petty revenge.'

With a look, Byrak closed Kale's mouth. 'I told you I would not repent nor regret my decisions. You and your friends are free to go with my blessing. This one, however, will die.'

'Your revenge... must wait until... we are safe,' groaned Kale.

'Honour is something you normals bleat on about,' sneered Byrak, 'That honour has cost your friends their lives.'

Crystal, watching horrified as Byrak continued to focus on Serac, advanced slowly with her staff levelled, and insisted, 'You cannot kill a man who cannot defend himself.'

'No, I can't, but I can kill a demon who was willing to strap me to a chair and torture me to death.'

'If you do this Byrak, if you kill an unarmed man, you are lost,' insisted Beria, 'there is no turning back. But you can change what you do to others.'

'Save your Balefire rhetoric. This is something that should have been done long before now. He will die a mindless zombie, like the manipulative dog he is.'

Crystal knew that if she didn't act now, she and all these people were going to be captured and killed. On the other hand, she couldn't just stand by and watch as Serac was slowly lobotomised. The black tendrils of dark matter that writhed towards her, however, made up her mind. Twisting and spinning, Crystal shrieked, 'Coward, what would your mentor think of his successor acting like a weakling Navarian sheep?'

Byrak, together with Serac, turned as one. 'He would be proud that I have taken up his mantel, his cause.'

Glancing at Kale, laid comatose on Beria's lap, made Crystal even more determined to end Byrak's threat. Grasped suddenly by the dark tendrils, Crystal, to her surprise, continued to forge forward.

'Your resolve is weakening, Byrak. I can sense your fatigue.'

His look of smug confidence turned to shocked surprise as she and her staff battled to within striking range.

Byrak pleaded, 'Crystal, please give me this one's life? Let me die, having fulfilled my one remaining purpose.'

'Compared to self-worth, self-satisfaction is such a fleeting thing, it leaves you empty and always craving more.'

'Wise words, Mistress, but an individual must pay for his or her actions, a life must pay for a life.' Concentrating harder, Byrak drove Crystal to her knees.

Then to her surprise the dark tangled bands released, as Byrak, like a boneless fish, flopped to the floor unconscious, together with Serac, revealing Bern stood holding aloft one of the table's broken legs.

'Are you alright?' asked Bern, his smile more like a grimace.

'Yes, thank you, Bern,' said Crystal.

Acknowledging her appreciation with a nod, Bern discarded the piece of wood, then began tending to the injured.

Kneeling next to Kale, Crystal searched his face.

'Thank you, Crystal, for what you did,' acknowledged Beria.

'Let's just be thankful he was weak, and he was hungry,' said Crystal.

'We have many dead and several wounded, together with a number of soldiers who are badly burnt,' reported Bern urgently.

'If we're found here, we can expect no leniency. Bern, Gable, we have to get our people ready to move as soon as possible,' commanded Beria. She then very gently turned Kale onto his back and looked into his eyes. Seeing Crystal's pained expression, she said, 'Kale will be all right, he just needs food and rest. I'll leave him in your capable hands.'

Crystal sank to her knees beside Kale, and with tears in her eyes, laid his head on her lap. Stroking his hair, she then searched his face. 'Are you OK?'

'Much better now you're here, although I....'

But before he could say another word, she embraced his face and kissed him tenderly.

When Crystal finally released him, Kale, grinning foolishly, said, 'Well, I think more time spent in the dungeons is called for.'

'Don't push your luck Kale Simm.' She wiped at a tear that had trickled down his cheek and smiling up at her, Kale did the same. 'Don't you ever disappear on me again, Kale Simm.' She looked around at their depressing surroundings. 'To think that a place like this exists in the so-called centre of learning!'

'It's Kuelack's way.' Kale then looked up at her gravely. 'I'm so sorry for what was done in my name,' he apologised. 'I was deceived, too easily it seems.'

'No apology needed. You are not responsible for what that man did to you.'

'Sorry to break up this tender reunion, Crystal. 'We have to go before more soldiers turn up,' said Beria urgently.

Those that could still stand got to their feet and helped those that couldn't. However, there was no helping those who lay dead on the dungeon floor.

Bringing up the rear as Beria led them up the stairs and along the corridor, it surprised Crystal to see that the fortress's small rear door was unguarded. No sooner had they exited the fortress than the sounds of urgent commands and frantic instructions could be heard, accompanied by soldiers, their armour and weapons clanking rhythmically on the bellowed commands. The sound of urgent voices calling throughout the night, they crossed the narrow, grassy courtyard to the worship hall.

'We're not going to make it,' despaired Keen.

'Always doom and gloom with you, isn't it?' cursed Bern.

'Do you have a plan?' hissed Keen aggressively. 'Do you?'

'If you want to live, let's have less worrying and more hurrying,' hissed Crystal aggressively.

'That's all right for you to say, you're a trained killer,' bemoaned Keen.

'So, what are we going to do?' queried Gable, adjusting the unconscious psychic draped over his shoulder.

'Hide,' said Crystal, standing and walking towards the ornate entrance-way.

'What are you doing?' despaired Beria.

'Saving your lives by leading the soldiers away. They still don't know I helped you, right?'

'But, when Serac awakes, he'll….'

'No, he won't Bern, he didn't see me, and if any of the soldiers recover, well, it's their word over mine.'

'But'….'

'Don't argue, Bern, just hide. I'll be fine.'

343

The doors leading from the courtyard suddenly reverberated to the sounds of soldiers entering the cathedral. Making as much noise as possible, Crystal turned, and hurrying as fast as she could through the assembly hall, ran towards the ornate entrance and opened the big double doors. Pulling the leather hood from her battle suit over her head, she stood in the entrance, and making sure that the soldiers saw her, exited the worship hall; the soldiers, yelling and screaming, chasing her outside into the night.

Waiting until the sounds of pounding feet had diminished, Keen whispered harshly, 'What are we waiting for? Let's go!'

'*We*, are not going to do anything,' said Beria. 'You and Gable are going to lead these people out of the school grounds towards Shadrack Valley, and then toward Leardon Quarry. As I recall, there's an old miner's hut. I'll meet you there.'

'And what are you going to do?'

'Acquire some food and medicine. If I don't, some of these people will not last the night.'

'But what about the school, our lives here?' asked another.

'Forget the school, forget your life here,' said Bern, 'a good friend of mine said, "it may take time, but if we're patient, and work together, and apply a bit of grey matter, we can achieve greatness."'

'Alfic?' mused Beria.

'Yes,' nodded Bern, 'He has a strong sense of intuition that more often than not turns out to be right. We would do well to heed his words and follow his example.'

'So, if we make it to this hut, then what?' hissed somebody in the crowd.

Beria, turning to the people now huddled in between the long wooden pews, said, 'One step at a time, one step at a time.'

EPILOGUE

In the cold but still night, the couple walked along the banks of the River Seddon beside Gonda's arboretum, the capital's multitude of lights twinkling from a myriad of windows, mirroring the stars in the cold, clear night sky.

Turning to Hethat, Narine purred, 'So, is this better?'

'Are you kidding? Of course, this is better. Who'd have thought me, Hethat, would be walking along the banks of the river beside such a beautiful woman out in the moonlight? Besides, that bartender was becoming far too familiar. Gods, I can't believe it.'

Turning towards him, she drew his face to hers and kissed him tenderly on the lips.

'Keep that up and the moonlight won't be the only highlight this evening,' said Hethat.'

'I'm counting on it,' purred Narine, and she kissed him again.

Disengaging abruptly, Hethat hissed, 'Did you hear that?'

'I heard nothing,' smiled Narine seductively, 'now where were we?'

Drawing him down to her, she kissed him again, but once more Hethat hissed... 'There it is again?'

'You're imagining things!' she dismissed casually.

Drawing her behind him, Hethat called, 'Hello, whoever you are, show yourself. I can hear you.'

'If you insist,' replied a voice dripping with malice.

From the shadows stepped a thin, anaemic creature, all gnarled and haggard, carrying a wickedly curved knife, and dressed in ragged, earthy, flowing robes.

'What in Praxis's name! Be gone foul creature,' hissed Hethat, producing a knife of his own. Abruptly, more of the deathly pale, yellow-skinned creatures appeared from the shadows.

Shielding Narine, Hethat waving his weapon threateningly, said, 'Run Narine, save yourself!'

'She's gone. You should be concerned with your own safety, human,' replied the creature in a voice like shale washing up on a shore. 'You've had your way with her; now we're going to have our way with you.'

Too late, Hethat span around, as in one quick movement the creature, called Narine, drew her razor-like fingernails across his throat.

Meanwhile, in the city suburb of Waterman situated around Gonda's docks, two men staggered home from the tavern, having had their fill...

'Sanwin there is no conshhpiracy, so shhhtop wittth the shhcare mongering, people jushhed want to get on with their livesh,' beseeched Tenser.

Sanwin, holding onto Tenser, disengaged himself rather clumsily and, struggling to stand upright, pulled his hood from his head.

'Asss true as I ssstand here, I talked to Mavishhh. She should know, she worksss at the palaish. Shheeee confirmed that the king isshh visited by shome kind of demon and is under shome sssort of shhpell.'

As the pair burst into another crescendo of claim and counterclaim, they didn't see the two hunched, gnarly figures stalking them from the shadows.

'The King isss a traitorousss runt and hasss no backbone,' shouted Sanwin. 'If I was the queen, I'd ring his ssscrawny neck, then trade him in for another one.'

'You, wringing the king's neck, don't make me laugh. You find it hard to wring the pissss from your jocksssshtrap,' said Tenser jokingly.

Sanwin turned to Tenser, looked at him seriously for a moment, then burst into fits of laughter. 'Nice one, Tenssher, come on buddy letssss go home,' and the two men singing out of tune staggered and swayed down the alleyway.

'Did you shee that?' stated Tenser.

'Shee what?'

'Over there in the alley. I thought I saw some kind of creature.'

'You've had too much to drink, you're just trying to mettthh with my head,' accused Sanwin, peering into the gloom. 'Your full of consshp...consshpir... wild theories, beshidessssss, monsssssters, don't venture into the capital anymore.'

Just then, the creature, looking more like a cross between a vulture and a turkey than a human, emerged from the grime and filth of the alley. She was quickly followed by several others, and the two men were quickly surrounded.

Advancing slowly, one of them said, 'You should have listened to your friend, human.'

Sanwin's and Tensor's raucous evening in the Hen and Feathers tavern, turned quickly sour, as despite their struggles and protestations, they were dragged into the shadows, their shrieks and screams cut off abruptly as they choked on their own blood.

Meanwhile, in the Firecracker Tavern situated on Gonda's Kings Way...

Agost took another mouthful of ale and exclaimed innocently, 'The carnival! I forgot all about it!'

'Don't be scared Agost, I won't torture you, well not much anyway.'

'Now look here, Rhea! I honestly don't know what you're talking about.'

'Don't act all innocent; you know I'm talking about the city's annual spring carnival, you know, the one where my display always trumps yours.'

'Oh, that carnival! To tell you the truth, I have more important things on my mind at the moment,' said Agost indifferently.

'I hope so,' she smiled, smoothing her long brown hair into a ponytail at the back of her neck, 'because if you were eavesdropping, you know that I'd have to kill you where you stand.'

'It's amazing the lengths some people will go to every year in an attempt to outdo each other,' joked Agost. Then, in an effort to regain a modicum of dignity, Agost said, 'Anyway, it's a good job I'm not competing this year. With my new secret design, you wouldn't stand a chance.'

'Oh, you mean like last year, second from last, wasn't it?' grinned Rhea.

'You can laugh, but you can't keep a determined man down.'

'I certainly hope not,' she purred, smiling back at him with large, hazel eyes.

Agost quickly turned around in embarrassment, stopped, and, looking at her nervously, asked, 'I don't suppose you would, you know, like to meet me in the tavern later?'

Smiling at him boldly, Rhea said, 'Why, Agost, are you asking me out on a date?' Revelling in Agost's awkwardness, she said, 'Yes, I would like that very much.'

'Oh, good. I'll meet you beside the Sterling memorial in, say, two hours?'

'I'll be there,' she smiled affectionately.

Annoyed at his foolishness and realising he had a silly grin on his face, Agost turned away quickly and, walking on cloud nine, strode purposefully around the corner. Suddenly a hand was clamped around his mouth and he felt the force of something sharp impact on his chest, followed quickly by a second and a third. As he tried to cry out, he felt the sting of another blade as it was drawn across his throat. As darkness took him; all he could think of was the disappointment on Rhea's face.

AFTERWORD

The third book of the Foundation series, **Prophecy and Allegiance**, offers a perspective into the struggles of humanity to control power, and delves deep into the human psyche, pushing the characters in this novel to their fates either by accident or by other actions — unearthing that sometimes, what drives humanity is our very own darkness.

This book teaches us that in the real-world people, who desperately want to cling to a power that isn't theirs, seek domination over the world. However, there are heroes like Aridain who will try to make a difference, reminding us that power comes with great responsibility. This chronicle will delve deeply into Aridain's story, revealing that even heroes can be corrupted by dark influences and struggle to control that power. This story reminds us that the Firebrand stone could be a stone, but there are other forces that drive us to do things we are not supposed to do, reminding us that even if someone is already a hero, he can be human, too.

But how do we really contain evil? There is no right way to answer that, but hopefully this book will give you, the reader, a peek into humanity's tendency to turn on each other for power. Perhaps this book will remind us that we should not fear who we are destined to become, even when we are struggling to take control of the darkness within ourselves. Evil may loom just out of sight, but the choice to battle against it is always in our hands.

GLOSSARY

ABADON: Falls. The River Storna, spills over these falls and then flows into the Parang swamp and estuary and into the Eastreach Sea.

ACUMEN: Head of Balefire coven

ADAXIAL: Wizard that killed the dragon Saloath.

AGRESTAL: Agrestal Mere, father of Gradine, Head of Gondian Central. Intelligence, Guild of Spies.

AGOTI: Deer native to Calabash

ALBAIN: Woodruff, Corporal, member of Pellagrin's guard; friend to Tance, Mace, and Vanir.

ALFIC: Bruin, married to Lascana, has a son Aridain. Supervisor and Head of Pellagrin's Workforce under his father Perak. His mother is Vara, his sister is Magen, and his brother is Kuelack.

ALLONAL: Most south westerly town in Durbah.

ALMAGEST: Head of Pellagrin's School and the Sivan Council, now deceased.

ALSIKE: Healer at Pellagrin's School.

ANIMISTIC: Title given to a charmer of animals.

ARDENT: Ardent Wolf, iridescent purple fur with streaks of orange that mate for life.

ARECA: Herbal magic teacher at Pellagrin's School.

ARHASS: Necromancer and teacher at Pellagrin's School; can enchant objects for others or himself. He is a devoted worshipper of Fornax.

ARIDAIN: Bruin, the First Elemental Wizard to be born for a thousand years. Balefire legend decrees he will destroy the Firebrand and Chimera stones.

ARRIAN: Bruin, brother of Aridain, whose father is Alfic and mother Lascana. Grandfather is Perak, and Grandmother Vara.

ARIES: Last Turkanian leader. Apposed Dacron before his kingdom was destroyed.

ARROWHEAD: Mountain, site of an ancient fortress called Collard Ray; location of one of the Firebrand shards.

AQUAR: The benevolent god of the sea, opulence and passion.

AYMARA: Continent consisting of the seven lands: Calabash, Chondite, Durbah, Navar, Srinigar, Turkana, and Zapata.

BALEFIRE: Cult of witches whose headquarters are in the capital Gonda. They are dedicated to healing and helping others.

BANTU: Magical creature living in the Monad Mountains, descended from Harvestmen, they dress in thick grey-layered cloak and snow boots. Cruel unblinking red eyes placed either side of a ridged nose-less grey face, thick platted shoulder length hair; a race strong in ritual magic.

BARFLEET: Small hamlet in Durbah.

BERIA: Dearing. Balefire witch and student of colour magic at Pellagrin's School.

BERN: Greengrocer loyal to Alfic working at Pellagrin's School.

BETRAYERS: Small door in the fortress wall, opened by a traitorous member of the school that allowed Zakan the Wicked into the Interior.

BHAREST: King. Ruler of fortress located in Chondite on a neck of land on the Navas straight in the Eastreach Sea.

BISMUTH: Forest, and hills, located south of Spalding, just beyond Firethorn hill.

BIT: Lowest of Durbah's currency in gold, silver or copper, one unit.

BLACK BROW: Outlaw, bandit leader, local smuggler, so called because of the tattoo of the poisonous Black Bistort plant across his forehead.

BLACK LOTUS: Narcotic associated with the god Fornax.

BLACK ROOT: Poisonous creeping black root that feeds off of other plants, also called Iron root.

BLINKS: Blinks Escarpment, containing remnants of ancient magical forest.

BLOCH: Milvus Bloch, undertaker at Pellagrin's School, allied to Kuelack.

BLUE: Painted devils, name given to barbarians living in Mycean Highlands in northern Durbah.

BOVID: (The Just), ruler of the Kingdom of Calabash.

BRYONY: Mining village and quarry located on the edge of the Blinks escarpment; suppliers of fine china to the capital Gonda.

BURDOCK: Orchid that shoots barbs in order to spread seeds, also a plant that makes a refreshing drink.

CABALA: Game played between teams on horseback with a leather ball and wooden club called a Paccar.

CABERARTUS: Legendary Mind Master who led the first Psychic uprising.

CALABASH: Land and dictatorship in the northeast of Aymara.

CANTLOCK: Village, home to Perak.

CARDIA: Former joint head teacher at Pellagrin's School.

CASEY: Defray, seamstress and stall holder at Pellagrin's. Secretly a Korda assassin and spy working for the Calabash government.

CEALEON: Desert, located south of Chondite Badlands, terminates at the Eastreach Sea in Southern Aymara.

CELIA: Corvuss, wife of Sorin and mother to Duran and Selva.

CELESTITE: Dynasty, family of King Bovid of Calabash.

CHANGLING: Creature told to scare children in bedtime stories.

CHIPPER: Dog and family pet of Aridain Bruin.

CHONDITE: Sparse, rugged land south of Durbah.

COLOUR MAGIC: Magic that through artwork and sculpture, manipulates daily events.

COLLARD RAY: Ancient fortress in Zapatian high Mountain plateaus, former home to two horned one-eyed giants.

CORNDON: Village in Durbah, home of Elimi and Elgin.

COVEN: Balefire Council situated in Durbah's capital Gonda.

CRESTAR: Highest Gondarian currency. One hundred units in Copper, Silver and Gold

CRYSTAL: Teacher of the fighting staff at Pellagrin's school of magic

CULT OF FORNAX: Ancient order who worship the dark god Fornax and the Firebrand stone.

CUREALL: Tonic made up of numerous ingredients that helps with healing body and soul.

DAPPERLING: Half plant, half pixie creatures related to Dryads.

DARKLINGS: Also known as Bitterlings. A friendly race who have an in bread hate of humans after their lands (Chondite) was deviated by Dacron in possession of the Firebrand stone. (Related to Pelts, living in the Orrin Marsh)

DEKTAR: Durbarian currency of ten units, in Copper, Silver and Gold.

DELRAN: Ryan, archery student and supporter of Kuelack's.

DRAGONLET: Cousin of dragons and Fire Lizards, the size of a mongoose.

DRAGONHAST: God of the dragons.

DRAGON'S VOICE: Flame projected from the mouth by a Dragon Lord.

DROVE: A flight of twelve dragons.

DRUMMER: Horse belonging to Elias Tan the school's baker.

DURAN: Corvus, brother to Selva and friend of Aridain.

ELEMENTAL: Name given to Aridain, as well as all the fairy creatures tied to the land.

ELGIN: Pike, farm worker, brother of Elimi.

ELIAS: Tan, Ex-Korda Prime, called Sujet, now renegade and defector working as a baker at Pellagrin's School.

ELIMI: Pike, farm worker, brother of Elgin.

ELOHIM: Most southerly town of Durbah located in the Southern wilds.

ENNUL: Queen of Durbah, wife to King Pheronis.

ERICA: Markeson, student of healing at Pellagrin's school.

EXEDRA: Mane, sorceress at Pellagrin's School and joint head of the Sivan Council.

FELDSPAR: Town and vale in Durbah, located south west of the capital Gonda.

FERULA: Breed. Daughter of Beaty and Magen

FEVERFEW: Spotted highly toxic sweet-smelling plant from the Darkling lands.

FINDER: Mr Finder, ex-pirate from Navar.

FIREBRAND: Stone. A powerful round, dark green stone with red inclusions; represents evil.

FIRELIGHT SPRITES: Night flying imps that give of light

FIRE LIZARD: Small, aggressive lizard, with skin the colour of fire.

FIRETHORN: Hill, located to the south of Spalding, also a type of lizard.

FLUTTER OF: Imps, sprites, dapperlings etc....

FORNAX: God of the underworld, lust and excess and violence.

FRENETIC FLAME: Rage induced when a dragon's life partner is killed.

FURNACES OF SERIDAL: Forge where Greysword's swords are forged.

GABION: Son of Kuelack and Gradine Bruin.

GABLE: Bagley, blacksmith from Leardon, employed by Pellagrin's School.

GALBAINUM: Grain producing town in the foothills of the Mycean highlands in northeast Durbah.

GONDA: Capital city of Durbah.

GRABBEN: River in Zapata.

GRADINE: Bruin, wife of Kuelack, daughter of Agrestal Mere, son Gabion.

GREAT KNIFE POINT: A vast inlet of the Butane Sea fed by the river Storna.

GREYSWORD: A weapon forged with magic in the forges of Seridal, that allows its owner to combat evil and magic.

GREYSWORDS: A brotherhood of four warriors chosen over the centuries to protect and defend Pellagrin's School and the Sivan Council.

HAIDA: Female dragon, killed whilst sleeping on Firethorn hill by drug runners, mate of Saloath.

HAROLD: Butler serving at Pellagrin's School of Magic.

HARVESTMEN: (Dreamcasters) Half dragonfly/half fury-like magical creature.

HASP: Founding members of Balefire witches, grounded in blood and ritual sacrifice.

HEAD CIRCLE: Ruling council of the Balefire witches consisting of, the Acumen and seven Magnates.

HEARKSON: Agricultural town located in northern of Durbah.

HEMLOCK: Town to the east of Gonda located on the border with Turkana.

HOGAN: Half giant, farm worker at Pellagrin's.

HORNET: Fly; aggressive form of wasp.

IMPS: Magical faerie creatures.

JACKAMAR: Youngest Greysword teacher and sword master at Pellagrin's School.

JARRAH: Sprites, that live in Farend woods behind Aridain's cottage.

JARAWAPE: Hairy ape-like creature with the face like a rat that lives in the trees.

KALE: Sim, former teacher/animistic at Pellagrin's, turned vigilante.

KARNACK: Moor, chief Greysword and teacher at Pellagrin's.

KEEGAN: Dax, former gamekeeper at Pellagrin's School, now a vigilante. Friend and ex-army colleague of Alfic Bruin and Mace Denobar.

KEEN: Superstitious butcher, works at Pellagrin's School.

KILLDEER: Large aggressive deer that hunt in packs possessing sharp teeth and claws.

KORDA: Hallide, guild of spies from Calabash; also, a special serrated Knife used by the Hallide's Korda agents.

KUELACK: Bruin, dark arts teacher, now First on the Sivan Council, sister Magen, brother Alfic, mother is Vara, father is Perak.

LANOS RAE: Dragon Lord Ramus's former home.

LASCANA: Bruin, mother to Aridain and wife to Alfic, born in town of Leardon. Proprietor of hardware and items of curiosity.

LAWNA: Reedman, proprietor of the apothecary at Pellagrin's School.

LEARDON: Town built on the profits of mining on the Leader River, situated east of Pellagrin's School, in the kingdom of Gonda.

LEADER: River that runs through the town of Leardon.

MACE: Denobar, Greysword and sword master teaching combat and strategies at Pellagrin's School. Served in the Gondarian army with Alfic and Keegan.

MAGEN: Breed; sorceress and teacher at Pellagrin's School, sister to Alfic and Kuelack.

MAGNATE: A member of the Balefire head council.

MALVERN: Town in northern Durbah in the Mycean Highlands.

MARANTA: Large cat living in Durbah's southern wilds.

MASS: Martin. Master Psychic and teacher at Pellagrin's School, deceased.

MEMBRAIN: Trap designed to initiate a response.

MERLE: Colour magic and eldest remaining female teacher at Pellagrin's School.

MICAS: Alfic's understudy.

MIDGE: Perak's horse.

MINDWALKER: Another name for Psychic's.

MIRA: Scosa, younger sister to Vara Bruin, mother Pion, sister, Vara.

MONAD: Mountain range in western Srinigar.

MORREL: River that runs from the Cammar uplands into Lake Storna.

MYCEAN: Highlands and mountain's situated chiefly in northern Durbah.

NAVAR: Land to the southwest of Durbah.

NAVARIAN GRAPE: A vine containing rare addictive juice.

NAVAS: Straight, narrow passage on the Navarian coast that connects the Navas Sea to the Eastreach Sea.

ORRINWELL: Town and old fort located to the southeast of Spalding on the road to Yarrow.

ORRIN MARSH: Marshland, southeast of Leardon.

OSCAN: Large black and white flightless bird, native to Navar.

PACCAR: Short wooden club used to strike a leather ball in the game of Cabala.

PACK RAT: Large destructive rodents.

PARANG: Swamp and delta. It is where the river Seddon flows into the Eastreach sea in the land of Cealeon.

PASSENGERING: The ability to hitch a ride in another's mind.

PELLAGRIN: Dragon Lord and founder of Pellagrin's School of Magic.

PELLAGRIN'S: School for the magically gifted, founded by the Dragon Lord Pellagrin.

PERAK: Bruin, in charge of the workforce at Pellagrin's School. Married to Vara they have three children, Alfic, Kuelack and Magen.

PHETON: Village on Capital Road.

PHERONIS: King of Durbah, married to Queen Ennul.

POLEEN: Keegan's home town in Calabash.

PRAXIS: God of the sky and the mind.

PRONGHORN: Woods near the village of Cantlock.

PROTECTORATE: A conglomerate of influential Barons that preside over Zapata.

PROVOST GUILD: Wizards headquarters located in Gonda.

QUELEA: Capital city of Calabash, land to the northeast.

RABIDON: Tree, famed for its intoxicating fruit, Native to Calabash.

RAMUS: Dragon Lord from northern Zapata, former teacher of dragon lore at Pellagrin's School.

RASBORA: Sorceress from the land of Zapata situated to the north of Durbah, now teacher of Elemental magic at Pellagrin's School.

REEDMACE: Moth from Navar.

ROCK STRIDER: Long legged, furry creature native to Navar, used by the Navar herdsmen to traverse the vast distances across the Navarian plains.

RUEBEN: Wizard, former head of Pellagrin's School.

RUMBLE TREE: Tree that vibrates, can move imperceptivity to feed on carrion.

SABRA: Name given to the dragonlet Treerinks by Aridain.

SALAMIS PASS: Wide valley that represents the border between Durbah and Srinigar.

SALOATH: Last dragon in Durbah, mate of Hiada, killed by the wizard Adaxial, when Saloath induced the frenetic flame and laid waste to Durbah.

SAPPHIRE SPRITES: Sprites enriched with magic.

SARAN: Casey Defrey's home province in Calabash.

SAVARIN: Destro, wizard and teacher of Weather magic at Pellagrin's School, from the town of Trover in the Southern wilds.

SCARRION: Species of aggressive scavenger lizard. Blue and Brown it has frills that it can raise around its neck and along its back.

SEDDON: River that originates in Zapata and runs south through Durbah and the capital Gonda, south to the Eastreach sea.

SELINE: Goddess of the earth and the heart.

SELVA: Corvus, playmate of Aridain, her brother is Duran, her father is Sorin, her mother is Celia.

SHADRACK: Village to the south of Pellagrin's School in the Kingdom of Durbah.

SHAN: River in eastern Zapata, joins with River Seddon and forms the border with Calabash.

SIAMANG: Dragon name for Firebrand stone.

SIMA: Town in northwest Durbah located in the Mycean Highlands on the border with Zapata.

SIMON: Tubney, new recruit to the workforce at Pellagrin's School.

SIVAN: Ancient council of four at Pellagrin's School.

SONTAR: Gondarian currency of five units; in copper, silver and gold.

SORIN: Corvus; runs the farm at Pellagrin's School and is married to Celia. They have a son Duran, and a daughter Selva.

SOUTHRON: Town in south western Durbah.

SPALDING: Village, home to Perak and Vara Bruin.

SPRAWL: A dragon nesting ground.

SPRITE: Magical imp-like creatures, species include Fire, Sapphire and Jarrah.

SQUILL: Derogatory name for any fire breathing animal.

SRINIGAR: Fanatical religious land to the west of Durbah.

SRIGARIAN: Rhododendron from Sringaria, possessing black and purple streaked blooms.

STORNA: River originating in the Mycean Mountain's, runs southeast through lake Storna then southwest to the Great Knife Edge in Navar.

TAAL: Balefire and Dark, Name given to the opposing combatants seeking the Firebrand shards.

TALLUS: Ramca, Animistic and wizard. Follower of Kuelack, now deceased.

TANCE: Melos, warrior from the ruined land of Turkana, now a member of Pellagrin's elite guard.

TANGLBANDS: Black ribbon like strands infused with dark magic, wielded by Serac.

TARO: Shoran. Colonel in the Gondarian army. Married to Umbra, they have three daughters, Lascana, Valeria and Neruda.

TARSUS: Capital of the land of Navar.

TEMPLAR: Town in eastern Durbah.

TIMBER RAT: Large destructive rodent.

TORSK: Former Animistic at Pellagrin's and head teacher, assassinated by Tallus Ramca.

TREERINKS: True name of the dragonlet chosen by Pellagrin to befriend and guide Aridain.

TROVER: Town located in southern wilds of Durbah.

TSANA: Town on Durbah's western border.

TURKANA: Once a powerful land to the east of Durbah, devastated by the Firebrand shards.

UMBRA: Taro, mother to Lascana, Valeria and Neruda, husband is Colonel Shoran Taro.

UNDINE: A small river running through the capital Gonda.

URAL: Hamlet in Durbah, on the road between Pellagrin's School and Gonda.

VALLEN: Town to the south of Durbah capital Gonda.

VANHARA: Broken lands to the south of Aymara, once the centre of the civilised world, devastated in series of atomic wars over millennia.

VANHARA: Sea of. Large body of water to the south that encompasses the broken lands of Vanhara.

VANIR: Ulrich, Greysword and weapons teacher at Pellagrin's School, from the town of Trover in the Southern Wilds.

VARA: Scosa, Witch and dedicated grandmother to Aridain, wife of Perak and mother to Magen, Alfic and Kuelack, sister Mira, mother Pion.

VIRION CAT: Large wild cat possessing venomous fangs, sometimes called a Shadow cat.

WATERMAN: Suburb in Gonda's dockland.

WIRRAL: Weapon's making town in western Durbah.

WHITLOW: Town on Durbah's north eastern border with Calabash.

WYTCHLEM: Creature inhabiting the Blinks escarpment, a distant ancestor of the Dark Taal.

YARROW: Town southeast of Gonda in Durbah.

YELLOW HAG: Derisory name given to the Hasp.

ZAKAN: Evil wizard from days gone by, whose name is used to scare children in bedtime stories.

ZAPATA: Rugged volcanic land to the north of Durbah.

ZYRLOT: Town in southern Zapata.

ABOUT THE AUTHOR

Born on a farm just outside Oxford, England, in 1961, Dean and his family's strong links to the land meant that he grew up with an inbred love of the countryside. He was never happier than when he was helping his father feed the animals, playing in the woods or playing beside the local stream, defeating imaginary goblins, ghouls and bandits. However, it wasn't to last, and he and his family had to move into the city.

Despite this, Dean's love of fantasy and adventure blossomed as he and his class listened to his English tutor read 'The Hobbit' over a series of afternoons; this inspired him to read many more books of this genre and to write his own short stories.

While at school, he excelled in many sports as well as studying art, history and creative writing. A love of music has followed him throughout his life.

On leaving school and with no clear direction career wise, he thought about joining the Navy to satisfy his need to see the world and adventure. However, before he could join up, his love of motorbikes took over and Dean found another way of seeing the world without the discipline that accompanies the Navy life, extensively exploring the British Isles from Land's End to John O'Groats. While travelling, which included time working in Australia and Europe, he discovered new landscapes and varied cultures, all of which now inspire his writing.

Over the years, Dean has worked in a myriad of professions, but his passion for fantasy has never left him. In his late twenties, Dean decided to make use of his overactive imagination to write short stories on a second-hand typewriter. These stories included fantasy, science fiction, and similar genres, including those about superheroes and monsters from the deep. Later in life, he became interested in geography, geology, the environment and astronomy; all of which feature in his novels.

In his free time, he loves listening to music and to keep fit he practiced Kenpo Karate and took up skiing until arthritis in his elbows and knees prevented him from pursuing the two sports he had come to love.

When it comes to writing, Dean considered completing a daily diary. However, he always preferred to live his life rather than record it in writing, so about fifteen years ago, Dean decided to write a series of fantasy novels.

Finishing the first version of The Dark Taal, he went down the agency route and sent manuscripts to numerous companies. Having no luck apart from one that fell at the final hurdle, Dean, like a lot of writers before him, became disenchanted.

But Dean didn't give up and in 2017 he decided to once again write professionally and concentrated on writing and reworking his first book, 'The Dark Taal'.

Having bought a camper van, Dean, when not writing, travels extensively; this allows him to re-set and think up fresh ideas.

Dean G E Matthews loves fun, adventure and the outdoors. You can't take life too seriously despite the knocks you receive along the way to success,' jokes Dean, 'as the song goes, you get knocked down, you get up again, they will never, ever keep you down, in that way I'm a typical Aries,' joked Dean.

Lightning Source UK Ltd.
Milton Keynes UK
UKHW042312081222
413589UK00015B/10

9 781952 750403